THE MUSIC PROGRAMME

THE MUSIC PROGRAMME

PAUL MICOU

A Birch Lane Press Book
Published by Carol Publishing Group

Published in the U.S. 1990 by Carol Publishing Group

Originally published 1989 in England by Bantam Press,
a division of Transworld Publishers Ltd., London

Copyright © 1989 by Paul Micou

A Citadel Press Book
Published by Carol Publishing Group

Editorial Offices
600 Madison Avenue
New York, NY 10022

Sales & Distribution Offices
120 Enterprise Avenue
Secaucus, NJ 07094

In Canada: Musson Book Company
A division of General Publishing Co. Limited
Don Mills, Ontario

Manufactured in the United States of America

5   4   3   2   1

Library of Congress Cataloging-in-Publication Data

Micou, Paul.
        The music programme / Paul Macou.
            p.   cm.
        "A Birch Lane Press book."
        ISBN 1-55972-023-9 : $16.95
        I. Title.
    PS3563.I354M8   1990
813'.54--dc20   89-71319
                                                        CIP

For Anna U

1

ON THE FIFTH ANNIVERSARY of his arrival in Timbali, Dr Humphrey Lord was informed that his second promotion had finally been approved. Mr Ng, Head of Personnel, brought Dr Lord the good news. Alerted to Ng's arrival by the sound of an electric golf-cart crunching up the gravel path to his hutch, the Englishman was able to hide his three-week-old *Times* and assume a business-like pose at his empty desk before Ng charged through the bead curtain and announced in a voice loud enough for Dr Lord's secretary to hear: 'You M-4!'

The months he had spent preparing himself for a dignified response to the news of his directorship could not prevent Dr Lord from standing to embrace the diminutive Ng; from pacing back and forth wringing his hands gratefully in the direction of the Supreme Director's palace; from touching every object within reach – paperweight, filing-cabinet, standard lamp, bust of Bach – as if each were the icon of a commonly held superstition; from moving through the beads to bask in his secretary's congratulations.

'Oh, Humphrey,' Mary Mbewa said, tugging back her tight mauve skirt so that she might stand. 'This is *very* good news.' Dr Lord skipped around behind Mary's desk and kissed her on a cheek caked with sweat-soaked violet make-up.

When Dr Lord had regained a portion of his composure, he paused to take in the scenery of Mary's office. The sight had startled and pleased him every day of his five-year employment for the Music Programme: all secretaries with the organization – and some low-level professionals – worked out of doors during the dry seasons. Their word processors were kept in a central storage-hut and delivered to their desks daily in a pick-up truck. Mary's desk was situated behind Dr Lord's hutch in the morning sun beneath four towering eucalyptus trees, an idyllic spot where each noon she and her boss fed Colobus monkeys the leftovers of their lunch and watched them preen on the cool grass. Mary's view beyond her computer monitor was of a gentle downhill slope to a river where giraffes fed and hippos bathed. Across the river was a higher plain where herds of zebra wafted back and forth like puffs of smoke, where bush pigs snorted and grovelled, where the occasional rhino trundled tank-like into view. The natural beauty was marred only by a distant electric fence, and behind it the diesel generator that supplied the compound's power.

On the morning of Dr Lord's ascendancy to full-fledged directorship there was a stillness over the plain. The only sound other than the faint chugging of the generator was the gurgling of water from a hippo bathing in one of the larger pools upstream. With a hand on Mary's shoulder Dr Lord stood imperiously before his domain, gulped a deep breath of dry Timbali air, and remarked to himself that he had never been more satisfied.

'Doctah Roared,' said Ng behind him. 'There is other news.'

'Well, what is it, Ng?' The correct pronunciation of Ng's name was not something for which Dr Lord strove: his adenoidal attempts could scarcely have been further off the mark than 'Roared'.

'You remember that man, that US man, they said he was coming?'

'Oh God, Christ, Jesus, Ng, yes, of course I do.' Dr Lord laughed, then hiccuped explosively.

Ng referred to the dreaded American advance man for an energetic United States Congressman whose only objective in foreign affairs, it appeared, was to see the Music Programme stripped of its Western funding. The Congressman's objections to the Music Programme ran deeper than a mere lack of love for music. He was unfriendly to all intergovernmental agencies, but for the Music Programme he reserved his loudest and fiercest criticism. The Congressman was said to have dispatched the much-feared Charles 'Crack' McCray to dig into the books, ask questions of the handful of comprehensible English-speakers on the premises, and report as negatively as possible on how the United States taxpayers' millions were spent.

Dr Lord now realized, with a rush of fear and self-doubt, that the news of his promotion was double-edged: he would be responsible for seeing to it that 'Crack' McCray was shown a bang-up time; that he was satisfied he had seen the real Music Programme; and, most important, that he was thwarted.

'Is that bad American man here yet, Ng?'

'At the airport in twenty minutes. He will be here' – Ng tapped the face of an enormous gold watch on his spindly wrist – 'two hours, maybe three hours.'

Dr Lord recalled his own trip through Customs five years ago. He had arrived in Timbali with four suitcases (anticipating a lengthy stay in underdeveloped circumstances), and had escaped from Customs with nothing more than a clear plastic bag containing his razor, a bar of soap, a facecloth, together with most of the clothes he had worn on the flight. The remainder of his possessions – including recording equipment of a quality unknown in Timbali at the time, and the six hundred cassette tapes he had deemed indispensable to the shortest stay – had been locked in a giant blue cage at the airport, guarded by a uniformed soldier pointing an assault-rifle at all who neared. 'We lock it up safe,' the smiling Customs official had said. 'You come back to leave, you get it, yes?' Dr Lord had not pressed the issue or impugned the official's honesty; he had decided instead to return the following day with formal letters and wax stamps – whatever it was the diplomatic community at the Music Programme used to lean on the locals.

Dr Lord later regretted that he had arrived in Timbali on the eve of an ill-fated coup. Like so many coups, this one was hatched at the airport, accompanied by satellite disturbances at the state-owned radio station. Dr Lord gathered from censored Western newspaper reports that the coup had spread no further than the main airport terminal (the radio-station takeover attempt had not come off at all), and that the only casualties were suffered by the naughty coupsters themselves: they were incinerated by a more or less loyal, or simply confused, strand of the Timbalian army, which happened to be in possession of untested flamethrowers. It was on his trip to the airport in a Music Programme car to retrieve his valuables that Dr Lord

9

learned that the rebels had taken refuge – before being torched – within the same blue cage that had contained his belongings, and which now housed nothing but charred remains.

'Don't be ridiculous, Ng,' Dr Lord said. 'The American will be lucky if he gets out to the compound today at all. I am quite sure he will have to stay the night in town. Touch wood.'

The Music Programme compound was best reached by four-wheel-drive vehicle, although the Timbalian government had built a splendid highway from the capital to within a few miles of its main gate. Having run out of funds – or will – so close to their destination, the road-builders had left some treacherous terrain between the place where the road trailed off into piles of gravel and broken-down dumper-trucks, and the entrance to the Music Programme compound. During the rainy seasons that part of the journey could take five hours all by itself; that is, if the vehicle suffered no punctures or overheatings, and if the marauding Land Pirates – desperate, often politically motivated highwaymen – left the traveller in possession of his life. The Supreme Director understandably retained a jet helicopter on call to avoid this considerable inconvenience on his way to and from the airport.

Dr Lord was therefore certain that 'Crack' McCray would not be on hand until the following day, at the earliest. A reprieve of twenty-four hours lifted his spirits, as if the American's arrival were made any less ominous by a single day's postponement.

'Here is an information-folder on the American,' said Mr Ng. 'Confidential. Someone will call you on the phone when he comes.' The terse and efficient Head of Personnel dropped the folder on Mary Mbewa's desk, then retraced his steps through the beads, into Dr Lord's hutch, and back out of the front door to his vehicle. Moments later Dr Lord watched him scoot northwards on his electric cart along the river in the direction of the Supreme Director's building, stumbling into the occasional aardvark hole but never slowing down.

'Good fellow,' Dr Lord said. Mary Mbewa nodded in agreement. 'I wonder if he has business with the SD today. He appeared even more nervous than usual. Well dressed, wasn't he?'

As for Dr Lord's own wardrobe, he felt secure enough in his position to wear shorts and sandals to work. He thought this gave him an air of eccentricity that was not unsuited to one whose title read 'Assistant to the Supreme Director, Late Baroque'. Stroking his light-red beatnik goatee, Dr Lord strolled around his office and Mary's in khaki knee-length shorts, his white belly protruding three or four inches over his belt-line, his

10

blue-and-white-striped polo-shirt untucked, his wire-rimmed glasses low on his long and pointed nose.

After Ng's departure Dr Lord was left to wonder whether his promotion had gone through solely in order to toss him in the path of 'Crack' McCray.

'Did you hear what Mr Ng said about that bad American, Mary?'

Mary stared up the hill in the direction Ng had gone. 'Yes, Humphrey, I heard.' Her eyes were wide and white with fear in her black and violet face. 'It's bad, isn't it?'

'You've got to help me, Mary,' Dr Lord said, with a mordent of panic cracking his voice. Instantly he realized that it might be *infra dig.* for a lofty M-4 to beg his secretary for assistance on an assignment that was more crucial by far than any he had faced in his entire bureaucratic career. 'What I mean is,' he corrected himself, 'the reputation of the Programme starts right here in your . . . office. If things are ship-shape here, why, it will rub off on the entire compound.'

'Yes, Humphrey.' Still, Mary Mbewa's eyes were fixed on the near horizon.

Dr Lord wondered at that moment if it might not be a good idea to request that Mary call him 'sir', or 'Doctor Lord', rather than 'Humphrey'. He was an M-4, after all. Practically an Insider. Almost ready to move into the SD's building. Had he been too relaxed and familiar with his secretary of two and a half years? His first secretary had called him 'sah' during office hours, 'bwana' while ironing his shirts, and 'bastahd, bastahd, bastahd!' when years of pent-up lust and a bottle of duty-free French wine under the eucalyptus trees had prompted him to reach just for a moment beneath her cotton shift, on to her pregnant belly, until a stinging slap sent him into retreat. On this occasion he chose not to make an issue of his grandiose new title. He strode back into his hutch, deep in gloomy thought.

On the day Ng informed him of his promotion, Dr Lord had nothing in particular on his agenda until late afternoon, when he would chair a meeting at which it was to be decided whether the Music Programme endorsed a recent recording of 'The Art of Fugue' played on crystal glasses more or less full of brandy. The young Danish artist and electrical engineer who had perpetrated the recording was a distant relative of a cousin of the wife of a powerful alternate member of the Music Programme's Board of Governors – the reason his recording had been selected for the Programme's scrutiny in the first place – so there was little sense listening to the performance in order to gauge its musical merits: it would be called 'supremely innovative'. One of the SD's

11

speech-writers would come up with a more expansive expression of the committee's praise.

This did not mean that the meeting would be a short one: Dr Lord knew perfectly well that his colleagues in Authentic Instruments would assail the recording – as they had done every offering that had ever come before the committee – believing as they did that the mere act of capturing pre-twentieth-century music on tape was counter to the spirit in which it was composed. Dr Lord usually responded with the question 'How would you twits ever hear this music in Timbali, were it not recorded digitally in Berlin or London or Tokyo or New York, then flown in here in great big aluminium-winged birds of a kind utterly unknown even in Vivaldi's day? Christ Almighty God.' The Romantics would yawn or bat their eyelashes; the Serialists would smirk impatiently and ask that the presentation be speeded along. The committed Bach-lovers, Dr Lord among them, would clutch at their hearts and gaze ceilingwards in silent praise of the sublime Father of Harmony.

Dr Lord entered his hutch and seated himself behind his desk. He had decided to face his new challenge head-on, to use the time until his afternoon meeting to dictate the appropriate memos, phone the concerned individuals, lay the groundwork for the loathsome 'Crack' McCray's arrival. He would call home and instruct one of his servants to remove from mothballs his one and only formal suit and a business-like tie. On a legal pad he jotted these and other items, conscious as he did so that he now performed his first duties as an M-4, that he had achieved an enviable stature in the organization, that his already bloated pay-packet would now be increased by an annual sum greater by far than the per-capita GNP of the impoverished African country in which he lived.

Dr Lord glowed with happiness at the thought of the Supreme Director, known among his anglophone employees simply as 'Ozymandias', signing the promotion papers that would entrust him with the delicate negotiations that would determine the future of an organization to which the Supreme Director had devoted his considerable energies for more than a decade. With this image came a dread of his confrontation with the American. Was he qualified, as a musical scholar and harpsichord-player, to act as public-relations representative of an intergovernmental organization, and to convince the envoy of a United States Congressman that the Music Programme was indeed a valid institution worthy of scarce American tax dollars in the coming year? Although Dr Lord had never visited the United States of America, he had read enough newspaper stories and seen

12

enough television documentaries in England to know that Americans possessed a quirky ruthlessness based on self-centredness and naïveté that could be both abhorrent and efficacious in the extreme: if European businessmen were said to be putty in their hands, how, then, could a mere specialist in Bach's music hope to compete with a man of 'Crack' McCray's experience?

'My intellect will out,' Dr Lord mumbled to himself. He pressed a button beneath his desk to start his tape-player, hoping he might be infused with strength by a recording of his own performance of Bach's Italian Concerto. Through the beads of his back door, Dr Lord saw Mary Mbewa at her desk, her green computer monitor glowing faintly in the eucalyptus shade, her hands folded on the desk before her, her eyes fixed on the near horizon.

Sipping a glass of airline champagne, Charles 'Crack' McCray mentally calculated that he had spent more time in the last six weeks flying through the air on commercial planes than he had in bed. First there had been his Congressman's whirlwind tour of Poland, then the Vienna conference on international tariffs and trade, then the twice-weekly hops between Paris and Washington ironing out the details of the Congressman's frontal assault on UNESCO, and finally this long flight from London to Timbali via Cairo, where he hoped to gather enough slander-ous intelligence on the Music Programme to put an end to its American funding for ever. Still, McCray was new enough to international travel and multinational intrigue for his energy reserves to be fuelled by the exotic locales and high-pressure meetings in which he had recently participated. Never having visited Africa before, the anticipation of doing so for the first time was enough to keep his eyes open and his adrenalin flowing.

He held before him a folder of evidence provided by a diverse array of informants who had worked for the Music Programme in the past: interviews with disgruntled American musical consultants; rash and destructive statements made by one of the few world-class musicians ever to grace the Nelson Mandela/Albert Schweitzer Auditorium (a tuba-player named Brendt-wood who had patience for neither the Third World nor sentimental international organizations); a Swedish Mahler expert who had defected from the Music Programme to the Organization for Economic Co-operation and Development, and had made something of a career out of his exposés both of what he considered to be the Music Programme's frivolous activities and of his wife's illuminating affair with a KGB agent in New York when the Swede had served as a member of his country's delegation to the General Assembly; and of course the transcripts of three years' worth of Music Programme telephone calls, official and private, intercepted by microwave equipment on the roof of the American embassy in Timbali's capital and stored conveniently on microfilm. None of this information did much to sort out the Music Programme's mysterious affiliation. A bastard child of a UNESCO project which had been abandoned in the wilderness of Timbali, the Music Programme had inexplicably taken root and blossomed like so much tropical rainforest into a forty-million-dollar-a-year operation. McCray had spent little time perusing the folder, but what he had seen had been more likely to bring a smile to his lips than an arch to his eyebrow: he had hoped to discover sinister – rather than simply lunatic – behaviour within the compound of the Music Programme.

Charles McCray sighed, poured himself more champagne, and decided to stretch his stay in Timbali into a vacation. He had heard about deserted beaches, land-rovers full of Italian girls, underfed children who nevertheless could produce a grilled lobster and basket of fruit at a moment's notice. This sounded like his kind of country. He leaned over and looked out the window behind the wing at Africa. He was surprised to see that the land was mountainous and arid; even from 30,000 feet McCray had expected to see waterfalls and jungle roofs, tribal villages, pygmies racing for cover. What he saw instead reminded him of Saudi Arabia, perhaps because he had flown into that country ten times in as many months. He looked at his watch and saw that arrival in Timbali was only an hour away. How could it be that a tropical paradise could exist only an hour's flight from the desiccated moonscape below? The pictures of Timbali he had seen were filled with wild animals grazing amid tall grass, gurgling hippos up to their ears in river water, colourfully dressed women transporting food along red-clay roads, dizzying tropical flowers. With nothing to look at down below – it was probably Ethiopia, he decided – McCray returned to the folder in his lap. Stapled to the first page was a photo and résumé of his contact at the Music Programme: Dr Humphrey Lord, Assistant to the Supreme Director, Late Baroque. A nice enough looking fellow, McCray thought: scholarly, serious . . . malleable.

'I say, Mary, would you be so kind as to bring in that file, the one Mr Ng brought, the confidential one about that atrocious American?'

'One moment, sah,' came Mary Mbewa's reply. Something in Dr Lord's tone had commanded that she respond respectfully.

A second later the folder knifed through the hanging beads. Mary Mbewa dropped it on his desk, and with an effortful swivel of her hips returned to her sunny out-of-doors.

Amused by his sudden feeling of power, Dr Lord took his time, carefully lighting his pipe before proceeding past the photograph of Charles 'Crack' McCray, which was stapled to the inside of the manila folder as if the information within were meant for the benefit of a hit-man. The passport-sized black-and-white photo showed a smiling rugged man of thirty-five or so, whose ample dark hair was parted so sharply that the line of scalp shone brightly beneath a tidy coiffure.

Dr Lord looked up from McCray's picture and followed a blue helix of pipe-smoke as it spiralled towards his thatch ceiling. It was not a good sign that the man looked physically imposing. If there were one word that summed up Dr Lord's own physique, he was afraid it was likely to be 'larval'. He had always been intimidated by tall athletic men and women, and something about the Timbalian diet and lifestyle had contributed to his feeling of lethargy and softness. The tropical sun had done nothing to his complexion except to dry his lips to cracking-point, to add a boozer's blush to his cheeks, and to turn his normally reddish hair a nauseating shade of light green. By contrast, 'Crack' McCray had the look of a person who would absorb a healthful tan on his way into town from the airport. Dr Lord was a victim of his cook's heavy reliance on butter, as well as the country's recent drought; the drought had reduced Timbali's vegetable crop to a trickle, depriving Dr Lord of his favourite salads and killing several hundred thousand people just to the north: his white belly now bulged unflatteringly between his ill-fitting shirts and shorts, an unsightly state of affairs for which he compensated by walking in a duck-footed stoop. Because he did not own a full-length mirror, Dr Lord had gone several months without seeing the deterioration of his body – until he had caught his reflection in the glass doors of the Supreme Director's building. On that occasion he had shuffled from side to side attempting to avoid the squat puffy old man coming towards him, trying in vain to avoid eye-contact, until by actually walking up to the hunched, goateed, pot-bellied person he had discovered his new self.

Mary Mbewa thoughtfully appeared through the beads when the music ended so that her boss would not have to leave his important work to turn over the tape.

15

'Oh, thank you so much,' said Dr Lord, listening to his own voice for a hint of new authority.

'What do you think of that American man?' Mary asked from across the room, referring to the photograph of 'Crack' McCray stapled to the inside of the confidential folder she had apparently been studying ever since Mr Ng had deposited it within her grasp.

'Pleasant-looking chap. But you know how Americans are. You do know how Americans are, Mrs Mbewa?'

Mary beamed. 'Very big friends, Americans,' she said, echoing the most recent government policy regarding the distant superpower.

'Yes, exactly. We're going to get along splendidly, this Charles McCray and I.'

'So we are hoping all to have jobs after he leaves, yes?'

'Oh, for God's sake, don't be ridiculous,' Dr Lord said. He tried in vain to prevent his voice from betraying his surprise that Mary Mbewa had surmised the vital nature of McCray's visit. He would have said more to disabuse her of this dangerous notion, but his mouth had filled with saliva and his throat had constricted tightly; this prevented him from doing anything more than gagging inaudibly, and pretending to be busy with his moribund pipe-bowl.

'You are M-4 now?' Mary asked, as if she might have hallucinated Ng's visit.

'That's right. Big boss.'

'I think maybe you will give me money now,' Mary said, and beamed again.

'That's quite possible, Mary, and now we must be getting to work. I must study this information and you, you . . . go on and ask bloody Gregory for some bloody coffee, yes?'

'Yes, sah.'

'There's a good girl.'

Mary Mbewa exited through the beads into the sunshine, squinting against the glare. She hobbled in her high heels over the gravel path to her desk in the cool shade. She sat down, folded her hands before her, and looked out across the river and into the trees. Half a dozen monkeys lazed among the branches waiting for lunch-time. Behind them a trio of giraffes, hounded by a Music Programme guard on horseback, performed their slow-motion gallop. High in the sky overhead a plane, heading for the Timbali International Airport, glinted in the equatorial sunlight. Mary had forgotten about the coffee.

A few minutes later Dr Lord emerged from his hutch, approached Mary's desk, and stood before her with his wrists crossed. 'Coffee!' he shouted, trying his emphatic best to perform in an administrative fashion. Mary leaped to her feet protesting that she remembered, that she would go tell bloody Gregory to fetch some bloody coffee.

'And a roll, and butter, if you please,' said the newly authoritative Dr Lord. Mary hurried away towards the nearest affiliate of the central canteen, where a young man named Gregory provided the staff on the south side of the compound with coffee, tea, snacks, cigarettes, and a powerful local beer known as 'Mister K' (before Independence as 'Kistenhoff Lager').

All alone in Mary's outdoor office, Dr Lord turned and faced the river. On the far bank, the Music Programme guard on horseback chased the family of giraffes away from the generator. The generator, one of Timbali's most frequently bombed objects, was guarded by a large force of guards imported from Somalia. Somalis made terrific guards, Dr Lord had heard, but the generator was blown up annually despite their efforts. The attacks were committed in the name of anti-imperialism, or as corollary violence to the main thrust of the ragged coup-attempts which the Timbalian President-for-Life quietly but ruthlessly put down every six months or so. The guards were good at chasing away rhinos and giraffes, but guerrillas struck at will.

A dull roar in the sky drew Dr Lord's attention to an airliner glinting in the noon-time tropical sun against a blue so deep it brought music to his ears.

'I'll wager the American chap is aboard that plane,' Dr Lord whispered aloud. 'Crash, crash, crash.'

2

PILED HIGH on Dan O'Connor's desk were two dozen memoranda, each entitled 'The Music Programme, Now and Tomorrow'. The highest-ranking professionals of the Music Programme had been ordered to report to O'Connor, a young member of the Supreme Director's prized stable of speech-writers, to aid him in the annual task of conveying the agency's *raison d'être* in a convincing manner. Although his draft was due by the end of the working day, diligent, driven, dedicated Dan O'Connor would submit his paper long before then: he was due at the Acacia Club pool at noon for lunch with Yvonne, the teenage daughter of the French ambassador to Timbali.

O'Connor reclined on his swivel chair, crossed his ankles on his desk, left his ringing phone unanswered. On his lap lay a memo from an Insider named Thwok, which read in full:

Oh! Thank You So Much Music Programme

> *You are made of such noble material.*
> *Our world can suffer so heavily, now*
> *Let the Music Programme*
> *Even more easily let it go.*
> *Of one thing, of all things: as they say.*
> *But! If sadness under music cannot blow,*
> *Then* GOD BLESS YOU, *You Music Programme.*

O'Connor knew Thwok socially; knew him to be warm-hearted, platinum-souled; knew him to be a harpist of considerable skill and dedication. It was Thwok's most endearing characteristic, O'Connor thought, that he seemed to spend his days quietly penning baroque and utterly meaningless memos to his colleagues, sealing them with a wax stamp of Telemann's profile, and sending them through the internal post as if he actually expected them to shape Music Programme policy. O'Connor smiled and placed Thwok's memo on the thin pile of the contributions he intended to incorporate into his draft.

Next on his stack of papers was a massive tract composed by a prolix team of keyboard specialists collectively known to most Westerners as 'The Bloody Bolshies', a group of three Soviet men and a Bulgarian woman whose devotion to Russian-style pianism would allow no quarter for representatives of less magnificent styles. The memo was single-spaced, double-sided, densely packed, printed in raised type, and sixty-five pages long.

'Mr Dan O'Connor,' the memo began. 'Undeniably it has crossed the appreciation of our esteemed colleague that under the circumstances the proliferation of independently scrutinized and approved affiliations there have been occasions when a supply of endless continuations for the remainder of . . .'

O'Connor knew and respected most of the Bloody Bolshies, but wasted no time in depositing their contribution in the dustbin with the majority of the memos he had received. He would leave them alone with Rachmaninov if they would leave him alone with the enunciation of policy.

Skipping through the next several missives, O'Connor found each to conclude in its own way that the purpose of the organization was to perpetuate its own existence. Variations on this theme included the above-all-my-department-must-be-spared argument and the equally self-righteous cost-cutting-in-rival-departments approach.

Soon O'Connor came upon a handwritten paragraph from the

desk of Dr Humphrey Lord, Assistant to the Supreme Director, Late Baroque, dated the same morning. 'O'Connor!' it read. 'Utmost freaking urgency. Am supposed to deter visiting American bent on our destruction. Afraid to use phone. Am M-4. Come down here, please, I beg you.'

O'Connor had established a friendly rapport with Dr Lord early on during his short stay in Timbali when the former was nearly killed by the latter's out-of-control four-wheel-drive vehicle. O'Connor drove a powerful stripped-down motorcycle with a gigantic fuel-reservoir and lug tyres, which had been incapacitated in its collision with Dr Lord's land-rover as they raced each other for the gate after work one afternoon. Neither could explain afterwards what had possessed him, but each man was suddenly gripped by a fierce desire to beat the other to the gate of the compound, a prize for which they both appeared willing to die. O'Connor cut across a hillside, front wheel bounding off the ground, back wheel spraying a rooster-tail of red Timbalian soil; Dr Lord, spying him from the paved road which covered the last mile to the gate, accelerated as fast as his sturdy car would allow him, and dashed for the fork where O'Connor, whom he had never met, would join the road for the sprint to the exit. It was at this juncture that Dr Lord's trusty car had left the loosely paved road, jounced up the hill to the right and then back down to the left. Dr Lord's efforts to bring his vehicle under control sent it skidding into O'Connor's path, and the speech-writer was catapulted over the bonnet of the land-rover. O'Connor flipped lazily in the air, then landed face-down on a soft sizeable anthill. Each man admitted at once to having behaved with exceptional stupidity. Because O'Connor was unhurt – though crawling with ants – they heaved the carcass of his motorcycle into the land-rover and drove together to the Acacia Club. There they chatted happily over a series of splendid gin and tonics in the Anthony Eden Room, ecstatic over the coincidence that they held a command of the English language in common.

O'Connor narrowed his eyebrows at Dr Lord's hysterical message. Rumours had circulated for months that a representative of the American Congressman would sweep into the Music Programme compound before long; yet, like contemplators of a nuclear holocaust, few on the staff could bring themselves to believe it would occur during their lifetime. It was bad enough that the American had materialized at last, but for O'Connor to miss an appointment with Yvonne would be catastrophic. O'Connor had invested a hundred days jockeying for position with the French girl, competing with a diplomatic community rife with eligible and qualified interlopers, some of them energetic and otherwise unemployed teenagers. But at last, O'Connor felt, his progress could be measured: Yvonne ate lunch at poolside with him at least twice a week; she insisted that he drive her at high speed on his newly refurbished motorcycle through the rolling tea-plantations bordering the Acacia Club; she had not ruled out the possibility of his visiting her at her father's residence.

With little time left before his appointment with Yvonne, and the need to drop by Dr Lord's office on his way to the club, O'Connor swept the remaining memos from his lap, sat up in his chair, and began typing furiously at the keyboard of his word processor. In half an hour he had composed, edited, proof-read and printed the draft of his report. His paper managed to convey the sentiments of the majority of the Music Programme's employees: 'We are paid therefore we are.'

After driving a staple through the corner of his masterpiece, O'Connor picked up, then quickly replaced the receiver of his phone (which had not stopped ringing in the past three hours), then picked it up again to summon his secretary, Pulma. When he had deposited the draft in Pulma's hands and looked her hard in the eyes while instructing her to distribute the appropriate copies, he seized his motorcycle helmet and loped down the stairs and out of the building to the car park.

Of the hundred spaces in the car park, only fifteen were occupied, all by off-road vehicles of some kind, including O'Connor's angry-looking black motorcycle. Jeeps, land-rovers, and three-wheel cycles with tyres like beer-barrels were parked together near the building, all owned and operated by courageous members of staff who, like O'Connor, lived beyond the electric fence of the compound in the land collectively known as 'Africa'.

Behind the car park, half a mile away, were six rows of concrete buildings where the majority of the Music Programme staff lived. The dwellings themselves were drab, but they were surrounded by freakish fauna and iridescent flora, sky-scraping eucalyptus trees, bushes bursting with colour as if ablaze, and many different kinds of poisonous and otherwise dangerous wild animal. Behind them, on a hill, was the residence of the Supreme Director, a place few if any of the staff had visited. The Supreme Director's mansion could have been designed and constructed by Ludwig II, so gaudy and fantastic were its appointments, so crippling was its cost. The Supreme Director appeared to share a peculiar quirk of American millionaires and antique despots: a tendency to have large objects – crenellated castle walls, Roman baths – transported piece by piece from distant parts of the planet and reassembled for his use. The overall impression one gained from the residential set-up within the electric fence of the Music Programme compound was of a medieval town surrounding its ruler's castle.

O'Connor donned his helmet, careful not to disturb the parting in his wavy brown hair, and kicked his motorcycle into life. The sound of its engine echoed off the concrete building he had just left. Its growl reminded him of buzz saws, the sound of his previous employment as a harvester of Christmas trees in New Hampshire. He accelerated across the car park and on to the downhill trail to the southern slope of the compound, and as the engine climbed through its gearbox he imagined the felling of trees amid fountains of sawdust.

Dan O'Connor, an American, had been indifferent to his nationality until the day he was hired by the Music Programme – as an Irishman. O'Connor was not a liar; he had not misled his employers. He had answered the man's question truthfully when asked, at a Munich music conference which he had mistaken for a beer-garden during Oktoberfest, if 'O'Connor' was an Irish name. 'Of course it is,' O'Connor had replied. Back home, when someone said 'Are you Irish?' the answer was 'Yes', even if he had never been to Ireland and knew no one who carried an Irish passport. Dan O'Connor was clearly of Irish extraction, but had nothing but neutral feelings about the fact until the day his ancestral Irishness had landed him an intriguing and lucrative job. How could he have known, in Munich, that the question had been asked in order to recruit O'Connor for a job so highly paid and unusual that to risk it by straightening out this little misunderstanding with Personnel would be, as O'Connor's brogue-feigning aunt would say, 'tantamount to folly'? During his few months on the job, O'Connor had been approached twice by the Head of Personnel (a man named Ng who drove a golf-cart even in the hallways of the Supreme Director's building) for clarification of his national origin. While this made O'Connor nervous, he argued to his conscience that thus far he had not lied to anyone either verbally or in print, except by omission, unless one counted the thick Irish brogue he put on in front of everyone who spoke English well enough to know the difference.

Only Dr Humphrey Lord, an Englishman, had caught on to Dan O'Connor's scheme. Over drinks in the Anthony Eden Room after their collision, Dr Lord had spotted O'Connor's true nationality after hearing only a word or two. Dr Lord found it hard to believe that O'Connor had fooled anyone with his

22

crude improvised Irishisms: 'Would ya be havin' another tip of the cup, friend?'

Dr Lord had winced at this question. 'That's a bloody silly brogue you have on,' he had said. 'Would you be so kind as to take it off?'

Like so many people who wrestle with a guilty conscience throbbing with secrets, O'Connor was more relieved than embarrassed when he found his cover blown. He was prepared to face the Music Programme authorities, let them do their worst, if Dr Lord betrayed him to Mr Ng. Instead, to O'Connor's even greater relief, Dr Lord showed not the slightest hint of disapproval, in fact appeared to welcome the news of the young speech-writer's duplicity. O'Connor sized up Dr Lord as an eccentric, a breed far outnumbered at the Music Programme by the kind of numb plodding bureaucrats who would have busted O'Connor in triplicate before he could say 'leprechaun'.

The young speech-writer enjoyed his occasional drink with Dr Lord, who after a gin and tonic or a Mister K became pleasantly giddy. He blushed as brightly as the flowering vines growing beneath the bar in the Anthony Eden Room, often humming snatches of his beloved Bach as if this substituted for normal conversation. Dr Lord was modest about his own musical accomplishments, but O'Connor had heard him described as one of the few genuinely gifted scholars ever to grace the Music Programme.

Roaring down the narrow trail to the southern edge of the compound, Dan O'Connor passed a team of Timbalian workers. Their job that day was to clear the underbrush with crude machetes, to implant diagonal bamboo branches across the face of the hill to allow drainage in anticipation of the short rains, and otherwise to beautify a path that was used for no other purpose than O'Connor's short-cut to the gate twice a day. They stood up from their stooped postures to smile and wave as he bounded by. Their khaki shorts were soaked with sweat, their naked legs caked with dried mud. Their faces bore expressions of happiness, as if O'Connor were a long-lost family member returning for the holidays. O'Connor waved without completely letting go of his handlebars; he was an accomplished motorcyclist, but it required all his skill to keep his front tyre aimed in the right direction and in contact with the slippery terrain.

The workers made O'Connor nervous. The Director of Security had briefed him, two days after he started work, on the problem the organization faced when it imported workers from beyond the electric fence: 'There are two kinds of Timbalian,' the Austrian former policeman had said. 'Thieves and expatriates.'

'Ah,' was O'Connor's tacit reaction. 'This man is a racist.'

Still, the security director's warning sank in, at least to the degree that O'Connor remembered it afterwards each time he was the victim of assault or robbery, which was unnervingly often. Twice he had feared for his life – identical midnight visits from groups of men wielding machetes and clubs – and of all the valuables he had brought into the country with him nothing remained but his wallet and his passport, which he had fought for successfully on two occasions.

At the bottom of the hill the terrain levelled off into dry grassy plain bordering a rushing river. O'Connor had once tried to impress Yvonne, the French ambassador's daughter, by jumping his motorcycle over this river at a narrowing where the water fell between two cliffs. He had practised the jump a dozen times (after first making one of his servants try it in exchange for the equivalent of fifteen US cents). The jump looked more spectacular than it was, because, although the bike left the ground on one side of a waterfall – after the rainy season the waterfall came complete with rainbow and deafening roar – and landed on the other side, the effect was mostly an optical illusion: on solid ground the jump would have been unimpressive, spanning only seven or eight feet. But, as a horrified Yvonne looked on, O'Connor had shamelessly pretended to attempt the jump spontaneously, building the tension by throttling loudly before launching down the gentle slope to the cliff – *vroom, vroom* – as Yvonne tried to make her protests heard over the combined din of engine and waterfall. Her yelps of pleasure when O'Connor bounced to a safe stop on the far side of the river had completely mitigated his fear. Without a second thought he had gathered speed and jumped back across the waterfall to accept Yvonne's ecstatic embraces.

O'Connor slowed down as he neared the spot and noticed as he did so the omnipresent Ng, Head of Personnel, approaching from the other direction on his silent electric golf-cart.

'Ng!' said O'Connor inside his helmet, where he could carry on a conversation with himself above his bike's high decibel-level. He wasted no time in veering uphill to the right, then back down towards the river again after a short pause to change into a lower gear. Gathering speed, leaning forward over his handle-bars, he steered towards the natural ramp created by the granite promontory on the near bank of the river. In Ng's clear view, O'Connor sailed across the waterfall on to the far bank just seconds before his path would have been blocked by the golf-cart and a conversation regarding national origin would have taken place.

On the other bank of the river, O'Connor bounded along in open country, signalling Ng with an appropriate fighter-pilot's wave. O'Connor stood up on his foot-rests to absorb the shock of the rough terrain. He travelled slowly for a hundred yards until he reached the widest stretch of river, just below the group of huts that included Dr Lord's office, where fording was possible. Cool water spattered his trouser legs as he slowly crossed the river. He steered towards Dr Lord and his secretary, who were seated together at a picnic-table on a grassy knoll beneath a quaternion of giant eucalyptus trees.

Of all the natural beauty to be found within the compound, O'Connor liked this spot best. In the absence of motorcycles, a profound silence reigned here, interrupted now and then by the soft noises of bathing hippos, splattering monkey droppings, and the *click-click-click* of Mary Mbewa's fingernails on her computer keyboard.

'I say, O'Connor,' said Dr Lord, when Dan had parked his bike in the shade of a tree and stifled its burping engine, 'have a Mister K?'

'Top o' the mornin' to you, Humphrey. And don't mind if I do,' said O'Connor, unwilling to drop his Irish accent in the presence of Dr Lord's secretary. 'And good day to you, Mary.'

'Hello, bwana.'

O'Connor could tell that the newly promoted Dr Lord had rehearsed this moment with his secretary: she had never called him anything but 'Danny' before.

'Congratulations, Humphrey. My goodness – M-4! I ought to have arrived bearing gifts.'

Dr Lord could not conceal his pride. He opened two Mister K's for toasting purposes: 'To Ozymandias.'

'Cheers.'

After the two men had swallowed refreshing gulps of beer, which was stored for refrigeration in a fishing-net at a nearby eddy in the river, Dr Lord made it clear to his secretary that he and the speech-writer wished to be alone. Bowing with a brand-new obsequiousness, Mary Mbewa walked up the hill to her desk and busied herself with a nail-file. (It was Dr Lord's little joke that when he told Mary to do some filing she addressed herself to her gaudy fingernails.)

'What a lovely spot you have down here. So peaceful.'

'We feed the monkeys tranquillizers. Couldn't hear ourselves think before Gregory came up with that brilliant idea. Biscuits soaked with tranquillizers.'

'Marvellous. Say, I crossed paths with that fellow Ng on the way down here. Almost had to stop to talk to him. He looked even more harried than usual.'

'O'Connor, the situation is grave. A sinister chap named McCray has arrived in Timbali. He'll come through the gate by tomorrow noon at the latest. I believe that was the reason for my promotion: the Insiders have hurled me in his path, God knows why.'

'We knew this would happen sooner or later. I'm sorry you had to be the one. It's a great deal of responsibility.'

'Precisely why I wanted to have this chat, O'Connor.'

'H'm?'

'I thought perhaps this responsibility could be . . . diffused, if you will.'

'Defused?'

'Yes.' Dr Lord made a swimming motion with his arms. '*Spread about.*'

'Ah.'

'Listen to me, O'Connor. You're an American – no offence, of course. But perhaps an American might have more insight than I into this "Crack" McCray's personality. I'm not suggesting you take full charge of the situation; simply that you give me a hand, as it were. Point me in the right direction. I've never been faced with such a problem. I'm just a musician, you see. And a scholar and a gentleman, of course. You, you are policy-orientated, are you not?'

'As much as anyone. But surely you aren't suggesting that I, a lowly speech-writer, assume responsibility for the fate of our organization?'

'Don't be sarcastic. I am merely asking for your advice.'

'Well, let's see. How would I handle this?'

As O'Connor mulled it over, the pair began to walk down the hill towards the river.

'I've got it,' O'Connor said, nudging Dr Lord in the arm. 'Take him on a grand tour.'

'Yes? Yes?'

'Why, of course. Take him to see old Kastostis.'

'You must be mad.'

Kastostis was the Music Programme's Composer-in-Residence, whose electronic mayhem consumed some ten per cent of the organization's budget and an even more disproportionate amount of its diesel-generated power-supply. Kastostis operated in secret in the northern hills of the compound not too far from the Supreme Director's palace. His fantastically expensive multi-media productions, performed once every two years, involved computers, laser light-shows, synthesizers, high explosives, and the occasional sample of local Timbalian wildlife (in Czech folk-costume). Although the reclusive Kastostis had been spotted in the flesh on only a handful of occasions, he was rumoured to be a most hateful little man, who cultivated his crazed-genius image as carefully as he groomed his Beethovenian mane of jet-black hair. The Czech composer billed himself as a 'MAXIMALIST', always spelled in capital letters, and to the extent that money was no object in his endeavours the rubric was apt enough. It was said of Kastostis' early piano works that they could be imitated in the following way: spill a sticky substance on all eighty-eight piano keys; use a moistened cloth and clean for fifteen minutes. Dan O'Connor, whose job did not necessarily depend upon his agreement with musical trends, said to Dr Lord after the most recent performance that it sounded 'like many different kinds of people and animals all being slaughtered at the same time in a small space'.

'Funny,' Dr Lord had replied earnestly, 'that's exactly what his wife says.'

Kastostis had been appointed to his position a few years after the Music Programme was inaugurated. He was characteristically absent from his own induction, and sent his young wife to read an acceptance speech in his place. 'Death, death, death,' his lovely wife Eleanor read carefully, in the presence of the invisible Supreme Director's official stand-in for the ceremony, 'it permeates my sound. We, the undead, communicate to our predecessors through music – the great lie is that music has been for our ears.' Kastostis' answer to the spiritual gap was apparently to be found in volume alone: seasoned staff members and dignitaries were careful to wear ear-plugs, if they could find them, or simply to stuff bits of saliva-moistened paper into their ears before subjecting themselves to one of his performances. 'Bach, Mozart, Beethoven, Schubert, Chopin, Mahler,' the impeccably translated speech concluded, 'were all nincompoops.' His attractive English wife blushed appropriately, bowed to the acting Supreme Director (who was then still receiving the tail end of the speech in a translation of his own), and strode from the dais with her chin pointed skywards and tears of embarrassment streaming down her face. She was not to be seen again until she turned up at one of the Security Director's monthly barbecues, where she remarked tipsily to Dr Lord, among others, that her husband 'must be near the end of Opus Nine, for he has not bathed since Easter'. It was then mid-August.

'Only kidding,' O'Connor said to Dr Lord, as the two

reached the bank of the river. 'But who knows? Our Mr McCray may be a MAXIMALIST himself.'

'You must help me. I've heard the most awful things about Mr McCray's boss, the member of Congress. This wouldn't be the first time he strangled the life out of an agency like ours.'

'I hear you.'

'What, then?'

'I still think a tour is the best way to get him on to our side before he jumps to conclusions. Don't show him the books until he's seen some of what we have to offer. I know: show him the front gate.'

'Ah.' Dr Lord's face glowed.

At the front gate of the compound was a statue said to be an abstract likeness of the Supreme Director; above the statue, carved into the Gothic arch over the road, was an inscription from Verlaine: 'De la musique avant toute chose.'

It was this inscription, more than anything within the gates, that gave the organization meaning. Dr Lord and Dan O'Connor agreed that they peered up through windscreen or visor to read those words as they raced, hours late, to work each day – and that the quotation tended to justify their tax-free pay. Yes, they said, Mr McCray would be moved to tears.

'Or you could take him to see Skip.'

'Again you jest,' said Dr Lord.

'Skip' was the nickname of an American consultant to the Music Programme who had started in a lowly temporary post, but had rocketed through the promotion system so fast that few other members of staff had had a chance to meet him before he landed his 'airline consultancy'. He had an office, a desk, a secretary, a database, a trombone collection – but Skip spent every working day *elsewhere*. 'Elsewhere' was the only way to describe where Skip was, because no one knew, not for sure, where the middle-aged consultant deplaned each day. 'He's in Beijing,' Skip's secretary might say, 'with Yehudi Menuhin.' 'Mr Skip? He's in Tibet,' another aide might suggest, 'studying finger-cymbals.'

'You know,' O'Connor said to his colleague Dr Lord, as the pair of suspicious hippos returned to their watering-hole, 'one of these days Skip will return. His time will turn out to have been well spent. He's a competent fellow, when sober. He will have soaked up a world of music during the last few months, and he will make it worth our while having kept the faith.'

'Only Ozymandias has faith in the man, God knows why,' said Dr Lord. 'Where the devil *is* Skip, after all – do you know?'

'Bangkok, is what I've heard. Something to do with organizing

28

a girls' choir. I kid you not, this is what they are saying. We just have to keep the faith. Skip will be back one day.'

'Our only chance is that Mr McCray will turn out to be an open-minded person. Not to be melodramatic, but our fate is in his hands. Our only chance is that our demise is not already a *fait accompli*. Do you think the man can be persuaded that we aren't like some of his past victims?'

'Yes, for several reasons. First, we are small beer compared to the others; hardly worth the trouble of shutting us down. Second, there is the matter of our true affiliation – and if McCray can pin that down he's a formidable investigator.'

O'Connor referred to the Music Programme's long-standing identity crisis. No one knew for sure whether or not the organization, clearly an offshoot of UNESCO, could still claim ties to any international body. Much of its funding was now derived from private sources, many of its buildings had been erected by individuals' donations, and few were the higher-ups in the United Nations who even admitted that the Music Programme existed; many veteran members of the Music Programme staff said privately that the agency had been set adrift from the mother organization rather early on.

'This could be our saving grace,' O'Connor said. 'We fear two things from Mr McCray: that he will publicize what some superficial Americans and others believe to be our frivolous use of taxpayers' monies; and that he will be instrumental in cutting off the substantial annual contribution of the US government, which as you know would spell our doom.'

'Oh, Christ, God, bloody hell, yes, I know,' said the agitated Dr Lord.

'But wait. If we were to explain immediately to Mr McCray that we may not be as closely affiliated with the hated United Nations as he previously believed, why, this might persuade him that even the paperwork involved in destroying us isn't worth his crusading Congressman's time.'

'You may be right. But do I have the authority to lay bare the Music Programme's bastard status?'

'I'm not sure. Let's think. Do you want to give the Supreme Director a call?'

Dr Lord shuddered and blanched as if he had been struck in the back by a poisoned spear.

'Surely', he gasped, 'you don't mean that.'

'Why not?'

'Have you ever . . .? Good lord, are you saying you have *met* the SD?'

'I'm one of his most important speech-writers, am I not?'

'Then, you *have* met him?'

'Well, not in the flesh, no. I have seen his motorcade on its way to the helicopter pad. And once – once – I spoke with him on the phone.'

'And? What was that like?'

'I was terrified, of course. I'm not very good on the phone in any case. I think I spoke too quickly. He didn't seem to understand anything I said. There are rumours, you know, that his English isn't what it should be. He reads most of his speeches in English, but he may do so phonetically, much the way the Pope reads his Christmas messages. And, at least since I've been here, he has never delivered one of his statements in person.'

'I see. So calling him now would be out of the question, thank God.'

'I suppose you're right.'

'You will help me, though, when the American arrives?'

O'Connor appraised Dr Lord, who looked rather pathetic standing in the mud on the bank of the river in his leather sandals, khaki shorts and striped polo-shirt.

'Of course I will. You may be right that as a compatriot I might be in a position to filter some of the more . . . exotic aspects of the agency so that they are not so glaring.'

'Thank you, thank you, thank you.'

'But now I must be going. I have an appointment at the club.'

'I see, yes. Well, jolly good. Have one on me, what?'

'You know you ought to do something about that,' O'Connor said, pointing up into a tree on the far bank of the river.

'What is it?'

'You see, there, hanging from that low branch? That is a green mamba.'

'Good heavens. I must learn to keep an eye out for snakes. Yes, yes, I will tell bloody Gregory to kill it.'

As Dr Lord spoke those words, the two men turned to walk up the hill to O'Connor's motorcycle. O'Connor waved goodbye to Mary Mbewa, donned his helmet, jumped into the saddle of his machine. He shook hands with Dr Lord, while behind them the deadly snake dropped from its branch, splashed into the river, swam with the current, then slithered with astonishing speed into the underbrush on the near bank.

Charles 'Crack' McCray looked on nervously as the woman in line ahead of him was harassed to the point of tears by a nonchalant Customs official who seemed intent on depriving her of everything she thought she would need in Timbali. This included her battery-operated toothbrush, two innocuous romance novels displaying preternatural flesh on their covers, and a portable video-camera with which she may have wished to record shaky images of the exotic land. Each item was placed in a cardboard box and removed to a giant, somewhat carbonized blue cage in the recesses of the terminal building. 'We lock it up safe,' said the official. 'You come back to leave, you get it, yes?'

McCray's first instinct was to come to the woman's aid, but when he saw the look in the Customs official's eye he thought again. As his turn arrived, he decided that to make waves might put his own tape-recorder in jeopardy. It took the Customs official three seconds to locate the device in the bottom of McCray's duffel bag.

'I need that for my business, do you understand?' McCray asked the official, who covetously fondled the sleek cassette-deck, holding it up like a newborn baby.

'What is your business?'

'I am a representative of the United States government. You have my papers there, do you see?'

The official looked carefully at McCray's passport and visa with an expression of utmost seriousness on his young face; he ignored the attached papers which explained the American's visit. McCray tried not to appear impatient as the informally uniformed official seemed to weigh the documents in one hand against the cassette-recorder in the other.

'We lock it up safe,' he finally said. 'You come back to leave, you get it, yes?'

'No, no,' McCray said. 'You don't understand. I am a foreign dignitary. Do you see? I am a United States Congressman.' Charles McCray hated to lie, but believed he could claim that the Customs official had misunderstood him, if it came to that.

'Thank you, sah,' said the official, saluting. 'We lock it up safe.'

McCray felt a distinct pressure at his temples, a tightening of the tendons leading to his hands, but decided he should save his natural combativeness for the Music Programme. At least the Customs official had left McCray's camera alone – he was an avid photographer in his own time, and had amassed an impressive collection of slides during his recent globe-trotting.

'And the camera, too,' said the official, removing it and the rest of McCray's photographic equipment and handing them to a subordinate for storage in the burned blue cage.

Stripped of his valuable equipment, but grateful to have held on to his briefcase full of incriminating documents, Charles 'Crack' McCray stepped into the bright sunshine outside the terminal. The glare was so bright he was momentarily blinded, and as he stumbled forward he bumped into a group of people standing on the pavement.

'Pardon me. Excuse me,' he said. He placed his briefcase and duffel bag on the ground and reached into his breast pocket for his dark glasses. 'I'm so sorry.'

Soon McCray's eyes had adjusted to the sunshine, so he could see that his briefcase and bag were no longer on the ground between his feet. The group of people he had stumbled into proved to be taxi-drivers, each of whom was now explaining that the others were criminals, and that he would never arrive safely in the capital in his colleagues' cabs. 'You come with me now,' they said, not quite touching him but giving him the impression that he was being frisked up and down. One of them, more aggressive than the others, a friendly-looking man with a bright smile, clutched McCray's briefcase to his chest and pointed to it and the duffel bag between his feet as if he intended to hold them for ransom. McCray was so happy to see his briefcase that he did not hesitate to throw in his lot with the evidently well-disposed man who had seized it, who had in any case already begun walking away towards his waiting car carrying McCray's remaining belongings. The driver courteously opened the back door of the car and handed McCray his briefcase and bag. The American sank into his seat and held tightly to the case's handle.

'Is that the city over there?' he asked, pointing to the left of the airport access-road towards a modest clutch of tall buildings.

'Yes, sah,' shouted the driver, turning right on to the highway.

'Good. Why did you turn right?'

'Sah?'

'I asked you why you turned right, away from the city.'

'We get petrol first, sah. Please give me money.'

'Damn,' said McCray. He had forgotten to change his dollars for local currency at the airport. 'I'll get money for you at the hotel,' he shouted to the driver.

'Your money is OK, sah. Are you German?'

'American.'

'American dollars very good, sah.'

'Fine. Proceed,' McCray commanded, although they were already travelling at high speed away from the city.

McCray reclined in the back seat and allowed the sweat to dry on his face from blasts of hot air blowing through the car's four open windows. He leaned out into the wind and took in the sights around him. He was struck especially by the uncannily vaulted sky: the dome of air overhead seemed to encompass a dozen distinct weather systems, both cloudy and clear, rainy and dry. It dizzied him to contemplate the overhead expanse for more than a few seconds at a time.

To one side, beyond a sparsely vegetated plain, a thunderstorm broke over an isolated range of rugged hills. A slow-moving train clattered along rickety tracks beside the modern highway. Groups of spindly-legged antelopes bounded in neurotic zigzags, while less nervous species sulked motionless even in the shadow of the passing train. In the distance a free-standing snow-capped mountain towered darkly over the plain, crowned by a halo of clouds.

'Where is this gas station?' McCray asked.

'The petrol, sah?'

'Yes.'

'In the suburbs,' said the driver, and with that he began hooting with laughter and striking his palm on the oversized steering wheel of his taxi.

'Soon, I hope.'

'Very soon, sah. One mile down the road, there.'

The mile passed in under a minute, and the countryside changed little, except that the city was no longer visible on the rear horizon. Two more miles passed, and the highway narrowed to one lane in each direction. McCray was about to assert himself, to tell the taxi-driver he had kidnapped the American Secretary of State, when the driver abruptly slowed and turned across the highway on to a dirt road pitted with holes deep enough almost to engulf the taxi.

'Petrol there, sah,' said the driver, pointing to a tarpapered shack on one side of the road.

'Surely we could have found petrol in the city,' McCray said.

'Yes, sah. Very expensive. My brother, he owns this petrol station. You give me your dollars now.'

The petrol station turned out to be a bucket and siphon, and the driver turned out to have a great deal of catching-up to do with his brother. McCray stretched his legs for a quarter of an hour, still holding tightly to the handle of his briefcase, breathing thin air, until his driver announced that it was time to go to the city. McCray still hoped to make it to the Music Programme headquarters before dark.

The drive into town was interrupted by a flat tyre and the demise of the taxi's meter. 'No problem, sah. You pay standard fare.' This 'standard fare' McCray managed to negotiate down from the equivalent of 400 US dollars to 25 US dollars, not including the ten he had paid for petrol, plus a pair of white boxer shorts. The porter at the entrance to the hotel had overheard the negotiations, but waited until McCray had paid the driver before informing the American that the airport was ten miles away and the standard fare, even for tourists, usually came to nine dollars plus whatever gratuity bwana thought appropriate.

'Well, then,' said McCray, 'how much to carry my bags to the front desk?' McCray could have handled his duffel bag by himself, both because he travelled light and because Timbalian Customs had been kind enough to store his heaviest belongings in the blue cage at the airport.

'Whatevah's fair, sah,' said the porter, thus ensuring himself double or triple the going rate.

McCray followed the porter up the front steps of the modern hotel, and noticed a pair of workmen plastering over what appeared to be horizontal lines of bullet holes in the building's stucco facade.

'Excuse me,' he said, catching up to the porter. 'Has there been some . . . disturbance?' McCray jerked his head in the direction of the workers.

'No, sah, never,' said the porter, quickening his pace and looking away.

At the front desk, McCray asked that his bags be taken to his room, then enquired of a uniformed receptionist as to the possibility of reaching the Music Programme compound by nightfall.

'It is far,' said the slender-shouldered man, who held in his hand a sheaf of credit-card receipts. 'One cannot take a taxi. One must rent a car.' The man looked down at his clutch of receipts, as if by being interrupted he could no longer act upon their existence. 'We have this service in the hotel.'

McCray was directed to a desk where a woman wearing the uniform of her rental-car agency sat reading the company's slim tourist brochure and map of Timbali. McCray cleared his throat and asked her about the journey to the Music Programme compound.

'Four-wheel drive,' said the woman, proffering the brochure and pointing to a photograph of a tractor-like vehicle. 'Two to five hours.'

'Then, it is not too late to go today?'

'Today?' The woman jumped from her stool, which was a shock to McCray because standing up she was six inches shorter than she had been sitting down.

'What's the matter?'

'I would not go today. Leave early in the morning.'

'But two to five hours – I could be there by sunset at the very latest.'

'Are you armed?' was the woman's unexpected question.

'Of course not. What do you mean?'

'You will have a driver, then, who will be prepared.'

'What exactly is the danger?'

'Pirates, sah.'

'I don't plan on going to sea.'

'No, sah. Land Pirates. They barricade the road. You stop your car, they rob you and kill you.'

'Kill me?' This was not the rent-a-car pitch McCray was used to.

'Your driver, he will know. You see something in the road – a dead elephant, a tree – you don't stop, you don't slow down, you speed up, yes?'

'Yes. I mean no: I'll go in the morning. Before the pirates wake up.'

'Yes, sah.' The woman seemed relieved as she filled in the papers for a car and driver. 'I will see you in the morning.'

McCray's next stop was the hotel's outdoor bar, where brightly dressed and sunburned tourists ate lunch and rolled film into their cameras. McCray found that his hotel was situated on the side of a hill, and the bar's terrace looked out upon the city and the Dark Continent beyond. With no empty tables available, McCray politely asked a man sitting alone if they might share.

'Sure, pal,' mumbled the man in an American accent detectable even through his drunken slur. 'Pull up a chair.'

The portly man wore a broad-brimmed hat and dark glasses, as if deliberately trying to disguise himself. Because his drink was nearly finished and its ice cubes had not begun to melt, McCray judged him to be on something of a binge. For several minutes the two men did not communicate, as McCray ordered a Mister K and the other American worked at a spaghetti-sauce spot on his white shirt with a napkin moistened with his plentiful saliva. When his second Mister K arrived, McCray was sufficiently refreshed to look up and take in his surroundings. The city was at his feet, much of it looking like the debris left by meteor impact. The central blossom of buildings could have been Los Angeles in miniature, and the ball of toxic smog choking the city was further proof that civilization had arrived in Timbali. McCray orientated himself by locating the tall snow-capped mountain on the horizon to his left, an open plain dead ahead where a commercial jet dragged itself from the airport runway, and to the right the rough hills that were pounded by a fierce thunderstorm even as McCray lounged in bright sunshine. The singing of birds could be heard above the drumming city noises, and the terrace walls were engulfed by clinging, hanging, jutting, exploding flowers that were so blazingly full of life that one almost expected them to pipe up and order a round of Mister K's from passing waiters.

'Hey there,' said McCray's table-mate, having finished with the spot on his shirt-front. He removed his hat and dark glasses.

'Hello.'

'You're an American?'

'That's right,' said McCray, than whom there was no more American-looking person. The drunk American was broad of belly, unkempt of hair, baggy of face, and coated in a film of sweat from the top of his freckled pate to the tips of his quaking fingers. McCray guessed the man's age to be fifty-two, doing so by subtracting ten from the age he appeared, in compensation for his drunkenness.

'Ewe heron bison?' the man asked.

'I beg your pardon?'

The man swallowed hard and forced himself to articulate his sentence: 'I say, *are you here on business?*'

'Correct. Was it my dark suit and tie or my briefcase that gave me away?' McCray was alarmed to hear the sarcasm in his own voice, and realized how tired he was from his long journey. It was for the best, he decided, that he would not be venturing off into the hinterland of pirates until the following morning. He would have one more Mister K on the terrace, then hit the hay for the afternoon before dinner. 'Yes, I'm here on business. And yourself?'

'I live here,' said the man. 'I've been here for years.' The man threw out an arm to encompass the landscape beyond the terrace wall, knocking McCray's half-empty Mister K to the ground. 'Next one's on me,' said the man, not bothering to reach down to retrieve the unbroken bottle.

'That's very kind of you.'

'We haveneven been introduced!' shouted the man, his eyes suddenly bulging from his glistening face.

'Charles McCray, from Washington, DC.' McCray extended a hairy hand across the table.

'Nice to meet you,' the man said, meeting McCray's firm dry hand with a limp moist palm. 'My name is Wendell Skinner. But you can call me Skip.'

'Skip,' McCray repeated, his voice betraying scepticism of the incongruous nickname. 'And what's your line, Skip?'

'I am a musician and an international civil servant.'

'Ah.'

'Get this,' said Skip, leaning forward, indulging in the conspirator's obligatory back-of-hand-to-the mouth. 'I work for the Music Programme here – maybe you've heard of it.'

'Yes,' said McCray, who had learned in his political life never to lie to strangers. 'That must be quite an interesting job.'

Skip Skinner began to laugh the laugh of a cuckolded man whose cheating wife has asked him about her position in his will. McCray waited patiently for the laugh to dissolve into an alveoli-wrenching cough, which it did.

'What a gig,' said Skip, when he had recovered. The laughing and coughing seemed to have oxygenated his blood: his eyes and voice had cleared considerably since he had stopped focusing on the spot on his shirt.

'How so?'

'I'll tell you,' Skip said, leaning even further across the table and lowering his voice. 'Right now, as we speak, I am earning one hundred and twenty five US tax-free dollars per day, every day, and the last time I went to my office was seven weeks ago. I've been in this hotel the whole time. The more I stay away,' he said, pausing to peep suspiciously through his fingers at the other people on the terrace, 'the more they believe I am indispensable.'

'That's remarkable,' said the Congressional envoy. 'Good for you.'

'Yes,' said Skip.

McCray intended to identify himself soon, because he didn't believe in doing business this way. It wasn't fair to the Music Programme to let a loose-lipped drunkard sink the ship, especially when it appeared the facts would speak for themselves on the premises.

'You say you are a musician?' McCray asked.

'Trombone. Twenty years of big bands.'

'Wonderful.'

'Oh, sure. You've obviously never played in a big band. Torture.' With a sarcastic expression on his face, using his hands to mime the playing of a trombone, Skip hummed a chorus of 'Satin Doll'.

'And what do you do – what are you supposed to do – for the Music Programme?'

'For starters, I studied the history of the trombone. Almost made me hate the instrument. Travelled around the world playing with its ancestors. Great travel, for a change. No buses, no motels, no schlepping drummers' equipment, music-stands, charts. I love Europe, I married a great gal in Amsterdam, and I played those funky horns. This was known as "field-work".'

37

Skip Skinner finished the last of his drink and looked around impatiently for a waiter. He belched into his fist, then continued: 'After two years I filed my report. I was promoted again and again during the year after that – to tell you the truth, I think it was some sort of computer screw-up, because my promotions were coming in two at a time. Honest to God. Normally a man would have to spend at least two years between each one. I didn't say anything. I found that everyone was supportive, that no one asked questions – I outranked everyone who was in a position to know what was going on, and everyone else knew I was about to go blazing past—*Waiter!*'

McCray recoiled, as did the waiter who had just been screamed at. Skip Skinner ordered another drink for himself, and a Mister K for his new friend.

' . . . For the last coupla years I have flown around the world on a great big open plane-ticket, seeing the sights, visiting my wife now and then, gathering info for my next report.'

'And what is your new topic?'

'The topic will reveal itself to me,' Skip said as his drink arrived.

McCray took a slow gulp of beer, smacked his lips, gathered in Skip's gaze, and spoke: 'I have been sent to Timbali by a United States Congressman who wants me to investigate the Music Programme and report to him on how the US taxpayers' money is spent.'

The corners of Skip's lips flickered like wind-blown flames, a waxy sheen dulled his stare, then a pained grin drew itself upon his face. McCray smiled back in a wry but unthreatening way and sipped again at his beer without losing eye-contact.

Skip attempted to speak, but required a shot of his drink before he could make his voice audible. He smiled even more broadly, and said: 'Would you like to hear about the origins of the slide trombone?'

3

LUDVIK KASTOSTIS stared menacingly at his piano keyboard, trying to unbosom himself of the last tortured chords of his Opus 9, 'Flamedance of Euphorion'. The four-hour piece was divided into three movements: a half-hour *adagio*, written 'For silent soprano and silent E-flat clarinet and silent pipe organ and silent timpani and silent cornet and silent cello and . . .' and so on through the orchestra (during which the audience was encouraged by the programme notes to talk among themselves at the top of their lungs); an hour-long *andante expressivo* 'For solo tenor', to be sung by a man bound and gagged and stuffed inside a black rubber bag; and an extended finale for full orchestra, Kastostis' own team of computer- and synthesizer-players, occasional solo piano ('To be played by someone who can prove he has never touched a piano before' – not hard to find in Timbali), and whatever racket the assembled wild animals chose to make. Kastostis hoped the piece would stand as the definitive MAXIMALIST statement, building in an afternoon-long crescendo into a sound so gigantic that all of Africa, from the most distant baboon plucking fleas from its offspring's scalp, to the Nile crocodile shimmying into its ancient waters, to the Afrikaner cleaning his firearms, to the Polisario knee-deep in a sand dune, would cock an ear and be amazed.

The problem at hand for Kastostis was one he encountered each time he entered the written realm of MAXIMALISM: his 200-stave manuscript paper already overflowed with the traditional stems and notes and ties, as well as stage markings, wine stains, and Kastostis trademark 'music blocks'. His 'music blocks' were the demarcations on a stave where the player was cued to perform the notes of his own choice, just as long as he played them as loudly as he possibly could or, as Kastostis could be counted on saying when he conducted an orchestra full of huffing, puffing, bowing, pounding players, 'Louder still!'

Whenever he reached the end of a piece, Kastostis found his last pages full of nothing but black music blocks. How could he have the French horns bleating like stuck sheep and keep the trombones quiet? No, every instrument had to shriek at highest volume. This waking of the dead made for a messy manuscript, and time-consuming music-block drawing. The piano, at this point, was virtually useless to the composer, who occasionally dropped a forearm on its middle register to remind himself of how marvellous dense dissonance sounded. Kastostis had to admit, way down inside himself, way back there behind his towering artistic integrity, that the gesture of a silent first movement had been at the very least a subconscious effort to save his aching back from days of debilitating composition.

As if the fatigue of MAXIMALIST composition weren't enough, Kastostis was further exhausted and discouraged by the faint sound of his wife practising the piano upstairs. With his mind full of a thundering orchestra and piercing synthesizer section combined in unparalleled cacophony, it was disorientating to continue to hear the gentle tinkling of his wife rehearsing her Mozart on the upstairs Steinway. His own music was so loud in his brain as to bring sweat to his temples, to fill his vision with bright hallucinations of Armageddon, but still the frilly-cuffed Mozart managed to trip down the stairs and dance daintily about his study.

Through the french doors beyond the black expanse of his concert-grand piano, Kastostis observed the comings and goings of his gardeners, four excitable brothers whose work-pattern ranged from prolonged sloth to destructive binges of defoliation. Kastostis' garden, built on ten man-made tiers descending to the same river that several miles later bordered Dr Lord's office area, was part jungle, part vegetable garden, part sculptured floral theme park. Distracted from his work by his wife's piano-playing, he watched with distaste as two of the gardener brothers carried the carcass of a wildebeest past the french doors and dropped it with a thump on the patio near the propane barbecue. Eager to profit from the slightest inspiration that presented itself, and sensitive to the international critics' unanimous belief that he was an entirely humourless composer, Kastostis quickly jotted a melody on the oboe stave of his manuscript, and wrote in the margin: 'You Make Me Feel Brand Gnu.'

'Let them find *that* when I'm dead and gone,' the composer muttered to himself in Czech, indulging the artist's comforting illusion of his efforts' immortality.

Gnashing   teeth, he plunged ahead into the music-block drawing, calculating that in another page or two he could safely draw the piece to its tumultuous close, or that if his wrist grew too tired he could simply add repeat marks at almost any point in the previous eighty leaves. 'Flamedance of Euphorion' meant more to the Czech than any piece he had yet completed, if only because a resident paranoia told him he had not proved himself entirely worthy of his lofty position, and that his cretinous enemies on the Music Programme staff had been biding their time waiting for him to write something so monstrously ugly that the Supreme Director would have no choice but to expel him from the agency. The avoidance of writing something 'ugly' meant to a composer of Kastostis' bent that he had to go beyond the merely dissonant, beyond the aurally unbearable, beyond the untamed volume of his early works: he had to create a work which was unassailably original in its interaction with the human ear, an effect not often achieved by muted strings or standard melodic, thematic and rhythmic interplay. No, that effect was most often achieved, Kastostis had learned, by drenching people in noise, clapping them about the ears, forcing them to watch a stage full of musicians and beasts in ever increasing stages of frenzy. A hostile critic might be offended, revolted, *deafened*, even. But could he say he had not been impressed?

'Of course not,' said Kastostis, hammering on his keyboard to drown out the sound of his wife's delicate negotiation of the piano part to Mozart's Concerto No. 17, which she intended to perform at a banquet the following weekend with a small chamber group made up of Kastostis' colleagues at the Music Programme. Twenty years of departure from the norm – really of flinging himself away from any given standard – had somehow not dulled his innate ability to recognize a beautiful and divinely organized sound when he heard one.

'Bastard,' he said in English, referring not so much to Mozart as to the overall programme of history that had plopped Kastostis down in an era of serious music when dominant-to-tonic progression and banal counterpoint were passé, when any attempt to have one's work go down in marble with those others seemed to require a superhuman effort of convention-blasting which went beyond the scope of sheer musicianship. Kastostis battled every day with his ink-spattered manuscript pages, squaring off not against the act of creation itself, but against the intrusion of doubt and fear that made him admit to himself, in the deepest recesses of his genius, that what he had created was inescapably . . . well, it was *shit*.

'Eleanor!' he shouted. His wife's playing tripped on through Mozart's antique phrasings. 'Eleanor!'

He heard the music ease to a halt with a gentle flourish.

'Yes, darling?' came his wife's clear voice.

Kastostis calmed himself by drawing his hands through his long black hair, plastering it against the sides of his head, and sweeping it down over his neck.

'Won't you come have a glass of wine in the garden? I want to ask those bloody fools why they killed a gnu.'

'They found it out at the fence, Ludvik. I told them if it was fresh we would eat it for dinner. It was electrocuted. No sense wasting it.' Her voice was louder now, as she had come halfway down the stairs. 'Vincent says he knows how to – you know, how to gut the thing and skin it and save the good parts. Our freezer is working again, so I thought—'

'You know I find game indigestible.'

'Lovely, darling,' said Eleanor, now at the bottom of the stairs, referring to her husband's able pronunciation and correct use of the word 'indigestible'. 'But I'm sure you've never had wildebeest. You've eaten some of those wretched skinny little antelopes with the bobbing tails. This is a larger, meatier creature.'

'Please. I have eaten okapi. I have eaten *elephant* – don't tell anyone. I have eaten caterpillars to be polite. I have eaten snake and buffalo and zebra and probably some human flesh mixed in along the way at some of these banquets. I'm in no mood for gnu.'

'As you wish, darling.'

How cheerful she is, and how beautiful, thought the Czech composer. I wonder if playing that pretty music makes her this way.

Inwardly, he narrowed his eyes. He didn't trust his wife when she was happy. In nine years of marriage she had gradually abandoned her musical ambitions, which had been based on an undeniable brilliance. Now, at twenty-nine, she seemed to ask nothing but to bask in her husband's glory and play the occasional concert on the side. It worried Kastostis that she still seemed satisfied with her life, when her musical tastes were so different from his own. She was suitably awed by his music, or at least she had learned never to *mention* his music. She had selflessly welcomed the move to Timbali, had in fact convinced her husband that the Composer-in-Residence post would be a boon to a career that threatened to flame out in its prime unless given some kind of official sanction. She had abandoned her plans to write a biography of Clara Wieck Schumann, which was to have contained a recording of the subject's husband's music as performed by the author. Kastostis had long entertained the fantasy that history would speak his name in the same breath as Schumann's, if only because they held marriage to great female pianists in common. He nearly always cringed when he made the mental comparison, both because a man of even Kastostis' ego thought it bad luck to second-guess posterity, and because he had somehow never got round to composing piano music of a kind his wife could perform publicly. The two 'Fantasia' he had managed to corral on to paper had met with the same reaction from Eleanor when she donned her glasses and attempted to comprehend the notes and music blocks on the manuscript. 'This is marvellous, darling,' she had said. 'Much too difficult. I couldn't possibly. My inhibitions.' This from a woman who once sight-read twenty-five minutes of obscure Scriabin at a Prague piano competition – where she met her future husband – without the slightest lapse in expressiveness.

The unbearable truth was that Kastostis had never quite reached a level of pianism that would permit him to compose truly worthy music for that instrument. Even Eleanor's undergraduate piano pieces – derivative as they were, and containing none of a post-modern composer's sense of artistic cul-de-sac – were more finely crafted than anything Kastostis had written for the instrument, even in playful moods when he allowed himself to be influenced by dead Germans. Midway through his controversial career, Kastostis had compensated for his sub-par keyboard technique by proclaiming the grand piano a 'dead instrument'. Mediocre pianists everywhere welcomed this news. Faithful Eleanor did not press her disagreement; she merely strove quietly onward to polish her skills to a world-class finish.

Eleanor approached her musing husband and gave him a kiss. 'I'll ask Vincent to bring us wine on the terrace, and to give away the gnu. What would you like for dinner?'

'Perch,' said Kastostis. 'And tell Vincent that if he locates the ingredients of a green salad I shall double his pay.'

'That's the spirit, darling.'

Eleanor left the room just as the phone rang on Kastostis' piano. The composer eyed the device suspiciously. He could tell by the tone of the ring – a faint buzz, really – that it was an outside call. Having tried to call home from the city, from the sea-shore, from remote hamlets where he had isolated himself for inspiration and been proudly shown the village phone, Kastostis considered the weak signal to be something of a miracle.

Because this was his first phone call in several years, Kastostis imagined the chances were great that bad news awaited the answerer. Only the knowledge that this room constituted his place of work, and the fact that technically speaking he held certain as yet untapped bureaucratic responsibilities, made him walk to the phone and answer it.

'Kashtoshtish?'

'Speaking.' Kastostis tried to imbue the tone of his one-word reply with the impatience of a man interrupted in the midst of ground-breaking artistic labour.

'It's Wendell Skinner. Skip.'

'Skip? Good God, are you in Timbali?'

'Maybe I am, maybe I'm not.'

'You're drunk.'

'Maybe I am, maybe I'm not.'

Over the years, Kastostis and Skip Skinner had established an alliance based on their mutual fear of losing their sinecures. They had answered the threat in similar ways: Skip Skinner by retreating into his airline consultancy; Kastostis by retreating further into his artistic fortress than he had even during his Prague education, when an artist's genius was measured in the main by his levels of reclusiveness, bitterness and unkemptness, and by the number of his relatives who had suffered at the hands of the Nazis and Russians.

There was a stronger, unmentioned bond between the men. Before his most recent departure for parts unknown, at a farewell banquet for a retiring sixty-year-old Insider, Skip had leaned over to the diminutive Kastostis and whispered in a breath redolent of peanut-butter sauce and whisky, 'Look at your wife with that creep,' the creep being a tall and handsome Jamaican Insider named Thomas (everyone called him Saint Thomas). The three seconds it took Kastostis to dismiss Skip Skinner's warning as a rude and drunken exaggeration saw the Czech composer's entire world-view shrunken into a single-minded loathing of Saint Thomas, of brown people, of his wife, of himself for being so blind. During the months since that

44

incident, Kastostis had reserved an almost mystical reverence for the drunk and leeringly observant Skip Skinner. 'Flamedance of Euphorion' contained an extended trombone solo written expressly for the American who, with his big-band background, was well suited to the Kastostis brand of improvisation-based writing.

Having now watched his wife's behaviour like the insanely jealous husband he had become, Kastostis had yet to gather the evidence he would need to prove her infidelity. On the other hand, he reminded himself by the minute, he had not disproved the possibility that she had found in Saint Thomas or another man a substitute for her husband's physical attention, meagre as it had been during his gruelling assault on Opus 9. It was enough of an insult, Kastostis believed, that his wife had behaved in a way, even for a moment, that would prompt a virtual stranger to remark that she appeared adulterous.

'Terrible,' said Skip Skinner over the phone. 'Awful.'

'Tell me what is the matter. You are in Timbali, aren't you?'

'Yes, yes, yes. All along. Pulling myself together.'

'And?'

'And I've really done it now. Just half an hour ago. I've really done it.'

'You've pulled yourself together?'

'No, I've *done* it. I've screwed up.'

'Relax and explain, old boy.'

Skip Skinner slurred his way through the story of his drinks on the terrace with the fierce American administrative assistant to Satan's own Congressman.

'He'll sink us all,' finished Skinner, nearly weeping. 'And it's all my fault.'

'You must calm down,' said Kastostis bravely, whose own hackles now stood like nails on the back of his neck. Eleanor had returned with glasses of wine, and the look in the eye of her husband stopped her in her tracks.

'What is it? My father . . .?'

Kastostis silenced her with a wag of his stumpy unpianistic forefinger. 'What you must do is calm down,' he said into the phone, his accent set back years by anxiety. 'You must be at work tomorrow, on time. Do you understand? Give your office a call today and tell them you are back from your . . . from your *travels*, and that you expect a tidy desk tomorrow at nine sharp. The American – what is his name?'

'Charles McCray.'

'Yes, God, I remember a circular that found its way here. Now that he has met you he will be sure to knock you up when he gets to the compound. Tell him you were pulling his leg. Tell him you try to pick up male tourists downtown by bragging untruthfully about your job.'

'Oh, great idea, Kastostis. Perfect.'

'Well, you know what I mean. Explain that you were drunk and depressed. You were drunk and depressed, weren't you, Wendell? Show him your trombone collection at the office. Tell him you've been fired, you're about to be replaced. Inefficiency, that sort of thing.'

'I'm going to tell him about you.'

'You wouldn't dare.' Now Kastostis truly did look like Beethoven, so narrowed were his eyebrows, so sneering was his lip. 'Would you?'

'You bet your ass I would. I'll play him your music.'

'Why? *Why*, Wendell?'

'I just don't want this all falling down on me. You're the guy with the most clout I know over there. I've been out of the swim for a few months. I need you to protect me. If this McCray tells anyone what I said, no matter what happens to the Programme, my gig is over. What if he just drops the word to the SD, saying there's a drunkard bone-player who earns more than the Congressman and hasn't been to work in weeks?'

'So you *are* threatening me, eh, Skinner?'

'Well. In a friendly sort of way? We're all in this together.'

'I don't know what you expect I can do, now that you've behaved like a right fool.'

'I'll tell you what, Kastostis. You can tell him and everyone else that I've been working with you all along. Travelling, researching, living with you and your wife when I'm in the country. Being good and productive. Playing your brass parts. Get it?'

'And what would it be that I got in return?' One of Kastostis' thick black eyebrows arched up his forehead like a caesura marking.

'I tell the American I love your music.'

'Done,' said Kastostis, taking one of the wine-glasses from his wife, sipping, smacking his lips.

O'Connor tip-toed across the lawn bordering the Acacia Club poolhouse and sneaked up behind Yvonne as she lay on a beach towel, sunning her seventeen-year-old body. The noon sun was so hot, and Yvonne's flesh was so brown, that O'Connor imagined he could smell the French girl cooking. She lay on her back wearing dark glasses and a white bikini manufactured almost entirely from a length of string. Her skin glistened with baby oil; the air above her flesh shimmered, as above sand dunes. Here was a girl in her mid-teens dooming herself to the leathery Riviera skin of her middle-aged platinum-blonde compatriots.

Next to her was another girl of similar shape who lay on her stomach, exhibiting buttocks brown as coconuts, between which was stretched the single strand that held her scanty garment in place. Her long sloping back was bare and brown, save for a dainty gold chain she had thrown over one shoulder. O'Connor recognized the girl as Yvonne's fifteen-year-old sister, Marie-Claire, whose nickname was Youpie. O'Connor knew that when together the French girls could be sulky, surly, and all too aware of the sexual aura that accompanied them wherever they went. He had learned to expect little conversation from them, just a lot of furtive cigarette-smoking and snarling sibling asides spoken rapidly in French.

As he approached he untied his tie, removed his jacket, kicked off his shoes, tugged off his socks, unbuttoned his shirt, and prepared for near-nudity. There was enough splashing noise of diplo-brats in the pool for O'Connor to be able to undress himself down to the swimsuit he always wore beneath his office attire and to stand over the sisters for a minute or so without their noticing. He signalled to the man behind the bar on the other side of the pool for a Mister K, the universal signal for which was a hand-sign composed of the right index finger held up across the second and third fingers of the left hand, forming a crude 'K'.

He cleared his throat as quietly as he could, and said: 'Yvonne.'

Yvonne cocked back her head, lifted her dark glasses to her forehead, and opened her green eyes. Youpie lazily rolled on to her back, leaving her bikini top behind. Calmly she covered her breasts with forearm and hand for the sake of the Acacia Club staff, who were shocked into physical convulsions by what French girls took for granted on their beaches at home.

'Danny, it's you,' said Yvonne, in a flat accent which she said she had picked up watching American movies with her father.

'I hope you haven't eaten. Hi, Marie-Claire.'

Marie-Clarie made a spitting noise and hoisted a corner of her mouth in disgust. This was her way of saying hello, and O'Connor was used to it. She removed her arm from her chest and stretched, revealing an evenly tanned bosom, which meant that she had been sneaking illicit exposure back at the ambassador's residence.

Dan O'Connor had learned not to feel foolish around these

47

girls, even as they stretched and posed their sleek young bodies like a pair of dolphins, and he pretended to find it merely amusing when they accused the rest of the human world of being shoddy goods by comparison to themselves. Normally, O'Connor would have allowed about a minute of their snobbish nonsense. Normally, he would have articulated his scorn for their Euro-élitism, their smug, puckered, smoke-sucking, upturned mouths fixed in the sneer of the internationally privileged. Normally, O'Connor would have done that, with relish. The reason he did not do that, the reason he put up with their foolishness, was now spread out before him in the form of Yvonne's remarkable shape and colour, her shining hair, her emerald eyes, her tense thighs, her élitist lips. He had come to grips with the sad fact that his lust was greater than his social conscience.

'We waited for you,' Yvonne said. 'We'll eat now, yeh?'

'Yeh.'

O'Connor's Mister K arrived on a tray carried by a beaming waiter wearing a dark brown uniform, nearly as dark as his skin. Sweat had soaked through his heavy costume at the neck, chest, waist, and under his arms. As O'Connor signed his chit, the waiter leaned down and picked up the detritus of the French sisters' sunbathing: used tissues, plates of half-eaten snacks, empty Coca-Cola bottles, discarded paper straws. Without thanking the man, in fact with rather definite disdain in their voices, the girls ordered a lunch of fried perch and chips, fruit salad, vanilla ice cream with chocolate sauce, extra napkins, coffee, lemonade, and a Mister K to share between them.

'And this time', said Youpie, sitting up with a jittering jounce of young breasts in order to strap on her bikini top, 'don't make us wait half an hour.'

'Yes, miss,' said the waiter, who still smiled broadly, but who had taken a step back from the glare of so much well-oiled French flesh.

'Charlie,' O'Connor said. 'Just the fish and chips for me – and another "K", thanks.'

Charlie bowed and retreated backwards, his gigantic teeth bared in a superficially sincere smile which O'Connor hoped only masked murderous designs on the French girls (just as O'Connor's own suave exterior veiled a ghastly lust). O'Connor knew it was the peculiar hang-up of Americans not to adjust to the cavalier treatment of the African servant class by diplomats, experienced tourists and privileged Timbalians themselves. During his stay in the country he had never been able to force himself, even as an experiment, to speak to a servant or a guard or a waiter in the way that unreconstructed colonialists did.

One friend of O'Connor's in particular, an archaeologist or spy named Durin Oakes, actually seemed to change his accent when addressing a laundress or barman or cook. Durin Oakes had pulled into O'Connor's driveway late one night only two weeks into O'Connor's stay in Timbali, looking for the previous occupant of the house. When O'Connor told Durin that the family had moved, Durin flopped on to the couch and ordered one of O'Connor's servants to carry his luggage from his jeep into the guest bedroom, and to prepare dinner for one. During dinner he had muttered a request for melted butter in a voice so low that even O'Connor could not understand him, much less the cowering servant standing at attention in the corner of the room. When O'Connor's servant failed to respond, Durin indicated with a smug grin that our darker brethren were a mite slow on the uptake, weren't they? O'Connor's only solace was that the servants didn't seem to notice Durin's callousness, and that each time Durin departed he left great wads of cash to be distributed among them.

Durin's frequent visits brought entertainingly cryptic tales of adventure in the north, and O'Connor grew to enjoy Oakes's company. He looked forward to Durin's stories, which were told over Mister K's in a peculiar accent that might have been South African, or just the result of too many linguistic influences spread out over a varied life of African travel.

'Weely wather wetched,' Durin might say when describing the living-quarters he had endured during the past two weeks. He invariably showed up with his clothes caked with mud and his hands black with motor oil. While Durin's stories centred around archaeological digs, O'Connor was suspicious of his true occupation because he always seemed to be fleeing from well-documented political and military mayhem. If O'Connor read in the local papers of a violent skirmish or particularly nasty troop build-up, Durin Oakes was sure to pop round within a couple of days.

'Fwightful bore,' Durin would report. 'Bwuddy bastards stwipped my car.'

Durin's hair was the colour of Timbali dust, his face was parched and leathery, his knees were bruised and skinned. No matter what misfortune had befallen him during a trip, he maintained an attitude best summed up by his frequent refrain, 'Can't let the cwetins get you down'. Being visited by Durin was like going to the movies every couple of weeks.

'Wuffed me up a bit this time, they did,' he had said the last time. 'Wanted me petrol. Left me two days' walk from a well wiffout me knoif. Once I'm wested, I'm off to kill the buggers.'

O'Connor had come far enough that he no longer felt the urgent impulse to do physical violence to anyone abusing the superficially servile nature of Timbalians, and he expected that in due course he would be heaping exploitation upon his own modest staff. But for the time being, poolside at the Acacia Club, it wrenched at his heart to see young girls of absolutely no substance treating Charlie – who with his waitress wife somehow fed and clothed eight children – like a pack animal.

'You look wonderful,' he said to Yvonne, as Youpie wrestled with the strap of her bikini. 'You could not possibly be darker.' O'Connor had discovered that bald flattery went exceedingly far on teenage girls.

'Thank you, Danny. Do you know your boss was at our house last night?'

It was all any employee of the Music Programme could do not to spit out his or her mouthful of Mister K at a personal mention of the Supreme Director. O'Connor swallowed hard, placed a finger on Yvonne's glistening thigh, and said: 'You can't possibly mean that.'

'It's true. I've told you, he and my father are friends. He came for dinner, along with about ten thousand bodyguards.'

That was Yvonne's teenage-exaggeration number: about ten thousand.

'Now, listen to me carefully, Yvonne,' O'Connor said, gripping her smooth brown thigh. 'You must tell me everything you saw and heard, from the moment you met him until the moment he left your house.' He thought that to ask for a detailed physical description of the Supreme Director would be to admit that he had never so much as shaken the hand of the man for whom he composed wildly provocative rhetoric.

'Oh, Danny, it was so boring. Youpie and I, we were not allowed to eat with the grown-ups, thank God. Actually, we were not even allowed to meet him. The same as once last year. I think your boss is a very secret person. Maybe we will see him finally at the reception?'

'Reception?'

'Saturday, at our house, in the garden. Everyone will be there.'

Invite me, invite me, O'Connor pleaded with his expressive eyes of Irish origin. He was one grade too low in the Music Programme hierarchy to be invited to the annual goodwill reception at the French ambassador's residence.

'Won't you come?' asked Yvonne.

'I suppose if *you* invited me. Saturday? Let's think . . .'

It flashed through O'Connor's mind that the visiting American troublemaker might have been invited to the reception, or might at least be amenable to invitation. The Supreme Director was said to be almost supernaturally charismatic: no one had ever denied him anything after having met him in person – although admittedly very few people had done so – not even the Arabs who objected to the Israeli architectural team that designed the Nelson Mandela/Albert Schweitzer Auditorium. The Supreme Director shook some hands and served braised lamb in his backyard, bread was broken between Arab and Jew, design and construction went ahead on schedule. With proper timing it might turn out that the Supreme Director was his organization's last best hope when it came to the marauding Congressional envoy. This was how O'Connor could help his desperate friend Dr Lord, by seeing to it that the American came along to Yvonne's house on Saturday. What a coup it would be if the big boss really did make an appearance at last.

'I would love to come,' O'Connor said. 'But an American friend will be staying with me. I don't suppose . . .'

'Bring him,' said Yvonne, with an insouciant gesture of dismissal that was bitchy beyond her years.

'Wonderful,' said O'Connor, jumping to his feet and hurling himself into the pool in one lurching movement, partly to get away before Yvonne reconsidered her offer, partly to squelch the arousal it was impossible to avoid when in view of, much less in physical contact with, the poolside sisters. Because he was so used to this routine, he took it for granted that the French sisters were aware of the reason all the boys tended to launch themselves into the water after a brief hello and did most of their talking from the pool, their arms folded on the deck, their bodies safely cooled and concealed.

From ground level, O'Connor was able to stare flirtatiously into Yvonne's eyes, doing so until she was forced to look away with a coy smile. Noticing this, her sister muttered to herself in French, rolled on to her back and closed her eyes. O'Connor suppressed the knowledge that this was shameless, ethically unsupportable, immature behaviour for a twenty-four-year-old man. Food and drink arrived in time to take O'Connor's mind off these considerations, and the trio retired to a shaded picnic-table a few yards away.

During their meal they were interrupted by a steady parade of Yvonne and Youpie's suitors. O'Connor had hoped his presence would keep the wolfish young men and boys at bay; he found instead that they not only ignored him, they seemed to mistake him for an elderly relative of the girls. The European boys, in their jock-strap bathing-suits, were particularly annoying. They spoke French, they seemed not to care that their sex organs were plainly visible between narrow teenage hips, they touched Yvonne's hair, and they kissed both girls on the cheeks with adult detachment during hellos and goodbyes and sometimes in between. There were even a few privileged black Timbalian youngsters – undoubtedly members of the President-for-Life's truly gigantic brood – who felt comfortable approaching the table and chatting with Yvonne and Marie-Claire. According to some Acacia Club bar-flies, the presence of blacks at poolside in any other capacity than busboy or waiter or gardener would have been unthinkable only five years ago; still, they reported, and thank God, even the President himself was not welcome in the snooker room.

Because O'Connor liked to bring his lunch-break in under two or three hours, he invited Yvonne to take a walk away from the pool, away from the bulging-suited hangers-on. He put on his trousers and shoes, confident that his tan and robust torso would constitute an asset during their stroll in the sun. Yvonne pulled on a pair of pink shorts, slipped her feet into white espadrilles and, in deference to the same indecent-exposure etiquette flouted by her younger sister, put on a T-shirt *before* removing her bikini top.

The Acacia Club, nestled between two flat-topped hills covered by tea-plantations to the north, also adjoined a splendid golf-course to the east, 'Embassy Row' to the west, and a recently nationalized horse-track to the south. Dominating the well-tended driveway into the Acacia Club grounds was a tall statue of Lord Percival Drek, an early settler in Timbali and founder of the Club; and next to it a towering likeness of Timbali's corpulent President-for-Life, which was erected in exchange for permission to keep the statue of Lord Drek on display. Stunted tea-bushes covered the pair of gently sloping hills above the Acacia Club (they had been dubbed 'Her Majesty's Bosom' by irreverent plantation-owners – perhaps even by Lord Drek himself – who had first observed them from the Wellington Terrace). The hills changed colour all day long, from dark green in the morning's shade, to luminiferous yellow in the evening's abrupt equatorial sunset, to a starlit silver at night. The golf-course boasted a rough so dense and unforgiving that its seed was exported to country clubs throughout the world. The course attracted golfing diplomats, and an especially depressed crowd of Timbalian government officials who were terrified of appearing at their offices, fearful of betraying the kind of ambitious bent which could invite disappearance.

O'Connor chose to walk beside the stream that divided Her Majesty's Bosom, along a path reached by crossing the eighteenth fairway of the golf-course. He marched out into the middle of the fairway, put up a hand like a traffic cop to stay an oncoming threesome, and gallantly ushered Yvonne across to safety. He caught up to her, cupped her elbow with his palm as they climbed up to the path, kept some form of contact as they ascended along the trickling stream, and finally grabbed her around the waist when they reached a promontory suitable for standing and staring out over the scenery below. He spun her around and held her from behind as they took in the view. From this vantage-point they could see behind the golf-course, to the south-east, where the dark roofs of shanties sprawled for miles on the flat dusty plain that accounted for the outskirts of the capital. Three-quarters of the city's unofficial population lived in those shacks; officially, they did not exist. O'Connor had looked out from this spot before. Never had he been able to allay the hackneyed emotions of someone who witnesses tarpaper and corrugated-iron shanties, with their dust and smoke and darkness, in the same line of sight with an exclusive pleasure-palace of a country club and a long row of ambassadors' residences bursting with colour and overflowing with appointments of the most superfluous kinds. Because it was several miles away, the black expanse of the shanty-city appeared to be no larger than the combined area of the Club, the golf-course, and the race-track; two million people lived there.

'I'm glad I got you alone,' O'Connor said, although the tragedy spread out at their feet tended to take some of the romance out of the occasion.

'Ah, la,' said Yvonne.

O'Connor took a quick look around for snakes before twisting Yvonne by the hips and kissing her. He had kissed her enough times during the last few weeks that he could now do so absent-mindedly, and he could release her from his grip without staring for too long into her eyes. Yvonne seemed sincere enough as she stroked his broad back, which was still hot from their walk in the midday sun. When he had finished kissing her, he spun her around and pointed her at the blotch of shanties where the majority of Timbalian city-dwellers lived.

'Bleh,' she said. 'That's where the criminals come from.'

'Have you been there?' O'Connor asked.

'Are you crazy? Have you?'

'Yes. On business.'

It was true: O'Connor, along with numerous consultants and experts and guards, had braved the supposed threat of cholera and armed robbery and seen up close how those people lived. Their ostensible purpose had been to record the singing voice of a certain young woman reputed to possess operatic promise. While they never managed to locate the woman, they were able instead to launch a fifteen-year-old girl on an international fashion-modelling career.

'They come and rob our houses,' said Yvonne.

'Yes.'

Insensitive as Yvonne's remark sounded, O'Connor knew it to be factual. The embassies themselves, wired, fenced in, patrolled by submachine-gun-toting guards and homicidal canines, were tolerably immune to common theft. Houses like O'Connor's, on the other hand, were targets of gang robberies of the most violent kind. The first time he experienced such a robbery, O'Connor awoke in the early-morning darkness to the sight of his cook standing in the doorway with a two-foot machete held to his throat by a particularly muscular thief. The scene was nightmarishly blurred by O'Connor's mosquito netting, but when he swept this aside he quickly realized that he was fully awake and a robbery was taking place. A red light on the wall next to the door told him – and the thieves – that the alarm system had been tripped, and that in five minutes a pick-up truck full of bludgeon-wielding security guards would come barrelling down the driveway to the rescue. Sounds of looting could be heard down the hall, as the colleagues of the hostage-holder hurriedly cleaned out whatever valuables they could find, including food. O'Connor sat quietly on the edge of his bed, looking away from his terrified cook, fearing that if he looked into the eyes of the man with the machete the Draconian Timbalian laws governing armed robbery would mean death to both the cook and himself. A shout from down the hall signalled the arrival of the security guards. Headlights from the pick-up truck danced on the bedroom wall. The head thief pushed the cook on to O'Connor's bed and slammed the door. The gang of robbers escaped through the back garden, past the swimming-pool, over a low fence, and into the jungle. The security forces then broke almost every window in the house with their clubs as O'Connor and his cook cowered in the master bedroom. When the guards finally broke into the bedroom, O'Connor could tell by their state of agitation that they would have pommelled any black person they chanced upon. Seeing O'Connor, they sheathed their clubs and began to strut about the wreckage of the house, explaining to the American that they had saved his life. O'Connor didn't notice for several minutes that his dog, Richard, had been uncharacteristically silent throughout the crisis. At daybreak O'Connor found Richard's body, in four pieces, next to the fence at the foot of the back lawn.

It was time for more kissing. O'Connor almost envied Yvonne's obliviousness to the colossal iniquity displayed before them like a generic tableau of the Third World. He held her tighter and wondered what she was thinking. Was she excited, to be kissing a tall strong man seven or eight years her senior? Was she mentally thumbing through her catalogue of suitors, making comparisons, wishing she had gone go-karting or roller-skating with one of those skinny teenagers? Or was her mind as empty as the Timbalian sky, with only the occasional cloud of doubt or curiosity drifting through its open expanse? O'Connor's own mind contained the usual thunderstorms of sexual desperation that any young man is heir to, made more severe by his concern about Yvonne's youth. Matters had improved significantly since he first met Yvonne, because he thought he had actually come to like her. His moral upbringing had been at least sturdy enough to leave him with the idea that he should be fond of under-age women he was in a position to corrupt.

O'Connor opened one eye to survey the blotch of shanties beyond Yvonne's smooth brown cheek, then retreated from her so that they could share the view.

'Look,' said Yvonne, pointing downhill towards Embassy Row. 'There is my house. You will come on Saturday?'

'Definitely.' O'Connor felt a poking poniard of guilt, since he didn't really belong at the reception, but he had come too far with Yvonne to be thwarted now. Besides, he would do Dr Lord a favour by taking 'Crack' McCray along.

'That is probably my brother André in the swimming-pool. Can you see from here?'

O'Connor could make out a splashing in the French ambassador's swimming-pool, a pool built among Greek columns, espaliered shrubbery and quaint garden gazebos.

'I've never met your brother. He's never at the Club, is he?'

'No. He stays alone at home. He is intellectual.'

'Too bad,' said O'Connor.

'And he is too old for the crowd at the pool.'

'Oh, yes?'

'He had twenty-one years yesterday.'

'Is that right? Shouldn't he have a job?'

'He works at the embassy, but will return to France soon for more school. André is going to be Prime Minister of France one day, then after that President.'

'How wonderful for him.'

'Now we should go back,' Yvonne suggested, arching her back and stretching as if waking from a nap.

'Yes, you're right. I should get back to work, ha ha.'

'What it is they all do there, at your job?' Yvonne asked, crinkling her brown nose, as they began to walk downhill along the stream towards the golf-course.

'Uhm.'

With a pang of panic O'Connor realized that this was precisely the kind of direct question 'Crack' McCray would be likely to ask. If one of the chief speech-writers for the organization couldn't answer the question to the satisfaction of a seventeen-year-old girl of questionable English fluency, how, then, to respond to a sharp American politico who would twist the slightest inaccuracy or inconsistency like a dagger in a chest wound?

'Why do you ask?' O'Connor knew this reply would be unlikely to impress Mr McCray.

'Why? Because my father, whenever he talks about the Music – you know—'

'The Music Programme?'

'Yes. Whenever my father talks about the Music Programme, he laughs.'

'He laughs? Ha ha ha?'

'Exactement.'

Marie-Clarie stared grimly into her glass of lemonade. Here was a fifteen-year-old girl in love. Why did Yvonne get *everything*? she asked herself. Or, if she did have to have everything *else*, why couldn't she leave Danny O'Connor alone? Had Danny even noticed her, almost every day at the pool with Yvonne? And now there they were, the two of them together, coming back across the golf-course from their walk, their romantic walk. Were they holding hands, almost? Marie-Claire knew she had never been so unhappy. These silly boys at the Acacia Club, running around and playing like children, their high voices, their skinny legs. Danny, Danny, Danny. Tall and handsome, a *man*.

Marie-Claire muttered to herself under her breath as she watched Danny retrieve his clothes and walk with Yvonne to his motorcycle where they said their goodbyes. He threw a leg over the bike's saddle, kicked over the high-pitched engine and waved in Marie-Claire's direction, just exactly as one would wave to a lover's *younger sister*. Instead of waving in return, Marie-Claire stood up, reached behind her back, removed her bikini top, tossed it over her shoulder, and stood bare-breasted for a two-count before throwing herself face-down on her towel in the sun.

Eleanor Kastostis stared into a swirling pool of butter and poked at her last remaining chunk of perch. She tried to organize an outdoor dinner at least three times a week alone with her husband, who if left to his own devices would probably skip food altogether and sulk into his brandy every evening, barking at the servants. The splendid view from their dinner-table at sunset took in a panorama of golden grass beyond their garden terraces, framed by flowering trees. After dark, a glow from the floodlit fence behind the house illuminated the trees and garden, while the plain on the horizon glistened like a starlit frozen lake. Vincent stood to one side wearing his clean white jacket and black bow-tie, hands clasped before him, hair free of dust. Eleanor's husband twirled his glass of wine, brushed his hair from his face in the warm evening breeze, seemed to sniff with pleasure at the pungent air around him.

'Happy?' she asked him.

'Look there,' said Kastostis, pointing out across the garden, over the river and to the plain beyond. 'Do you see that light?'

A tiny cone of light bumped across the hillside.

'A guard with a torch?' Eleanor asked.

'Ng,' said Kastostis.

'I beg your pardon?'

'Ng. Mr Ng, Head of Personnel. Drives a golf-cart. Indefatigable.'

'Lovely word, darling. You are something.'

'I am *something*?'

'Something. An idiomatic expression. It means extraordinary. In this case it means your command of English amazes me.'

'Thanks to you. And except for certain idiomatic expressions.'

'You are something, Ludie.'

Eleanor was acutely conscious of having to act a role during these dinners. She deliberately set a stage for herself and her husband on the terrace, under the glow of the electric fence, under the gleaming carpet of stars, with Vincent standing by scrubbed and proper, their intimate conversations uttered beneath the muted gurgle of the river below the garden. Eleanor told herself that her motives were golden, that she exhausted herself with kindness to her husband for the sake of his work, which he executed with all the ease of a woman giving birth to quintuplets.

It was in this same spirit that she congratulated herself on keeping her recent affair on a purely physical level. In this way she satisfied the itch her husband could not begin to scratch, she preserved an epic spiritual love for the manic genius she had married, and she maintained the even sexual keel required to continue heaping affection and adulation on a not-always-deserving man whose music she respected but could not stand to hear.

As long as the world received Kastostis' productions with outraged encouragement, Eleanor believed he would be satisfied as an artist, and that some place in the history of music might even be reserved for him. Her only worry was that the crucial ingredient of his genius – namely overconfidence – might have begun to ebb in the wilds of Africa, removed as he was from the international machinery of artistic renown, which was greased as much by social contact and self-promotion as by musical output. The disturbing phone call she had overheard that afternoon, and her husband's later explanation of the conversation, made her fear that Kastostis' legendary arrogance had been replaced by a defensive willingness to bargain with mere mortals to protect his position. If a clumsy instrumentalist like Skip Skinner could ring him at home and make him tremble with threats – the only real threat being that his music would be played for an American bureaucrat – then had he not lost the blind faith in himself that would permit him to complete the wretched 'Flamedance of Euphorion'?

'I'll show him,' Kastostis said, tossing back the last swallow of his wine. 'I'll show that American so-and-so that he cannot—'

'Darling Ludie,' Eleanor interrupted. 'You mustn't become exercised over this insignificant matter. What does this bureaucratic scuffle have to do with your own agenda?'

This seemed to catch Kastostis off-guard, as if he should have thought of how insecure and petty his actions appeared before confiding in his wife.

'It is a minor matter, you are correct,' he said casually, gesturing at Vincent with his glass for a refill.

'You won't let it ruffle you, my sweet?'

'You above all people would know that I am imperturbable where my craft is concerned.'

'Lovely, darling.'

Eleanor pretended to adjust the vase of flowers at the centre of the table to get a surreptitious glance at her wristwatch in the candlelight. Still plenty of time for her husband to drink too much and go to bed before she would race to the river at the bottom of the property for her long-planned assignation with Saint Thomas.

4

WENDELL 'SKIP' SKINNER squinted disgustedly into his toilet-bowl. When he had finished vomiting, he shaved his baggy face, combed what hair he had, brushed the slime from his gums, dried the sweat from his body, and dressed himself in his sharpest suit. He picked up the phone and hoarsely called for his jeep to meet him at the hotel entrance. He could not remember the last time he had dragged his hung-over self from bed at daybreak. Fear had fed life into his sodden corpulence. Without so much as a cup of coffee to cut through his nausea, he hoisted his suitcase and departed, taking the short-cut to reception via the swimming-pool.

Charles McCray stared greedily into the bowl of fresh fruit room service had delivered at the break of dawn. He took the bowl and coffee service on to his terrace to enjoy breakfast beneath the pale morning sky. The terrace was so alive with plant life that McCray checked beneath his wicker chair for snakes before sitting. The low sun angled in over the misty foothills to the east and illuminated the western plains in crisp detail. Snow-capped Mount Timbali sparkled like a wet jewel on the horizon. Just below McCray's terrace a young woman swam laps in the hotel swimming pool. Sweet birdsong and the lapping of water were the only sounds to be heard.

McCray knifed his way through a rather spongy mango, washed it down with rancid local coffee, wished he had a newspaper. Reluctantly, he looked ahead to his journey to the Music Programme compound; part of him wanted to spend one relaxing day at the hotel or exploring the city before getting back to the unpleasant business of slaying an international organization. He watched the young woman's flip-turn at the near end of the pool, and his mind automatically raced through a fantasy of their day together buying souvenirs, feasting on lobster, making love before nightfall on starched hotel sheets as yet another coup rumbled on outside.

McCray's reverie was interrupted by the sight of Skip Skinner lugging a heavy suitcase past the swimming-pool, one hand to a forehead that was almost visibly pounding with pain. The lithe and athletic woman in the pool stopped at the far end to watch Skip drag his bag up the dozen steps to a landing. When Skip had disappeared into the reception area, the girl leaped from the water as if someone had dragged her by the hand, and began to towel herself dry.

'That's it, then,' McCray sighed to himself. He would have to leave now and catch up to Skip before the trombonist had a chance to spread word of his arrival.

Standing up on his terrace, he drew the girl's attention. He waved farewell to her and to the day he had planned for them. She smiled prettily as she dried one of her thighs; McCray had to close his eyes and remind himself of his duty to the Congressman.

Skip Skinner removed the top of his jeep, then drove down eucalyptus-lined avenues with the cool morning air drying the sweat on his scalp. The first leg of his journey wound up increasingly narrow paved roads over the low hills to the north of the capital. The chief danger during this section of the trip came not from Land Pirates or wild animals, but from brakeless city buses overloaded with passengers, belching black fumes, gravity hurtling them out of control towards the city. Skip kept well over to his side of the road, crept cautiously around corners, held his breath when buses roared by. Burned-out skeletons of vehicles that had failed to negotiate tight corners littered the roadside every few hundred yards.

The second leg took Skip through undulating tea-plantations, yellow-green in the morning sun, where labourers had begun toiling among the bushes. At regular intervals natives worked on broken-down trucks or cars. Women carried enormous burdens of firewood, while men smoked cigarettes and urged their spouses on.

It was only during this drive that Skip was exposed to what he thought of as authentic Timbali. Its effect on him was that of driving through a movie set, as if the labourers and bus passengers and wood-gatherers had been placed there entirely for his benefit. Not a lover of nature, Skip was affected by the uncanny beauty of the countryside only to the extent that taking in the fantastic colours and infinite sky above made his suffering stomach churn. He gritted his teeth and pressed on.

Charles McCray's driver wore a khaki military uniform, dark glasses, a black beret, and drove as if pursued at all times by Land Pirates. McCray gripped his door-handle and searched his mind for long-forgotten prayers. With each narrowly missed head-on collision with wildly out-of-control buses, McCray's driver let out a war whoop and accelerated. Terrified, McCray's only comfort was that he would undoubtedly pass Mr Skinner on the way to the Music Programme compound. In an effort to calm himself, and to gauge his driver's character, McCray attempted to converse with the intense paramilitary figure behind the wheel.

'Do you make this trip often?'

'Oh, yes. Many times. The diplomats come this way. Five miles, that is where the embassy residences are. You, you are going further.'

'Is it very dangerous, beyond the embassies? I heard something about . . . Land Pirates.'

The driver reached behind his seat and extracted a particularly evil-looking machine-pistol. 'If I have to shoot, you pay for bullets, OK?'

'Oh, yes. Fine,' said McCray, wondering why such imminent danger hadn't been mentioned in his briefing papers. How did the Music Programme staff carry on, if mortal danger lurked around every curve in the road to their place of employment? 'How often have you had trouble on this road?'

'Me, never. My brother, he had trouble.' The driver made machine-gun noises and pantomimed the strafing of the road ahead with his weapon.

'What was the result of this trouble?'

'Four punctures, a wounded shifter. My brother was arrested for ownership of this gun. I visit him in gaol on Fridays.'

'Seems unfair.'

'Yes, sah.'

With the treacherous hills behind them, McCray and his driver sped through lush terrain on a beautifully paved road. After a few miles, the road abruptly petered out into a graveyard of dumper-trucks and piles of gravel. The highway itself was transformed in the space of a mile from two lanes of asphalt on an open plateau to a narrow dirt road snaking uphill into a rainforest.

'Danger now,' said the driver.

McCray raised a hand and placed it between his skull and the roof of the vehicle as the car jerked and jounced uphill over rocks and dried mud. The driver bit his lip in concentration and worked the steering-wheel like the horns of a bull. The car climbed up the steep path under a dripping canopy of rainforest. After fifteen minutes of this, they surfaced on to a hillside road bordered on one side by a cliff dropping hundreds of feet to the jungle, on the other by a scrubby mountainside ascending into a wispy mist.

'So far so good,' offered McCray hopefully. He was relieved to be out of the darkness of the jungle, but his driver didn't appear to share this optimism: sweat dripped in opaque droplets from beneath his black beret.

'Do you have a cigarette, sah?' asked the driver.

'No, I'm sorry, I don't smoke any more. Is there any place we could stop to buy some?'

The driver let out a screeching laugh of ridicule, which modulated into the even more disconcerting sound he made when he spotted trouble around the bend.

McCray didn't have to ask what the trouble was. Just ahead lay a barricade of rocks, and behind it a group of people surrounding a red and white jeep.

'Shifters!' shouted the driver.

'Skip Skinner!' shouted McCray.

The application of brakes sent McCray's vehicle into a controlled skid on the dirt road, and stopped it only twenty yards from the gun- and machete-wielding Land Pirates.

'They kill us now,' said the driver resignedly, resting his head between his black fists on the steering-wheel. 'We are dead men.'

McCray had long since decided during his travels that he would meet emergencies with exaggerated heroics. He calmly dismounted from his vehicle and approached the scene. Skip Skinner had sunk to his knees before them, and sobbed his plea for leniency in a foreign tongue. The Land Pirates themselves were a dishevelled and impatient lot, but appeared to enjoy the coincidence of having two vehicles stopped at the same road-block. They were dressed in a mish-mash of modern clothes and rags. One wore expensive tennis-shoes, another scuffed brogues that were several sizes too large. All wore filthy turbans.

'Mr McCray,' moaned Skip, only now recognizing his compatriot. 'They're going to cut my head off.'

'Nonsense,' said McCray, if only to say something hopeful. 'You aren't going to behead him, are you?' he asked the closest Land Pirate, who indeed held a machete high over Skip's bowed head.

'They don't speak English,' whispered Skip Skinner. 'Don't make them angry.'

One of the Land Pirates rummaged in the back of Skip's jeep, having already removed the trombonist's suitcase. Another, carrying an old-fashioned revolver, approached McCray's car. He grabbed McCray's driver by the wrist and jerked him to the ground.

'No need for that,' said McCray, with artificial valour.

The Land Pirate who had flung the driver to the ground quickly discovered the machine-pistol behind the seat. He held it aloft and fired a short burst, which caused Skip Skinner to place his nose on the ground between the shoes of the Land Pirates' leader.

'That's all we have,' said McCray in a loud voice. 'Take it and go along.'

Even if they could not understand him, the Land Pirates appeared to be incensed by the American's lack of fear. They shouted amongst themselves and gestured with their weapons for McCray to lie on the ground.

'Do what they say,' said Skip. 'They're desperate. They kill everyone they rob, because if the Army finds them they're shot on sight. They're ruining the tourist industry.'

McCray obliged by slowly kneeling. One of the Land Pirates had removed McCray's briefcase and bag from the back of the car. Skip sobbed quietly while McCray's driver crawled beneath his vehicle. Another Land Pirate ran over to poke at the driver with his machete until he crawled back out again next to McCray and lay face down on the road.

'We are dead men, we are dead men,' was what the driver chose to say once more.

'Shut up, man,' said McCray, determined to go to his doom with the sang-froid of a British army officer at Ypres.

'This is it,' said Skip, as the group of Land Pirates assembled around them, their booty now stored in packs.

And then, from the distance, like the sound of a cavalry bugle, came the beating of helicopter blades. The terrified Land Pirates wasted no time in wrapping up their goods and fleeing down the road, then on to a footpath leading uphill into the scrub. Thirty seconds after their departure, as the three reprieved victims rose to their feet, a helicopter roared into view from behind the hillside and shot overhead.

'Good timing,' said McCray. 'Thank God for the Timbalian armed forces.'

'Armed forces nothing,' said Skip, brushing the tears of gratitude from his eyes, wringing his hands thankfully towards the horizon over which the chopper had disappeared. 'That was the Supreme Director.'

'He'll be here any moment, Mary,' said a harried Dr Humphrey Lord. 'Americans are said to be viciously prompt. Can't you bring up something on your monitor, just in case he looks over your shoulder? A memo? A letter? Better yet, a *chart* of some kind?'

Forewarned of the American's arrival, Mary Mbewa had slathered on an extra layer of mauve make-up, which had already begun to melt in the sun.

'Yes, sah. Maybe that Christmas greeting?'

'No, no. Business, please.'

'Yes, sah.'

Mary Mbewa gazed intently into her computer screen, nudged the space bar, gave up.

Dr Lord paced nervously back and forth outside his hutch, pulling now and then at the crotch of his ill-fitting grey suit. He had gained so much weight that he could no longer button his collar or jacket. A faint smell of ozone alerted him to the possibility of an afternoon thunderstorm, which he welcomed. In the rain the compound tended to appear more solemnly business-like, less like a tropical pleasure-dome.

Dr Lord sniffed at the smell of mothballs on his sleeve; he admired the pattern of treble clefs on his burgundy tie. 'Try to relax,' he said to himself, even as the Supreme Director's jet helicopter pounded overhead. Lord watched it beat past, slowing as it neared the crest of the hill. Wrenched awake from their drug-induced torpor, monkeys screeched and swung from branch to branch, and one even dropped to the ground with a thud.

Dr Lord's only consolation was that in an unprecedented burst of energy he had planned a full schedule of events for the visiting American: a tour of the compound, neatly avoiding the residence of the Supreme Director; an audio tape of the Supreme Director's speech lamenting South African musical rights violations; a sherry-party in the Wagner Courtyard (weather permitting) with a dozen hand-picked professionals who had been alerted to the importance of the American's visit and had been instructed to be on their best behaviour ('Each of you must be able to convey concisely – in one sentence, if possible – what it is you have been doing for the last, say, ten days'). As for himself, just in case Mr 'Crack' McCray should ask, Dr Lord intended to impart a brief discourse on preservation techniques for antique harpsichords.

By pacing back and forth and swatting at flies, Dr Lord hoped to distract himself and avoid a failure of nerve.

Dan O'Connor sat with his feet crossed on his desk, an official-looking folder open on his lap, his computer alive and glowing on his desk, a sharpened pencil held between his fingers like a cigarette. He was sound asleep. He often slept this way, so that in the event of interruption it was only a matter of opening his eyes to appear to be hard at work.

When his phone rang, O'Connor was jerked from a dream involving Yvonne and crashing surf.

'Yes?'

'O'Connor, you must come down here immediately.'

'Humphrey?'

'Yes, yes. You must be here when he arrives. What have you got for him?'

'Well, I . . .'

'Good, good. Whatever it is, I'm counting on you. He'll be here any second. Please hurry.'

It was not encouraging to O'Connor that Dr Lord had so plainly lost his cool. He had hoped to play only a peripheral part in the thwarting of 'Crack' McCray. Nevertheless he picked up his motorcycle helmet and made his way, via a cup of coffee, to the car park.

After their close call, Charles McCray and Wendell Skinner worked quickly to remove the boulders from the road in front of Skip's jeep. McCray had paid his driver with the few notes that remained on his person, grateful to be alive, if penniless. The driver had wasted no time in turning his car around and heaving it downhill towards the relative safety of the capital. In ten minutes the two Americans had rolled the rocks out of the way and were *en route* to the compound.

McCray tactfully avoided his knowledge of Skip's early-morning escape from the hotel, his transparent effort to beat the Congressional envoy to the compound.

'Back to work, eh?' was all he said.

'Oh, lots to do. Get cracking on that report . . .'

Kastostis sipped his fifth cup of tea, still waiting for word from Skip Skinner.

'Leave it to Skinner to oversleep on a day such as this,' he said to himself.

'Flamedance of Euphorion' lay before him in a neat pile: the composer had pronounced it complete. His plan, should he come face to face with the visiting American, was to show him the manuscript and describe it in painstaking detail, hoping to confuse or simply bore the man into believing that the piece must be unrivalled in contemporary musical composition. From the little intelligence passed on by Dr Lord, Charles 'Crack' McCray was known not to be musically knowledgeable. During his early career Kastostis had often counted on such ignorance for standing ovations.

Skinner and McCray reached the gate of the compound, where a uniformed white-gloved guard inspected Skip's identification. It embarrassed Skinner somewhat that the guard didn't remember him, a fact Mr McCray would no doubt register. After a phone call the guard saluted and waved Skip on.

'Here we are,' said Skip, 'safe and sound.'

'What a trip,' said McCray. 'Maybe on my way out I can bum a lift on the Supreme Director's helicopter.'

'Most people never venture as far as the capital,' Skip said. 'They find their entertainment nearby at the Acacia Club, and in the local villages that cater to the ambassadors' residences and politicians' homes. Actually very few employees ever leave the compound.'

'I can see why. It's beautiful here.'

'Do you think so?'

Skinner had deliberately taken the scenic route along the river to Dr Lord's hutch. McCray took in the scenery with pleasure after so harrowing an experience beyond the electric fence.

'Look, water buffalo,' said Skip.

'Oh, yes.'

'And scads of antelope and zebra over near the fence, look.'

'Look at *that*,' said McCray.

'What? Where?'

'Over there. That guy on a motorcycle. Coming down the hill.'

Skip Skinner spotted O'Connor just in time to see him launch his motorcycle over the river, taking the shorter route to Dr Lord's office.

'That's a new employee,' said Skip. 'A crazy Irishman. He's one of the SD's speech-writers.'

'Something of a daredevil, isn't he?'

'Well. Irish, you know. A crack writer, I hear.'

'Thank God you're here in time, O'Connor,' said Dr Lord. 'I just received the warning from the guardhouse. You aren't going to believe this.'

'What is it?'

'McCray didn't arrive alone. He was *escorted*.'

'Yes? By whom?'

'Skip.'

'Skip! You see? I *told* you old Skippy would return one day. I hope he's had lots to say to the American. Told him about his Thai chorus, perhaps.'

'I hope you're right. My God, here they come.'

Dr Lord and Dan O'Connor stood side by side as they watched Wendell Skinner's jeep ford the river. O'Connor cleared his throat and prepared to feign his Irish accent. The new arrivals stepped from their jeep with sighs of profound relief.

'May I present Mr Charles McCray?' said Skip Skinner. 'Dr Humphrey Lord, Mr Daniel O'Connor. Men, we were robbed by Land Pirates.'

'Good heavens,' said Dr Lord, grasping McCray's hand and wringing it rather too forcefully. 'No injuries, I hope?'

'None,' said McCray, now shaking O'Connor's hand. 'They were driven off by the Supreme Director's helicopter. All of our belongings are gone, though.'

''Tis a shame,' said O'Connor, 'but at least life and limb were spared. A wee bit barbaric, some of the natives.'

Dr Lord caught O'Connor's eye and winced.

'How about some tea, then?' Dr Lord suggested, then added seriously: 'Before we get down to business.'

'A Mister K would be more like it,' said Skip. 'Don't you think, Mr McCray?'

With McCray's assent, Dr Lord first introduced his beaming secretary, then sent her off to Gregory's canteen for a tray of lagers. The four men retreated to the shade amid the eucalyptus trees, where Dr Lord had placed extra chairs around his picnic-table.

'This is lovely,' said McCray, inhaling an air so delicate and pure that it was less like breathing than simple ventilation of the lungs.

O'Connor was relieved to find that, although McCray certainly *looked* the part of a bureaucratic hit-man, he showed appreciation of the scenery and a willingness to drink a cold beer before lunch. The Congressional envoy, despite having been robbed during a voyage that even uninterrupted could be quite taxing, had maintained the crisp parting in his hair, the ruddy complexion in his cheeks, the steady hand that now gripped a frosty bottle of Mister K.

'Aah,' said the four English-speakers in unison.

There was an awkward pause before Dr Lord toasted McCray's arrival. 'We will try to keep you entertained,' he said.

'Because I understand you are to be my main liaison, Dr Lord,' McCray said with admirable directness, 'I thought I might tell you right off the bat that, despite what you may have heard, I am not an entirely closed-minded person.'

'Marvellous,' said Dr Lord with all-too-evident credulousness and relief.

'While your organization suffers from, shall we say, a certain PR problem—'

'Oh, does it?'

'– I'm not here solely to bolster that negative image. I am open to persuasion that what goes on here' – McCray swept a hand across the horizon in the direction of the electric fence, where mounted guards patrolled the perimeter – 'might very well be a valuable asset. Certainly I expect it to be unusual.'

'So nice of you to get that out in the open, Mr McCray.'

At this point Skip Skinner rose to leave. 'I must get to work,' he said, which drew involuntary smiles from Dr Lord and O'Connor.

'So nice to see you again,' O'Connor said, not aware that his sarcasm was bound to be picked up by Charles McCray, who had heard Skinner's confession on the hotel terrace the day before.

'Yes, well, I'll be in touch. Thanks for your help, Mr McCray. I might have been killed without you.'

'Nonsense. We were all saved by the Supreme Director.'

'Bless him,' said Dr Lord. 'Goodbye, Mr Skinner.'

Skip trudged off to his jeep and drove away.

'Any chance of my thanking the Supreme Director in person?' asked McCray.

'Possibly,' said Dr Lord, with the instinctive diplomatic caution of a programme director.

'Certainly,' said O'Connor, with the carelessness of an under-ling. 'There's a reception Saturday at the French ambassador's residence. I've been authorized to invite you. The Supreme Director will be there.'

Dr Lord's eyes widened at his new information.

'Sounds good,' said McCray. 'The man's reputation is . . . astonishing.'

'He is a remarkable man,' said Dr Lord. 'Remarkable. One of a kind.'

'Do you work closely with him?' McCray wanted to know.

'I wouldn't say *closely*,' said Dr Lord. 'My field is rather narrow. I'm not involved with policy or fund-raising.' Dr Lord brightened when it occurred to him that O'Connor actually worked in the SD's building, amid those frightful Insiders and their luxurious attire. 'But O'Connor here is one of the SD's speech-writers. Works closely with the man.'

'Is that so, O'Connor?'

'That it is, that it is. While I meet with him infrequently, I am often the recipient of his handwritten missives. A very impressive and persuasive human being, he is.'

'The man has élan,' Dr Lord was able to say, although O'Connor's accent had sent a shiver down his spine.

'Listen, O'Connor,' McCray said, changing the subject. 'I know this is an imposition, but you appear to be about my size, and I'm fresh out of clothing. Do you think I might . . .?'

'Absolutely. I have everything you'll need. You might want to leave with me at the end of the day, come to my house and be outfitted with a few days' worth. And listen: if you find your accommodation anything less than satisfactory, you might stay with me. I have plenty of room, and a young man who cooks the most excellent mint lamb chops.' This was the longest speech O'Connor had ever delivered in his crude Irish accent.

'Outstanding. I believe I'll take you up on that. Valuable insight, to see how the employees live.'

'Quite so,' said Dr Lord, nodding happily, pleased that even more of the onus of McCray's visit had been lifted from his frail shoulders. 'And now how about a quick tour? My land-rover is parked behind my office.'

'That would be fine. Join us, O'Connor?'

'Oh, no, I'll have to be back to the salt mines.' And back to the Acacia Club for lunch with Yvonne.

'Working on a speech, are you?'

'More of an . . . a position paper.'

'Subject?'

'A numerologist now living in Kuala Lampur claims to have broken a code in Scarlatti's keyboard sonatas that sheds light on Old Testament prophecies. We don't believe him.'

Dr Lord gave O'Connor a puzzled but encouraging look. O'Connor shrugged his shoulders almost imperceptibly.

'How interesting,' said McCray. 'Who knew?'

Eleanor Kastostis laboured through her morning piano exercises, fighting off the exhaustion that inevitably stemmed from spending half the night trysting in the rainforest with a Jamaican lover. The assignation had not gone well; in fact the night of seduction had nearly ended in tragedy.

Saint Thomas had been waiting for Eleanor as planned, equipped with a blanket and suitable potables, dressed in complete colonial adventurer's gear, including hunting-jacket and pith helmet. A cuckolder of Saint Thomas's accomplishments needed something out of the ordinary, in this case a Great White Hunter fantasy, to inject zest into what had become his routine midnight exercise.

The pair reclined on the blanket by the river – the same river that would snake downstream past Dr Lord's picnic-area, then pass over the waterfall where Dan O'Connor performed his motorcycle stunt. Eleanor obliged Saint Thomas's fantasy by acquiescing to a fabricated tale of the day's rhino hunt, which was spiced with an aside about a fourteen-year-old gun-bearer named Jonah whom Saint Thomas had been forced to shoot for insubordination and cowardice.

'Pitiful kaffir,' said Saint Thomas, unbuttoning his fly.

Overhead, between the overhanging trees, the sky was thick with stars. Eleanor watched patiently for streaking meteorites while Saint Thomas finished his story and discarded his jodhpurs.

'Tomorrow, rogue elephant,' he concluded, addressing his attention to Eleanor's blouse.

This was the part Eleanor liked. She had only to reciprocate with appropriate noises and muscular resistance as the wiry and athletic Saint Thomas moved over her body like a spider wrapping a fly. In the thick of the act her view of the stars was obscured by her partner's pith helmet, but soon this, too, was cast aside in the excitement. With the helmet gone she opened her eyes and enjoyed the stars and rising moon. Eleanor allowed herself the luxury of nature-watching at this juncture, for she knew from previous grapplings with Saint Thomas that she could count on a relatively uninterrupted hour and a half of precisely this.

It was light enough beneath the stars and the moon to make out individual leaves and vines in the trees above. Eleanor alternated between focusing on Saint Thomas's energetic and relentless physical attention, humming the French-horn part to the *Tannhäuser* overture, and tracing the lines of Orion.

While staring up at the trees and the stars, perhaps three-quarters of an hour after Saint Thomas had begun performing in earnest, Eleanor caught a glimpse of something in a tree directly overhead that caused her to tense up spasmodically. Saint Thomas noticed.

'What is the matter?' he asked, not sounding even the slightest bit out of breath.

Eleanor found her voice-box paralysed at the sight of a glistening green mamba hanging by the last few inches of its body. While she couldn't speak, she could move. She wriggled out from underneath Saint Thomas in a manner that caused him considerable pain and surprise. He quickly understood, though, and rolled to one side. He turned and watched the green mamba drop on to the blanket, as he would later tell his fellow-Insiders, 'right where my perineum had been only a moment before'.

Eleanor and her lover knew that the green mamba was a slim, long, speedy, deadly snake; its nearly phosphorescent colouring screamed out evidence of toxicity. Eleanor jumped into Saint Thomas's arms and just barely stifled a shriek that might otherwise have wakened her husband back in the house. Shining in the starlight, the green mamba turned on the blanket and seemed to stare with its needle eyes at the naked couple trembling nearby. It twisted around Saint Thomas's bottle of port, shot its tongue over the rim of Eleanor's half-empty glass, then slithered with tremendous acceleration uphill towards Kastostis' house.

'It's gone,' said Saint Thomas.

'My God,' said Eleanor. 'We might have been killed. How would we have explained that?'

Saint Thomas didn't dare escort Eleanor any closer to her husband's house, for fear that servants or guards might spot them. Therefore it was a terrified Eleanor who made her solitary way up the hill, in the slimy tracks of the mamba, to the safety of her house.

Eleanor shivered at the recollection of this journey as she completed her scales and began a cursory study of the Mozart concerto she had been rehearsing for the weekend's reception. What clearer sign did she need than a close call with a poisonous snake to show her how irresponsibly she had behaved? In the clear thought of daylight, she realized that she would rather have been killed by the mamba than have her husband discover her infidelity. Ludvik Kastostis' artistic self-confidence was fragile enough without the monumental insult of his wife's having it off with a near-stranger in the jungle.

Dr Lord thought the tour was going very well. The dreaded Charles 'Crack' McCray turned out to be as affable as could be. The American asked pertinent but moderate questions, and seemed to understand each time Dr Lord confessed his ignorance or asserted his unwillingness to answer for others.

The first stop on their tour was Gregory's canteen, where they picked up another couple of Mister K's: McCray's nerves still needed calming after his run-in with the Land Pirates, and of course Dr Lord needed all the personality he could metabolize. Next, Dr Lord drove to 'The Special Place', the grave of a Norwegian artist who had sculpted the bust of Wagner for the Wagner Courtyard. The artist had thrown himself from the roof of the Music Programme headquarters just after, or in many people's opinion well before, the completion of his work.

'And now', announced Dr Lord, bounding over a dirt track away from the Norwegian's grave, 'what you've all been waiting for.'

The headquarters of the Music Programme now came into view: the massive central building surrounded by groomed lawns and shaded walking-paths; the conference-hall complex, gleaming white in the sun; the auditorium, rearing back on its ribcage of steel flying buttresses; the Supreme Director's pent-house office, revolving slowly with the path of the sun to maintain a consistent southern exposure on the organization's penetralia. While gathering in these sights, McCray took the opportunity to check some of his figures with Dr Lord – number of employees, number of divisions, salaries, pensions, benefits. Dr Lord answered as truthfully as he could given his limited knowledge of the organization, and was quick to admit that he was not the person to ask about specifics. 'It's Mr Ng you'll want to see,' he said.

It took all of Dr Lord's concentration to drive, to field McCray's questions, and to avoid any road or trail that might reveal a glimpse of the Supreme Director's palace on the hill. It was inevitable that McCray would spot the mansion at some point during his stay, but Dr Lord didn't want to be the one to explain it to him.

'My God. Stop. What's that?' said McCray.

'What? Where?' said Dr Lord, accelerating.

'Stop. Go back. What was that fantastic thing up on the hill?'

★   ★   ★

Skip Skinner ground to a halt in Ludvik Kastostis' gravel drive-way, emerging from his vehicle into a white cloud of his own dust. Coughing and waving at the air, he marched to the front door where he was greeted by the composer's firm handshake and look of searching expectation.

'Good news and bad news,' said Skip.

'Well? Well?'

'The bad news is that "Crack" McCray is here, right here in the compound.'

'My God. And the good news?'

'The good news is that the SD saved McCray's life on the way up here.'

'I suppose that is something.'

'No doubt he'll stop by here this afternoon on his tour. Humphrey already has him bumping around in his land-rover.'

'I had anticipated that,' said Kastostis, standing taller and folding his arms across his chest. 'I have completed my Opus Nine.'

'Congratulations. Shall we drink to that?'

'Vincent!' shouted Kastostis. 'Ginny tonics!'

When their drinks arrived, Kastostis warily presented Skinner with his bulky 'Flamedance of Euphorion' manuscript. He spread it out on the coffee-table in the living-room for the American's perusal.

'H'm, yes,' said Skinner, extracting a pair of shaded reading-glasses from his jacket pocket, 'let's see here.'

Kastostis held his breath. It wasn't that he trusted Skip Skinner's opinion more than anyone else's, nor that he thought any musician could judge such a piece without hearing it performed; it was simply that like all artists of gigantic self-esteem Ludvik Kastostis trembled with insecurity at the thought that someone might misunderstand his work to the point of actually *disliking* it.

'Very impressive,' said Skinner, who had spent the previous three minutes rehearsing in his mind exactly what to say and in what tone.

Kastostis exhaled with relief, then gathered himself up for a remark that would smack of arrogant genius. 'It is my most magnificent work,' he said flatly.

'I can see that,' said Skinner. 'The black rubber bag is particularly . . . Iron Curtain of you.'

'I'm so glad you appreciated that.'

'And this ending', said Skinner, flipping through the dense pages of black-ink blocks, 'will blow their minds.'

'Do you think it can be explained to the American, this Mr McCray?'

'Absolutely not.'

'Good,' said Kastostis. 'Vincent! More ginny tonics!'

As Dr Lord and Charles McCray approached the outdoor cafeteria on foot, Dr Lord used subtle but urgent twitches of his facial muscles to warn all those seated there that he was accompanied by the enemy.

'Oh, good,' said McCray. 'I can meet some of your colleagues.'

Dr Lord turned pale when he saw McCray take his tray of food and head directly towards a table occupied not only by Thwok and the Bloody Bolshies, but also by a French lunatic named Jean-Baptiste Grandmarie, whose adoration of what he called 'neo-tonal music' had brought Dr Lord close to physical violence against him on numerous occasions. Grandmarie was saved in Dr Lord's esteem only by his great skill as an organist. Dr Lord caught up too late to steer McCray clear, and was forced to make introductions.

'Hello,' nodded the communists in unison.

'Bienvenue à Timbali,' said the Frenchman.

'So happy to meet you,' said Thwok. This amazed Dr Lord, who hadn't known that Thwok could speak English.

Seated between Thwok and one of the Bloody Bolshies, McCray was treated to a confusing debate on the subject of embouchure. A dental reconstruction technique had been developed in Finland that would alter the embouchure of brass-players who suffered from the lack of a powerful upper register. Jean-Baptiste Grandmarie supported the idea; the Bloody Bolshies argued that if the technique were allowed to continue only the rich could produce clear high notes; Thwok babbled incoherently during pauses in the conversation.

'Do you mind if I ask a question?' McCray interjected. All eyes turned to him. 'When you've worked this out, then what happens? A formal resolution? Funds for dental surgery in the developing world?'

'Mais non,' said the Frenchman.

'What, then?' McCray wanted to know.

'Nothing,' said one of the Bloody Bolshies. 'This is not business. This is our lunch-hour.'

'I see,' said McCray reasonably. 'And may I ask what you've been working on, business-wise? It's my task, you see, to investigate the Music Programme.'

Dr Lord nodded frantically at his colleagues. 'Go on,' he said. 'Tell him. Not you, Thwok.'

Jean-Baptiste Grandmarie brushed a forelock of greasy black

75

hair from his brow, and spoke. 'Schoenberg's middle years', he said, 'have been a great concern of mine of late.' The Frenchman left it at that, as if this vague statement explained how his days were spent.

One of the Bloody Bolshies, an attractive elderly Bulgarian woman named Lyudmila, stepped in: 'Am helping to organize December conference for women instrumentalists.'

'How interesting,' said McCray, much to Dr Lord's relief.

'Yes,' said Lyudmila. 'Very simple. We try to encourage young women to think of themselves professional quality. Fill world orchestras with women.'

'I see.'

'Yes, yes,' said Dr Lord. 'Very important work.'

'Salope,' said the Frenchman, spitting a speck of food on to the table. He did not approve of females playing their instruments anywhere but in the salons of their husbands' homes. No one at the table understood the word; Thwok repeated it anyway, as if to practise it.

'And this conference in December,' McCray asked, 'will it be well attended?'

'We hope,' said Lyudmila. 'Many women speakers. Many all-women performances. Composing clinics for women, by women.'

'Wonderful,' said McCray.

Dr Lord found himself beaming at Lyudmila.

'Never mind, never mind,' said Thwok, standing and smiling at McCray and Dr Lord. 'God will please bless all of you one at a time.' Thwok turned and departed.

McCray seemed unfazed, but Dr Lord thought it wise to smile at him apologetically. 'Thwok is a superb harpist,' he explained. 'Good man. No real English. His calling-card is the absurd *non sequitur*.'

'Look over there,' said McCray, allowing himself a *non sequitur* of his own.

'Where?'

'There, near the gate. There goes that crazy Irishman again. What's his name?'

'O'Connor. Yes. Probably off to lunch at the Club.'

'And look at *that*,' McCray went on. 'That motorcade.'

'Ah. That would be the Supreme Director on *his* way to lunch. Probably an official banquet of some kind. Such a busy man.'

'Is his life in danger, by any chance?'

'H'm?'

'All those guards. The armoured vehicles.'

76

'Not my field, really,' said Dr Lord. 'There have been rumours of threats, of course. He is a prominent dignitary, and the existence of the Music Programme headquarters here is something of a boon to the government in power. Opposition groups – well, guerrillas, frankly – look for opportunities to destabilize . . . Well, you would know better than I.'

'I think I understand.'

'Our generator has been blown up six times during my five years in the country. Do you see it there, on the horizon? It's hell on the computer system, I hear.'

Jean-Baptiste Grandmarie and the Bloody Bolshies had finished their meal and excused themselves, the Frenchman doing so with a stiff bow and an entire sentence in French which no one else at the table understood.

'Horrible man,' said Dr Lord. 'I *must* say.'

'I wish I knew more about music,' said McCray. 'What's all that about Schoenberg?'

'Bloody ghastly twentieth-century noise. Hyper-intellectualized, atonal, random, spiritless—'

'Well, Grandmarie obviously doesn't think so.'

'Frog bastard.' Dr Lord could not be diplomatic, or even polite, when it came to serial music.

'I gather that your speciality is Bach.'

Dr Lord's expression softened, and he bowed his head, as if he had just been reminded of his mother's death. He clutched at the air with his right hand, then looked McCray in the eye. 'During your stay I will attempt to explain.'

'I sense that there must be considerable in-fighting around here. You do adopt musical *policies*, do you not?'

'That is correct. But it is far from a democratic process, as you can imagine. Conferences are held, papers are written, but in the end the Insiders – I mean the Supreme Director and his cabinet – make policy.'

'And what are his tastes?'

'He's terribly open-minded. Rather too tolerant of aberrant music, if you ask me. I suppose a man in his position must attempt to please a broad spectrum of musical interests, but my feeling is that boycotts are in order for certain of the lesser forms.'

'For example?'

Dr Lord picked at his goatee. 'For example, all music composed after the death of Bach.'

'I sense that you are a radical. I thought everyone liked Mozart . . . and the others.'

Dr Lord looked pitifully at the American, like a priest at an unrepentant sinner. 'That's what I believe the Music Programme is for,' he said. 'To dispel such a notion.'

Dr Lord hoped he had not gone too far. He simply couldn't hold back when it came to his musical tenets, which he held more firmly than the most committed religious zealot. But on the whole he thought his tack was an improvement over the one he had fully expected to pursue, namely that of a grovelling know-nothing begging on his knees for mercy from the super-power's plenipotentiary.

The pair sat in silence for a few moments, soaking up a hot sun beneath the fluttering flags of a hundred-odd nations. Dr Lord wondered what the American could possibly be thinking, what his impressions had been so far. Rumour had it that McCray's boss accused the Music Programme not only of waste and inefficiency, but also of an anti-American bias: his fear was that the organization tended to favour obscure folk-music in the developing world – as well as esoteric and unprofitable classical music – that if allowed to prosper would cripple the monolithic American corporate pop-music machine that set the taste trends of the industrialized world. Dr Lord had unconsciously decided not to challenge such an indictment, and instead to assert the importance of promoting non-commercial music. Something about his new position as director had instilled in Dr Lord a strength of conviction he never knew he possessed. He was determined to win over the American by drenching him in the majesty of Bach, letting the Master's works speak for themselves, leaving it to McCray to discover the unassailable integrity of the music the Programme did so much to support.

'So,' said McCray. 'When do I get to meet your Composer-in-Residence?'

5

DAN O'CONNOR found Yvonne alone at poolside, wearing a pair of pink sun-glasses that matched her bikini bottom, which was her only article of clothing.

'You are awfully dark. Darker than yesterday, if possible.'

'I want to be black, if I am going to live in Africa.'

Dan undressed and ordered his usual lunch from a particularly harried-looking Charlie.

'Where is your sister?'

'Oh la-la, la-la.'

'H'm?'

'Youpie says she will not come to the Club with me any longer.'

'Why?'

'She will not talk to me, but I think I know.' Yvonne held up her hand, her thumb and forefinger pinched together. 'She has a little crush on you, I think.'

'Who, *me*?' O'Connor blushed with gratitude.

Yvonne rolled on to her stomach and sat up, an impossibly

brown forearm held over her chest for the sake of the staff. 'She is so young,' she said. 'She's only fifteen, you know.'

'Yes, of course. There must be a tremendous gulf separating fifteen and seventeen . . .'

Dan's lunch and Mister K had arrived.

'I'm looking forward to that reception at your house tomorrow. I invited that friend I mentioned.' Yvonne seemed not to remember. 'The American friend I said I would invite?'

'Good. Fine.'

'But, sweetie, you have to do me a favour. You can't tell anyone I'm from the United States. Do you understand? They don't know I'm American, and my job sort of depends on their not finding out.'

'You work at such a funny place.'

'You wouldn't tell anyone, would you?'

'Why would I?'

'And you won't laugh when you hear me speak in a strange accent?'

'I'll try,' said Yvonne, already giggling. She looked at him with bright green eyes over the tops of her pink sun-glasses. 'Finish your lunch so we can walk.'

O'Connor gulped down his food as Yvonne took her time putting on a white T-shirt with the Music Programme logo on the front (the logo consisted of the globe encircled by a transparent staff of musical notes: B flat, A, C, B, repeating in quarters, eights and sixteenths as it wound around the planet).

'When you gave this shirt to me,' Yvonne said, 'my sister, she cried for a day.'

'Poor thing.'

Yvonne then asked suggestively if O'Connor would like to take the rest of the day off. 'My father won't return until six. My mother will return from France only just in time for the party tomorrow. Youpie is sulking in her room. My brother is adjudicating a debate at the French school.'

'What could be clearer?' said Dan. 'We could take a swim, we could—'

Yvonne gave him a squeeze.

'Wait, wait,' O'Connor said, grimacing as he remembered his appointment with 'Crack' McCray. 'I have very important work this afternoon.'

'Don't be silly,' said Yvonne. 'You have never had important work until now.'

'This is different. That American fellow I told you about. I have to take care of him at my house.'

'Bof,' said Yvonne.

'But tomorrow,' Dan said in a rather desperate tone. 'I'll see you at the party tomorrow, won't I?'

'I suppose so.'

'Cheer up, sweetie. Give me a kiss.'

'Danny?'

'H'm?'

'I have decided to fall in love with you for a little while.'

'Good idea,' said O'Connor.

'Oh Christ, they're here already,' said Wendell Skinner, peeping through the curtains. 'I'll escape out the back.'

'Stay where you are,' commanded Kostastis, drawing both hands backwards through his hair.

'What's the matter?' called Eleanor from upstairs.

'Dr Lord has brought the American, my dear. No need for panic. Come down and be introduced. Vincent! Get the door!'

With a nervous glance at his master, Vincent shuffled to the front door and opened it for the visitors. Wendell Skinner was surprised to see that Kastostis, rather than approach the door to greet his new guests, retreated to the opposite side of the room and turned his back. His short dark shape was silhouetted against the french doors leading to the terrace. This left it to Eleanor to make introductions, to arrange for refreshments, and finally, during an inevitable pause in the banter, to point across the room and explain that her husband the maestro appeared to be deep in thought.

Eleanor, for her part, was grateful for this interesting diversion from her piano scales. The much-feared American turned out to be a rather dashing gentleman with the kind of toothy smile not usually found outside North America. She scolded herself for being immediately attracted to the rugged 'Crack' McCray, but mentally threw up her hands and asked herself what she was *supposed* to do when her husband had no energy for anything but his noise-making compositions.

Charles McCray, for his part, welcomed the self-confident smile of Eleanor Kastostis, whom Skip Skinner had introduced by describing her as 'on the top tier of pianists in the world'. When they shook hands, he took care not to squeeze her slender fingers too forcefully. He found himself beaming at her, as if he had not been introduced to so attractive a woman in months, which was in fact the case.

Skip Skinner told Eleanor of their brush with the Land Pirates, implying that McCray had fought off the brigands single-handedly.

'But, then, you have no clothes!' said Eleanor. 'I'm afraid my husband isn't . . .'

'It's all taken care of, thank you anyway. A speech-writer, my size, has offered to help.'

Skinner cleared his throat loudly, hoping to wake Kastostis from what Skip assumed was a panic-induced trance.

'Is he OK?' McCray asked.

'Oh—' started Skip.

'He'll be fine,' said Eleanor, improvising. 'He has only recently completed a major work, and . . . and he has felt a little *depleted* during the past two days. Darling? I say, Ludie, sweetheart?'

Kastostis held on as long as he could under the excruciating strain of pretending to be in the grip of a mystical stupor. He counted the stones on his terrace outside, he squinted into the distance to see if he could make out the roof of the Supreme Director's palace through the trees, he hummed one of the internal motifs of his Opus 9. When he finally turned round to meet his enemy face to face, he did so with as contorted an expression of genius as he could muster, followed by a show of surprise that a group of people stood in his living-room staring at him.

'Ah,' he said distractedly, turning to his wife for an explanation. 'Company!'

'Darling, this is Mr McCray, from America. And you remember Mr Skinner, he's been here for hours. And of course Dr Humphrey Lord, the Bach specialist.'

Dr Lord scowled despite himself. He had seldom met Ludvik Kastostis in person, and on each occasion it was all he could do to restrain himself from spitting on the man's shoes. Dr Lord did not like the Czech's music.

Kastostis moved across the room to shake the Congressional envoy's hand. 'Welcome, Mr McCray. To what do we owe this honour?'

Skinner winced, and hoped an objective observer would find the composer's act convincing.

McCray stated his case with what Kastostis thought was admirable directness and clarity.

'I see,' said Kastostis when the American had finished. 'Have you ever been to Czechoslovakia?'

McCray seemed to take the change of subject in his stride. 'As a matter of fact, I have. Only three months ago I was—'

'Vincent!' shouted Kastostis, then looked at his wife for support.

'Yes, Vincent,' she said. 'Cheesy crackers, lagers, please. Will that be all right?' she asked McCray.

'Wonderful,' he said, full of admiration for the poised and elegant Eleanor.

'Mr McCray,' said Wendell Skinner, 'I have worked closely with Mr Kastostis on his most recent work. The maestro has been kind enough to write a special trombone part for me. It is a towering work, I'm sure you'll find.'

'Oh,' said Kastostis absent-mindedly, raising a limp forefinger and pointing behind McCray. 'There it is on the coffee-table.'

'I'm afraid I don't read music,' said McCray. This comment triggered a quick meeting of eyes between Kastostis and Skinner. 'But I'll take a look, if that would be all right.'

'Certainly,' said Kastostis.

McCray leafed slowly through the massive manuscript. His eye was caught by the unusual markings written in English: 'A black rubber bag is brought from the wings by two women in ancient Egyptian garb'; 'A backcloth descends behind the set with the word 'PAIN' stencilled upon it in all the world's languages'; 'The Four Men begin digging'.

'I'd say this is quite unusual,' McCray remarked.

Kastostis fiddled with his hair, as Eleanor and Skinner nodded emphatically. Dr Lord only just prevented himself from issuing audible signs of his disapproval.

'Animals?' McCray asked, not quite masking his disbelief.

'"Such sweet compulsion doth in music lie",' said Kastostis.

McCray looked to Eleanor for an explanation.

'Milton,' she said, then addressed her husband: 'Lovely, darling.'

Earlier in the day, Kastostis had taken a peep into his wife's *Bartlett's* in search of just such a vague gem of antique poesy to toss out when detailed elucidation of his work might prove counter-productive. It seemed to have done the trick, for McCray replaced the manuscript on the table and changed the subject.

'Such a beautiful house. We are still within the compound?'

Kastostis forced his expression to turn blank in the face of such a mundane query, and once again turned his back on his company.

'Thank you,' said Eleanor. 'It is the permanent residence of those holding my husband's post. He has been the only one, of course. And, yes, we are still within the fence, if that's what you asked.'

McCray was charmed by Eleanor's English accent. 'I'd imagine the fence would be dangerous for children.'

Eleanor was charmed by McCray's manly American intonation. 'We have no children, but your point is well taken, Mr McCray. Quite a few animals have come to grief on the fence. On the other hand, there is no better place to raise a family. Timbalian women are wonderful with babies.'

'I would think so,' said McCray. 'They have ten each of their own. Sorry, I don't mean to be sarcastic. I was reading about birth rates on the plane yesterday.'

Wendell Skinner thought everything was going well. Vincent had brought beer; McCray and Eleanor had hit it off; Kastostis really did look like a brooding genius.

Dr Lord wanted to leave; this was enough excitement for one day. He thought it too much to ask that he feign approval of Ludvik Kastostis. Could the American possibly be fooled by the composer's music blocks and synthetic sounds and wild animals dropping excrement all over the stage between the singers' feet? 'Computer music indeed,' he had once written in an unsent memo to the Supreme Director. 'A composer may employ whatever instrument he wishes, but in my opinion high technology does not excuse cacophony. A great composer may explore the possibilities of computers and synthesizers if he chooses, but that does not prevent the rest of us from informing him that the resulting noises are distasteful. When a computer makes a recognizably beautiful sound, I will be the first to admit it.' As an instrumentalist it offended Dr Lord that highly trained musicians, men and women who had devoted years of study and practice to their craft, were forced under Ludvik Kastostis' baton to perform sounds that were unnatural to their instruments and could just as easily be made by unskilled amateurs: growls and shakes in the brass; screeches and honks in the reeds; pianists forced to grovel amid their precious strings, plucking and stroking them with artificial aids. It upset Dr Lord greatly.

'I'm afraid I must excuse myself,' he finally said, just as Kastostis came out of his most recent trance and began explaining his 'Flamedance of Euphorion' in more detail. He had decided to cancel his sherry-party. 'I'll contact Dan O'Connor and have him pick you up here, Mr McCray.'

'Thank you for the tour, Dr Lord. See you tomorrow?'

Dr Lord nodded to his colleagues and retreated with a sigh of relief.

Eleanor moved close to McCray and said: 'He loathes my husband's music.'

'Is that so?'

'Poor dear. Dr Lord is a purist. He lives for the B-Minor Mass. Sometimes' – she lowered her voice as her husband neared – 'sometimes I don't blame him.'

Kastostis now pretended not to know who McCray was.

Eleanor patiently reminded him. Skinner surreptitiously signalled Vincent to bring more drinks. McCray tried to ask Kastostis
specific questions about his post, but was met with what
sounded like harsh epithets in a foreign language – Czech, he
assumed. Finally Kastostis shook his head violently, as if fending
off a troublesome insect, and left the room. Wendell Skinner
followed on his heels.

'You must forgive him,' said the ever poised Eleanor. 'My
husband lives in a different world from the rest of us.' She
surprised herself with this show of loyalty; she could just as
easily have asserted that Kastostis was a fraud.

'I hear a motorcycle. Could that be the speech-writer?'

'No doubt. Must you leave so soon? When will we meet
again?' Her eagerness was unmistakable.

'I have very little planned. A reception tomorrow, I gather,
at—'

'The French ambassador's residence? My husband and I will
be there. It is an annual event. Wonderful.'

McCray shook her hand and departed, pausing in the doorway to listen to a high-pitched singing that must have been
Kastostis in the kitchen with Skip Skinner. Eleanor shrugged her
shoulders and smiled apologetically.

'Climb on,' shouted O'Connor over the din of his motorcycle
engine, careful to maintain his brogue. 'You'll be needin' this
helmet.'

'Has he gone?' asked Kastostis, peering around the doorway
from the kitchen.

Eleanor narrowed her eyes at her husband. 'Yes, just now.'

'How was I?'

'Marvellous, darling.'

'And what do you think, Wendell?'

'Vincent! Ginny tonic!'

O'Connor and McCray bounded out of the driveway leaving a
spray of gravel behind. Soon they were on the Ring Road,
bordering the electric fence, buzzing along at high speed.
McCray raised the visor of his helmet to take in the countryside:
a broad plain to the right, beyond the fence, where a lone acacia
tree stood like a beach umbrella; a downhill slope to the left
towards the river that wound through the compound; a hillside
beyond where the Music Programme headquarters shone in the
waning sunlight; and above it . . .

'What the hell is *that*?' shouted McCray, leaning forward on the bike and pointing towards the hillside.

O'Connor throttled down. 'What? Where?'

'That . . . that *thing* on the hill above the main buildings!'

'Oh, *that*,' shouted O'Connor, speeding up again. 'The residence of the Supreme Director!'

'I'd like to see it!'

'Wouldn't we all!'

Once beyond the gate, where those leaving work were saluted daily by a pair of erect Music Programme guards, O'Connor weaved neatly along the familiar road among the tea-plantations. When they arrived at the crest of a hill and O'Connor slowed to a stop for the sake of the view, McCray thought he might never have seen so beautiful a sunset. Flaming red and violet clouds seemed to wrap well below the point of horizon, as if Timbali were a mountain-top kingdom surrounded on all sides by bottomless cliffs. He removed his helmet and felt the rush of warm air climbing the hillside. He knew the country to be overpopulated to a dire extent, and yet there was not a human being or habitation to be seen in the entire magnificent landscape before him. Mount Timbali, a dark cone when the sun set behind it, brooded in the distance. The wilderness of the distant plain contrasted movingly with the sculpted tea-bushes in the foreground. It might have been exhaustion, jet lag, perhaps a touch of loneliness, or his jarring attraction to Eleanor Kastostis that affected McCray so deeply: he felt himself shiver with emotion. He pursed his lips and donned his helmet once again as tears formed in the corners of his eyes.

''Tis a pretty sight,' said O'Connor, feeling that his dishonest accent was shamed before a natural beauty to which he had never become inured. 'I stop here nearly every evening in the dry season. At this latitude, you can set your watch by the sunset.'

Just as he spoke the sun broke from behind the rubicund clouds and settled on the horizon. It appeared to expand and bulge like a ball bouncing in slow motion, as if trying to come to rest on the earth.

O'Connor kicked his engine to life and continued on his way, and felt McCray's fingers digging hard into his ribcage. He was unaware that the vicious nemesis of the Music Programme, a man someone had nicknamed 'Crack', now sobbed ecstatically inside his crash helmet.

6

AT DAWN ON SATURDAY, McCray was wakened in O'Connor's house by the sound of a knock on his door. This was followed by the entrance of a woman pushing a low trolley laden with breakfast: tea, orange juice, buttered toast, marmalade, sliced bananas and cantaloup. McCray thanked the woman, who did not speak or look up before leaving his room. McCray reflected that, if this were the way a lowly speechwriter lived, the Supreme Director's pad must be something to behold.

As he ate his breakfast in bed, McCray mused about the evening he had spent with his host, Dan O'Connor. There was something peculiar about the young man. He was not exactly evasive when it came to the Music Programme – indeed, he was often critical of the organization while still standing behind its principles. But McCray got the distinct impression that O'Connor had something to hide. There was a nervousness behind his otherwise pleasant personality, which McCray had chalked up to an Irish mannerism or neurosis of some kind. His speech was garbled, while his words followed one another in pefectly grammatical form. When he thought back, McCray remembered that his more personal questions were the ones O'Connor had failed to answer satisfactorily. Without success, McCray had tried to establish the whereabouts of O'Connor's family in Ireland (North or Republic of? he had asked, to no avail).

Despite this stumbling-block, McCray was grateful for O'Connor's hospitality, as well as for the young man's precision of thought if not always of articulation. The speech-writer had put the Music Programme in clear perspective as no one else had been able to do. 'At the root of our organization is a belief that musical education leads to enhanced musical enjoyment,' O'Connor had asserted. 'With comprehension comes love, with love comes a demand for excellence. A demand for excellence employs skilled musicians, and without élitism diminishes interest in commercialized faddish music, broadens society's cultural base. The power of music is the power of harmony: those who adore music are peaceful and contented. The drive to make and hear music is primal, and it is represented in all individuals and societies; our purpose is to protect and foster musical justice.'

McCray appreciated this noble stance, but had his doubts that the organization he had glimpsed wielded much influence. And already he could hear the arguments of his boss, who quite honestly believed that serious musical education represented a threat to national security. When the Music Programme published withering reports on the Americanization of world music, which it equated with cheap exploitation, the Congressman cried: 'Commies.' While perhaps one in every ten thousand Americans had ever heard of the organization, it was a rare speech of the Congressman's that failed to mention the Music Programme in the context of a fist tightening around the neck of American free will.

McCray stretched and poured himself more tea. He thought of Eleanor and her strange little husband. Was it wise for the American people to pay part of that Czech maniac's salary? Should tax dollars contribute to 'Flamedance of Euphorion'? Was this communist music?

Eleanor opened her eyes and shook off the remnants of a nightmare in which her left hand had become a right hand, and vice versa, so that to play the piano she was forced to cross her arms. Breakfast had not yet arrived, and her husband was still asleep next to her, whistling an F-sharp through his nose. Kastostis slept in a black turtleneck.

88

Eleanor sat up in bed and looked at her husband. He seemed to have shrunk, physically, since the day he took the Composer-in-Residence post. Years ago, as an *enfant terrible*, his stature had been indisputable. Even Eleanor had studied, if not really *listened to*, his music. At the time it had seemed so extravagantly ambitious (penniless Kastostis had written music for companies of musicians, computer programmers, lighting engineers and set designers that only millions of pounds could unite) that Eleanor had always assumed a prodigious musical technique lay behind his post-modernist works. It would have been enough if his confidence had held, but in the isolation of Timbali – with no sycophants and back-slappers to buoy his spirits – his self-image had been dashed. Unfortunately, in Eleanor's opinion, his music depended on the composer's hubris for its validity. Eleanor believed that her husband's apparent physical diminishment was a result of his progressive artistic deflation.

Despite her disappointment, Eleanor retained a deep affection for the man she had impetuously married at twenty. She had not only loved him for his musical reputation, of course; any personality that could cause international attention and acclaim to gravitate towards increasingly noisy and even health-threatening music belonged to a man of impressive charisma. He sprang from literally Bohemian roots and burst upon the musical scene with an éclat heard round the world.

Eleanor mulled this over and watched her husband gradually stir from sleep. She had never before observed this phenomenon at such close range, for it was usually she who outslept him, and it disturbed her to see that her husband's face took on the aspect of a small child gasping for air, as if surfacing from a great depth of water. Kastostis choked and hacked, his eyes flickered open and closed without showing signs of consciousness. His first guttural words were Czech.

Dr Humphrey Lord's weekday morning routine never varied: breakfast in bed accompanied by Bach's Magnificat; dressing-gown and slippers for the journey to the glassed-in terrace, where he sipped a second cup of tea and warmed his hands in specially prepared hot towels; half an hour of harpsichord-playing in his drawing-room on an instrument brought overland from Tunis a year into his stay when he could no longer stand abstinence from the keyboard; shorts, sandals and polo-shirt, then into the land-rover for the drive to work. At weekends the routine was the same, but instead of driving to the compound he installed himself at his desk in his study and added touches to his long-standing scholarly hobby, a dissertation which attempted to prove that J. S. Bach was an atheist. He found the going really rather tough, but he was dogged.

On the day of the reception, when he had finished his extra-long session of harpsichord-playing, he spent an hour clipping his hair and grooming his goatee, suppressing the chills he felt each time he remembered that he might soon be introduced to the Supreme Director.

A few miles from the compound, across the street from the Acacia Club, the staff at the French ambassador's residence began the preparations for the annual goodwill reception in honour of the Music Programme. The French government had been the staunchest Western ally of the Music Programme since the organization's inception, a public relationship that was said to be bolstered, if not wholly sustained, by the private mutual admiration of the ambassador and the Supreme Director.

Uniformed servants hauled food from a trio of catering-vans in the driveway to the cooking-area and barbecue-pit in the backyard: tubs of iced shrimp and lobster; butchered beef, buffalo, antelope; a gutted, glazed bush pig; crates of glistening plump vegetables and fruit; platters of gaudy pastry specially imported for the occasion, along with their creator, from Lyons. Chairs and music-stands were erected in front of an acoustic shell on the patio near the swimming-pool, where Eleanor Kastostis and a group of Music Programme staff members were scheduled to perform a Mozart concerto. The grand piano had been moved from upstairs in the ambassador's residence, then expertly tuned by Jean-Baptiste Grandmarie. Yvonne and You-pie, on opposite sides of the swimming-pool and still not speaking to each other, gathered last-minute solar exposure before beginning their elaborate process of self-beautification.

Dan O'Connor was worried about contraceptives. After dispatching his morning maid with breakfast for Charles McCray, he ransacked his cupboards and cabinets in search of protection, but found none. Would it be unseemly to request contraceptives from his house guest, whom he had determined at dinner the previous night to be unmarried? No, no, he decided, an Irishman asking for condoms might provoke suspicion.

To relax, he took his breakfast out on to the terrace. The previous occupant of his house had left a powerful telescope behind, which O'Connor used to observe monkeys and birds in the trees, and on clear days to focus on the Supreme Director's palace, part of which was visible from the vantage-point of his terrace. His ambition was to catch a glimpse of the boss himself, but the best sighting he had ever managed was of a limousine leaving the palace grounds between gilt-tipped gates. On this morning all was quiet, except for a pair of gardeners using hand scissors to manicure a topiary tree into the shape of a three-dimensional treble clef.

Wendell Skinner had returned from Kastostis' house the previous evening to find his home emptied of its movable contents. At least he had shown the foresight to borrow a bottle of Scotch from Ludvik, which he drank seated on the floor in his unfurnished living-room. The absence of servants hinted at the perpetrators of the thorough robbery, and between sips from his bottle of booze he spat their names into his echoing rooms.

When he came to the following morning, stiff and sore from having passed out on a cold stone floor, his first order of business was to clean his clothing – now his *only* clothing – so as to make an impressively kempt re-entry into the Music Programme at the French ambassador's reception. He washed his shirt, socks and underwear in the shower, and placed them in the sun to dry. His suit he merely hung in the steam-filled bathroom. Naked, he strolled about his utterly empty house whistling the second trombone part to 'Take the A Train'.

'So 'appy you could come,' said the French ambassador to Dr Lord. ''Ow nice to see you. Rebonjour, Monsieur Grandmarie, et merci. Please, come in. The garden is through there.'

In the garden, the first arrivals had begun to mingle and nibble on baby shrimp.

'I don't think I've been this nervous since my début,' said Dr Lord, who had found O'Connor up to his elbow in a cooler full of ice, fishing for a Mister K.

'Relax, Humphrey. What's the problem?'

'For God's sake, man, the Supreme Director! He could be among us at this very moment.'

'I think we'd know it. I hear he has a man walking three steps behind him at all times, a bodyguard-cum-chopper-pilot for protection and hasty exits.'

'He knows all of us, doesn't he?'

Dr Lord referred to the SD's legendary memory, and the rumour that he studied photographs of his employees as he surveyed their output.

'So they tell me,' agreed O'Connor.

'I say, what have you done with our Mr McCray?'

'Left him at the entrance with the ambassador's wife. He seems to adore women.'

'Good man.'

'What a turnout,' said O'Connor.

'Look, there's Thwok. I suppose he'll play his harp in the chamber group. He can sight-read the full score and make up his own part as he goes along; that's what I hear, at any rate.'

'Have you heard Eleanor Kastostis play?'

'She's marvellous. If you like Mozart, that is. I must say I'm quite smitten by Eleanor. Partly pity, I suppose, since she must live with that madman. What a lovely young woman she is. Have some shrimp.'

O'Connor tried to be as subtle as possible as he stood on the tips of his toes and craned his neck searching for Yvonne.

On the other side of the garden, next to a latticework crawling with indecently vivid flowers, Wendell Skinner choked down a stiff restorative drink and tried to understand a portion of what was being explained to him by a fiercely opinionated Pakistani double-reed expert. The Pakistani was trying to determine whether the jigger bites from which he suffered might be infected. He wanted to show Skinner his toes, where he claimed a hideous pus – might even be larval jiggers, the Pakistani said – had evidenced itself beneath his skin. Skinner wondered if vomiting on the man might deter him from taking off his socks.

The Composer-in-Residence arrived with his glowing wife on his arm. Word quickly circulated that he was in a vile mood, that he had shrugged off his introduction to the French ambassador. One persistent rumour held that Kastostis himself was the Supreme Director – which might have explained a portion of his arrogance – a rumour that would only be dispelled by seeing the two together.

Eleanor caught the eye of Saint Thomas, whose job it was to assign seating. They shivered in unison, even though separated by fifty feet, as the memory of the green mamba reared its fangs between them.

Kastostis surveyed the guests with a fanatically hostile leer. With the early-afternoon sun beating down, he regretted having worn his heavy black cape.

'Oh my God,' said O'Connor. 'It's Ng.'

'Ng?' asked Dr Lord.

O'Connor pretended to have dropped something, and

squatted down on the ground. 'He's talking to McCray. Oh, hell. Humphrey, could you do me an enormous favour?'

'I'll try . . .'

'Go over there and interrupt them. Don't let Ng ask about me. He's sure to, when he finds out where McCray is staying.'

'Are you going to remain squatting there?'

'I'm going back in the house to look for someone.'

'I'll do my best,' said the loyal Dr Lord.

O'Connor carefully walked the perimeter of the garden, keeping his back on Ng. He said a few words to each party of his colleagues along the way, keeping his head down and an eye on Dr Lord's progress. Along the way he came across a pale Wendell Skinner who was deep in conversation with a Pakistani member of staff.

'Help,' said Skinner.

'Top o' the mornin' to you,' said O'Connor. 'Must run. The bladder, you know . . .'

O'Connor tip-toed behind the acoustic shell near the swimming-pool, climbed a terraced garden, sneaked behind the ambassador's house, and came face to face with a pair of guards, machine-guns slung over their shoulders, sharing a cigarette.

'Jolly good,' said O'Connor. 'Keep up the good work. I'm going around the front to come back in again, ha ha. Tally ho.'

At the main entrance of the house O'Connor was reintroduced to the French ambassador and the other members of the receiving-line.

'I am so 'appy you could come,' said the distinguished Frenchman, whose green eyes Yvonne had inherited. 'The garden is through there.' Next in line was Yvonne's mother, whose dark-brown skin indicated an addiction to sunshine shared by her daughters. After her came Yvonne's politically ambitious older brother, André, who wore tasselled black loafers, argyle socks, tight brand-new blue jeans, and a white button-down shirt; his abundant hair was greased straight back from his forehead. 'You'll go far,' said O'Connor, smiling cordially.

O'Connor dawdled in the living-room on his way to the garden, pretending to be fascinated by a brass clock on the mantelpiece. He kept his eye on the main staircase, hoping he hadn't missed Yvonne's entrance while circumventing Ng.

In the garden, Dr Lord had done his duty well, engaging McCray in conversation about African flora and practically elbowing Mr Ng in the teeth to keep him quiet. He owed O'Connor this favour. Remembering how well McCray and

Eleanor Kastostis had seemed to get along the day before, Dr Lord suggested they go over and say hello to her, which McCray eagerly agreed. Ng pouted.

Youpie was first to descend the staircase. She spotted O'Connor in her own living-room, alone: a fantasy had materialized before her eyes. She wore a simple turquoise backless cotton dress, and a bow in her hair to match. She wafted over to O'Connor and kissed him on each cheek in her usual offhand manner. Her scent was a mixture of perfume, shampoo, sun-tan lotion and skin cream, a fragrance of profound cleanliness. She stood gazing up adoringly at Dan O'Connor until her sister came down the stairs, whereupon her expression changed to one of childish rage; without speaking, she raced out of the room and into the garden.

'You two shouldn't fight,' said O'Connor after kissing Yvonne hello. Like her sister, Yvonne wore a simple dress, the only difference being that Yvonne's was cut so as best to display the nut-brown rounded cleavage she had worked so hard to tan. In the pit of O'Connor's stomach an awesome force began its work. Nothing mattered any more – not Ng, not McCray, not expulsion from the country – nothing mattered except finding a place to be alone with this exceptional girl.

'Marie-Claire is a beach,' said Yvonne.

'You look awfully pretty,' O'Connor said. 'Really very, very lovely.'

'Thank you, Danny. Have you been outside?'

'Yes. I came back inside to hide. And to find you.'

'You are hiding?'

'Look there, through the window. Do you see that small man next to the tall, extremely American-looking person? That's Ng. He mustn't see me.'

'What have you done?'

'I told you. Nothing serious, except that my nationality is a bit of an issue, and that man Ng is a stickler for detail. He won't rest until he has my papers in order.'

'I'll hide you,' said Yvonne. 'Come upstairs.'

Outside, Wendell Skinner had escaped from the Pakistani jigger victim, and felt wonderful. It was as if he had never left the Music Programme. Members of his own department chatted with him without asking where he had been. His only discomfort was the fear that anyone he didn't know on sight might turn out to be the Supreme Director. By drinking heavily he hoped to maintain his composure.

★   ★   ★

94

Across the way, Charles McCray extracted gossip from Eleanor Kastostis. She seemed to know everyone, even though she was not an employee of the organization.

'There are some interesting cliques,' she said. 'You say you've met some of the Bloody Bolshies? What about the Terrible Teutons?'

'Not yet.'

'Some of their representatives are huddled over there, do you see, near the barbecue-pit? A grim lot. Full of themselves. They think simply because they invented all the world's great music that they can lord it over us to this day. Watch, when I perform. They claim Mozart as their own, Austrian or not.'

'They claimed Hitler, Austrian or not.'

'Shh. Don't be wicked.'

'Is the Supreme Director here yet?'

'Everyone keeps asking *me* that question. I wouldn't know the Supreme Director if he spilled his drink on me.'

McCray hoped no one would spill any drinks on the lovely Eleanor. She had dressed for her performance in a silk gown the colour of champagne, which accentuated her height and slimness. Her hair was drawn back and pinned above her neck. Pearl earrings constituted her only jewellery. Standing next to her, McCray could feel the pressure of the entire group's attention, and particularly that of Eleanor's husband, who was circling the perimeter of the party in his black cape like a feeding bat.

'I hope I don't ask too many questions, Eleanor.' They had already agreed to use first names. 'But you understand my assignment.'

'Oh, yes, it's frightfully clear. You are here to torpedo the Music Programme. Without your funding the place will go under, I guarantee it. It will be reclaimed by the jungle.'

'It isn't *my* funding.'

'You know what I mean.'

'Yes, but I am only here to investigate, not to jump to conclusions.'

'Please, there's no reason to be diplomatic with me. If your Senator or Congressman or whatever he is has sent you here, it is not so that you can return and report to him that what he has been saying for five years is utter bunk. I do read the news-papers, you know.'

Over by the bar, Wendell Skinner thought he had sprained his ankle trying to dig a Mister K out of the bottom of the ice-chest. He bent over to untie his shoe, and felt a twinge of pain shoot through his lower back. 'Easy now,' he said, bent double and staring at the ground between his feet. He was afraid to move, afraid he had already set off a chain reaction that would result in his self-inflicted death. With one hand on his back he carefully tried to stand straight, and with the other hand he reached out for support on the edge of the barman's table. His hand clutched at the air, his fingertips brushed a checked tablecloth, and Skinner fell to the ground under the bar.

Waiters and colleagues rushed to his aid. From beneath the table Skinner saw a dark brown hand extended to him, which he grasped, and felt himself pulled to his feet by a powerful arm. When he had brushed the grass from his suit, Skinner realized that the dark brown hand belonged not to a servant, but to Saint Thomas, the handsome Insider.

'I do thank you,' said Skinner, attempting to bow in gratitude and nearly slipping a disc.

'You are all right, aren't you?' asked Saint Thomas.

'Oh, yes, perfectly fine.'

It was then that Skinner noticed another man next to Saint Thomas, someone he had never seen before, a short man with a shock of white hair, wearing dark glasses and a fine dark suit. Skinner swallowed hard and extended a trembling hand to be introduced.

'What rot,' said Dr Lord for the third time, 'what utter bloody rot.' One of the Terrible Teutons had just vented considerable spleen concerning his view that truly great music, that is, German music dating from the first performance of Beethoven's 'Eroica' symphony, had never been intended for mass consumption, and that the fewer people who understood or appreciated a composer, the greater the composer's artistic contribution. The modern popularity of Bach's music disqualified him from the pantheon. 'The contrapuntal Thuringian was a vulgar plagiarist,' said the German. 'A caterer to the unwashed.'

Dr Lord clenched his fists, raised his chin and apologized heavenward for the Terrible Teuton's blasphemy.

'Now, look here, you miserable bastard,' he said. Rational discourse had never been Dr Lord's forte. 'I wouldn't trade any eight bars of Bach's *oeuvre* for all the chest-thumping Nietzsche-isms ever regurgitated on to a staff.' What Dr Lord did not say was the word 'Nazi', a word that was so prominent in his mind at this moment that his field of vision was ablaze with hallucinated swastikas.

A different sort of *Sturm und Drang* had cropped up on the other side of the garden, all of it centred within Wendell Skinner's fragile emotional state as he tried to decide whether he had just met the Supreme Director. The white-haired man had walked away after shaking hands, but Skinner had not heard his name. He was left standing by the bar, favouring his good ankle, his jaw slackened by the experience. Dr Lord had once told him that the existence of the Supreme Director, like the existence of God, was something best doubted until revealed by personal exposure to the phenomenon. Had Skinner just seen his burning bush?

The musicians had begun to assemble for the performance of the Mozart concerto. Eleanor had warmed up at home, and waited until the others were seated before moving over to the piano amid a smattering of applause. The French ambassador shushed the crowd and encouraged everyone to gather round. The pleasant sound of the orchestra tuning up was added to the clink of ice against glass, as well as a nervous clearing of throats that seemed to come automatically to the Music Programme staff before a musical performance. Ludvik Kastostis positioned himself so as to be conspicuously disdainful of his wife's enterprise.

'They've gone quiet,' said O'Connor, upstairs in Yvonne's bedroom. 'What do you think happened?' His question was answered when the music started.

Eleanor conducted the introduction from the piano. Various factions of the Music Programme stood together exchanging looks of approval or condescension, depending on their particular orientations. Adherents to Authentic Instruments bit their cheeks: the performance of this 1784 work on a Pleyel piano was plainly factitious. The Bloody Bolshies took this performance as a personal affront: no Russian composer, not even the decadent bourgeois homosexual Tchaikovsky, had ever been represented at one of the ambassador's receptions.

Dr Lord, in a faction all his own, had to admit that what he heard was quite beautiful, even if Bach had not written it, and that Eleanor's delicate feminine touch suited the music divinely. Dr Lord admired her keyboard posture: she managed to concentrate without looking tortured, to appear emotionally involved without undue physical movement; she sat stoically upright and watched the keyboard down her beautiful nose. Dr Lord had to take slow deep breaths to maintain his composure in the presence of such grace.

Charles McCray asked the person next to him, a short white-haired man wearing dark glasses, if he didn't think Eleanor was a striking woman. The white-haired man nodded solemnly.

Youpie, standing next to her father, scanned the crowd for her sister and Dan O'Connor. Not seeing them, she glowered. She had made up her mind to do something, anything, to come between them.

Although sexual arousal was for Dan O'Connor an almost constant companion, he found as he slowly undressed Yvonne that he had been transported on to an altogether higher plane of desire than he had ever feared possible. Her body was hot to the touch, even though it had been removed from the sunlight for some hours now. And when she whispered something to the effect that caution be employed because she had never done this before O'Connor was afraid he would swallow his own tongue.

All of the beds in the house, even Yvonne's, were king-sized. Through the open windows, which gave on to the garden and the Acacia Club beyond, they could hear the orchestra and Mozart's petite melodies. O'Connor, to the extent that he could think straight at all, was pleased that there was no rush: the concerto would be followed by lunch and prolonged toasts of mutual self-congratulation. For long minutes he was more than content to stroke Yvonne's miraculous physique from scalp to Achilles tendon, and she, too, appeared relaxed and delighted with this novel pastime.

As the first movement of the concerto neared its close, Eleanor allowed herself a lapse in concentration long enough to wonder what she would play as an encore. With this audience, she knew, her selection would be regarded as a political statement, and by the more paranoid among them as a statement of the Supreme Director's tastes indicating which camp was currently in favour. She had four short solo pieces to choose from: Byrd, Schumann, Scriabin and Sibelius. William Byrd would be considered imperialist when played by a British pianist; if she played the Schumann, she would be accused once again of trying to fill Clara Wieck's shoes; Scriabin was out of the question because it would appear to endorse the Bloody Bolshies; neutral Scandinavians were always safe in international organizations, she knew, so by the time she reached the beginning of Mozart's moving second movement she had decided on a Sibelius sonatina for her encore.

★   ★   ★

When Dan O'Connor was entirely naked, Yvonne had some technical and linguistic questions for him.

Youpie, inflamed by sibling jealousy and puppy love, left her father's side and headed for the house.

The white-haired man felt a powerful need to relieve himself.

McCray had now fallen in love with Eleanor in earnest, as if he had never heard music before hearing her play. He was not alone: Dr Lord, Wendell Skinner, and every other heterosexual male member of the Music Programme staff now daydreamed of a life spent at Eleanor's side.

Kastostis' stubborn antagonism was soon penetrated by the music, and the phrase 'innately beautiful' rose to the surface of his thoughts. He had given quite a lot of cerebration to the concept of innate beauty recently, although he knew it was dangerous to explore theoretical aesthetics when one's genius demanded constant departure from the common conception of 'beauty'. Kastostis had concluded that MAXIMALISM, while not innately beautiful, was at least a form of music with an *agenda*.

'S-C-R-O-T-U-M,' spelled O'Connor.

Thwok strummed and plucked and pedalled delightedly; he lived for public performance.

Youpie entered her house and gripped the banister of the main stairway while trying to decide on a plan.

The white-haired man, calculating that the concerto would last at least ten or fifteen minutes more, elected to slip away and find a bathroom in the ambassador's residence.

Wendell Skinner sidled up to Dr Lord and whispered, too loudly: 'I wonder where those saucy little French daughters are. Remember them from last year?'

'Ouch,' said O'Connor. 'No.'

By the third movement of the concerto the orchestra had warmed up and were giving it their all. Many of them were accomplished musicians, although none was of Thwok and Eleanor's calibre. Eleanor's demeanour at the keyboard was one of almost impossible restraint. She prided herself on the fact that, no matter how emotional or grandiose a piece might be, she never moved any part of her body except for her shoulders, arms, fingers and right foot. Members of her audience sometimes commented that they found this a peculiarly British style of performance. Charles McCray found it erotic.

Yvonne had stopped asking questions, and was no longer a virgin.

An electrical overload in O'Connor's brain had stiffened his body, clamped shut his eyes, prohibited audio response in his ears, deadened all sensation save for that in his rather active loins. He was no longer in the ambassador's residence, in Timbali, in Africa; he was in Yvonne.

Youpie was at the top of the stairs, still undecided. For a minute she listened for incriminating sounds, her head cocked in the direction of her sister's room. She might have stayed there longer, but there were footsteps at the bottom of the staircase. She caught a glimpse of a short white-haired man wearing dark glasses, and dashed into her own room before he spotted her. She listened at her door and heard the man pass by outside.

In the garden, during the applause that preceded Eleanor's solo encore, the French ambassador searched the crowd for his daughters. Naughty little girls, he thought. What could they be up to? Taking advantage of the audience's rapt attention on Eleanor, the French ambassador stepped backwards into the clear and headed towards his house.

Youpie had made up her mind. She undressed entirely, save for the gold chain round her neck, which she had not removed for three years. She listened at her door, heard nothing, and crept out across the hall to her sister's bedroom door. There were sounds inside, the same sounds a maid might make fluffing pillows. Her ill-informed plan encompassed no more than her vision of joining Dan O'Connor in bed, even if Yvonne happened to be there, too.

The French ambassador took a quick look round downstairs, and caught one of his cooks drinking from a bottle of expensive Cognac. The ambassador fired the cook, then headed for the staircase.

With Eleanor's careful exploration of the Sibelius sonatina under way, Dr Lord lit his pipe and decided to lobby for a performance of his own at next year's reception. He saw himself playing the Italian Concerto or the Chromatic Fantasy before an audience of hostile Teutons and Bolshies, only to have them fall to their knees in awe. Eleanor's divorce would soon follow, and she would join him on an extended vacation behind the Iron Curtain fondling keyboards Bach had played.

Youpie twisted the knob on Yvonne's bedroom door and slowly pushed it open. It was noticeably warmer in Yvonne's room.

Yvonne thought she heard something, but was not about to move at what she considered a critical juncture in the sexual exercise.

O'Connor's obliviousness would have blocked out the entrance of a charging rhino, much less the stealthy naked Youpie.

The French ambassador reached the top of the stairs just as the white-haired man emerged from the bathroom at the opposite end of the corridor. They smiled and waved warmly, then walked towards each other, meeting at the centre of the corridor outside Yvonne's room.

Inside, Youpie padded across the room to her sister's bed, which got Yvonne's attention. Youpie was fascinated by the activity of O'Connor's body. Yvonne was unable to shriek, and it was likely that if she had done so O'Connor would have taken it as a good sign; as it was, he took the sudden stiffening of her body as a signal of climax.

The French ambassador asked the white-haired man to wait a moment while he looked in Youpie's room. He was surprised to find her clothes and shoes in the middle of the floor. When he emerged into the hallway he was plainly angry, and the white-haired man asked him what was the matter.

'Zose girls,' said the irate ambassador. With the white-haired man behind him, he crossed the hall and strode into Yvonne's room.

The ambassador's entrance coincided with Youpie's reckless leap on to the free side of Yvonne's bed and with O'Connor's heart-stopping orgasm.

7

MARY MBEWA hiked up her orange skirt to board a public bus outside the gates of the Music Programme compound. She travelled alone to the capital each Saturday to visit her family, and to shop for articles not stocked by the Music Programme facilities. The rickety bus was packed with people on their way to visit relatives, to search for work, or to purchase goods they couldn't buy or produce in their villages and towns. Mary Mbewa pushed between the bodies and bundles of belongings, and squeezed her way to a window where she could breathe fresh air. She recognized many of her fellow-passengers on the bus who took the same trip to the city each week from a small town north of the compound. Each Saturday they asked for news of Mary's job, wide-eyed with envy. Mary tried not to appear too self-satisfied when she described to them her apartment in the compound, her outdoor desk and word processor, the communal nursery that looked after her children during the day, the new clothes she bought with her generous pay-packet, and the other perquisites she enjoyed working for an international organization. Mary's

102

friends viewed life in the compound as Utopian: pay comparable to the best salaries in the city, safe housing, medical benefits. With special jealousy they resented Mary's added bonus, which was that her husband, a chauffeur for the Music Programme who lived within the compound, had few opportunities for late-night carousing: living with irresponsible mates was the uxorial lot of Timbalian wives on the other side of the electric fence.

What Mary did not tell her covetous acquaintances on the bus was that her job was often unsatisfying. It bored her to stare at the same scenery every day with practically no work to do, and during her department's infrequent crises she felt ill at ease around her strangely uncommunicative boss. She liked the Englishman well enough, but when he instructed her to do something it was usually too late, through no fault of her own, to finish the job on time. Mary sensed that Dr Lord held her in disdain because she rarely had anything to do, even though he never gave her reports to type or papers to organize. These were precisely Mary's skills, she enjoyed using them, and she resented Dr Lord for appearing to blame her for the inactivity of his department.

The past week was a good example. By the time Mr Ng told Dr Lord of the American's arrival in Timbali no one, not even Mary, should have been surprised. In preparation for the envoy's visit, Mary would have been happy to type business-like memos, acquire pertinent documents from other departments of the organization – anything her boss requested. Instead, Dr Lord seemed to hold her responsible for the American's sudden visit (sudden only because he had repressed his knowledge of its imminence); he had nearly made her cry when he angrily repeated his request for coffee. Mary had forgotten about the coffee because it didn't seem important when all their jobs were at stake and so much work had to be done to impress the American. Not wanting to shed tears or betray her concern in the presence of her high-strung boss, she had concentrated so hard on controlling her emotions that Dr Lord's request for coffee had slipped her mind. When Dr Lord had raised his voice at her she had run off to Gregory's canteen with tears dissolving her make-up.

The bus ride to the capital was a dangerous one, downhill along steep ravines almost all the way, but mercifully short because the buses were able to achieve such high speeds. The trip in the other direction was long and dangerous, because the Land Pirates, not satisfied with robbing rich diplomats in private cars, sometimes plundered the buses leaving the city full of urban treasures, such as food.

Leaning out the window of the bus, Mary Mbewa chatted with two women who occupied the window next to hers. They shouted to each other over an engine that seemed to run in perpetual backfire. Mary made them laugh with stories about her employment. In her native tongue Mary was a born storyteller, amusing and descriptive. Although she was not proud, Mary still enjoyed her stylish clothes and liberally applied make-up. Part of her hoped that the other women on the bus thought that even the President's wife could not possibly live so well.

Her companions on the bus urged Mary to repeat the story of the day she had visited her boss at his house. Mary told this story every week. They listened with a mixture of awe and disapproval as Mary described the single man living in a large house in the forest among servants and gardeners and guards. They assumed Dr Lord was the boss of bosses at the Music Programme, and Mary was more than ready to foster this grandiose image of the Late Baroque specialist. She painted a picture of Dr Lord's life as if the scholar were a European prince who retired nightly to his drawing-room to fill his pipe-bowl with the finest tobacco, his glass with the smoothest brandy, his ears with the loftiest music, all of these emoluments produced at the snap of his fingers by a crew of devoted minions. Much as Mary tried to embellish this story, her description of Dr Lord's private life could not really count as gross exaggeration.

Mary Mbewa was more apprehensive than usual about her visit to her older brother's house, for she had heard disturbing news from him during recent weeks. Robert Mbewa, though only thirty-three years old, had already seen his share of political turmoil. He had started as the protégé of the President's Interior Minister, had been groomed by him, had hoped one day to succeed him. Robert's worst fears came true when his mentor fell out of favour over a seemingly insignificant property dispute with the President-for-Life. Mary's brother had been trapped in political limbo for three years, going cautiously about his duties under the new Interior Minister, waiting for a sign from above to determine his future. In the meantime the former Interior Minister, enraged, risked his neck by speaking out publicly against corruption in the government, mincing no words in criticizing the President's gigantic land-holdings and blatant cronyism. The former Minister's name, Ndana, had become synonymous with the country's growing movement of opposition to the President-for-Life. Robert was torn between his loyalty to Ndana and his desire to live a long and comfortable life. While he had kept his post at the Ministry, he had also kept lines of communication open with the former Minister, who was said to be living across the border in a historically hostile country, fomenting periodic coups in his homeland.

Mary Mbewa had learned all of this directly from her brother, who said he confided in practically no one but his eight brothers and sisters. He was clearly overextended, and Mary worried that he might flee the country to join Ndana in exile. During her visits to his house in the city she rarely brought up the subject of his political difficulties, choosing instead to talk of family matters. Mary and her numerous siblings had long planned to buy a house for their parents; for five years, each had contributed an annual tithe to a bank account controlled by Robert, the oldest, and their sensible savings plan had now mounted to the point that a two-room house with plumbing on a small plot of land was easily within reach. Mary would discuss the matter with her brother, and hoped to avoid any mention of Ndana if it could be avoided. She respected her brother's accomplishments, but she knew him to be mercurial and prone to rash decisions under pressure. If she had thought he would listen to her advice, she would have told Robert to get out of government and start a business. Presidents-for-Life would come and go, Mary suspected, but a country always needed lumber and cement and baskets and spare engine parts. She knew even Robert realized that the best an up-and-coming bureaucrat could hope for the future was a position of sufficient power to make him spend his days in constant fear of assassination.

Mary shrugged off these concerns and crossed her arms on the window-sill. The bus travelled momentarily on paved roads, near the fabulous residences of ambassadors, Music Programme higher-ups and some wealthy Timbalians. The women in the next window stopped their conversation as a series of gilded gates and groomed lawns passed by like a slide-show of Heaven. Turbaned guards sat in phone-booth-sized huts outside the gates. Gardeners wearing white T-shirts sweated in the sun as they engaged southern Timbali's inexorable plant growth in battle.

As the bus rumbled past one of these gates, Mary spotted a familiar figure running out of the drive. It was Dan O'Connor, Dr Lord's good friend, his brown hair pressed back in the wind created by his full sprint. An alarmed guard stood up in his hut and shouted as O'Connor dashed out on to the road. The speech-writer paused for a moment to turn round and check for pursuit, then jogged away. Mary lost sight of him as the bus turned a corner and regained the precipitous dirt road leading to the capital.

Dan O'Connor lay flat on his back in bed, staring through the gauzy haze of his mosquito netting, waiting for his pounding pulse to abate. His servants had seen him gallop down the drive, burst through the front door, race down the hallway and cast himself head first through the netting on to his bed. They had peeped in on him and heard him moan and rustle beneath the diaphanous shroud. O'Connor's cook recognized a crisis and courageously entered his master's bedroom with a bottle of bourbon and a glass of ice (his previous master had required this brand of thoughtfulness on a regular basis). O'Connor flailed at the netting and shooed the cook away. The noises he made sounded to his servants like the death rattle of a tubercular old man.

O'Connor burrowed beneath his sheets and half-smothered himself with a pillow. He bit on the corner of his mattress like a nineteenth-century soldier undergoing amputation in a field-hospital. He kicked his legs in the air and flopped about as if experiencing electrocution. He opened his eyes and clenched his fists in the air and ground his teeth and expelled all the air from his lungs. He pressed at his temples to drive all memory from his brain, succeeding only in imprinting on to his synapses an enhanced image of the wide-eyed French ambassador standing over him and the naked bodies of the diplomat's daughters.

There was no question of rational thought or action now. O'Connor was at the mercy of an emotional constitution that shut down to the point of paralysis under the stress of even a minor *faux pas*, much less a *Gotterdammerung* of a misstep such as the one he had so recently executed. He could only re-create, over and over again, the point at which he had shifted gears instantaneously from physical ecstasy to psychological seizure. O'Connor knew that a stronger man would have asserted himself without compunction, chastised the ambassador for bursting into the room, declared himself immune to the diplomat's incomprehensible insults, clothed himself while grumbling to the girls about their father's impudence, and marched into the garden for a taste of charcoal-broiled gazelle. A stronger man would have done all of that.

A new spasm of remorse jerked O'Connor's body about on his bed. He had learned long ago that he possessed only one major psychic quirk: an inability to tolerate embarrassment. This accounted for his deranged evasion of Mr Ng, his failure ever to announce himself to the Supreme Director, his clinging to an Irish accent, and scores of other games he played to avoid the slightest discomfiture, much less the mortification that now gripped him like an anaconda.

From past experience O'Connor knew that the physical symptoms of his embarrassment would take six to eight hours to subside: they would break like a fever in the middle of the

night, leaving him smiling witlessly, and would return spasmodically during the next five or six years. O'Connor worried
that if he accumulated too many episodes of abashment, and if
his fits of retro-mortification struck simultaneously, the sympathetic vibrations of stress might rip him open like a water-
melon dropped from the battlements of the Supreme Director's
penthouse office.

O'Connor's most immediate problem was the return of
'Crack' McCray. The reception, if it had continued at all after
O'Connor's apocalyptic confrontation with the French ambassador, would soon be over. McCray would find his way back to
O'Connor's house, O'Connor would feign malaria, and it was
quite possible that McCray would have heard rumours of
O'Connor's heinous behaviour through a Music Programme
grapevine that lived for gossip of this magnitude. McCray
would be left without a tour guide, wondering what had gone
wrong. Poor big bad American, O'Connor thought.

'More wine, Charles?' Eleanor asked, signalling Vincent to fill
her guest's glass.

'Your cook is very talented,' said McCray. 'I'm glad I didn't
spoil my appetite at the reception.'

'Game can be rather filling. I'm afraid Ludvik must have
overdone it with bush pig.'

'Yes, too bad he couldn't join us. Are you sure he's all right?'

'Oh, yes. Spit spot to bed, though. He was quite exhausted
even before the reception. His labours, you know.'

McCray wondered just how sarcastic Eleanor had meant to
sound.

'Your performance this afternoon was thrilling. Everyone
said so. I'm just sorry I haven't spent more time listening to
music, trying to understand it. I'm afraid I don't know Mozart
from . . .'

'Monteverdi?'

'Right.'

'One needn't study music in the academic sense to appreciate
it.'

'I think I'd have to study to appreciate your husband's . . .'

'Output?'

'Right.'

'Poor dear. It isn't easy carrying the mantle of the Masters.'

'Are you sure he isn't upset about something? When we
arrived here he seemed to be in a bad mood. Marching around in
his cape that way. Not joining us for dinner.'

'Don't be silly. He's tired, and he ate too much. Thompson's gazelle has never agreed with him. That's all. Off to bed, and he'll feel much better in the morning.'

Ludvik Kastostis stood in his darkened bedroom, glaring down through his open window at his wife and Charles McCray as they dined on the terrace under a bright moon. Two candles flickered in the breeze between them. While he couldn't make out their words, he did catch the occasional titter from Eleanor, and he could plainly see that every so often they tossed their heads in appreciation of something the other had said. It had become Kastostis' artistic ambition to express in music the jealousy he felt, the extreme possessiveness that overcame him, when his wife talked to other men. He wished to create a work that would first set a scene aurally descriptive of Eleanor's astonishing charms, then dash the whole mess about the stage like the contents of a ruptured *piñata*. Wagner could have done it justice, Kastostis thought, so why can't I? Already he heard the primary theme in his mind, a flute lilting tunefully above a bed of murmuring strings – a little *too* tunefully, really. This would continue for five minutes or so until the ear was lulled into a false sense of security, whereupon the low brass would enter (from offstage, perhaps?) with a macho juggernaut of a theme, *bim-pom bom, bim-pom bom*, and march right over the flute, covering it, drowning it out, until the flute would be forced to join the brass part in an unnaturally low register. The remainder of the orchestra, unable to look on complacently any longer, would fight the brass theme with the kind of manic mayhem for which Kastostis was most famous. A MAXIMALIST, bow-breaking, reed-snapping, timpani-head-bursting crescendo would finally succeed in driving the brass section away, leaving the flute alone once more.

Kastostis' Opus 10 was born.

McCray felt like someone who had drunk too much at a dinner-party with his prospective in-laws and hoped they hadn't noticed. Could Eleanor see through his casual manner, his exaggerated calm, his steady voice? Could she see that he could barely conceal his infatuation, that each sentence he spoke wanted to trail off into a pitiful admission of love? McCray found himself staring at Eleanor's skilful hands, watching her fingers raise the wine-glass to her lips, watching them conduct her speech, watching them lie dormant on the white tablecloth betraying none of their potential; her hands were symbols to McCray of this woman's grace and excellence.

'If there is a Beethoven living in the world today,' Eleanor said, 'it is my husband Kastostis.'

108

'High praise,' said McCray, allowing himself just the tiniest interrogative inflection.

'H'm,' said Eleanor, with a perceptible twitch of her eyebrows.

'It must be difficult for you in Timbali,' McCray suggested, hoping this wasn't too bold a conversational tack.

'In what way?'

'To pursue your own musical ambitions?'

'I relinquished all ambition years ago. It was more important that Ludvik find a peaceful place to work – and the built-in approbation of the Music Programme is nothing to sneeze at. As marvellous as they may seem, instrumentalists are common enough; composers who manage to reach the level of recognition my husband has are as rare as unicorns.'

'That's awfully selfless of you.'

'Not at all. I was afraid that Ludvik had peaked, and that without a structure such as his present post he would never work again. What he does is awfully difficult.'

'Composing?'

'Not so much composing. I meant the maintenance of his sanity. He would have been murdered in an academic post. He needed a place to work freely, with computer equipment at his disposal, and a comfortable place to live. There is no money in being an *enfant terrible*, or an angry young man, or a furious middle-aged artist, or a wrathful grandfather. One needs a framework, and you can imagine how attractive the Music Programme appeared to both of us during that difficult time in England.'

'I think you've been very generous.'

'I am a saint,' said Eleanor, dismissing this notion with a wave of her trim right hand.

McCray clenched his fists beneath the table in an effort to dampen the waves of longing for Eleanor that had begun to dizzy him. He tried to reason with himself, even as he continued to converse with Eleanor, arguing inwardly that he had travelled too much, worked too hard, denied himself the routine exposure to women that would make someone like Eleanor seem common enough by comparison. His internal arguments proved fruitless each time he met Eleanor's gaze. McCray wondered if he had somehow been transformed into a romantic since the days of his more conventional amorous adventures when he lived in Washington full time. He replaced his hands on the table and steeled himself against the possibility of blurting out his innermost thoughts.

★   ★   ★

109

Mary Mbewa's brother Robert seemed even more agitated and distraught than usual. As soon as Mary arrived he insisted that they walk outside, near the University, where they could talk without worry of surveillance. He spoke rapidly and sometimes incoherently, gripping Mary by the forearm for emphasis. He told her that his position was untenable, that he might as well blindfold himself and shoot himself in the chest if he wanted to continue at the Ministry. When Mary asked him what had changed he said only that his links to Ndana, always common knowledge, were now being used against him. He had protested that his only tie to Ndana was that of friendship and gratitude for past sponsorship, but now it seemed people were accusing him behind his back of being in direct cahoots with the former Interior Minister. The pressure was on, Robert said, to quit the Ministry or risk the wrath of the President-for-Life.

'Why do you tell me this?' Mary asked. 'Why can't you simply leave, without making a drama out of everything? You have put yourself in this position, even though we warned you long ago.'

'I need your help,' Robert said.

That was when Mary tried to walk away, to return to her brother's house and the rest of the family. Robert grabbed her by the wrist and looked her in the eye. 'I'm in danger, and I need you to help me.'

'What could I possibly do? I know nothing about your situation, and I don't want to know anything. I came here to talk about our money.'

'Don't worry about the money.'

'I *am* worried. I want you to take it out of the bank and get started on the house. We have enough.'

'We won't have enough, if you don't help me.'

'What do you mean?'

'I need the money, Mary.'

'You wouldn't dare . . .'

'Listen to me. I'm going to Ndana.'

'Fool.'

'I've made up my mind. It is fate.'

'And you are taking the money?'

'Of course I don't *want* to. But I need something. I am in danger and I have to go into hiding. Isn't that more important than a house right now? I have not spoken to Ndana in three years, only to his people. They say I have taken too long to make up my mind, that I have not shown loyalty. They say Ndana needs an incentive to have me join him.'

'And these are the people you are going to run away for? What incentive are they asking?'

'The opposition struggle needs funds.'

'Robert, you are no brother of mine. Think what will happen to us if you go.'

'Nonsense. Think what will happen to us if Ndana returns, victorious.'

'I won't discuss it. That is not only your money. Take your share, if you want, but I won't speak to you again if you take the rest.'

'It isn't enough. Listen to me. If you help me, I won't be needing the money.'

'What are you talking about?'

'I just need one bit of information that you can provide. Ndana has asked me.'

'How dare you involve me in this? It isn't enough that you are a fool; you have to put your own family in danger too?'

'There is no danger. It's a simple matter. You could help me right now.'

'How?'

'Ndana wants to know the description of your man at work.'

'What? Dr Lord? You met him, when you came to see my office.'

'No, not that man. The big man.'

'The Supreme Director?' Mary shuddered, a habit she had picked up from watching people at the compound when they heard the words 'Supreme Director'.

'Right.'

'You are really crazy. How can I have such a crazy brother?'

'You won't tell me?'

'Oh, who cares? You are hopeless. I don't even *know* what the man looks like.'

'How can that be?'

'No one has seen him, ever. Only his car and his helicopter.'

'I say how can that be?'

'Why do you ask me these things? I am a secretary.'

'But you could find out. You could ask Dr Lord.'

Dr Lord shivered to the core of his spine and ordered another drink in the Anthony Eden Room of the Acacia Club.

'Oh, yes, old chap, I'm quite certain. No doubt at all. This afternoon we both met – I should say we both *touched* – the Supreme Director himself.'

Skip Skinner wished he belonged to a religious cult so that he could cross himself, flagellate himself, crawl over broken glass, spin a prayer-wheel, count beads, or merely stare at the ceiling of the bar and consider himself tapped into a helpful line of communication. He had already relived the moment when he had shaken the white-haired man's hand; he simply couldn't remember if he had heard the Supreme Director's name, or even his title, from the handsome Jamaican Insider who had introduced them. He was not quite sure that he would recognize the man again if he saw him. Dr Lord agreed that the visitation of the white-haired man had been of an ethereal nature.

Skinner sloshed some of his drink on to his coaster as he gestured in disbelief: 'Man, what *is* it with this Supreme Director? Since when are employees not allowed to know the name of their boss?' He crinkled up his nose, which accentuated its bright red colour.

'Again, we must rely on rumours,' said Dr Lord, who had in the last twenty minutes achieved a plane of alcohol-induced beatitude that made him wonder why he didn't imbibe heavily more often. 'Here are the facts,' he said. 'We have a Supreme Director. Neither of us has met anyone, save perhaps for a tight-lipped Insider or two, who has met Ozymandias in person before today. We know the Supreme Director is secretive, according to the few Insiders who have been so indiscreet as to leak this information, because he is a man of such staggering power and influence that to reveal his identity in a volatile country such as Timbali would provide interested parties with a target for terrorism and blackmail.'

'Come on,' said Skinner.

'This much we know,' affirmed Dr Lord. 'We know through the rather active Music Programme rumour-mill that our leader is a tireless worker, a man who possesses a photographic memory, a pathological eye for detail, and a temper that has resulted in the summary dismissal of half a dozen of my colleagues since the day I arrived. On the other hand we know, quite firsthand, that the Supreme Director has shown himself loath to provide specific direction.'

'Right,' said Skinner. 'All we *don't* know is who the man *is*.'

'Until today,' added Dr Lord, like a lawyer resting his case. 'Everyone said that was he. I say, Solomon, once more!'

While they waited for their next round, the Music Programme colleagues inspected their fellow-drinkers in the Anthony Eden Room, a grizzled collection of colonial throwbacks, each of whom had probably lived in Timbali longer than the President-for-Life. In one corner a pair of elderly men wearing heavy wool suits played backgammon and washed down their snack of greasy chips with pink gin. Nearby, a trio of similarly dressed gentlemen engaged in a spirited reminiscence of ancient cavalry battles fought further south on the continent. At the bar a group of younger men, who might have been European diplomats, discussed their most recent treks into the bush, telling tales of inconceivable danger and fantastic luxury.

'Well, Skinner,' said Dr Lord, 'what do you say we take these drinks into the snooker room?'

'God,' said Skinner. 'My God, we met *the man*.'

'Never mind, old chap. I'm certain we made a marvellous impression. Snooker?'

'And what about that . . . commotion?'

'At the reception? H'm, yes. Something of a domestic spat, I should say. No one was rude enough to ask, of course.'

'I asked like crazy,' confessed Wendell Skinner. 'I asked the *servants*. I wanted to know what had happened. Did you hear that shouting? And what happened to the white-haired man – I mean, the Supreme Director? Why did he disappear? The ambassador came back looking like someone whose country has just been blown off the map. Is France OK?'

'As far as I know. Actually I heard it had something to do with the dismissal of a cook. That can be quite unpleasant, believe me.'

'I thought you said you hadn't asked.'

'That much I overheard. I'm sure that explains it.'

'You're probably right. OK, snooker it is.'

As they moved towards the door to the snooker room it occurred to Dr Lord that Dan O'Connor had never returned to the reception after the peculiar outburst was heard from within the ambassador's residence. As a scholar and a bureaucrat, Dr Lord did not consider himself prone to belief in conspiracy theories or any other brand of paranoia; still, he hoped that the disturbance had not involved the young man on whose shoulders McCray's satisfactory impressions now rested. Dr Lord had been forced to believe implicitly in Dan O'Connor's ability to soothe the American invader; he had rationalized the avoidance of his own duties by decreeing to himself that he had instructed rather than begged O'Connor to take charge of the envoy.

Dr Lord's own recollection of the reception disturbance was as confused as anyone's. He remembered being entranced by Eleanor's wintry interpretation of the Sibelius sonatina, then wrenched out of this state by sounds of shouting, in French, and of objects being broken. Already near the end of her performance, Eleanor had continued to play. The applause that followed her completion of the sonatina served to camouflage the disconcerting female screams emanating from the main house. Always attuned to the possibility of international incident, the knowing

113

members of the Music Programme staff had mingled loudly and pretended not to notice when a stuffed animal had flown out of an upstairs window and splashed into the swimming-pool. Only a few people, Dr Lord among them, had noticed when the white-haired man emerged from the residence, followed closely by a uniformed chauffeur, and hurried to the gate.

Dr Lord was troubled enough by the simultaneous disappearance of Dan O'Connor and the presumed Supreme Director that he paused at a telephone on the way to the snooker room. 'I'll just be a moment,' he said to Skinner. 'Select a cue and I'll join you shortly.' Skinner nodded and moved unsteadily into the next room.

'I am a director, I am a director,' he said to himself as he dialled. 'I am a director acting responsibly, even at the weekend.'

When the phone rang next to O'Connor's bed the young speech-writer had only recently survived the most severe and sustained wave of cringing he had yet undergone. He swept aside his mosquito netting and scrutinized his buzzing telephone as if by close inspection he could divine the caller. His mind raced through the possibilities: Yvonne, McCray, Ng, the police, the French ambassador, Youpie. As someone accustomed to not answering his phone at work, he let it continue to ring, picking up the receiver only when he could stand the suspense no longer.

'Is that you, O'Connor?'

When he heard Dr Lord's voice, O'Connor collapsed back on to his bed in relief. 'Thank God, an ally,' he said, finding that his voice was oddly muffled inside the web of mosquito netting.

'You sound strange.'

'I'm in bed.'

'Not ill, I hope?'

'No . . .'

'I was just checking in, you see. I didn't see you at the reception, after the – Are you quite sure you're all right?'

Dr Lord had been interrupted by the sound of O'Connor gagging.

'Fine, fine,' said O'Connor breathlessly. He had wrapped the receiver cord around his own neck and had resolved to strangle himself at the slightest hint that the entire Music Programme staff had learned of his fate.

'You see, it just occurred to me that I should check in on you

114

and Mr McCray. I noticed that he stayed on at the reception after you left. Why did you leave?'

O'Connor loosened the phone cord. 'To be honest,' he said, which was the last thing he intended to be, 'I had something of a spat with the ambassador's daughter.'

'I see. That wasn't the cause of the . . . disturbance, was it?'

'What disturbance?'

'Oh, well, in that case never mind.'

'No, I mean, tell me about it.'

'It's all very worrying, O'Connor. You see, I believe the Supreme Director was there and that his abrupt departure was caused by some sort of contretemps with the French ambassador.'

'The Su . . . the Su . . .'

'O'Connor? Are you there?'

'You saw the Supreme—?'

'Yes, yes. I'm certain. He was the white-haired man who was being introduced to people by that Jamaican chap, Mr Thomas.'

'Dark glasses?' asked O'Connor.

'Yes, that's the one. So, you see, I was simply calling to ask if you had any more intelligence on this matter.'

'None,' croaked O'Connor, the phone cord tightened once again around his neck.

'Well, that's fine, then. And Mr McCray was not put out by any of this, one hopes.'

'Yes, one hopes he was not.'

'Is he there, by any chance?'

'Who?'

'Why, Mr McCray, of course.'

'Sure, yes, absolutely, of course, certainly, you're right, he's here. Taking a nap, I think.'

'Right-ho, then. Well done, Dan old man. That's a relief. I'm off to the snooker room with old Skinner.'

'Thank you for calling.'

The phone went dead in O'Connor's hand. 'Oh, good,' he said to himself. 'That man behind Yvonne's father, that horrified-looking man with the white hair and dark glasses. That was the Supreme Director. That was my boss.'

What must he have seen, O'Connor wondered. A pair of naked nubilities bouncing off a mattress; his speech-writer wearing nothing but the expression of someone interrupted in the act of ejaculation; a murderous ambassador prevented from killing the speech-writer on the spot only by his own incapacitating fury. That's what he had seen.

O'Connor tunnelled deeper into his bedclothes. He dug the fingertips of each hand into his solar plexus and attempted to rip his own ribcage asunder. That will show them I'm sorry, he thought, if they find me gnawing on my own still-beating heart.

'SAVE PERHAPS for alcohol,' said the German speaker in English, 'music is the world's most pervasive distraction.'

This remark was translated simultaneously into nine languages and dialects, and piped into the ears of the audience through sterilized disposable headsets. Dr Lord smoked his pipe at the back of the auditorium and doodled on a yellow pad, happy to be back at work after such a nerve-racking weekend. Although he spoke German fluently and understood Italian, Dr Lord had selected the unintelligible Arabic translation on his dial, just for the sake of hearing an interesting sound. The guttural language in his ears emanated from the throat of a young man seated inside a glass booth on the balcony behind the audience's heads.

'Imagine the gypsy's guitar, its strings shining in the campfire light,' continued the speaker. 'The Tibetan monk's burdensome trumpet hauled to clifftop at sunrise. The American mountain-dweller's homemade banjo. The hoop-skirted Spanish maiden's castanets. The Eskimo's walrus-tooth flute. And tiny bells, tiny bells, tiny bells.'

117

Dr Lord tapped at his headset and jiggled its cord, for the translation seemed to have petered out. Finally he removed his headset and put it aside, digging at his pipe-bowl as the speaker went on:

'. . . mathematicians, woodcarvers, acousticians, metal-workers, electrical engineers, united throughout history for the sake of musical sound.'

Always willing to give a distinguished speaker the opportunity to reach his point, Dr Lord patiently scanned the audience for familiar faces. There was Jean-Baptiste Grandmarie, near the front, intense as usual, jotting notes in his anal-retentive penmanship; over there was Thwok, smiling amiably; in the front row the Terrible Teutons inspected their compatriot with a mixture of pride and trepidation, perhaps fearful that one of their jobs was in danger; two rows in front of Dr Lord a Dutch jazz expert and Music Programme long-timer dozed in his seat, emitting the reek of home-grown Timbalian marijuana that always permeated his clothing; a pair of Bloody Bolshies entered the hall, then departed in a noisy huff when they saw that yet another Western speaker controlled the microphone.

'Distinguished visitors, colleagues, good friends, Mr Chairman,' said the speaker, having concluded his half-hour introduction. Dr Lord had to consult his printed programme to remind himself that the speaker's name was Friedrich Weissmann (DTh, MD, DPhil, Hamburg; Hon. DMus, Dublin; Hon. DD, Oxon; LLD, Muirfield), whose most recent published work recounted the difficulty he had met publishing his next-to-most-recent work, which had somehow linked and then vilified Sigmund Freud and Alban Berg.

'We stand, dear friends, at the brink of a musical apocalypse. Without concerted international effort, I foresee the doom of our precious musical heritage – a heritage stemming from one of mankind's most primal needs, and encompassing its most fantastically gifted individuals.'

Dr Lord thought he recognized the stamp of Dan O'Connor on this part of the speech, which was not altogether unlikely: O'Connor was farmed out gratis to visiting speakers and consultants who wished to spice up their presentations and conform to the protocol of Music Programme gatherings. Thinking of O'Connor reminded Dr Lord that Charles McCray was probably somewhere on the premises.

'Before continuing to the body of my discussion I wish to salute the fine work of the Music Programme, and in particular the tireless labours of its Supreme Director' – here Herr Weissmann appeared to sigh, as if unwilling any longer to put up with

118

the pretence of sincerity during introductory remarks – 'whose ardent pursuit of musical justice makes it easier to sleep at night for those of us worried about the world's musical horizons.'

Definitely O'Connor, thought Dr Lord, who disapproved of the young man's hyperbole. Dr Lord drafted his own speeches, which were invariably dry, overly opinionated (some said offensive), and so brief that his colleagues usually asked him afterwards if he were ill.

'I was pleased to find that the subject of this week's discussion coincided with my current research,' said the speaker, as if this might be a coincidence. 'As some of you know, the musical response of animals has been a subject dear to my heart since my earliest work at gymnasium, where I met, through my Russian mother, among others, Herr Doktor Pavlov. As all of you surely know, the salivation of Pavlov's dog, after prolonged associative foreplay, was induced by the sound of a *tiny bell*. Perhaps only the imagination of a child – and I was a child at the time – and the curiosity of a rather precociously musical child – at that time, at least my mother said so, I was a precociously musical child – would prompt the question, which I asked: "Herr Doktor, what *pitch* was your tiny bell?"'

A snort of laughter came from the Dutch jazz expert, who had regained consciousness in time to hear only the last few sentences, and perhaps was unaware that he was no longer asleep. Dr Lord crossed his bare legs and drew on his pipe, certain now that Herr Weissmann's speech would last the better part of two hours before ending in one of O'Connor's patented pleas for international harmony and, in this particular case, sympathy for animals, who might, for all we bloody well know, enjoy music as much as we do. Dr Lord shook his head and turned his glazed eyes away from the speaker in time to see the entrance of Charles 'Crack' McCray into the hall. Happily, he was not unescorted: Eleanor Kastostis, the radiant Eleanor about whom Dr Lord had dreamed all day Sunday while sleeping through the worst hangover of his life, led McCray by the hand to a seat near the door.

'Jolly good,' said Dr Lord, none too loudly, but loudly enough so that the smelly Dutch jazz expert turned round and gave him a quizzical look, as if Dr Lord had meant the speaker was jolly good, rather than the accompaniment of McCray by the one individual at the Music Programme who might conceivably persuade him that sane and talented people were affiliated, if only by marriage, to the organization.

'Shh,' said Dr Lord, putting an index finger to his lips. 'Go back to sleep.'

*   *   *

119

Mary Mbewa sat at her desk, tossing tranquillizer cakes to a shrewdness of strung-out monkeys. Her brow was furrowed with worry. She had made up her mind to ask Dr Lord for a description of the Supreme Director, hoping that this last favour before disowning her brother might permit her to recover the full contents of their bank account. She had not asked her brother why Ndana's people needed this information and, while not wanting to know, she thought she did. A glance at her schedule showed that Dr Lord would be back from his conference any moment now. By the time his land-rover forded the river and pulled into its parking-place behind his hutch, Mary had landed on a reasonable ploy for extracting the information without arousing suspicion.

'Ah, good morning, Mary,' said Dr Lord, who had left the conference early with elaborate glances at his watch and the sour expression of someone who only wished he had time to stay and hang on Herr Weissmann's every word.

'Good morning, sah.'

'Did you have a pleasant weekend?'

'Very nice, sah,' said Mary. 'I went to see my oldest brother.'

'Oh, yes, uhm . . .'

'Robert.'

'Right, yes, I remember.' Dr Lord remembered a good-looking excitable fellow in a white suit who had visited the compound one day.

'He remembers you, too, sah,' said Mary.

'Oh, does he now?'

'He thought you were the Supreme Director.' Mary raised a hand to mask her giggle.

'Oh, did he now?'

'Yes. I thought that was funny.'

'Oh, did you now?'

'My bus passed the party on Saturday.'

'Party? Oh, yes.'

'You met the Supreme Director there?'

'Yes, naturally, of course I did,' said Dr Lord, whose pride had been slightly wounded by Mary's giggle.

'I have never seen the Supreme Director.'

'Well, I suppose few people have,' said Dr Lord, showing Mary that, if he was not the Supreme Director, at least he was in a position to know the man intimately.

'Is he very frightening-looking?'

'H'm? No, of course not. Charming fellow. Friendly.'

'What does he look like? Is he a white man?'

'Somewhere between you and me, Mary. His outstanding

120

feature is his thick white hair. He's not a tall man, no. He's shorter even than I. But a great mass of white hair stands on top of his head, and he may be blind, for all I know, because he wears dark glasses when one might even say it was impolite to do so. I say, don't you think those monkeys have had enough? Are they still alive, those two?'

'*Dolphins?*' whispered McCray into Eleanor's ear. 'Did he say *dolphins?*'

Eleanor nodded and turned her palms upwards as if to say that she had no explanation for the speaker's having brought up aquatic mammals.

Having leaned so close to Eleanor's head, McCray could no longer hear the speaker over the drumming of blood in his ears. Her hands were folded on her crossed knees, her bright eyes were raised towards the platform where Herr Weissmann droned on about the capacity of flora and fauna to appreciate Palestrina, her cheeks shone with good health and – McCray dared to hope – reciprocated attraction.

McCray had been in love only twice before. In retrospect the emotion he had felt for those women resembled nothing more than a tender pity compared to the all-conquering admiration and desire he felt for Eleanor. Here, McCray decided, was a challenging woman. Because he had chatted so long after dinner with Eleanor, he had spent the night in the Kastostis guest room – sleepless, an ear cocked to the door for the slightest sound of approaching footsteps. It had reminded him of the adolescent sexual anticipation of his distant past. The fact that she had not visited the guest room did not discourage him; she would need more than a day to get used to the idea of leaving her husband for all time.

When McCray had felt it was safe to emerge from his bedroom in the morning he had found Ludvik Kastostis sitting silently at the downstairs piano grimacing as if in pain, having just swallowed a sip of sour coffee. Conversation with the composer had proved impossible, and McCray soon accepted a ride with Eleanor to Dan O'Connor's house. There he looked in on the bedridden speech-writer, who was apparently a victim of food-poisoning, and borrowed a change of clothes. He spent the day alone, having planned to meet Eleanor on Monday morning to hear the German speaker.

' . . . which I call neutral bio-aphasia,' said Herr Weissmann, with an accent and a fermata, as if he expected rousing applause to meet the announcement of his breakthrough.

'They aren't usually academics,' whispered Eleanor, leaning

over to McCray so that her hair brushed his neck. 'More often they are ministers of education, directors of foundations, that sort of thing.'

'I take it field-work is not the Music Programme's strong suit.'

'I don't suppose I should comment in depth. You're the investigator, and I don't even work here.'

'Don't worry. As you say, my opinions have been formed for me in advance.'

'I'm sorry I said that. I was anxious about my performance. I didn't mean that you weren't personally open-minded . . .' McCray wanted so badly to place his hand on hers that he suffered a dizzy spell and missed part of Eleanor's remark. ' . . . perfectly marvellous programmes.'

'I'm sure.'

' . . . for the good of man', said Herr Weissmann, 'and beast.' He dropped his chin to his chest like a spent conductor at the end of the Brahms First Symphony, a clear indication that applause was recommended. This he received, in a sufficient dose for him to be able to smile triumphantly to the back of the near-empty hall and clasp his hands over his head like a victorious boxer.

'Where to now?' Eleanor asked. 'What have they planned for you?'

'Nothing. Isn't that strange? You'd think they would lavish me with impressive examples of their productivity. Or give me an audience with the Supreme Director, at least. Dr Lord said he was at the reception on Saturday, but I never met him. What does he look like?'

'Haven't the foggiest. It was said that he might have attended my husband's induction ceremony years ago, incognito, but it was never made clear which of the dark-suited fellows he was. You'd think in all these years I would have spotted him, but I'm afraid he's something of a shadowy figure.'

'So I gather.'

'Lives in that monstrosity on the hill, somehow runs the show through a team of rather tension-crazed cabinet members. In some ways it is an effective managerial technique, based on fear of the unknown. One always has the feeling that he could be among us at any time, like a disguised king among his subjects.'

'I hope I'm not keeping you away from your piano practice. This is awfully nice of you to show me around.' McCray hoped that the way he felt, namely like a drooling, tail-wagging sheepdog seeing his master for the first time in fifteen years, was not evident in his facial expression.

'Not at all. I think Ludvik preferred that I stay out of the

122

house. Surprisingly enough, he claims to have begun a new work, which I have never known him to do before the first performance of his last composition.'

'And when will that be?'

'Several months, surely. His manuscript is at the copyist. The artistic directors have been presented with his material requirements. The computer people are on full alert. The game reserve will have to be persuaded to give up a creature or two. God, I hate the animal parts.' Eleanor shivered, because she had thought of the green mamba.

'Are you cold?' With the strength of ten thousand men, McCray did not put his arm around her shoulders, even though he and Eleanor were now alone in the gigantic conference-hall.

'A little. Let's go outside into the sunshine.'

Outside, in the Richard Wagner Courtyard, those who had persevered through Herr Weissmann's speech gobbled up cakes and sipped tea served by white-jacketed waiters. Thwok happily strummed his harp in the shade to one side. The Terrible Teutons had surrounded Herr Weissmann beneath the dead Norwegian artist's bust of Wagner; their German conversation sounded important. A Daliesque statue of Paganini-as-Satan leaned grotesquely into its violin playing in the centre of a sputtering fountain, which itself was surrounded by a modest Japanese rock garden. (Dr Lord called this part of the compound 'The Axis'.)

'I should mingle,' McCray said.

'By all means. Let me introduce you to someone.'

All the men in the courtyard were in a state of some arousal now that Eleanor was on the scene. She wore the kind of light sun-dress that McCray imagined no one owned, or had any need for, in England. As she moved towards one of the groups, guiding McCray by the elbow, two dozen heads turned in unison.

'It must be nice being you,' McCray whispered, although it wasn't bad being McCray, either, at this point.

'Hush,' she said, and pulled him harder by the arm. 'I want you to meet Mr Aarndt. Here we are.'

McCray had once had a college room-mate who smelt the way Mr Aarndt smelt, who smelt this way even in the breezy African outdoors.

'Hey, man,' said Mr Aarndt, in a Dutch accent that was even more surprising than the words he chose to speak. 'You from the States?'

Eleanor intervened and sternly explained McCray's mission.

'Heavy,' said the Dutchman. 'What do you want to know?

123

Last week I wrote a letter to the Sultan of Brunei, trying to get him to buy musical instruments for every child in Asia. Man could afford it, too. Man has deep pockets.'

'Best of luck,' said McCray, indicating to Eleanor by his tone of voice that he wished to move on.

'He always wanted to be a New York hipster in the fifties,' said Eleanor, when they were out of Aarndt's earshot. 'He has written an important essay on the pros and cons of the ascendancy of the stand-up bass to the level of solo instrument in jazz groups.'

'Heavy,' said McCray.

'I'm sure he's quite worthwhile,' suggested Eleanor. 'A gifted fund-raiser, or so I gather. Persistent. Asks for the world, gets Pakistan, if you follow.'

'Good for him.'

'And, for someone who is stoned much of the time, he is an effective proponent of what he calls "America's One Indigenous Art".'

'A patriot. My boss would like that.'

'Wonderful. Chalk one up for the Music Programme.'

'Could you tell me something, Eleanor? Who is that man over there playing the harp? I met him when I first arrived.'

'Thwok?'

'Right. I knew his name was a sound-effect. He played in the group with you at the reception.'

'A darling man. Believe it or not, one of the best musicians I've ever met. Completely photographic visual and tactile memory. Never looked at a piece of music twice. Rather handicapped by his instrument of choice, if you ask me, but he loves the harp as if it were a woman. Look at the way he strokes it. Such beautiful hands. And it says something, I believe, that Thwok – I don't know if it's *Mr* Thwok, or just *Thwok* – simply adores my husband's music. I don't know if poor Ludvik could have carried on without his encouragement.'

'I should meet some more of these people, I suppose,' said McCray, who didn't like being reminded of Eleanor's husband. 'If you're sure you can spare the time. I'm afraid your husband won't approve.' McCray was glad to get this one bit of honest concern off his chest, and finally to table the possibility that there might be something going on which would cause Ludvik Kastostis some distress.

'Not at all. Ludvik will be eating his lunch on the terrace about now, not a care in the world. I'm sure he's in fine spirits.'

Ludvik Kastostis selected a crystal vase from a kitchen cabinet,

124

brought it upstairs to his bedroom, and cast it through the window on to the terrace. That was the effect he wanted: the sight and sound of something beautiful exploding irrevocably into worthless dust. He went back downstairs and ordered Vincent to clean up the mess, then cautiously approached his piano like a hunter stalking a rogue elephant from downwind.

Much as he might publicly disdain conventional musical keys, Kastostis instinctively lowered his left hand on to the keyboard and formed the root, fifth and third of a C-sharp-minor chord. His intention was to stake out this key and explore its nuances until history remembered it only as Kastostis' Key. It would become synonymous with the anguish of the wronged lover, the pure artist trodden upon by mortal woman.

He continued to toy with the key with both hands, until he could no longer deny that he was playing the Moonlight Sonata.

'Vincent!' he shouted. 'Sherry!'

With drink in one hand and the new key of B-flat minor in the other, Kastostis worked at his new composition until it was indistinguishable from Chopin's 'Marche Funèbre'.

Kastostis slammed the piano shut, then stormed around his house in search of more objects to destroy. Vincent stayed out of his master's way while the composer first broke his emptied sherry-glass, then went to work on an intricately inlaid, lac-quered Japanese jewel-box, which with the aid of an empty vodka-bottle he succeeded in reducing to unrecognizable slivers in slightly less than one hour.

When he returned to his piano he found that his ideas had crystallized, and that with a sufficient number of keys depressed simultaneously the tonal centre of his Opus 10, as in all his other works, was irrelevant. In a matter of minutes he felt comfortable with the piano rendition of what would become his bed of murmuring strings. He flipped a blank two-hour cassette into his tape-recorder, turned on the machine, and played this portion of the piece. Once finished, he retired upstairs for a nap, happy with his day's work.

While O'Connor's fever of embarrassment had broken some time during Sunday night, he was still not psychologically prepared to go to work on Monday. Instead, enlisting the help of his not-quite-comprehending servants, O'Connor gathered together a disguise comprised of an Australian bush-hat, a mud-spattered safari-jacket with black epaulettes, khaki shorts, heavy knee-high motorcycling-boots and reflecting sun-glasses. Each of these articles was part of the eclectic wardrobe belongng to O'Connor's friend Durin Oakes, the archaeologist/spy. A large wardrobe in the guest bedroom contained nothing but Durin's filthy cast-off clothes and a collection of what O'Connor took to be souvenirs of battle.

It was wearing the disguise provided by these items that O'Connor intended to present himself at the Acacia Club pool around lunch-time. He was unable to think clearly enough to know exactly from whom he was hiding, but he went so far as to leave his motorcycle behind and make his way to the Club on foot. He was more than halfway to the Club when he realized that he must look exactly like a rebel soldier stumbling back into the city from a catastrophic guerrilla attack in the bush. He raised the brim of his hat slightly so that his white skin was visible, but not his hair. He passed the French ambassador's residence, walking on the far side of the street, and averted his eyes from the guard in the booth near the gate. He clumped along in Durin's heavy boots until he reached the driveway of the Acacia Club. It was here that O'Connor wished he had a plan. He knew only that life demanded action. Two days enshrouded within his mosquito netting had convinced him that retreat was no answer to his problems. His hearty forebears would have told him something about grasping the bull by its sharp charging horns. There were even some members of his family who would argue that he had done nothing wrong, that it was the French ambassador who owed O'Connor an apology for barging in on his manly right to enjoy himself, that his wisest course of action would be to call the Supreme Director on the phone and complain to him that his friend the ambassador had behaved very badly indeed. O'Connor's constitution would not allow for such heroics; the best he could muster was a disguised visit to the pool, hoping that seeing Yvonne might dispel most of his regrets.

He stopped first at the poolside bar for a Mister K and a good view of the pool. Yvonne wasn't hard to spot, standing at the far end near the diving-board in her white bikini, holding a glass of lemonade with one hand and bunching her wet hair on top of her head with the other, talking to a freakishly tanned teenaged boy. At this point O'Connor wondered exactly what it was an international civil servant thought he was doing dressed as a mercenary soldier fresh from battle, ogling the diplo-brats while he sipped a Mister K in the shade of the snack bar of the Acacia Club. He had almost decided to rethink his actions when Yvonne glanced over at him and seemed to strip him bare of Durin Oakes's dishevelled clothing.

Well, here is a momentous occasion, O'Connor thought to himself, draining his Mister K: the French girl spots her deflowerer across the way only forty-eight hours after the immutable fact. She looks away, pretends she hasn't seen me, continues her conversation with the hormonally preposterous boy at her side.

It took O'Connor a moment to realize that Yvonne had looked away again because she had not recognized her conqueror wearing Durin Oakes's archaeologist/spy costume. He removed his hat and dark glasses, and waited for her to return her gaze in his direction.

Now we'll get the reaction, O'Connor thought. Her frozen stare, her rigid body; her hands will drop to her sides and the glass of lemonade will shatter on the concrete deck.

When Yvonne recognized O'Connor her expression was that of a hostess watching a dinner-guest spill a glass of claret on the tablecloth, but she quickly regained her composure, waved nonchalantly, then resumed her conversation with the bronzed teenager.

O'Connor turned to order another Mister K, and found Youpie standing just behind him at armpit level, close enough to feel the heat radiating from her body. O'Connor replaced his bush-hat and dark glasses, and tried to smile.

'Strange clothes,' said Youpie. 'I love you, Danny. Papa is going to kill you.'

Mary Mbewa made the phone call to her brother while Dr Lord napped in a hammock strung between two of the eucalyptus trees outside his hutch. With all the authority she could muster, she told Robert that she had held up her part of the bargain by giving him a description of the Supreme Director, and that she had better not hear any more idle threats about his keeping all the money in their bank account for himself. Robert told her not to worry, that she was a good sister, and that she would not regret having helped him. Unfortunately, he said, he would need some time to get together all the money the Mbewa children had set aside. Mary thought she knew what this meant. It meant the money was probably all gone, that he had never saved one penny of it. She slammed the receiver in its cradle and buried her face in her hands. Dr Lord stirred in his hammock and saw Mary sobbing at her desk. From twenty yards away he could see the mascara dripping through her fingers.

Charles and Eleanor stood in the Kastostís living-room, toasting each other with white wine. McCray felt sunburned, tipsy, jet-lagged, in love. All day he had restrained himself from any overt suggestion of his fervid feelings for Eleanor. But now, with the sun slanting through the french doors, and Eleanor before him leaning one elbow on her husband's grand piano, McCray could no longer contain himself. He took one step towards her, which covered the distance between them, and like an ape inspecting a television screen he brushed at her cheek with his fingertips.

'Oh, Charles,' Eleanor said.

'Oh, Eleanor,' Charles said.

The wheels of Ludvik Kastostis' tape-recorder turned noiselessly on the piano.

9

At dawn on Tuesday morning Skip Skinner could not remember Monday, but thought he was handling the blackout well. In his empty bedroom, naked, he stood before the full-length mirror the thieves had left behind, and vowed that his drinking would not defeat him. Looking as objectively as he could at his own body, he thought he did *Homo sapiens* a terrible injustice; if it hadn't been his own body, he would have looked away in revulsion. Only his legs looked familiar, bony and hairless; but above them a belly worthy of a railroad tycoon had sprouted, starting years before as a mound between his hips and gaining momentum over time until it seemed to begin somewhere in the middle of his chest, and wrapped around his body like a tightly fitted sack of dough. He poked at his stomach near the entrance to his navel, and wondered what material could have accumulated this way beneath his skin, and what relation it had to the substances he ate and drank. Could clean liquid booze settle in the body in the form of what felt like baked potato?

Clearly a major revamping of his life was in order, starting with the customary vow never to drink again; daily attendance at work would be a distinct improvement; three or four hours a day practising the trombone would lend order and spirituality to his existence. He would focus on subsequent birthdays in anticipation of retiring with a sufficient pension that he and his wife could live out his days in comfort.

Skip Skinner missed his wife terribly. Since she had left Timbali five years before for a career of her own, he had seen her only two months a year. When sober he thought of Tina with a spine-bending shudder of self-loathing. What had he ever done to deserve pure sweet Tina, who had put up with the excesses of a drunkard for so long?

His fantasy was to return to Tina in Amsterdam, clean and sober, with enough money for them to be able to start a family. For some time now Skinner had believed that sixty was the appropriate age for a man to begin the reproductive process. Tina would still be in her early forties when Skinner retired, so that at least one child was a theoretical possibility. Theoretical, that is, because Skinner was not convinced he could muster fruitful activity from the quarters beneath his extravagant belly, a region he had drunk into dormancy.

Skinner knew that to live out his fantasy he had to keep his job; to keep his job he needed to issue a fresh report on the State of the Trombone. He wished he had Dr Lord's gift for scholarly R & R (Research and Regurgitation), or at least Dan O'Connor's ability to flood a page with words as fast as others might spatter it with spilled coffee. One common technique used by Music Programme staff when faced with the need to produce what were referred to as Tangible Results was to take their speciality to the Timbalian locals and organize a highly concrete example of the Music Programme's contribution to world music. A musical-education specialist at a loss for Tangible Results might recruit a dozen children from one of the city orphanages and dramatize over a six-month period the way their moods and expectations improved when they were exposed to rigorous music-appreciation classes. Dr Lord had logged an invaluable record of Tangible Results by directing the B-Minor Mass each year with his enormous orchestra and chorus composed mostly of local talent. And of course there was the time-honoured symposium or conference format, which could produce Tangible Results in the form of a fat document written and signed by parties who were often at war with one another in the real world. Because it was the central issue at all Music Programme conferences, music was inevitably used as a metaphor for world peace: the most Tangible of Results stemming from even the smallest of gatherings was usually a bathetic statement of hand-holding musical solidarity against the baser instincts of man.

Skinner could not decide how to solve his dearth of Tangible Results, except perhaps to enlist the services of the prolific Music Programme publishing department and produce a colourful book on the history of the trombone. While this might not qualify as an entirely humanitarian endeavour, it was commonly believed that the Supreme Director was a big fan of colourfully illustrated books bearing the Music Programme logo on the cover. The more he thought about it, the more Skinner liked the idea: plenty of work, an autobiographical foreword written by himself or ghost-written by O'Connor, a jewel in the Supreme Director's crown, and no drinking, no drinking, no drinking.

Wearing his black bathrobe over his black turtleneck and his black pyjama bottoms, Ludvik Kastostis watched the sunrise through the french doors of his living-room. In his right hand he held a cassette tape; in his left hand he held the crumbs of a roll he had crushed in his fingers when he rewound and played the tape. He stared into the rising orange sun and felt tears of anger spring to his eyes. He waited until the last frayed edge of the star had cleared the horizon, then returned to his audio equipment for another listen. He used headphones, because Eleanor was still upstairs asleep.

'Oh, Charles,' Eleanor said.

'Oh, Eleanor,' Charles said.

There followed the muffled sound of a clench and kiss, the tapping of wine-glasses deposited on the piano, the smacking of lips, the lapping of tongues, the rustling of clothing, and an amount of moaning and breathing and whispering of endearments that served almost to arouse the composer *trompé* himself.

This is the sound I'm after, Kastostis thought, fiddling with his equalizer, adding digital reverb and compressor, working with the recording until he had a highly amplified and well-filtered audio version of his wife's adulterous passion. Already he could hear these sound-effects sampled, digitalized, looped and fed into his computer blanks, amplified over his Opus 10 at such volume that the rest of the orchestra would be subsumed in a thunderous roar of high-fidelity infidelity.

Dan O'Connor's hands were poised above his word-processor keyboard as if he were about to launch into the *presto* finale of a Beethoven piano sonata. A memo from the Supreme Director's office had arrived asking him to compose a statement suitable for presentation at the Music Programme's tenth anniversary celebration. The event would be observed in one week's time. The memo, marked 'Confidential', signed by the Supreme Director but written by Saint Thomas, clearly indicated that the big boss would attend the occasion in person to address his staff. At past anniversaries the SD had been conspicuously absent as usual, but the import of a decade's existence apparently demanded his physical attendance.

O'Connor had locked his door against the possibility of a visit from the Head of Personnel; his telephone would go unanswered. He had arrived at work with a fatalistic attitude, prepared to discover his walking-papers waiting on his desk. He would not have been surprised if the security guards at the gate had prevented his entering the compound. Instead he had discovered the confidential business-as-usual memo, which made him wonder whether the Supreme Director had even recognized him in bed with Yvonne and Youpie. It also crossed O'Connor's mind that the Supreme Director might be something of an admiring co-voluptuary.

'Dear friends,' O'Connor wrote, 'my dearest friends. I look out at your faces, at your warm smiles, and I am filled with pride. How far we have come together. What great progress we have made. What a long, long road we have travelled. What a twisted path through dangerous jungle we have negotiated *ensemble*. Who would have thought that such a lengthy treacherous voyage would lead us all to . . .'

O'Connor had begun to daydream about his escape from the Music Programme. Before coming to work in the morning he had thought through his firing, which he would have taken like a man, and his departure, which he would have taken at high speed on the back wheel of his bike.

' . . . help to guide our endeavours into our next decade and beyond,' O'Connor typed. 'I'm certain everyone in this room realizes how lucky we are to be able to devote our energies and skills to one of man's highest and most ineffable callings. Our purpose is to assure democratic access to serious music; to promulgate sensible governmental attitudes towards this art; to transcend the political differences which divide the world and reach humanity with the divine gift of harmony . . .'

O'Connor yawned, and tried to type faster.

' . . . I enjoin you therefore to redouble your efforts, to rededicate yourselves to our cause, to rekindle the flame we lighted only ten years ago, to march into our second decade with the great masters our standard-bearers, their celestial sounds our anthems.'

O'Connor wondered how long he had before Ng or someone more muscular would break down the door and send him on his way.

' . . . our day for self-congratulation, but tomorrow we forge ahead, united, as we hope the world will some day be, by our common adoration of music,'

O'Connor read his speech aloud, and pronounced it finished. When he looked up from his monitor, he noticed that someone had slipped an envelope under his door. He took the time to start his printer before walking over to pick up the envelope. He brought it back to his desk and inspected it for official markings, but found none. He asked himself if news of his firing or deportation would come in such a thin unmarked package.

With a sigh of resignation he opened the envelope and extracted the single sheet of paper it contained. Still standing, he read:

> *Above man's need to see himself as God,*
> *Our reason tells us no such high regard*
> *Will slay the odds of one day lying cold*
> *Beneath the frozen earth, a mossy mould.*
> *Beware the curse of mighty, learned men,*
> *Who live with expectations and a ken*
> *For having more than is their rightful lot;*
> *Their fate we trust is simply ours, to rot –*
> *To rot away and blend into the soil,*
> *To melt like so much butter on the boil –*
> *How pleasant for us all, alive, to know*
> *Where every living, dying man will go:*
> *Our business done, we bow just like the dear*
> *Kalima; we fold our wings and disappear.*

O'Connor examined the typed unsigned sonnet for an indication of its authorship, then reread it several times for a hint of its meaning. It took him only a few minutes to notice that the last five lines began with the five letters spelling T-H-W-O-K.

'I'm so glad we could have this chat,' said McCray, sitting across the desk from the Head of Personnel. McCray was in such a fine mood that nothing Mr Ng told the American irked him in the slightest: not the top-heavy staff with grossly inflated salaries; not the astronomical upkeep fees; not the gardeners, limousines, guards, caterers, busboys and janitors, whose cost alone might keep a more low-profile organization in business for five years; not even the Kastostis Budget fazed McCray on this beautiful morning.

No one could accuse Mr Ng of reticence. At each request for specific information the tiny man darted to his filing-cabinets and deftly retrieved the pertinent document. His English was ungrammatical but direct. What impressed McCray most was that Mr Ng did not seem the least bit intimidated, nor did he seem to find anything at all embarrassing about the information he turned over. He was proud of his files, proud of his thoroughness, proud of his organization. He was particularly pleased with the distaff side of the Music Programme, showing McCray that women made up just slightly more than half of its professional members.

When McCray rose to leave, Mr Ng shook his hand and walked him to the door.

'I have one question for you now,' Mr Ng said, his hand on the doorknob.

'Yes?'

'You are staying with Mr O'Connor?'

'Sure,' said McCray. This was not strictly true, since he had seen the Irishman only briefly over the weekend, and had spent the rest of his time with Eleanor.

'You tell O'Connor I want to see him,' said Ng.

'Can't you call him?'

'He doesn't answer the phone.'

'Visit his office?'

'His door is always locked.'

'I see. Is he in some sort of trouble I should know about?'

'I have chased him many weeks. I suspect he is not Irish.'

'Really? How strange.'

McCray was not in the least disturbed by Mr Ng's puzzling assertion. He whistled to himself as he exited the building into the sunshine, and headed straight for the cafeteria for a Mister K and a seat in the shade. Seated near him were some familiar faces and several strangers, some of them playing small tape-recorders for their companions, others poring over sheet music, others conversing in a pleasant babble of foreign tongues. McCray liked it here.

Night fell abruptly in Timbali. The day's collected heat vanished in a rush. Villagers built bonfires in the streets or in metal drums, and watched the sparks dance in the quavering heat. On the great plains, tribesmen retreated to their brambly huts. In the city, empty shop-stalls were locked shut, and the avenues filled with warmly dressed strollers.

134

In the hills above the capital, the lights of a Mercedes limousine knifed through the sudden gloom. In the back seat, a white-haired man studied a folder beneath the yellow cone of a reading-light. A uniformed driver hunched over his steering-wheel and peered intently into the darkness, watching for roadblocks. In the front passenger-seat a guard watched the sides of the road and fiddled with the shoulder-strap of his machine-gun. Even in the darkness of the limousine, the white-haired man wore dark glasses.

Reading became impossible for the white-haired man once his limousine had begun the descent from Embassy Row towards the city on an uneven unpaved road. He switched off his reading-light and rubbed his eyes behind his glasses.

When the driver saw the roadblock he had to make a quick decision: he could accelerate and try to break through the tree-limbs and rocks, risking a precipitous drop on the left and gunfire from the right; or he could apply the brakes and try to turn round before the Land Pirates disabled his car. The white-haired man had already made the decision for him, and shouted from the back seat for him to speed up. The guard rolled down his window and propped his weapon on the sill. He fired three short bursts into the darkness to the right of the roadblock before the car rammed into a heavy log, then into a group of tyre-sized boulders. When the car stopped bouncing the driver thought they had made it through. There was no sign of Land Pirates, and the car was still moving. A hundred yards later all four tyres of the limousine were flat, and a slight uphill gradient made further progress impossible. Shouts were heard from the underbrush to the side of the road, and the white-haired man instructed his guard to throw out his weapon. His instructions were hardly necessary, because both the driver and the guard opened their doors and jumped from the limousine and threw themselves face-down on the ground. The white-haired man, who had rehearsed this predicament in his mind a hundred times, turned his reading-light back on, emptied his pockets, removed his watch, and separated documents from valuables in his briefcase.

He was almost done with this chore when the muzzle of a rifle poked through the driver's open door. The white-haired man slowly opened his own door and got out of the limousine, expecting an orderly theft of everything in the car. He deliberately did not look at the Land Pirates, and was therefore caught entirely by surprise by the rifle-butt to the back of his head, which knocked him to the ground next to his prostrate guard.

*   *   *

When O'Connor heard the knock on his door he was certain Durin Oakes had come back from the bush for another few days of rest and personal hygiene. It wouldn't have been unusual at all for Durin to wake O'Connor after midnight and insist that they build a fire and drink beer for three hours while the archaeologist/spy went about debriefing himself. Barefoot, wearing only his boxer shorts and an anti-apartheid T-shirt which read 'I know whose side God is on', O'Connor opened his front door. It didn't take him long to realize that the person waiting outside was not Durin Oakes, because Durin Oakes looked nothing at all like Yvonne.

'Yvonne.'

'Danny,' said the French girl. 'Please let me come in.'

'Just whisper. I have a guest.' Charles McCray had finally returned, in high spirits, interested mainly in a shower, a change of O'Connor's clothes, and rest. 'Come into my room.'

O'Connor guided Yvonne into his room and drew back the mosquito netting so there was room for them both to sit on his bed. Yvonne wore a bulky Scandinavian sweater and jeans, which was a radical departure from her usual attire, or lack of it.

'I saw you at the pool, Danny. I saw you talking to Youpie.' Yvonne was clearly upset.

'Nonsense. She snuck up behind me. I was looking for you, of course. She told me your father was going to kill me.'

'Correct. He said so to us both. Of course that is only a manner of speaking. I tried to explain that nothing happened.'

'What do you mean nothing happened . . .?' O'Connor checked himself.

'I said that's what I tried to *explain*. He didn't believe me, of course. He said he was going to have you fired first, then killed – so to speak. Papa is not really that way, but nothing of this . . .'

' . . . magnitude . . .'

' . . . has happened before.'

'I should hope not. But so far your father hasn't acted, that I know of. I haven't been fired. In fact I have received new assignments.'

'Papa has been busy. And something awful has happened tonight. I should tell you. You remember my father's friend, that man we saw with the white hair?'

O'Connor fixed his eyes on Yvonne's and waited.

'Tonight he was kidnapped on the road to town.'

'Ah.'

'Papa is terribly upset. It is an international incident. It would be worse if he were a Frenchman, but still . . .'

'Yes. Still.'

O'Connor knew it was his duty to wake up McCray and tell him that the Supreme Director had been abducted, but he waited until he was able fully to digest Yvonne's shattering news.

'I am very worried about my father. He took the same road into the city after he heard the news. He has gone to talk to officials in the capital, then he is going to France.'

'Jesus, they ought to do something about that road.'

'Always before it has been robbery. But this is different, no?'

'I would think so. Sounds sort of political to me.'

No matter what this development might signify for his own short-term position, O'Connor was worried about the Supreme Director. Oddly enough, he had grown attached to the mysterious invisible man for whom he wrote speeches. The SD, hidden in the clouds of his palace on the hill, was like an all-powerful but usually benevolent god. The act of writing such a man's words had made O'Connor feel more intimately attached to him than anyone else at the Music Programme. And now where was he? Dragged from a car in the middle of the night by murderous Land Pirates – or worse. Why had he not taken his helicopter?

'I thought you should know,' said Yvonne. 'I suppose that is why I came here.' She looked down at her hands, and O'Connor recognized the signs of a need for emotional comfort.

'Here,' he said. 'Don't worry. Come here.'

Yvonne moved closer and leaned her head against his collarbone. With one arm around her back and a hand on the back of her head, O'Connor held her tightly for several minutes, whispering to her not to worry about her father. She shook her head silently, and soon he felt her tears soaking through his shirt on to his chest. 'Shh,' he said. 'You mustn't worry. Your father is well protected. He's made the same journey many times. He must have alerted the Army before he left.' Yvonne sniffled, and rubbed her nose while still pressing it against his shirt. 'There,' said O'Connor. 'Please don't cry. We'll call the embassy in the morning and find out that he has arrived safely.'

'I hate it here,' Yvonne said. 'I hate this ugly country.'

Under different circumstances O'Connor might have tried to argue that the only ugliness in Timbali was political and economic, and that much of that was traceable to unrelenting waves of foreign interference during the past century and a half. True, Timbalians had robbed him and sliced his dog Richard into four separate pieces; but one does not generalize about a country based on the behaviour of its most barbaric citizens.

'It's like a prison,' Yvonne said, her voice still muffled by O'Connor's shirt. She sniffled again, but seemed to have stopped the flow of tears.

137

'I know,' said O'Connor. 'I know.' What he really knew was that to be imprisoned at the Acacia Club pool and behind the impregnable walls of the ambassador's residence was most people's idea of heaven. He stroked the back of Yvonne's head and stared up at the ceiling, wondering what to do next. From a purely selfish point of view, he hoped to dispel the nagging worry – a major component of his near-nervous-breakdown over the weekend – that he had taken advantage of Yvonne. He found it distasteful, if unavoidable, that his prurience could so overwhelm his judgement.

'Yvonne?' He reached up and grasped a handful of mosquito netting, and when Yvonne looked up he used it to dry her cheeks. He kissed one of her eyes and drew her hair behind her ears. When he looked at her face he felt a powerful pang of tenderness, a physical sensation well north of the area from which he was more accustomed to receiving powerful pangs. 'I have to ask you something. This might not be the time . . .'

This is it, thought O'Connor. I'm behaving in a mature fashion. I am verbalizing.

'Saturday. Remember?'

'Yes. I remember.'

'Was that a . . .?'

O'Connor paused long enough to wonder if he hadn't been let down by his Irish gene-pool, whose gift of the gab didn't appear to extend beyond banter and blarney.

'Was that a terrible idea, what we did? What we tried to do?'

Elliptical, thought O'Connor, but 'twill serve. He awaited her reply with a pre-emptive flinch and the squint-eyed expression of a person about to be struck on the side of the head.

Yvonne had dried her eyes, and answered his maladroit question by smiling. There was no end to O'Connor's relief. The great vice on his spinal cord had been loosened a notch. He smiled back and kissed her other eye.

'This is great,' he said. 'I'm happy. I'm relieved . . .'

'You're so funny,' said Yvonne. 'So nervous.'

'Who, me? Don't be—'

'Do you know why I came here?'

'The . . . kidnapping?'

'No, not that. Because I saw you with my sister at the pool.'

'Oh, that was—'

'Because I like you, Danny?'

'That was why you were . . .?' O'Connor wished he could complete just one sentence.

He gave his social ineptitude further thought while he rearranged his mosquito netting, until he and Yvonne were safely enclosed within the womb-like shroud and Yvonne had begun to remove her clothing.

With the late-night chill in the air it was important to get under the covers immediately when they were naked. With that accomplished, O'Connor found that words came more easily. 'This is wonderful,' he was able to say. 'Doesn't this feel good?' Yvonne nodded. 'Aren't we happy?' She nodded again.

It alarmed O'Connor, in a vague sort of way, that he felt so relaxed and comfortable once there remained nothing for him to do but experience the serenity of lying next to a beautiful warmer-than-room-temperature girl. There was no need for rationalization. They smiled at each other in the snowy inside of the mosquito netting. Calmly, happily, he traced her ribs and collarbones and jaw with a lazy index finger. He told her she was so soft that she seemed to be dusted by a supernaturally fine powder. She wrapped a leg over his, and O'Connor let out a sigh that surprised him by its volume and profundity. 'Aren't we happy?' he asked again, and once again she nodded. He held her as tightly as he dared without appearing extreme or murderous, delighted with the feeling of warmth and closeness. Unlike the previous occasion at the ambassador's residence, Yvonne had no specific questions to ask. Her intellectual curiosity had evidently been sated, and she had turned over the operation to her emotional and physical senses. 'You're a beautiful girl,' O'Connor told her. She rolled on top of him and smiled. Under her weight O'Connor sank deeply into his soft mattress and felt happily enclosed on all sides. He gripped one of Yvonne's feet between his own, and drew his palms down the long slope of her back.

O'Connor's thought processes gradually slowed to a cottony low gear, so that nothing surfaced in his mind above the calmly lapping waters of his physical pleasure. With his eyes tightly shut he was aware of swirling colours and shapes; with Yvonne's hands cupped over his ears he heard nothing but the sea. He let himself float along among these colours and sounds, warm and happy under Yvonne's body, distracted only the slightest bit by what he assumed was a hallucination: he heard a voice. 'Hey there, Dan,' said the distant masculine voice. O'Connor put his arms further around Yvonne's back and pulled her down on top of him. 'Hey, Dan, are you there?' said the voice. It sounded like his late father. Oh, no, thought O'Connor, I'm having an out-of-body experience.

'Danny?' whispered Yvonne, whose mouth was next to his ear.

'H'm?'

'There's someone in the room.'

Still attached to Yvonne, O'Connor gave his mouth some room and raised his voice: 'Who's there?' He could see nothing through the mosquito netting but a lunar glow.

'It's McCray,' said the voice. For a moment O'Connor didn't remember the name. 'I'm sorry, are you asleep? I saw the light on, and couldn't sleep myself. Went to bed too early.'

'Yes, I'm here,' said O'Connor. 'I've got a girl here, actually.'

'Oh, hell, I'm sorry, I'll—'

'No, wait. I have something to tell you. Listen.' O'Connor hoped he wasn't speaking too loudly, but it was an eerie sensation to be carrying on a conversation while buried beneath Yvonne in a cocoon of netting and sheets and flesh.

'I'm listening.'

As he spoke, O'Connor rocked himself – and by extension, Yvonne – back and forth with his heels.

'I've gotten word that the Supreme Director has been kid-napped.'

'What?'

'I said I've gotten word that the—'

'No, no, I heard you fine. I can't believe it. Why didn't you wake me?'

'What would you have done?'

'Jesus,' said McCray.

'I know, it's—'

'No,' interrupted McCray, rather forcefully. 'I mean, Jesus, you *are* American, aren't you?'

O'Connor had discovered too late that he could not make love and fake an Irish accent at the same time.

10

AT THE CONTROLS of his equipment in the Computer Centre, Ludvik Kastostis felt like a despot of the distant future, exerting his omnipotence through the touch of a button. At his fingertips a semicircular panel of flashing lights and glowing monitors surrounded his controller keyboard. To one side stood two refrigerator-sized memory-banks, which contained all the electronic elements of his recent *oeuvre*, as well as the sampled sounds needed to perform them. Behind his control panel a pane of glass separated him from a small studio where the few live musicians he required could record their parts.

It was past midnight. Kastostis' engineers had gone home hours before. With a sketchy score of his still-untitled Opus 10 propped above the keyboard, Kastostis played part after part into his computer system. He had never felt so capable, nor so inspired. Each pass through the piece went off flawlessly, as if the notes he conveyed to the computer through his brain and fingers had been there all along, waiting within the circuitry to be awakened by his awareness of their existence. After twelve

141

passes, the bed of murmuring strings lived apart from the composer's imagination, existed as an independent entity in the world's canon of man-made sound. A single pass more and the too-tuneful flute sang above the bed of murmuring strings in a melody of such poignancy that Kastostis' right hand trembled as he performed it and his hair stood up from tingling follicles. With delight he added a foreboding timpani part, executing the rolls with his index fingers on two keys of his synthesizer keyboard. When it came time to add the juggernaut of a brass part, the composer did so without a moment's hesitation or conscious thought. It was as if a lifetime's inspiration had finally overflowed into effortless creativity. He began with the bass trombone – *bim-pom bom, bim-pom bom* – then quickly added two higher trombone parts; the trumpets were next, a syncopated echo of the trombones; and finally the French horns entered in a fantastically inspired three-against-four feel that ate up the flute and bed of murmuring strings like a set of gigantic mechanical jaws. The reeds were a simple matter of frenetic trills and dissonant clusters. After a dozen more surgical passes his strings had crescendoed to a pitch dense and powerful enough to drive the brass part into submission. Typing frantically on the computer keyboard, he excised the too-tuneful flute and pasted it above the cacophony he had created by pitting the strings and bass against one another, then slowly modulated the volume of the combatants until the flute melody re-emerged unscathed and floated off to the end of the piece like a human soul.

'Mahler never had it so good,' Kastostis said gleefully in Czech, as he pressed the button that would store his composition on hard disk.

In half an hour he had mixed and panned and equalized his creation, and added enough acoustical effects that it might as well have been performed in Westminster Abbey. He dumped it to eighteen tracks of digital tape, and cracked his knuckles in preparation for the *coup de grâce*. His engineers, sworn to secrecy, had worked for hours to break the recording of Eleanor's passionate infidelity into its smallest components. These bits had been sampled into the computer system and arranged on Kastostis' keyboard so that each key played a different segment of Eleanor's rapture. After ten minutes of rehearsal, Kastostis performed what he thought of as the descant part of his Opus 10. He accompanied the introduction with vague sighs and moans. To the approaching storm of brass he added more recognizable grunts and groans. At the peak of the musical confrontation he injected the most overt fragments of his recording, in which Eleanor's whispering voice soared into the stratosphere of ecstasy. If these weren't musical sounds, he didn't know music. McCray's sounds, on the other hand, were harsh – just like the brass part – and distinctly MAXIMALIST. It made Kastostis deliciously angry to hear the dissonance of their passion, as he felt the competing emotions of spousal jealousy and artistic triumph.

His inspiration might have been fuelled by fury, but he was objective enough an artist to know that what he had composed was a masterpiece. He listened to the finished version once through, timed it at twenty-eight minutes, and simultaneously dumped the finished mix to two-track and digital cassette. He hid the sampled eavesdropping in secret sub-directories of his computer system, locked the two-track version in his safe, and left the studio with the cassette tucked in the inner pocket of his black cape.

He emerged from the darkness of his studio into the bright clear dawn of the Music Programme compound. With one arm he drew his cape over his face until his eyes grew accustomed to the light. The studio was situated on the side of a steep hill overlooking the compound, roughly equidistant from the Supreme Director's palace and Kastostis' own house. The composer blinked into the washed-out sunrise, then inspected the nearby palace for signs of life. Viewing it from above was a thrill reserved only for those few whose security clearances allowed them to visit the Computer Centre. He saw the palace so rarely in daylight that each time it was a matter of several minutes before he had his fill of its magnificence. Kastostis loved its ornate architecture, its excessive luxury, its wanton squandering of resources. The Supreme Director's was a MAXIMALIST palace constructed in a small space, something with which Kastostis could identify, especially when he squeezed the pocket of his cape and felt the cassette inside.

'I think I understand,' said McCray. 'I might have done the same thing.'

'I'm so glad to hear you say that,' replied O'Connor, 'but I'm still in a bind. I ought to resign, I suppose.'

'I wouldn't be too hasty.'

They sat together on O'Connor's terrace in the brilliant light of morning, drinking their third cup of coffee. Yvonne, whom McCray had not yet met, could be heard indoors taking a shower.

'You've had quite an adventure, then, haven't you?' said McCray, standing up to stretch his legs. 'I'd imagine it's exhilarating to live as an imposter, especially here, a million miles from anywhere.'

'I don't know about that,' said O'Connor. 'I'm not cut out for intrigue, I assure you. If I've lost sleep over such a minor affair, just imagine if I were in your—' O'Connor stopped himself before rashly accusing McCray of extracurricular intelligence work.

'I'm used to people thinking that,' McCray said understandingly, having caught O'Connor's implication. That was all he said. He sat down on the stone wall of the terrace and swivelled O'Connor's telescope from side to side.

'I suppose with this new development my little scandal will pale into insignificance.' O'Connor referred to the Supreme Director's disappearance.

'And my little investigation, too, really,' said McCray. 'In the midst of such a crisis it would be unseemly for me to interfere by burrowing into things the way I had intended.' He turned the telescope around and tested the viewfinder.

'Take a look,' said O'Connor. 'You can see some of the compound through it, up the valley there.'

McCray stood up behind the telescope and aimed it in the direction O'Connor had pointed.

'God,' said McCray. 'That palace is something.'

'Isn't it?'

'Have you ever seen the man come out of there?'

'Never. I've tried almost every morning. Saw his car once, I think.'

'The place is dead right now, understandably. I hope the guy's OK. Do you think that's real gold on the dome?'

'Certainly.'

'You know it's part of my job to look into the Supreme Director and his private funds. If that's a taxpayer's gold dome, he's in trouble.' McCray could hear the ravings of his Washington boss, who didn't want to see Federal spending on anything but defence and tobacco subsidies in his own district.

'They insist it's a private house, and they won't let you anywhere near it – or near the Supreme Director, for that matter.'

'It's tempting to try anyway. Especially now that the man isn't home.'

'You *are* a spy.'

McCray swivelled the telescope a few degrees to the left.

'What's that white building?' he asked.

'Up on the hill there? That's the Computer Centre. Where the Composer-in-Residence works. Not allowed up there, either.'

McCray focused the telescope on the one-storey stucco building, bright white in the sun. He was about to look away again when a red door opened in the centre of the building. The figure

144

that emerged was recognizable even from this great distance. In his black cape, Ludvik Kastostis was sharply outlined against the white stucco wall as he drew a bat-like wing over his eyes.

'There he is,' said McCray. 'Kastostis. After a long night's work, I suppose.'

'It's a good thing that studio is so well insulated. We might have heard his music from here.'

'What do you make of that stuff anyway?' McCray asked, as the black figure skirted the white building and disappeared around a corner with his black cape billowing behind him.

'I'm not sure. I've written speeches about it. I've said he is in the vanguard of contemporary composers, that sort of thing.'

'Can that be true?'

'Someone has to be. Would he have this job if he weren't?'

'I suppose,' said McCray, whose spirits were buoyed when he thought of Eleanor. 'Mrs Kastostis says quite bluntly that she hates his music, but she claims to respect it in the grander scheme of things.'

'She's a very direct woman. I think she has the right attitude.'

'Yes. What a lucky man Kastostis is.'

'So everyone thinks— Oh, hello, Yvonne.'

Yvonne came out on to the terrace wearing one of O'Connor's work-shirts over her jeans. Her wet hair was tucked behind her ears.

'Yvonne, this is Charles McCray. My American friend.'

McCray had great difficulty concealing his dismay when he saw that O'Connor's girlfriend was practically a child. He glanced quickly at O'Connor as if an apology or explanation might be forthcoming, then hastily said hello to Yvonne in the flattest tone of voice he could manage.

'Do you have a cigarette?' Yvonne asked.

McCray shook his head, and wanted to tell her she was too young to smoke. 'You're French?' he asked.

Yvonne sniffed.

'Yes,' O'Connor answered for her. He guessed that Yvonne always appeared grumpy and rude when she was introduced to people. Shyness, that's all it was.

Yvonne plonked herself down in a wicker chair and poured herself a cup of coffee from the pot. She took a sip before announcing, to McCray, that she had run away from home. 'I'm going to stay with Danny now,' she said.

'Now, Yvonne,' O'Connor said, 'you don't mean that.'

'Of course I do. I can't stay with Papa any longer.'

'The French ambassador,' O'Connor said to McCray, shrugging his shoulders.

'And Youpie is a beach.'

'Her sister,' said O'Connor. He could tell McCray was troubled by this arrangement. He had turned his back on them and was scanning the valley below the house with the telescope.

With her wet hair and pouting expression, Yvonne really did look terrifically young.

'Wow,' said McCray, focusing the telescope. 'There's a big green snake in a tree down there.'

'A mamba,' said O'Connor. 'I saw one last week in the compound. That could be the same one, actually. The same stream runs right through this valley.'

Yvonne shivered. 'That's what I hate most. Snakes. My brother André was almost killed by a puff adder. They had to send him home to France for a month.'

'It's gone,' said McCray. 'It fell out of the tree into the stream.'

'Well,' said O'Connor, standing up. 'Some of us have to go to work today.'

'Business as usual, Supreme Director or no Supreme Director?' asked McCray.

'It's going to be wild.'

'I'll stay here,' said Yvonne. 'I'll get your cook to go buy me cigarettes and Coca-Cola.'

'You're going home,' O'Connor said. He almost said 'You're going home, *young lady*'.

'Will you give me a lift to the compound?' asked McCray.

'Absolutely. Off we go. Do you promise me you'll go home, Yvonne? Your mother will worry.'

'My mother is in Iraq,' said Yvonne. 'And she wouldn't worry anyway. She doesn't care. And my father is in Paris.'

'You'll be terribly bored here, believe me.'

'Not after you get back from work,' she said.

'Oh *Christ*,' said McCray, who could no longer contain his disapproval.

'Now, now,' said O'Connor. 'Everything is going to be all right. We'll discuss this later.'

McCray left the terrace without saying goodbye to Yvonne. O'Connor leaned over to peck her on the cheek, but she grasped him by the hair and pulled him down to her mouth for a prolonged and expressive kiss. When O'Connor finally left the terrace, McCray was waiting for him at the front door, shaking his head.

'O'Connor,' he said. 'Are you sure that's wise?'

'Trust me,' O'Connor said. 'Nothing I do is wise.'

★　　★　　★

146

'Sanctus!' sang Dr Lord's chorus. 'Dominus!'

Dr Lord stood on the podium, his hands raised high, his mouth opened wide, his glasses fogged from the sweat on his brow. The baton in his right hand trembled as he held out the sustained notes, swept like a sabre when the music soared into motion. He conducted the B-Minor Mass without a score, for he knew every nuance of the piece as if he had composed it himself. He glared at his stern male singers during the giant descending strides of the *Sanctus* as if the slightest hint of holding back would mean their summary execution. He shut his eyes and raised his face to the ceiling when the sopranos ascended to their celestial heights. He arched his back and spread his hands to encompass the entire chorus, exposing a half-moon of white belly beneath his polo-shirt.

More than a hundred singers had gathered for this rehearsal, most of them veterans of previous masses under Dr Lord's baton. Once-weekly during the four months they prepared for the performance, three Music Programme buses picked up the singers in the city and brought them to the compound. Some of them were university students, others were church chorus members, still others were unaffiliated to formal singing groups but were hand-picked by Dr Lord at open auditions. All of them loved to sing more than anything else in their lives, so that Dr Lord's was a highly motivated, disciplined, passionate chorus.

They looked beautiful. Whenever a pause in the rapture of conducting allowed Dr Lord to open his eyes and survey his singers, he was filled with love and satisfaction by their eager radiant faces. They ranged in age from nine to seventy-six. Most of the men wore white shirts and jeans, their most proper clothes, and the women wore colourful city dresses. For indoor performances the Music Programme supplied them with dinner-jackets and black evening gowns; outdoors, they wore modified cricket costumes. Their rich voices sprang from expressions ardent with the ambition to please their conductor. When they opened their mouths to sing it was a visual sensation akin to the collective sound they made: a hundred mouths of bright white teeth flashed as one like a curtain drawn open on a morning sun. Dr Lord was moved in particular by the children in the group, whose angelic black faces and keen high voices lent a bright and hopeful spirit to the ensemble. Dr Lord often reminded himself that the miraculous Bach was first noted not for his instrumental virtuosity but for his pure and noble singing voice. Dr Lord therefore saw a little of the Master in every child he taught or conducted, and in their singing he heard all the potential genius of humanity.

147

For the purposes of rehearsal, Dr Lord assembled a pick-up orchestra of Music Programme staff and some competent Timbalians who worked within the compound. At the organ was Jean-Baptiste Grandmarie, whose petulant personality Dr Lord put up with only because the Frenchman was a disciplined and masterful player. The ability of music to defy boundaries of prejudice and hatred was clearly evidenced in that Dr Lord overcame his ingrained antipathy towards all people born within the borders of France when he heard Grandmarie play.

'Sanctus!' the chorus sang. 'Dominus!'

This was the greatest pleasure in Dr Lord's life. He relished music-making in all its facets. As an intellectual expression he found it unparalleled. For nearly half a century he had been wholly absorbed in the magical combination of science, skill and sensitivity known as music, the sole purpose of which was to render people's lives more livable.

Bach's sacred choral music ranked highest of all in Dr Lord's esteem, and this without the useful foundation of a religious outlook that might lend the music its power for the credulous listener. For years Dr Lord had scoured the record for evidence to back up his theory that only an atheist – or at least a man whose only true allegiances were to the intellect – could possibly have created a body of work so magnificently universal and complete. He was not the first scholar to work backwards from a conclusion towards its underpinnings; he would not be the last to inject a massive dose of his own preference and ideology into a treatise. With trembling fingers he had leafed through the scant documentation of Bach's life, looking for the one nugget of unbelief among the *pro forma* genuflections that would settle once and for all the issue of Bach's faith, or lack of it. It was insufficient that the Bach family were known to begin their annual musical get-togethers with quodlibets as bawdy as they were complex. But the lack of a definitive find proved nothing, of course. A man in Bach's position would never breathe a word of his infidelity, and why should he? Bach was as likely to rebel against his employer the Church as a man like Ludvik Kastostis was to embrace it.

Without documentary evidence, Dr Lord had turned to the music itself for his proof, searching for one of Bach's famous codes and riddles proclaiming his disdain for the Saviour he celebrated in his music. Just because he hadn't found it didn't mean it wasn't there. The best Dr Lord could do in the early draft of his thesis was to claim that, ironically, it was the perfection with which Bach pulled off his religious works that betrayed a less than pious mind at work: the truly devout composer would hardly sully his holy music with Bach's snide numerological gags, in-jokes and puzzles. True to the nature of the scholar, it never once occurred to Dr Lord that his *idée fixe* was unprovable, arcane and entirely irrelevant to the enjoyment of Bach's music.

Dr Lord shook a fist high overhead and glowered at the tenors. 'More!' he shouted. 'Give me *you*!' He was rewarded with the gratifying punch of their renewed vigour. Against his better judgement, because he was enjoying himself so much, he overlooked several lapses in energy and allowed his chorus to sing to the end of the *Sanctus* without interruption. When they were finished he blew them all a kiss, then abruptly soured his expression and said: 'We have a lot of work to do. Sopranos and altos, from the top, if you please.' He raised his baton and waited for the rustling of their sheet music to dwindle.

He was about to deliver the downbeat when a side-door of the auditorium clanged shut. Dr Lord turned, and was about to berate the author of this unthinkable intrusion when he saw that it was Dan O'Connor and Charles McCray. He motioned for his chorus to wait for a moment, and descended from the podium to greet the visitors.

'I hate to interrupt,' said O'Connor. 'But have you heard the news?'

'News?'

'The Supreme Director?'

'What? What is it?'

'Kidnapped,' said McCray. 'On the road to town.'

'Good heavens,' said Dr Lord. He looked back over his shoulder at his singers, as if they might now be taken away from him. He turned back to O'Connor. 'What do we do now?'

'No idea,' O'Connor said. 'Carry on, I suppose. We've asked around, and no one seems to have more information. The radio station isn't saying anything, but of course they wouldn't. We're not in any danger that we know of.'

'This is terrible. This is awful news.'

'I just thought we should tell you.'

'Well, I'm so glad you did. Do we know yet what steps are being taken to free him? Have there been any demands?' Dr Lord thought it odd that O'Connor could be so relaxed around the American visitor. His brogue was gone. Could it be that the two had become confidants?

'We assume there is an Acting Director. Also that the Timbalian government will have to be the ones to act. It must be a political move.'

'Good heavens,' repeated Dr Lord.

'Dr Lord,' said McCray, 'I wonder if I might stay a while and listen to your group. I know this is a crisis situation but, as O'Connor says, we must carry on until we have more information.'

'By all means,' said Dr Lord. It pleased him to have an opportunity to impress the American on his own terms.

McCray and O'Connor took their seats in the centre of the auditorium. Dr Lord returned to his podium beaming with pride at his chorus, no member of which had moved a muscle during the conductor's absence, as if he had held the baton aloft and maintained eye-contact with each one of them the entire time.

Rumours, big or small, swept down the corridors of the Music Programme headquarters like seasonal winds. By the time the rumour of the Supreme Director's kidnapping reached Skip Skinner's office it howled like an arctic cold front, sending chills through all who heard it and passed it on. The blast reached Skip just as he had applied a spritz of water to his trombone slide and put the mouthpiece of the instrument to his lips for the first time in nearly two months. Without playing a note he locked the slide, replaced the trombone on its stand, and sat down at his desk to take stock of the situation. He couldn't help thinking that his noble resolutions had something to do with bringing on the crisis. Here he was, showered and shaved; the hair surrounding his bald pate still wet and even neatly combed where this was an option; his suit passably wrinkle-free after another humidification in the shower; his bloodstream completely free of alcohol for the first time since the great booze drought during the October Coup five years before; his trombone oiled and ready for playing. And what happened? The support structure he counted on for making it back from rock bottom had been dealt its severest blow. The organization had been decapitated. He was reminded of ancient conquering armies suddenly forced into retreat upon the death of their leader.

Skinner picked up the silver-framed photograph of his wife and stared into her eyes. He knew it was impossible for anyone else in the world to love a woman as much as he loved Tina. He wanted to reach inside the photograph and pull her out into his arms, to hear her soothing voice, to see her dancing eyes when she laughed. He stared at the picture so hard that he knew, wherever she was, Tina could feel the warmth of his love for her. The frame trembled in his hands, and he knew it did so only partly out of emotion, but mostly out of what had become an aching need for drink.

He put the frame down and called for his assistant, the able and stalwart Mrs Maria Grayson, a Venezuelan who had married an Australian colleague at the Music Programme. She was a dark, plain, round woman whose great energy and loyalty had probably accounted for Skinner's mysterious series of promotions. She had been the one to bring her boss the news of the Supreme Director's disappearance.

'Maria,' Skinner said, clasping his hands together to prevent their shaking. 'My dear Maria, we are facing a crisis. But I've been thinking. If the SD were here, what would *he* say?'

Mrs Grayson shook her head.

'He would say "Have courage",' said Skinner. '"Continue," he would say. And that is precisely what I intend to do. To continue. I want you to assemble our trombone research. Everything. We are going to write a book.'

Mrs Grayson grinned and said she was game as always.

'We are going to make the SD proud. When he returns, he will see that we didn't let him down.' He looked once again at Tina's photograph, then back at his assistant. 'We're going to do the right thing, Maria.'

Mrs Grayson turned and left Skinner's office with new vigour in her step. Skinner found himself reaching instinctively for the drawer that used to contain his quart flask, but remembered that he had poured its contents into the toilet first thing after arriving in the morning. He nodded emphatically to himself that this was the right thing to have done, that there was neither time nor place in his life for liquor, that the gleaming trombone on its stand in the corner and the silver-framed photograph of Tina were the only idols he worshipped. He would write Tina a letter announcing his change of life, and when Mrs Grayson returned with the documents and photographs the serious work would begin.

He was halfway through the letter, in the middle of a sentence in which he expressed the hope that their child, if male, could be named Louis Armstrong Skinner, when Mrs Grayson brought him the day's mail. Among the business letters was an airmail envelope from Tina. He kissed it before tearing it open, his eyes wet with happiness.

'Skippy my love,' the letter began, 'I'm sorry I haven't telephoned in so long. But I would much rather write than call to tell you what I have to say.'

Skinner flattened the letter before him and gripped the corners of his desk. As he read on he felt his body begin to quake. The sack of dough attached to his front bobbed and shook. Before long the tears poured from his eyes and splashed on the desk. He opened his mouth and cried, a long croaking below that quickly brought Mrs Grayson back into the room. She ran round behind his desk and put her hands on his shoulders as he ground his fists into the damp letter and sobbed.

'Wendell, Wendell,' she said. 'What has happened? It's your wife?'

Skip tried to calm himself, but it took a minute for his pitiful whimpering to abate.

'Oh, Maria,' he said, through an oesophagus choked with emotion. He shook his head in disbelief and rubbed the tears from his eyes. Then he looked up at Maria, and she could see that he was grinning broadly. 'Maria, Maria, Maria.'

'What is it, then?'

'What is it? What *is* it? I'll tell you what it is, Ma-Maria.' Skip had the hiccups. 'I am married to the world's most wonderful woman. She – *hic* – loves me, Maria. She says she *knows* I'm doing good work, and that we'll be together soon.'

Maria seemed rather disappointed by this news, as if her efforts to console him had been a waste of precious office-time. 'Well, of course you are, and you will, Wendell,' she said. 'You are going to write a beautiful book, and the Supreme Director will come back, and your wife will visit you in the spring. Why do you cry over this?' She gave his shoulders one more squeeze, then patted him firmly on the back.

'Who's crying?' said Skinner. He opened what used to be his liquor-drawer to get a tissue. The letter on his desk was wrinkled and stained with running ink. He wiped his face and blew his nose and looked brightly at Mrs Grayson. 'I'm – *hic* – elated!'

Wendell Skinner's were not the only tears flowing within the compound. Charles McCray crossed his legs and turned his head away from Dan O'Connor, and half-covered his face with one hand so that the speech-writer wouldn't see the moisture building up in his eyes. The more he thought how peculiar it was that he had developed a sentimental component to his personality since coming to Timbali, the more he was moved to tears by the pathos of such a transformation.

He had seen so much in the last few years. He had logged so many miles, witnessed so much pointless bickering, participated in so much acrimonious debate, observed so much poverty and illness that he was disarmed by this chorus of African singers belting out a joyful mass. He was touched and proud to see Dr Lord in his element. The man had seemed so off-puttingly anxious and fidgety at first, so exactly like the kind of sinecure-holding bureaucratic leech McCray had been expected to find.

But here he stood, his arms outstretched, his white belly poking out from beneath his polo-shirt, extracting a sound from his singers that massaged McCray's tear-ducts like a bite of lemon.

McCray couldn't see himself trying to explain to his Congressman boss that he had been reduced to tears by a Timbalian chorus singing Bach in an empty auditorium, all thanks to Dr Lord, Assistant to the Supreme Director, Late Baroque. Was this a waste of money? How much money? How much of a waste? He had to look away from the beaming black faces of the singers to prevent himself from breaking down altogether and blubbering on O'Connor's shoulder. He concentrated instead on Dr Lord, whose red goatee bobbed in time with the libretto as he sang along with the tenors. What a good man, McCray thought. What a fine, talented individual. Nothing at all like the petty adversaries McCray had encountered during his recent travels, representatives of kings and generals and presidents-for-life, who bargained like hostage-holders over the slightest disagreement and could be trusted only to go against their word as soon as the ink dried. He had seen pestilence and starvation ignored over political squabbles, he had seen billions appropriated for hydrogen bombs, he had toasted leaders with champagne who allowed their compatriots to live like animals, he had seen his own self-righteous Congressman publicly defend leaders so savage they belonged in the despotic hall of fame. McCray sniffled as quietly as he could and wiped at his eyes while pretending to smooth his hair.

He saw no problem here, not unless the Supreme Director's golden dome had been paid for by farmers' tax dollars. If he could clear up that one issue, he would quit his job rather than pull the rug from under an organization that gave a hundred Timbalians an opportunity to sing. McCray had been in Timbali only a matter of days, and already he had fallen in love with the countryside, with Eleanor and with music. He'd be damned if he would be the one to draw the curtain on a place that had exerted such an extraordinary influence on him in so short a time. Where is the waste? he asked himself, drowning in the harmonies of Dr Lord's chorus. Show me waste.

Dan O'Connor pretended he hadn't seen that Charles McCray had been dabbing at tears in the corners of his eyes. When Dr Lord brought his chorus to a halt and told them it was time for their break, O'Connor stood up and walked to the door with the sniffling McCray. They both waved a thank-you to Dr Lord, and O'Connor held the door for McCray to exit. When McCray was out the door, O'Connor turned round and caught Dr

Lord's eye. The speech-writer raised a thumb and winked. Dr Lord slowly bowed, placed his baton on the empty music-stand of the podium, and left the stage to join his beloved singers for tea and biscuits.

11

'DARLING LUDIE,' said Eleanor, 'you must be exhausted. You've done good work, I trust?'

Kastostis screwed up his face into an expression of contemptuous disbelief that anyone could doubt for one second that his work had been good.

'You haven't worked through the night in ages. Won't you take off your cape and relax? Vincent could draw you a bath.'

'Please, Eleanor. Could you leave me alone for a few minutes? I have a telephone call to make.'

'Of course. If it won't bother you, I'll begin my practising upstairs.'

'Do.'

'And one more thing, my sweet – I hope you don't mind. I loaned your little Peugeot car to Mr McCray. Do you remember the American who came to visit?' Kastostis nodded slowly. 'I sent one of the boys to deliver it to him at the headquarters early this morning.'

Kastostis made a gesture with his hand that signified his

155

unwillingness to be bothered with details of car loans, long-dead composers, Americans, or anything else outside the universe of his own awesome creativity.

'Mr McCray will be back here in half an hour or so,' Eleanor said offhandedly. 'I promised to take him on yet another tour.' Kastostis had already noticed that she wore an outdoor-excursion outfit: jeans and a heavy shirt and sturdy shoes.

'Good,' said Kastostis. 'Vincent! Brandy!'

'Ludie, do you think you ought to? You need to get some sleep.'

'Pfff,' said Kastostis.

'All right, then, suit yourself. I won't disturb you.'

Eleanor climbed the stairs, leaving her husband staring demonically from within the frame of his jet-black hair. Soon he heard her playing her warm-up scales, a brand of music he had always associated with the pain and loneliness of his own musical education. The dutiful Vincent arrived with the brandy-bottle and glass, which Kastostis took without looking at his servant. 'Do, re, bugger mi,' he said. He took a swig of brandy from the bottle and hurled the glass across the room. Vincent sighed and retreated to the kitchen to fetch a broom. Kastostis knew that if it were ever his misfortune to have a child he would do the creature a favour and not demand that it play the piano as well as Franz Liszt at the age of five. His own father had set such standards, and reacted to his son's failure to take the world by storm before puberty by whipping the back of the boy's clumsy hands with a thong.

In preparation for his phone call, Kastostis took another sip of brandy and breathed deeply. His plan was to première his Opus 10 at the tenth-anniversary celebration over the weekend. This would require clearance from the Supreme Director's office, if not from the big boss himself. He went to his phone on the piano and dialled the number of the revolving inner sanctum of the Supreme Director's headquarters.

'Office of the Supreme Director,' said a male voice.

'This is the Composer-in-Residence,' said Kastostis, whose pulse had quickened from the knowledge that the voice on the other end was probably only a few metres away from the great man.

'So nice to hear from you, Mr Kastostis,' said the voice, which Kastostis now thought he recognized as Saint Thomas's. 'One moment, please. I can put you through.'

Through? thought Kastostis. *Through?*

'No, wait!' he shouted into the phone, but it was too late; he was on hold. He pulled the receiver away from his ear and looked at it in horror. Saint Thomas could not possibly have meant 'through' in the deepest sense of the word. Could he?

Kastostis put the receiver back to his ear and waited, in a kind of trance.

'Mr Kastostis?' It was Saint Thomas's voice again.

Thank God, thought the Composer-in-Residence. He was about to go on, to request – no, to demand – half an hour at some point during the weekend's festivities, when Saint Thomas said: 'One moment, please.'

There was a buzz and a click, and a strange voice said: 'Ah, my dear Kastostis. What may I do for you?'

Kastostis swallowed hard and stood at attention. From upstairs came the faint sound of his wife's Czerny exercises. Vincent entered with a broom and paper bag, but Kastostis swiped at him violently and the servant retraced his steps into the kitchen.

'Good day,' said Kastostis into the phone. 'I wish to announce that I have composed a work for the tenth-anniversary celebration.'

'Marvellous,' said the voice.

'Yes,' said Kastostis. 'It is finished, on tape. I had hoped I could reserve half an hour at some point for a performance. No musicians will be required.'

'This is wonderful news,' said the voice, a rather high voice with an accent Kastostis could not have placed for anything. 'I had hoped you would compose something for the occasion, but I didn't feel it was proper for me to ask. I have always held that complete artistic freedom is the most important aspect of your post.'

'Yes,' said Kastostis.

'Half an hour, you say? Your piece will close the festivities, then.'

'I am honoured,' said Kastostis.

'Nonsense,' said the voice. 'It is *I* who will be honoured to witness the première of your work.'

'You will be there, then?' Kastostis asked, by now almost at ease with the friendly voice, but still standing erect in his black cape.

'Oh, certainly.'

'And we will meet?'

'We have met many times, my dear Kastostis. I do apologize that I have not introduced myself.'

'I understand,' said Kastostis, not understanding at all.

'On Saturday I will be happy to see you.'

'I am so glad,' said Kastostis. 'See you, then.'

157

'God bless you,' said the voice.

'Thank you,' said Kastostis uncertainly, and the line went dead.

Kastostis paced slowly across the room to his brandy. After a sip from the bottle he removed and discarded his cape and black turtleneck sweater. He felt drained from his long hours in the studio and his shocking conversation with the Supreme Director. After so many years living in dread of the secretive figure in the palace, it surprised him to hear a pleasant voice and exquisite manners instead of drooling lupine growls and ghastly threats. The weary Kastostis sighed out loud and sat down on the couch. He called Vincent into the room to apologize for his abruptness and to offer him a gigantic rise. Moments later he heard the sound of a car in the gravel driveway.

Eleanor's playing abruptly ceased. 'I'll get the door, darling,' she said, as she practically fell down the stairs.

Kastostis crossed his legs nonchalantly and said nothing. Eleanor sprinted to the door and opened it just as McCray was about to knock.

'How nice to see you again, Mr McCray,' she said. Kastostis winced. He had spent the entire night listening over and over again to their most intimate, primitive noises. 'Won't you please come in? I won't be a moment.'

The cheerful-looking McCray entered the house and said hello to Kastostis, who looked blankly at him for a long time before nodding hello in return.

'Hey, wait a minute,' McCray said, 'you haven't heard, have you?' He didn't look cheerful any more.

'What is it?' Eleanor asked. Her husband yawned and looked out the window.

'The Supreme Director. He was kidnapped last night on the road to town.'

Kastostis stopped yawning, in fact clamped his mouth shut so hard his teeth knocked together with a hollow click.

'No!' said Eleanor.

'That's right. Things are really jumping at headquarters.'

'Just a moment,' said Kastostis. 'You don't know what you're saying. I spoke to him not five minutes ago.' Eleanor looked at her husband as if he had just burst into flame. 'That's right,' said the Composer-in-Residence. He recrossed his legs in the opposite direction and drew a stray strand of hair behind his left ear. 'I gave him a call.'

'How can this be?' McCray wanted to know. 'Did the kidnappers let him go?'

'He didn't say,' Kastostis said. He allowed himself to yawn

again, as if he spoke to his friend the Supreme Director every day.

'This is awfully confusing,' said Eleanor.

'Pfff,' said Kastostis. 'Vile rumours, nothing more. Vincent! Clean up this mess!'

'Now, now, you mustn't be upset, Mary. Please, don't cry.'

Dr Lord crouched next to Mary's desk with one arm around her shoulders. Her face in her hands, her torso heaving, Mary Mbewa sobbed and shuddered. Dr Lord had just returned from his rehearsal and found Mary this way, alone at her desk under the eucalyptus trees, her face stained with mascara. 'There, there,' he said. 'Everything will turn out fine, you'll see.' During a short pause between bouts of weeping Dr Lord had ascertained that the cause of her sadness was evidently the kidnapping of the Supreme Director. Gregory had told her the news, she said, when she went to the canteen to get a cup of tea.

'There's no need to cry, Mary,' said Dr Lord, giving her shoulders a reassuring squeeze. 'Of course everyone is very worried, but as far as we know he is not in imminent danger. What I'm saying is you shouldn't be upset until more is known about the situation.' Dr Lord didn't know this to be the case, but he chose to be optimistic.

'It can't just be the Supreme Director, can it? Please tell me, Mary. I'm worried about you. Family trouble?' Mary shook her head and sobbed more loudly still. 'I know these have been stressful days. I was a bit shaken myself when Mr McCray arrived. But he's not so bad, is he? In fact he's getting along swimmingly with Mr O'Connor and Mrs Kastostis. Why, look there,' Dr Lord said, pointing across the river. 'Look, Mary.'

With difficulty Mary looked up from her hands through blurry tear-filled eyes and saw what Dr Lord was pointing at. It was Charles McCray behind the wheel of Kastostis' white Peugeot, with Eleanor in the seat next to him, fording the river at its shallowest spot and waving in their direction.

Dr Lord removed his arm from Mary's shoulders and waved back. 'They seem to be coming from the Ring Road,' said Dr Lord. 'Did you see how happy they were?'

Mary nodded.

'Now, can't you tell me what's the matter?'

Mary shook her head and began to cry again. Dr Lord stroked her shoulders and decided to let her get it out of her system for a few more minutes before asking her once more what was the matter.

An unusually hot and humid atmosphere had settled over the compound. Towering cumulus clouds on the horizon announced an afternoon thunderstorm, if not the arrival of the short rains themselves. The monkeys lazed overhead in the trees, inspecting each other's scalp, relieving themselves hideously from a great height, or sleeping off their lunch-time fix of tranquillizers. A small herd of zebra, which had been scattered by McCray's car, warily returned to the river for a drink. The diesel generator chugged bravely beyond the electric fence, its smoke ascending into an increasingly threatening sky.

'Now, Mary,' said Dr Lord, handing his secretary another tissue. 'Let's pull ourselves together.'

'Yes, sah,' she said. She blew her nose and shivered.

'Please,' said Dr Lord. 'You have always called me Humphrey.'

'Yes, Humphrey.'

'Now. What can be the matter?'

Before she could compose herself enough to answer, a pick-up truck appeared on the near bank of the river. Three men had come to remove Mary's word processor before the rains came. They wore light-blue overalls with the Music Programme logo stitched on their breast pockets. It rained so predictably in this part of Timbali that for most of the year their services were not required before nightfall. Dr Lord thanked the men and escorted Mary Mbewa into his hutch so that they would be out of the way. He pointed to a bamboo armchair for her to sit in, then installed himself behind his desk with his pipe.

'Perhaps you should go home,' he said to her. 'You do seem terribly upset.'

'I'm so sorry,' Mary said. 'I should not cry. I am worried about the big boss.'

Dr Lord was touched. He had never known that the lower-level Music Programme employees harboured such a fondness for the Supreme Director. For a moment outside he had feared that Mary might have been upset about her position, about the work she had to do, about her eccentric boss. He hadn't always been the ideal supervisor, he knew. These fears were difficult for Dr Lord to express, but because he pitied Mary Mbewa he made an effort.

'I hope you weren't ever . . . well, *annoyed* with me, Mary. I know that during the past few days it has all been rather difficult, hard on everyone.'

'Well, sah – Humphrey. I was a bit worried that we weren't doing enough for the American. I wanted to help.' Dr Lord could see that she was about to erupt into tears again, so he put down his pipe and walked around his desk to give her another tissue.

'Now, Mary dear, please don't cry. I don't want you to think . . . please. You're a marvellous woman, Mary. A splendid secretary. I rely on you more than you can imagine. I wouldn't want to think that you were unhappy here.'

Mary blew her nose again, but this time when she finished she looked up hopefully and smiled. Dr Lord thought he had her coming out of it. He pointed at his paper-strewn desk and said: 'Why, just look there. Do you see the work piling up? Everyone seems to have burst into a frenzy of activity. I don't know if it is because of Mr McCray's arrival, or because of this recent crisis – don't cry, my dear – but everyone now has a project. It's amazing, don't you think, the way people have pulled themselves together in a pinch?' Mary nodded. 'Why, I had the most marvellous rehearsal this morning. Mr McCray was there. I think perhaps we got through to him.'

'I'm glad,' said Mary hoarsely.

'So, you see, we must be strong. The Supreme Director would want it this way.'

'Of course,' Mary said.

'Do you feel better now?'

'Yes.'

'I'm so glad. Listen, the rains are starting.'

Heavy raindrops drummed like snare brushes on the thatch roof of Dr Lord's hutch. He stood up, walked to the hanging beads of his door, and looked outside. There was never any such thing as a single weather system in Timbali. While it rained on the compound, the grassy plain beyond the electric fence basked in bright sunshine. The white tails of frisky antelope glinted as they hopped. Gloomy water buffalo chewed the cud and seemed to shake their heavy heads in disapproval of the more fleet-footed species. A lone rhinoceros stood immobile on a knoll, ready for anything, ready for nothing. Far away, Mount Timbali was obscured by tenebrous clouds, while the foothills nearer the capital were awash with sunshine.

Dr Lord had always thought the climatic disarray and geographic diversity of Timbali were symbolic of a deeper chaos and of a deeper beauty. Icy mountains, humid jungles, powdery beaches, grassy savannah and infinite deserts coexisted within Timbali's borders; myriad tribes of humans lived there, too, whose sensational pullulation threatened to leave the country looking like a vulture-stripped carcass in a matter of years. Unlike some of his more adventurous colleagues, Dr Lord had rarely ventured out into the African countryside. What he had

161

seen was so arrestingly beautiful, but so painfully depressing, that he lacked the nerve to risk its hazards more often. While he sometimes felt lonely and isolated staring into the distance outside his office door, today's uplifting rehearsal had invigorated him to the point that the view acted as an energizing catalyst.

He looked back over his shoulder at Mary Mbewa, who stood up, sniffling, awaiting instructions.

'If you're up to it,' Dr Lord said, 'I say we get to work.'

Fording the river at the lower end of the compound, McCray waved out the car window at Dr Lord and his secretary, who seemed to be embracing each other behind her desk under the eucalyptus trees. Eleanor reached her free hand over the roof of the car and waved; her other hand was on McCray's leg.

'Don't they look happy?' he said. 'Where are we going anyway?'

'You'll see. Follow the track into the forest.'

They climbed slowly uphill through the trees, reached a grassy plateau, then climbed still higher until the dirt track bordered the electric fence.

'This is the north-easternmost corner of the compound,' said Eleanor. 'There are plans to build here, I gather. More housing for the professional staff. It will mean extending the Ring Road along the way we just came. If you continue uphill there, we'll have an excellent view.'

After a steep climb they reached a natural promontory from which they could survey all but the most distant southern reaches of the compound. McCray turned on his windscreen-wipers, for it had started to rain. In the centre of the compound reared the behemoth headquarters. McCray recognized other landmarks, such as Dr Lord's miniature village, the front gate, the auditorium, the amphitheatre and the Computer Centre. He even thought he could make out O'Connor's house and terrace beyond the fence, near the road to the Acacia Club. But what interested him most was the Supreme Director's palace, inexcusably vast, its central golden dome glistening wet in the rain.

'Now,' said Eleanor. 'Just what do you make of my husband's having talked to the Supreme Director this morning?'

'Is he likely to lie about such a thing?'

'Yes, I'm afraid he is. He's been working so hard. Add to that his occasional delusions of grandeur and, yes, he might tell us he had spoken to the Supreme Director when in fact he hadn't. I find it hard to believe he would be that nonchalant about it if it were true. He was practically gloating, wasn't he?'

'Still, why would he react to my news with a lie? Don't you

think it would have come as a shock to him to find out that the boss had disappeared?'

'Perhaps you are right. But it sounds preposterous that he should have rung up the SD so casually and had a chat. No one has ever done that, I don't think.'

'Maybe no one ever tried.'

'You see, Charles, and perhaps I shouldn't even be voicing my suspicions this way . . .'

'Off the record.'

'As you say. You see, it's been my feeling all along that there's more to the Supreme Director's secrecy than simple reclusiveness. Just look at the place he lives in. How is it possible for the Music Programme to support such a monstrosity?'

'That's what I want to know. But what's your point?'

'My point is, Charles, that whoever he is the Supreme Director is more powerful than a man in his position has a right to be, which makes me wonder about the old question of exactly who is in charge of the Music Programme.'

'The Board of Governors.'

'Really? Do you think that they willingly put up with a man who lives in a palace and refuses to be seen even by his own staff?'

'I have some experience in this, Eleanor. I have seen corrupt agencies in action before, after all. And governments.'

'Yes, but that's of an entirely different scale, isn't it?'

'You understand, don't you, that if what you are implying is correct, if this man has spent international tax dollars on some sort of private Utopia for himself, then I'm going to have to bring it out?'

'Of course you must.'

'That will be the end. The end for your husband, too.'

Eleanor shrugged, and cracked open her window to defog the windscreen. 'There's so much good here,' she said. 'I mean it.'

McCray took her hand and examined her magical fingers. He thought of all he had seen during his stay: Eleanor's concert; Ng's beloved files; a speech on musical animals; O'Connor and his under-age girlfriend; Dr Lord's inspirational chorus; Kastostis' little black figure outside the Computer Centre. Only one thing was glaringly unacceptable, and that was the palace on the hill.

'I'm going up there tonight,' McCray said.

'Where?'

'There,' said McCray, clearing the windscreen with his palm and pointing. 'The palace.'

'They'll never allow it, I'm sure of that.'

163

'I'm not going to ask permission.'

'What do you expect to find?'

'Whatever I find.'

'You will be careful, won't you?'

'I can't see well enough from inside the car to plan a route. I'll get soaked out there, but I have to take a quick look.'

'It's a warm rain. I'll come with you.'

McCray could see immediately the route he would take. If he started at Eleanor's house he could descend through the garden to the grove of fever trees by the stream. Crossing that, he could climb the first hill to the Computer Centre without running into a road. From there it would be a simple matter of moving slowly so as not to be spotted by the palace guards. He could see that the way to get over the fence would be to climb one of the enormous topiary hedges at the front gate. It would all depend on the presence of guards.

McCray felt comfortable in Dan O'Connor's young man's clothes. He had selected well-worn khaki trousers, a blue cotton button-down shirt, and tennis-shoes. He hadn't dressed this way since college. O'Connor's clothes made him feel limber and agile, even though he had not exerted himself in months. He hoped the Land Pirates were enjoying his flannel suits and boxer shorts and silk ties.

Eleanor seemed to like his clothes, too. She stood close to him, an arm around his waist, a hand on his hip. McCray looked down at her, and saw that raindrops had collected in her long eyelashes. He turned and hugged her and kissed her hair. The raindrops were fat and warm, and exuded a strong mineral odour. When he kissed Eleanor, he felt the agreeable moisture of her cheek. He liked it in Timbali.

McCray felt like a teenager with no place to take his girl-friend, but this ceased to be an issue when Eleanor put her arms around his neck and pulled him to the ground, as if she were accustomed to doing this sort of thing out of doors. The ground consisted of a wet mossy clay. As a courtesy he lay down on his back and pulled Eleanor on top of him. While she kissed his neck and tore at the buttons of O'Connor's shirt, McCray arched his back and looked behind him, up the hill, and hoped he had put on the Peugeot's emergency brake.

'I like it in Timbali,' he said.

'Sometimes it's very nice,' Eleanor agreed. 'Help me with this.'

McCray helped her. Raindrops dripped from her hair into his mouth, and he thought he could taste her shampoo. When she moved her head down his body he tried to keep his eyes open in the rain, but the drops were so heavy he shut them tightly again. His shirt was open and his trousers were around his ankles and he was wet all over. He was as relaxed as a person can possibly be who is lying on mossy clay in the rain in a state of extreme sexual arousal. The part of his brain that could still think told him he wished his Congressman could see him now. This thought spawned a more disturbing one, which was that the Music Programme had arranged for the lovely Eleanor to distract him during his stay, to take him out into the countryside and take his mind off the Supreme Director's palace.

'You aren't *laughing*, are you?' Eleanor said, pausing in her activity so that she could speak.

'Here we are in Africa,' said McCray. 'All naked and wet.'

'Well, I'll be . . .,' said O'Connor, staring through his telescope. 'Yvonne, come here and take a look at this.'

'Oh la-la,' said Yvonne.

It had only just started to rain at O'Connor's house. His lunch-break had stretched into its second hour. Yvonne had spent the morning sunbathing in the nude on the terrace, which O'Connor could have guessed by the look of terror on the servants' faces when he returned from the compound.

'Oh la-la la-la,' she said.

'Let me take a look.' It took some convincing to get Yvonne to relinquish the telescope, even though it had begun to rain rather hard. 'Yup. That's McCray all right. Atta boy, Charles.'

'That is your American friend?'

'Yes. Getting my clothes all dirty.' O'Connor used his shirt-tail to wipe off the eyepiece of the telescope. 'I think he's taking the SD's disappearance very well indeed.'

'I want to watch some more,' said Yvonne.

O'Connor handed over the telescope again, thinking what a corrupting influence he had been. At work that morning, during Dr Lord's rehearsal, he had thought through the Important Talk he was going to have with Yvonne as soon as he got home. The Important Talk would detail his concerns about her age, her parents, her having run away from home, and the need for a girl to know exactly what she wanted before she jumped into bed with a man. Predictably, the Important Talk lasted from the front door into his bedroom, to which Yvonne pulled him by the wrist, where she asked him if she could try some of the things she had heard about in school and seen in movies on home leave. Buckling like a shot elk, O'Connor threw himself into this activity with praiseworthy vigour, and went so far as to request that Yvonne speak in French to him for the duration of

165

their prolonged session. This experience taught him never to rely on his cerebellum where women were concerned, that for the foreseeable future his actions would always be guided by forces infinitely more powerful than conscience or intellect.

On the terrace, Yvonne refused to give up the telescope.

'Come on,' O'Connor said, 'Let's get out of the rain.'

'Wait,' said Yvonne.

'Please. This spying isn't very nice.'

'Oh, yes, I think it is. I think they are almost done now.'

'Jesus, Yvonne.' By squinting through the rain O'Connor could just make out the white car near where he knew Charles and Eleanor to be.

'Oh la-la.'

'What? What is it?'

'Finis,' said Yvonne.

'Good. Let's go inside now, shall we?'

Yvonne turned away from the telescope and gave O'Connor a devilish look. O'Connor sighed. It was hopeless. He would not be back at work today. And what difference did it really make, he thought, when the Supreme Director was probably locked in a dark room in a hideout in the middle of the bush, naked, lashed to a wooden post, suffering interrogation and torture at the hands of savage kidnappers?

Skip Skinner could not recall having concentrated so hard on any one thing for as long as he had this day. He had skipped lunch, partly because he feared the temptation of those ice-cold Mister K's, but mostly because the ever-increasing pile of trombone-related information demanded his undivided attention if he were to finish his book proposal before the end of the week. Mrs Grayson was positively frolicsome as she entered and exited his office bearing pamphlets, photographs, acoustical charts, and cup after cup of black coffee. Each time she left she pumped a little fist in the air to rally on her newly invigorated boss.

It was at about four in the afternoon, as a warm rain pounded the headquarters, that Skip noticed with some astonishment his first involuntary erection in more than three years, since the days of his rapid and unexplained promotions. He was so happy that he wanted to show it to Mrs Grayson, but he quickly decided she might not understand. This was not the poetical ache in the belly, nor the ambiguous stirring-of-the-loins, nor the quasi-tumescence of the aristocrat climbing the gallows to the guillotine. This was an out-and-out Chrysler Building of an erection, which Skinner attributed directly to his day without drink. If only he had time to send a telegram to Tina with this news.

A second manifestation of his booze-free lifestyle was an ability to think clearly for hours at a stretch, in fact to make practical progress during that time. He could see the trombone book so clearly now. It didn't daunt him for one moment that there already existed dozens of books on the subject: books by metalworkers who had built trombones, books by archaeologists who had dug ancient trumpets out of King Tut's tomb, books by scholars who had researched all biblical references to metal instruments, books by people who had actually been present at the creation of the valve. He was undaunted because this would be *his* book: a slim volume, exquisitely made, translated into dozens of languages, distributed free of charge to schoolchildren in the developing world.

Skinner had already made great progress on his proposal, which outlined a quick romp through the history of lip-reed instruments, from the mollusc to the sackbut to the *zugtrompete* to the Posaun. His intention was to show the inevitability of the slide principle, the near-perfection of its acoustical properties, its clear superiority over valve instruments in terms of tuning and inflection. This historical overview would be entitled *From Jericho to Jazz*. In the true spirit of nearly all Music Programme publications, Skinner's book would be opinionated to the point of propaganda, and hopeful to the point of hysteria. If possible, it would also include a tape-recording of Wendell 'Skip' Skinner himself, demonstrating the various techniques and styles of trombone-playing.

Skinner's hope was that his book would circumvent all committees on its way to publication, especially the Committee on the Future. The Committee on the Future, known as 'Cough', was liable to shoot down most historical work, just as it regularly attempted to derail Dr Lord's efforts to preserve and perform music from the Baroque period. The kidnapping of the Supreme Director didn't help matters, because Cough would undoubtedly gain power and influence during the leader's absence. Skinner's book was also likely to meet resistance from Authentic Instruments, stressing as he hoped it would the deterministic nature of instrument craftsmanship. 'Is the electric light an improvement over the wax candle?' he would ask them. 'Yes and no,' they would reply with one voice. 'Different? Yes. An improvement? Not necessarily.' Thus the modern concert-grand piano was different from, but not necessarily an improvement on, the tragic little clavichords of the sixteenth century; and thus the glorious tenor trombone standing in the corner of Skinner's office was different from, but not necessarily an improvement on, a grimy little Posaun in the same key but built

167

four hundred years before out of inferior metals. Skinner's only hope was that when and if a confrontation with Authentic Instruments took place Dr Lord would be on hand to silence them with one of his caustic diatribes about their inability to separate musical from technological progress, their personal tendency to be socially inadequate, their spouses' propensity to sleep with more likeable people.

Deep thought and concentration had not put a stop to Skinner's physical arousal, which heightened his sensation of being a veritable fountainhead of productivity, intellectual and biological. His resulting happiness was easily sufficient to cancel out the nagging aches and queasiness of his addiction, and he resolved to do some research in order to ascertain the likely duration of these unpleasant withdrawal symptoms. He had associated with enough drinkers and drug addicts during his big-band years to know that it was not a problem to be taken lightly, nor one that was normally solved through willpower alone. And yet he was a man with an agenda. He would continue to throw himself into his work, and surface into social life only when every trace of alcohol had been cleansed from his organs by a steady liquid diet of fruit juice and black coffee, when he would scoff at imbibers as if they were eaters of human flesh.

It would take some of the pressure off if the Supreme Director could be released in time for the weekend festivities. It didn't look good, during the American envoy's visit, for the organization to be running around in search of its brain. Skinner couldn't stand the thought of the Supreme Director, whom he took on faith to be a pacific, scholarly, introverted genius of a gentleman, locked in a shed somewhere in the shanty towns of the capital, feeding on caterpillars, contracting tuberculosis, chained to a wall, perhaps even hanging by his heels from a corrugated-iron roof. That was no way for a gentleman and a musician to live.

Fifty miles north of the Music Programme compound, the hilly tea-plantations and valleys of moderate jungle finally yielded to a rocky desert that continued for hundreds of miles to the country's border and beyond it was a new desert, virtually man-made. The red rocks and soil made the north country indistinguishable from the surface of Mars, and just as arable. For exactly twelve hours every day, a scorching sun made life unlivable for all but the most unattractive and spiteful animals. Scorpions loved it there, scuttling happily about their business; snakes put up with the environment for lack of a lusher place to slither, evolving gradually more devastating toxins just in case.

168

The white-haired man hated it in the desert. His only companion above the altitude of rocks and scorpions was a dark hill or mountain, which for all he knew could be five hundred miles away. Nevertheless he walked towards it, his only friend, for the sake of walking in a straight line. His dark glasses were a great help, but he wished they had left him with more protection from the sun than his underwear and undershirt and socks.

He wasn't thirsty at all, but, then, he had only been walking for fifteen minutes since they had driven away and left him stranded. What a curious journey it had been. He had evidently witnessed a mini-coup within the group of unsavoury hostage-takers. Ever since his abduction, for hour after hour of unpleasantly bumpy driving in the back of the heavy troop-transport truck, his ten kidnappers had argued ceaselessly while they finished off the two bottles of vodka they had found in the white-haired man's car, shouting at each other in a language he couldn't understand. They had a two-way radio, and after each communication their argument became more heated. The truck bounced along at daybreak on the outskirts of the desert, while the men continued to berate one another with epithets whose obscenity transcended the language-barrier.

It was plain to the white-haired man that they were arguing over the fate of their prisoner. One of the men, who looked eighteen years old and wore a clean camouflage-uniform, pointed at him every so often and shrieked at the others while making death-orientated hand-gestures. Another man, wearing white city clothes, shook his head and appeared to be trying to reason with his accomplice, perhaps telling him that the white-haired man was a valuable commodity. Most of the others had taken sides by morning, while one or two were too drunk to care. The white-haired man wished he spoke their language so that he could enter into the debate: he considered himself a valuable commodity, and that is what he would have told them.

The white-haired man knew that such a power struggle usually went to the side of the most violent elements in the group, which was not reassuring. It confused him, therefore, when they stopped the truck for a lunch- and water-break, then stripped his suit from his back and drove off into the desert without him. Was this a compromise, or a successful coup on the part of the young man in the white suit? The white-haired man had watched the truck as it disappeared into the shimmering desert, shaking his head in disapproval of its occupants.

Alone at last, the white-haired man wished he were more important. If that had been the case, the sky would be swarming with jet aircraft and helicopters, and his captors would already have been blasted across the desert in strips of bloody meat. The white-haired man's lack of clout would be his undoing. He would be baked or frozen to death during the next few hours, if the snakes and scorpions didn't get him first. As he walked, he focused his mind on the imagined sound and sight of a rescuing army patrol, hoping that concentration alone might make it materialize.

12

LUDVIK KASTOSTIS knew that Richard Wagner would have tolerated this degrading scene just long enough to call in the guards and flay the brute alive: Charles 'Crack' McCray, naked above the waist except for a white towel around his neck, drinking a glass of the finest wine available on the continent, chatting with Vincent, waiting for Eleanor to return with his laundered shirt. Engine trouble indeed, thought Kastostis. Ah, but never mind that Wagner would have strangled such an interloper before writing him into the interminable death scene of an interminable opera, never mind: Kastostis could bide his time. Like his music, he had an agenda. He had already made sure, with a politeness that must have caught the American off-guard, that McCray would attend the première of the Kastostis Opus 10. 'I do hope you will listen carefully to my new composition, Mr McCray,' he had said, handing the half-naked American the glass of wine. Kastostis possessed the patience of a trained assassin and could afford to wait a couple of days before his triumph, before he would revel in the

American's humiliation, before he would see his wife shrunk to womanly size once again.

'Crack' McCray, indeed. Look at the way he talked to Vincent as if the little black man were a visiting African head of state: his head cocked in genuine interest, his wide white teeth bared with pleasure at having met such a sympathetic native, his posture informal so that Vincent wouldn't think for a moment that he was in the presence of a superior. Would Americans never learn to deal properly with servants? And look at McCray's body, would you? Only an American, thought Kastostis, could actually walk around in a body such as that one. He was broad of shoulder and tidy of waist, with a perfect V of not-too-primeval hair nestled between rounded muscles that had not existed on Kastostis' body even in youth. At least he had the decency not to remove his trousers, which were tight around his thighs and soiled with the same red clay that Eleanor was now removing by hand from his shirt in the laundry room. Eleanor hadn't done the washing in nine years, but suddenly she had been able to say 'Won't take a moment. No, it's no bother', as she removed the American's shirt and took it away over Vincent's protests that it was his job to do the laundry. The reason McCray now stood in the centre of the living-room half-naked was that no article of clothing Kastostis owned would fit over the American's hair, much less his chest. 'Crack' McCray, indeed.

Kastostis' mind was flooded with his own brilliant musical ideas. Never before would he have chosen the word 'catchy' to describe any one snippet of his own work, but at long last he found himself inwardly humming the too-tuneful flute, the bed of murmuring strings and the goose-stepping onslaught of brass. Did he dare admit to himself that he had been musically barren for a disconcertingly long period of time? That he had reached the unthinkable point of self-doubt not long before his creative juices were unfrozen by the arrival of this marauding American civil servant? Could he admit that the slightest inkling of unworthiness had set in during the completion of 'Flame-dance of Euphorion'? Of course not; he could admit none of these things. It was simply the case of a master coming into his own.

Look at 'Crack' McCray, Kastostis thought. Just look at the athletic cretin with his chest dominating my living-room and his animal cries of passion recorded digitally on the cassette in my cape pocket. What woman – especially a woman of Eleanor's refined sensibilities – could waste more than a curious glance at such a man when *Kastostis* was in the room? It could only be the

172

glance a Spanish *señorita* might give the bull before her adoring gaze settled permanently on the toreador.

His conversation with the Supreme Director had changed his life. He wished he had recorded it, so that the Supreme Director's voice might be added to the climax of his Opus 10. 'Ah, my dear Kastostis,' the voice would boom. 'God bless you. Ah, my dear Kastostis. God bless you.' Kastostis felt a spiritual bond with the Supreme Director. Was anyone in the Music Programme closer to the boss than he? Had anyone else even spoken to him, much less received his blessing? Their conversation offered the promise that some day the palace gates might part before Kastostis, and under the golden dome the two great men would share their biographies, their dreams for mankind, their deep and symbiotic intelligence.

'Excuse me, Mr Kastostis,' said McCray, who had evidently noticed that the composer was lost in profound thought.

'Kastostis!' shouted the composer. No one called him *Mr* Kastostis.

'Yes,' drawled McCray. 'I have to thank you for your hospitality. Your car, your guest room . . .'

My *wife*, Kastostis said to himself.

'My stay would have been so difficult without your assistance. I was robbed on the way here, you see, and—'

'Pfff,' said Kastostis. 'It is a country of thieves. Vincent, for example, is a most satisfactory servant, but I wouldn't leave him alone for ten minutes with the smallest amount of cash. One lives in fear of one's gardeners. One is aware that they are naturally bloodthirsty, and that they are as likely to butcher a human being as they are to gut those wild animals they find on the fence. The stories one hears.'

'Have you seen much of the country?' McCray asked, which Kastostis immediately took as an affront to his masculinity. Early on during his tenure he had ventured out into Africa, hoping for inspiration, but found himself constitutionally unfit for mingling with the natives.

'Of course,' said Kastostis. 'Vincent! More wine for our guest.'

'I'm eager to get out and see the countryside. Extend my stay.'

'Of course you must.' Your headless body will be found in a ravine, thought the composer. 'Take my car if you wish.'

'You're too generous.'

'Not at all.' Swine, thought Kastostis. Mortal, ignorant, bestial swine.

A flushed Eleanor returned at last with the American's borrowed blue button-down shirt.

'You're very lucky,' she said. 'We have the only mechanical

drier in the compound, with the possible exception of the SD's palace – but, then, who knows?'

'H'm,' said McCray.

Kastostis scrutinized their transparent expressions, and wondered if he would have recognized the attraction between them without recorded proof. Eleanor's face shone like a Christmas ornament; McCray's stomach muscles were distinct as piano keys as he put his arms through the sleeves of his shirt. Somehow he would win back this woman, prove to her that what he offered went beyond love, beyond friendship, beyond physical attraction. What Kastostis had to offer was a grand MAXIMALIST obsession that made the Romantics look like schoolchildren passing notes to one another in the classroom.

'Will Mr McCray be staying for dinner?' he asked his wife. 'I'm sure Vincent could find the ingredients to one of his marvellous salads. I told him yesterday that if he could get his hands on some spinach I would pay for his next child's education.'

'Oh, Ludie darling, aren't you something?'

'I'm afraid I can't,' said McCray. 'I'm expected back at Dan O'Connor's house.'

Kastostis thought he detected just the slightest conspiratorial glance between McCray and Eleanor. 'What a shame,' he said. You shameless bastard, he thought. The brass section of his Opus 10 trudged on through the Siberian landscape in his mind. 'Do be careful out there in Africa. Frightfully violent people, Timbalians.'

'His house is only fifteen minutes away.'

'Yes, but it's after dark. You've seen how quickly darkness comes. And just as quickly the hills are filled with villains.'

'I'll try to be careful.'

'Yes, do,' said Eleanor. 'Darling, I will see Mr McCray to the door.'

'Yes, do,' said Kastostis, with the most barely perceptible mockery. He fell back on to his sofa and stared out the window into the darkness. 'Crack' McCray, indeed.

McCray knew he shouldn't linger too long at the door with Eleanor, and that he would have to restrain himself from kissing her goodbye. In a loud voice he thanked her for the tour and for laundering his shirt, then he whispered that he missed her already. In her own version of the casual goodbye she raised her voice and said, 'Not at all, Mr McCray,' then lowered it again to wish him luck during his assault on the palace. McCray pursed his lips and exhaled quickly through his nose, which indicated that a man of his courage and ability would scarcely be in need of luck on so routine a mission. He paused only a few moments longer to etch her lovely face into his mind, to smile the smile of a shy but supremely heroic warrior on his way to battle, then walked through the rain to the car.

Before dark, with Eleanor's help, he had picked out a spot where he could leave the Peugeot during his visit to the palace. Fifty yards away from the Kastostis driveway a dirt track led into the forest to a toolshed used by the composer's gardeners. With the headlights turned off, McCray nosed down the track and stopped the car. He got out and closed the car door as quietly as he could. He walked to the end of the track, passed the toolshed and began his descent to the valley stream. McCray found a narrow footpath which had been cut by the gardeners, and was able to follow it even in the pitch darkness because the jungle on either side was impassable. Every so often a fat wet leaf slapped him in the face, and he groped around until he felt the clearing in front of him, then continued until another floppy sloppy piece of vegetation interfered. In only ten minutes he reached a clearing next to the stream at the bottom of the valley. He took off his shirt, socks, shoes, trousers and underwear, and held them at shoulder-level while he stepped into the cold river water. Eleanor had told him that at this time of year the stream was only just waist-high to a man at its deepest point. She had assured him there were no crocodiles in the stream, or at least no one had ever seen one, and that the hippos used only the deepest pools on the southern edge of the compound. When McCray enquired about snakes, she squirmed herpetophobically. When he told her he had seen a green mamba through Dan O'Connor's telescope, she shuddered to her core and begged him to stop talking about snakes.

Halfway across the stream, he wished he hadn't thought of that conversation about crocodiles and snakes. He wished he hadn't seen the green mamba. He clutched his shoes and clothing to his chest with one hand, and with the other hand reached down and gathered in his floating genitals to protect them from whatever ˙creatures might at this moment be slithering by. He wished he had a photograph of himself in this position to show back in Washington. If this wasn't beyond the call, he didn't know what was. The riverbed was tolerable enough under his feet, flat rocks and tiny pebbles, spongy moss near the bank; but every ripple in the river, every splash of rain, looked like the head or eyes of a swimming snake. The only sounds he heard were of dripping and squashing and lapping and oozing, the sort of sounds one heard when in the presence of

slimy poisonous animals. He wondered how the Music Programme would react if he were bitten by a snake and his naked
corpse washed up somewhere downstream, perhaps in the
eddies of Dr Lord's office-area. With this thought in mind, he
pushed through the mild current until he reached the far bank.
He let go of his genitals and reached up with his hand for a vine
hanging from a low tree. There was just enough light in the
valley to make out the shape of the vine, which was snake-like
enough to make him pause with his hand six inches away, just to
make sure. When he saw the vine raise its brilliant green head
and twist in the air, his reaction was to fall backwards into the
river with a shriek. His yell sounded like a dull thud in the
echoless dripping jungle. The current carried him downstream
along the bank for twenty yards until he found his footing and
scrambled into the undergrowth. The wetness of the jungle on
the shore was in no way preferable to the wetness in the river, in
fact far worse because there were so many wet clinging things
touching his legs and buttocks and neck. He swiped at the
foliage around him with his free hand, and when his arm became
entangled in something even slimier and more snake-like than a
real snake probably would have been he gave up this show of
calm and started to run away from the river into the dense plant
life, in a crouch, holding a forearm in front of his face, as if he
were running through a swarm of anopheles mosquitoes.
Almost immediately he was knocked to the ground by the fat
trunk of a fever tree. He crawled past the tree, stood up again,
and pressed on at a slower pace. With every barefoot step he
took he imagined the hollow teeth of a mamba sinking into his
calf. His flesh was torn by brambles and twigs, his feet were
ripped by sticks and thorns. None of this mattered to him, not
so long as he avoided the tiny toxic jaws of the green mamba.
He tripped over roots and banged against fever trees, but he kept
moving.

The first sign of relief was a steep incline, which meant he was
moving away from the river rather than along it, but the surest
proof of his safety came to him in the form of a smell: he smelt
the clay and earth and grass of a drier terrain, the smell of the
ground where he had muddied his clothing with Eleanor earlier
in the day. He fell to the ground, panting, and gave himself
thirty seconds to die of a mamba bite before he would be certain
of survival. He rolled on to his back and hoped the rain would
wash the grime and blood and ooze from his body, but it had
nearly stopped raining. He looked up at the sky and saw patches
of stars between swiftly moving clouds.

*   *   *

The white-haired man looked up at a sky so completely overwhelmed with stars that he wondered how primitive people could have hoped for one moment that they existed at the centre of such a roiling mass of astral movement. He had stopped walking shortly after nightfall, not because he was cold but because, to his surprise, his muscles and joints were no longer strong and supple enough to walk for long distances. He squatted on the ground with his arms around his bare knees, shivering, aching, staring up at the star-glutted sky.

He clung to one flimsy strand of hope for survival, which was that just before sunset he had stumbled across a seldom-used car-track, probably the same one his abductors had followed into the desert from the city. He had walked along the track in the general direction of his friend the mountain, which had grown no larger on the horizon after several hours' march. Now he squatted on one side of the track, wishing he could support his back with one of the larger boulders scattered around, but fearful that snakes or scorpions might be coiled there. He felt minuscule. He was a ball of flesh, the size of a small boulder, sitting on his coccyx in his underwear, somewhere in a desert that stretched from the Indian Ocean to the Red Sea to the Mediterranean to the Atlantic. His limbs and joints were numb; the only conceivable advantage to be gained sitting in a vast cold desert, he decided, was that his head no longer hurt from the blow he had taken from the rifle-butt, not compared to his neck and his spine and his feet. Especially his feet, which burned like branding-irons on the ends of his ice-cold legs.

The white-haired man tried to concentrate on his image of a rescuing army patrol. With his head between his knees, he would not see their headlights – the sound would come first. The sound would start as a desert wind, then climb into the realm of the unnatural, until it was unmistakably the sound of an internal combustion engine. He thought of engines he had known and loved. Motor boats, racing cars, rocket engines roaring around the planet on lakes, on highways, in outer space, almost everywhere but here, in his desert, on his rocky red track. He concentrated so hard on the sound of an engine that his head filled with sputtering, grinding, popping, humming motors, motors he had known and loved. When he shook his head the humming didn't go away, so that he realized with a sinking rush in his empty belly that he had begun to lose his mind. The sound of the motor wouldn't go away. The noise grew so insistent that the white-haired man decided he had better stand up and walk like a man instead of sitting on his coccyx on the outskirts of nowhere, a ball of hallucinating flesh.

177

He stood up and brushed red dust from his underwear. He stood as erect as possible on the balls of his burning feet, still unable to clear the roaring engine from his mind, and tried to locate his mountain by starlight. The sky was as before, like being hit in the face with a snowball, except brighter – brighter because there appeared to be two yellow suns on the horizon.

When the rains abated, Yvonne asked O'Connor if he would take her on a motorcycle ride under the stars. He equipped her with one of the leather jackets Durin Oakes had left behind, but she refused to wear a helmet. She said she wanted to feel the wind in her hair.

O'Connor loved his motorcycle. He loved its spongy suspension, its terrific power, and the pressure in his chest when it accelerated. When they rocketed out of his steep driveway he felt Yvonne's arms squeeze around his waist. The paved roads of Embassy Row were still wet, so he kept his speed down even when Yvonne leaned forward and shouted: 'Faster, Danny, faster!' The air was cool and moist, and rushed into his nostrils with a wintry chill. On a long straight he roared through his gearbox and blazed past Yvonne's house with his head low over the handlebars and Yvonne's arms gripping him like a wrestler. They zipped past the gates of the Acacia Club, changed down for the long downhill turn to the racetrack. O'Connor took them around the track at high speed, banking into the gradual turns, spraying a fountain of sloppy wet turf behind them. Yvonne yodelled with pleasure. O'Connor felt the exhilaration of speed, which made him bellow and hoot into the rushing wind. Evidently Yvonne's bare hands were cold in the wet wind, because she warmed them inside the front of O'Connor's trousers. O'Connor throttled up and accelerated into the last turn of his third lap.

A small white van appeared from beneath the grandstands at the finishing line – the authorities, such as they were – so O'Connor raced to the main exit and escaped on to the main road. Back up the hill in high gear to Embassy Row, a sharp turn across the fourth fairway of the golf-course, up the walking-path next to the stream, they climbed and climbed in a bright starlight now that the clouds had passed. O'Connor slowed down and bounded off the path between two rows of tea-bushes on the hillside called Her Majesty's Bosom, part of a plantation belonging to the President-for-Life, formerly to Lord Drek himself. The wet tea-bushes glinted in the starlight. Yvonne squealed with delight as they bumped and bounced up the hill. O'Connor avoided the road that would have led to the main plantation-house, and kept his front wheel pointed straight uphill to the high plateau on the real-world side of the Music Programme's electric fence. Once there, on a sloping plain of bright silver grass, they accelerated once again and raced along beside the fence until they reached the highest point anywhere in the region of the compound, the place known as Top of the World.

Top of the World could be seen from the capital, and looked from that perspective like a shining dome over the pleasure-palace of the rich. In daylight the panoramic view from Top of the World encompassed not only Mount Timbali to the south, beyond the city, but also the great western plains, as well as the ominous red line to the north that was the beginning of an infinite desert. At night the outlines of these landmarks were easily distinguished, but it was the truly jaded observer who could keep his eyes on the ground when surrounded by such a swirling skyful of celestial objects.

O'Connor shut off his engine, leaned the bike on its kick-stand, then sat side-saddle on its seat with Yvonne in his arms. They stayed that way in silence for several minutes, as if their voices could not possibly be heard in the limitless cavern arching overhead. O'Connor gently rested his chin on top of Yvonne's head. The curvature of the horizon seemed so exaggerated, and so completely dwarfed and surrounded by sky, that the feeling of being precariously attached to the surface of a rolling, spinning ball was almost sick-making. O'Connor lowered his eyes and held Yvonne more tightly still. In the valley beyond the fence was the Music Programme compound, and above it the Supreme Director's palace, its golden dome turned silvery by reflected stars. All was peaceful in the compound. Lights burned in the windows of the staff housing complex and in the guardhouse at the main gate. The auditorium shone like a surfacing white whale.

He leaned forward to one side of Yvonne's sweet-smelling head and put his cheek against hers. He closed his eyes.

'We're very lucky to be here.'

'My brother André says there are lions up here.'

'Oh God.'

'And he says they once found one of our guards hanged in those trees.'

'Now, now.'

'Are you scared?'

'No.'

'I'm not, either.'

'Good.'

179

'It's a very dangerous country, though.'

'Sometimes.'

'Did you hear about the German?'

'What German?'

'A few years ago, when I was little, a German man came here on business. He had been in the war, where he lost one arm. He went to the beach in Hamana, and a shark bit off his other arm. Too bad, no?'

'Too bad, yes.'

'My father would not stop laughing. My grandfather was in the war, too, you see.'

'I see.'

'My father thought I was too young to understand. Now when I remind him that he laughed about the German he gets very angry.'

'You shouldn't taunt your father.'

'It isn't nice to laugh at people who are eaten by sharks.'

'Good point.'

'Even Germans.'

'That's what I say.'

'If we are eaten by a lion here, my father will be very angry that we were together.'

'But he won't laugh this time.'

'I don't think so.'

O'Connor opened his eyes, just in time to catch a needle-thin meteor flaming out over the Indian Ocean.

Charles McCray regained his feet and tested his body for incapacitating wounds. He gave no thought to turning back, which would have meant crossing the river again, re-entering the mamba's territory. When he put on his clothes, though they were sopping wet, they gave him a feeling of strength and security. He scrambled up a hill, over an outcropping of loose rocks and on to a ledge in the hillside from which he could survey most of the compound. He was exactly where he wanted to be. The Computer Centre was at the top of the hill, the palace was a ten-minute hike from there. He paused long enough to catch his breath and take in the magnificent sky. On a dome-like hill across the way, the electric fence glinted like a knife-blade. Behind it, McCray made out what appeared to be the single headlight of a motorcycle.

Hand over hand he climbed the steep incline to the Computer Centre. Just below eye-level across the way loomed the Supreme Director's palace, McCray's closest look yet. He could make out the gilt tips of the iron fence, the clef-shaped topiaries,

180

the fabulous dome. All else was hidden in darkness, but the starlit silhouettes hinted at hugeness.

McCray descended the other side of the hill from the direction he had come, slipped down a few yards of scree, picked his way down 'to the rocky valley. It was time to start thinking about being quiet and invisible. Clambering up the incline to the palace, he kept his body close to the ground and his head up, like a mamba. He moved deliberately, aware that the altitude of the Timbalian high plains accounted for his shortness of breath. Near the top of the hill he kept within a narrow gully where he could move silently on the larger rocks and keep his body out of sight. Finally he stood up on a boulder and found that he had reached the tarmac drive leading to the main gate of the palace. There were no guards to be seen. He squinted through the iron gates and saw nothing but a driveway and manicured lawn. The only sign of life was the raucous sound of birds, lots of birds. Some birds sang, some cawed, some chirped, and one bird, if McCray was not mistaken, spoke French.

The treble-clef-shaped topiary standing on the left side of the gate looked sturdier and taller than the bass clef on the right. McCray trotted across the drive, crouched behind the treble clef, and peered between the bars of the fence. An albino peacock stared back at him. McCray liked peacocks. They bore practically no resemblance to green mambas. Behind the peacock was a low crenellated wall, and behind that the eerie blue glow of a lighted swimming-pool. The blue glow shimmied and wavered, indicating the presence of a swimmer.

The side of the hedge next to the fence was ladder-like and easily climbed. McCray kept as low as possible as he traversed the gilt arrows atop the fence. He dropped to the ground on all fours into a bed of roses and crouched quietly for a moment, staring the peacock in the eyes, listening to the lapping in the swimming-pool. He detected a slight increase in volume among the birds nearby, but they had been making plenty of racket in the first place. Inexperienced in breaking and entering though he was, McCray was still able to deduce that a dangerous guard dog would not be kept side by side with exotic birds and, even if that could somehow be arranged, a dangerous guard dog would already have made off with his oesophagus.

He thought it unwise to head directly towards the pool, which would mean crossing open ground. Instead he followed the fence to his left, just inside the wide bed of roses that ringed the grounds. The white peacock followed him around the perimeter until he reached a low stone wall. He hopped over the wall and landed knee-deep in a fish-pond, which was surrounded by an extensive rock garden. He waded dejectedly across the shallow pond thinking about piranhas, and stepped out into a bed of pebbles in the rock garden. He crunched as quietly as he could across the gravel, squelching sloppily in O'Connor's sodden shoes. A parrot perched on a bonsai tree said: 'Thank you for coming, Johann Strauss. Thank you for coming, Johann Strauss.' He reached the border of the rock garden, and his footsteps were silenced by the putting-green lawn underfoot. High overhead gleamed the golden dome, atop the red-tiled roof of the central white villa.

As McCray tip-toed towards the wall of the villa, he began to hear music, a sound so faint that he could not make out the instrument. It could have been a harpsichord or a guitar. He passed a penguin and a duck, who looked like two elderly socialites chatting at the intermission of a play. He sneaked along the wall of the house, back in the direction of the swimming-pool, where the music grew louder. He reached the corner of the main house and paused to listen before peeping around it. The sound he heard was now identifiable as that of a harp, which caused McCray to wonder just for a moment if he hadn't been killed by the mamba and gone to his reward. Without turning the corner he could see the shadows of statuary lining the pool, Greek profiles stretched across the lawn. The splashing in the pool was terrifically loud, McCray thought, as if an Olympic swimmer had come to this altitude for training.

He waited one more minute to be absolutely sure he had gone undetected, then eased his head around the corner to take a look. All in a flash he took in the sight of a dolphin, gleaming in the starlight, five feet out of the water in a twisting leap, dropping back into the pool tail first with a splash that sent water spilling over the sides. In the ensuing silence McCray heard the harp once again, and looked to the far side of the pool where a man wearing a white toga plucked and strummed, watching the dolphin perform. The dolphin leaped again, and this time it arced gracefully in the air and entered the water nose first. The harpist continued to play. McCray found it difficult to absorb this astonishing sight, and turned back around the corner to regroup. Without warning, a pair of powerful black arms encircled him, squeezed the air out of his lungs in a rush and picked him up off the ground.

The two yellow suns on the horizon bobbed and swerved. The white-haired man scratched his head in puzzlement and squinted into the glare through his dark glasses. He was bewildered by the light and sound, and even after he felt himself being helped

182

into the seat of a car it took a long time for him to understand the reality of his situation. A blanket was draped over his shoulders; a cup of water was placed to his lips.

'Well, then,' said a voice, as the car began to bounce along the rocky track. 'Feewing a wittle better?'

The white-haired man nodded and looked at the driver, a bright-faced man with shining blue eyes wearing a dusty safari-jacket.

'Durin Oakes,' said the man, 'that's my name.'

'Thank you, Mr Oakes,' said the white-haired man. He wanted to expand on his gratitude, but found himself too exhausted to speak.

'Bwuddy siwwy place to take a walk,' said Durin Oakes. 'If you pardon the observation.'

'Kidnapped,' grunted the white-haired man.

'Ah. Just as I suspected. Left you for dead, did they? Bastards. Why, last time that happened to me I thought I'd kill every bweeding bwack bastard in Timbawi. There's no getting even, though.'

'Wouldn't occur to me,' said the white-haired man, who had regained part of his voice. His gratitude to Mr Oakes was not tempered in the slightest by the man's harsh remarks. 'I'm just glad to be alive.'

'And lucky you are. Why'd they let you go, do you think?'

'They had a disagreement. They may have heard something about me on the radio. I believe one wanted to kill me, but a saner one prevailed upon him merely to throw me unprotected into the desert.'

'Chawitable bastards, aren't they?'

'If you hadn't come along, I'd surely have frozen to death.'

'Yes, well, you'll be happy to know I came across those chaps on my way here. Dwove straight past them. They had two flats and one spare. Poor buggers'll be patching all the night through. They yelled at me to stop, and I gave 'em one o' these.' Durin Oakes raised his hand in a complicated obscene gesture which the white-haired man could not make out in the darkness of the cab. 'If I'd known about you, they'd be leaking into the sand by now.'

'My goodness,' said the white-haired man.

'Filthy cwetins,' said Durin Oakes. 'Mustn't let them get you down.'

13

'I BELIEVE Mr McCray has been favourably impressed so far, all things considered. Wouldn't you agree, Ludie dear? Why are you looking at me that way? Are you ill, darling?'

'You should call me Kastostis. Not this "Ludie". It sounds ludicrous.'

'Lovely pun, darling.'

'Thank you.'

'But I'm your wife. May I not have my diminutive for you?'

'Don't call me diminutive. I am Kastostis.'

'Of course you are.'

'History will call me Kastostis. Beethoven's wife did not call him "Ludie", I promise you.'

'If poor Beethoven had married, darling, and his wife had called him "Ludie", he would not have heard her.'

'Very well, very well. But you grasp my point, surely.'

'I grasp your point.'

'Did I tell you the Supreme Director has asked me to première my Opus Ten at the anniversary reception tomorrow?'

'Opus Ten? It's finished?'

'That it is. I have it here on this cassette.'

'What a lot of work you've done.'

'You are my inspiration.'

'Nonsense. Thank you.'

'I am weary.'

'You haven't slept properly in days.'

'You are trying to get rid of me?'

'Not at all. Stay up with me, if you like.'

'I want you to play the piano for me.'

'I would be happy to.'

'What will you play? Vincent! Brandy!'

'Something soothing for you, Kastostis. Something you won't object to too much.'

'Schumann. "Childhood." Begin.'

'Good heavens, Ludie– I mean Kastostis. You are asking a great deal.'

'Thank you, Vincent, you may go. Begin, my dear. I've heard you do it before. You have it all in your head.'

'I've drunk two glasses of wine; it won't be perfect.'

'Begin.'

'If it will make you happy.'

'It will make me very happy indeed to watch you play. You are the most beautiful pianist who ever lived.'

'How lovely of you to think so.'

'Don't stop when you hear me start to weep.'

When O'Connor heard the chugging of an engine in his driveway he thought the local robbers had come back for their monthly thieving.

'Don't move,' he said to Yvonne. 'Stay in bed. I'll handle this.'

He took Durin Oakes's cricket bat from beneath his bed and crept to the front door, still entirely naked. He didn't dare turn on a light. He heard a rattling at the flimsy oft-broken lock and saw the door begin to open. He stood to one side and raised the cricket bat over his head. He had prepared himself for this moment ever since the day he had found his dog Richard cut into four separate pieces. He bent his knees and firmly gripped the bat-handle. First one figure, then another, came through the door. O'Connor extended the bat higher into the air and was about to bring it crashing down when the beam of a flashlight hit him in the face.

'I say, O'Connor,' said the holder of the flashlight. 'A bit pawanoid, aren't we?'

'Durin?'

The hall light came on. O'Connor froze in his position of attack when he saw that Durin Oakes was accompanied by the white-haired man, the Supreme Director, who wore a frayed blanket over his shoulders. Recoiling from O'Connor's naked threat, the white-haired man had pulled the blanket halfway over his head.

'Is this the way we gweet our guests?' said Durin. 'My friend here has been through enough already. There's a good fellow. Put the bat down, Dan. For God's sake, put some clothes on.'

O'Connor lowered the cricket bat and used it to cover himself. 'I'm sorry. Come in.' He thought it grossly unfair that he had been naked the first two times he had met the Supreme Director.

'And some clothes for my friend, too,' said Durin. 'The poor man's been wobbed of everything.'

'Yes, right away. I'm so sorry, sir,' O'Connor said to the white-haired man.

He tip-toed back into his bedroom and began to scour his wardrobe for clothes that might fit the Supreme Director.

'Oh, man,' he whispered to Yvonne, who still lay on the bed inside the mosquito netting. 'Stay where you are. It's the freaking SD.' He found a large polo-shirt and a pair of Durin Oakes's baggy archaeologist/spy shorts. He trotted out into the hall, then remembered that he needed some covering of his own before he clothed the Supreme Director. He went back into his room, pulled on a T-shirt and a pair of jeans, then jogged down the hall to find Durin Oakes and the white-haired man in the kitchen preparing tea. The white-haired man warmed his hands over the kettle. Durin cracked open a Mister K from the refrigerator and located his supply of cigarettes in a cupboard.

'What a lot of excitement,' said Durin. 'Chap here was left for dead in the desert. I saved the day.'

O'Connor winced at Durin Oakes's familiarity with the Supreme Director. Had Durin not discovered the white-haired man's identity? Was the Supreme Director so secretive that he did not reveal himself even to the man who saved him from certain death in the savage wilds of Africa? O'Connor thought it an amazing display of nerve that the Supreme Director – even now, standing in the kitchen of his speech-writer – could act as if he were not O'Connor's employer.

'Anything else, Durin?' he asked, wide-eyed, after the white-haired man had slipped into the unattractive outfit O'Connor had provided. He tried his best to make these words sound Irish. 'Should I try to call a doctor? Is everything under control?'

'Do welax,' said Durin, who appeared puzzled by O'Connor's new accent. 'I'll take my friend the west of the way home when he's finished his tea. It isn't far. I thought we would stop here on the way for clothing and sustenance. I'm sure he could use some toast and jam, if you'd be so kind. We could wake your cook.'

'I can handle it, I can handle it.' O'Connor's servants lived in a shack in the forest two hundred feet away, which he had never seen. He wasn't about to walk over there in the middle of the night.

O'Connor busied himself with the toast, wishing the Supreme Director would talk to him. It was such a relief to have him back. Would he want to discuss the tenth-anniversary speech right now? No, he wanted to finish his tea and toast, then hurry back to his palace in the compound.

It was something of a thrill for O'Connor to be so close to the action. He would have to concentrate on being a model of discretion when he bragged about this close encounter to his colleagues at the Music Programme. He could already hear his conversation with Dr Lord: 'Did I tell you old Ozymandias dropped by the other night? Charming fellow, really. Gave him some chow and clothing, bucked him right up. He was ever so grateful.'

'Wight, then,' said Durin Oakes. He stubbed out his cigarette and tossed his empty bottle into the trash-can. 'Shall we be on our way?' The white-haired man nodded. 'And, O'Connor, do wemember that I shall weturn in an hour or so. No need to dash out my bwains.'

'I'm sorry about that. I'll leave the door open for you.'

'Off we go, then, what?'

O'Connor escorted them to the door, and shook hands with the Supreme Director with as many components of a knowing look as he could possibly work into his expression at once. When he heard Durin's land-rover rumble out of the driveway, he returned to his bedroom, where Yvonne was asleep. He crawled inside the mosquito netting and touched her bare shoulder.

'Hey,' he said, gently waking her. 'Are you asleep?' She opened one green eye. 'We've had a little excitement. I just had a nice visit from the Supreme Director – you know, my big boss? What a fantastic guy, what a wonderful gentleman. You can tell your father that I helped to save his life. Won't he be impressed?'

McCray awoke inside the palace lying on an enormous circular bed. Someone had dressed him in burgundy-coloured silk pyjamas, which were slightly too small but awfully comfortable. The bed took up only a small corner of a long and complicated room, which seemed to be decorated wholly in silk. A dizzying full-colour hologram of a string quartet hung over the bed. At the foot of the bed, which was quite far away, a magnificent silver samovar as tall as a man stood on a circular brass tray. Next to the samovar stood a white-haired man holding a syringe.

'Feeling a little better?' asked the man.

In fact McCray had begun to feel distinctly *well*. He noted a small bandage on his forearm, an indication that the white-haired man had injected something into his vein – a substance which, judging by its marvellous effects, would probably rank as a national security risk back in McCray's drug-soaked land.

'Terrific,' said McCray. 'Thank you.'

'Mr McCray,' said another voice, 'won't you have some tea?' The voice descended from the ceiling, but when McCray looked up he failed to detect a loudspeaker.

'Yes, please,' said McCray. He crawled down the length of the bed and accepted a cup from the white-haired man, who had put away the syringe and now smiled amiably. He nodded goodbye and left the room.

'Please make yourself comfortable,' said the voice from above, in an unfamiliar accent. 'I will be with you in a moment. I am feeding my fish. She is exhausted.'

'All right,' said McCray. He wasn't sure if his voice could be communicated to the man who spoke through the ceiling, but he wanted to be as polite as possible. Thanks to the white-haired man's syringe, he felt an almost unbearably pleasurable sense of well-being.

McCray propped himself up in the pillows and sipped happily at his china cup of tea, and thought to himself that the room around him was hideous beyond all imagination. The whole place was the colour of fresh blood; the plentiful mirrors reflected more of the same. Two small fountains, one on each side of a massive bronze door at the far end of the room, were illuminated by crimson spotlights. Scarlet curtains covered whatever windows there might have been, assuming the room was above ground-level. The overall impression, thought McCray, was that of lying inside a human body.

He had just finished his tea when the bronze doors opened again, revealing the slight figure of the toga-sporting harpist. McCray had thought he recognized him at poolside, although the leaping dolphin had distracted him before he had been able to take a closer look: it was Thwok.

'Hello again, Mr McCray,' said Thwok. 'Won't you please have some more tea?'

'No, thank you very much. I'm absolutely perfect. Really.'

'It was such a beautiful night. After the rains the skies are clearer than one would think possible. I sat beside the pool for hours, playing my harp, enjoying my fish, inspecting our galaxy for signs of wear.'

'Yes,' said McCray. 'I saw you.' McCray wondered if Thwok were going to sit down. He stood near the foot of the bed, his wrists crossed in front of him, his tiny toga still loose on his miniature body. His wavy black hair was combed straight back from his forehead, ending in a single sculpted curl at his neck. His bright bony features seemed to emit a light of their own.

'Won't you come with me, please, Mr McCray?' Thwok gestured towards the brass doors with a spindly hand. 'There is a robe for you at the door. Your clothes were dirty and wet. They will be clean and dry shortly. You are feeling well, I trust? I'm afraid my powerful friend cannot distinguish between friend and foe when he happens upon prowlers in the garden. And you have been in the care of my personal physician, who is a miracle-worker. What a night he's had, poor fellow. Only just returned from his own kidnapping.'

McCray followed Thwok to the door, donned a silk robe and puffy slippers that matched his ill-fitting pyjamas, and was ushered into a long dark passageway. This led to an enclosed terrace, through the glass ceiling of which McCray could see that it was still night. He looked out at the swimming-pool and saw the black giant lugging Thwok's harp away. The giant wore a larger version of Thwok's white toga, secured at the waist with a burgundy sash.

'I am afraid I could not lift my harp by myself,' said Thwok, still leading the way. 'My friend there could lift two at a time, no doubt. Here. After you.'

McCray entered a vast room decorated in part like a mosque, beneath the golden dome. Dozens of prayer-carpets were arrayed on the stone floor, but there was none of the mustiness of a normal mosque or cathedral and signs of secular activity abounded: one entire wall was occupied by shelves of record-albums and music-books; another wall was partly taken up by stereo equipment, television screens, and at least a dozen life-sized bronze busts of grim-looking composers.

Thwok showed McCray to a semi-circular couch surrounding a low glass table of the same shape.

'Would you like some grapes?' asked Thwok.

McCray nodded.

'Grapes,' said Thwok in a normal tone of voice, and seconds later a plump woman in a costume like the giant's entered through a hidden door in the record collection, bearing a crystal bowl. She placed the bowl of grapes on the table between the two men, then retreated.

'I do love grapes,' said Thwok. 'Please help yourself.'

McCray had begun to compose a report in his head. No, nothing out of the ordinary. A typical bureaucracy; a few fine individuals sprinkled in. Waste? No, no waste. Show me waste. He tapped his slippers on the rug and beamed involuntarily at Thwok.

'Tell me, McCray,' said Thwok, inspecting a grape held between delicate fingers. 'Do you love music?'

'I'm afraid I—'

'Such a silly question. I do apologize. "Every man is mindful of music", as they say. Or as *I* say. I wrote that. I am a poet. I will give you a book of my poetry in English.'

'Thank you.'

'And you have seen that I am a harpist as well. I play the harp.'

'Everyone says you are—'

'There is no better harpist alive, is what they probably say.'

'Well. Yes.'

'They are too kind. But enough. Mr McCray, I am so glad you are here. I have been so busy, and I am sorry to say I was unable to prepare properly for your visit. I gather there is some concern in certain quarters of your American government regarding the usefulness of the Music Programme?'

'No, no. Well, yes. That is—'

'We are so isolated here. Even our Board of Governors, you see, tends to hold meetings by conference phone. It is no surprise to me that some misconceptions exist in your country among the uninformed.'

'Well, really they—'

'At the risk of sounding impolite, the man who sent you here is a dullard. Is he not?'

'You mean Congressman—'

'Yes.'

'He is my boss. He's—'

'A simpleton. Oh, please forgive me, Mr McCray.'

McCray decided he should simply sit quietly and let this strange little musical genius sort out his train of thought. At least it was true, McCray had to admit, that Thwok knew more about McCray's boss than the Congressman knew about the Music Programme.

'I am awfully sorry. Already I have been rude to my guest. I am no diplomat. I believe in bluntness. My people have become accustomed to this trait of mine. I know so few Americans. When I discovered you had chosen to visit me in this unorthodox manner, I wondered to myself if all Americans acted so impulsively.'

McCray continued to smile like a madman.

'But now that you are here you are more than welcome. Frankly, I had not intended to meet with you at all, or even to have one of my intermediaries search you out. I thought you could draw your own conclusions from the lower-level staff. Evidently you were not satisfied, or why would you have gone to the trouble of visiting me here?'

'Do you know something, I have no idea,' said McCray happily.

'You see, I try to separate my life in two. I have a strong philosophy which requires that I live in a certain way.' Thwok drew two circles in the air with his hands, indicating that the gaudy splendour McCray had seen was the 'certain way' in which Thwok felt himself philosophically compelled to live. 'And then there is my sense of duty, my obligation to music.'

Thwok paused to eat another grape, then raised his hands in the air like a conductor. As he did so, a bank of electronic equipment clicked into life. He issued a gentle downbeat, and on cue the stereo system emitted the cat's-hair melodies of a string quartet. Thwok conducted for a measure or two, then looked back at McCray and sighed with satisfaction.

'Does your Congressman, I wonder, think of the Music Programme as a business?'

'To the extent that he can think at all, he . . .' Hold on, McCray said to himself, whose side am I on? There seemed to have been something of a truth serum in the white-haired man's syringe.

'I wonder if that is an American penchant as well, thinking in terms of cost versus benefit, even if the subject cannot objectively be quantified. There were members of my family, my younger brother especially, who were Americanized, or perhaps simply modernized, in this way. He learned how to gauge the value of an object or a concept by an estimate of the number of dollars it would be worth in the future. It would never occur to him, even though he is well educated, that there were aspects of life and human endeavour that are automatically cheapened by the assignment of material value. It seems a simple enough argument, but my brother never even began to understand it. He visited us here once, and he walked around with an expression of pity on his face, as if I had handed my fortune over to a band of criminals. My brother buys and sells gigantic three-dimensional objects.'

McCray crossed his legs, then uncrossed them again when his

silk pyjamas rode up to reveal a hairy calf. He wondered where the white-haired doctor had gone, and if he might be coming back with more of that champagne for the vein.

'My education centred on music, of course. It was something of a disappointment to my father, I would say, that I showed such an unusual aptitude for this discipline. There were no musicians in our family. Musicians were street people who sang songs at our parties in exchange for scraps of food. Teachers and psychologists from around the world tried to explain to my father that his oldest boy was exceptional – you will take this in the right spirit, I hope. I retained music by ear and by sight as if I were a human tape-recorder. My father's repeated failures to interest me in commerce led to my running away from home on five occasions. Of course I was forced to return in shame each time – because I was a child I lacked the physical strength that would seem to account for your presence here tonight, and I could not scale the wall surrounding our grounds. My father disapproved of my musical inclinations until the time of his death, which occurred not long after my eleventh birthday, may he reside in Heaven. From that moment on I was able to throw myself into the art of music without the slightest hindrance. Do you drink spirits?'

McCray nodded, assuming that Thwok meant alcohol.

'Wine,' said Thwok. The hidden door opened again, and the plump woman entered with an uncorked bottle of red wine and one glass.

'"The merest drop of wine maketh my mind a maze,"' quoted Thwok. 'But feel free.'

Thwok filled McCray's glass and handed it to him. The wine was the colour of McCray's pyjamas, and tasted as silky smooth. He reclined even further into the pillows, smacked his lips, tried to focus on Thwok's face. McCray had the impression that Thwok had been speaking for some time now. Concentration was essential.

'. . . come to the point,' Thwok was saying, 'as a careful investigation into our books may have shown you, that each year a greater percentage of the Programme's budget is paid by private individuals. One of these individuals is my brother, who gives us a small truck each year. All the other individuals are pseudonyms for me.' Thwok poked an index finger into his own chest. 'This is my answer to fund-raising obstacles: I write a cheque. Last year, if you must know – and it pains me to tell you this – I contributed slightly more than twice the amount your government did. I am no superpower, Mr McCray; but, then, again, I have no other expenses, and I gather your

192

government has other bills to pay. Perhaps all of this bores you, Mr McCray?'

Bored was the last thing McCray was.

'Life is short, Mr McCray. Or had you already noticed that?'

McCray nodded energetically.

'For this reason I prefer not to quibble. I will continue to write my little cheque. I will write larger cheques if your Congressman has his way. He has his own priorities, and I have mine.'

'Of course you have,' said McCray.

'Perhaps you overestimate my involvement in such matters,' Thwok said. 'Or my interest in them. Music will sing for itself, my friend. Take the Composer-in-Residence, for example. It is no concern of mine if someone like Kastostis persuades people centuries from now that his was a valuable music. I wish to shepherd his works along, because he is what the world has to offer at the moment. For that reason alone he is worth listening to. Besides, if the Kastostis *oeuvre* survives any apocalypse your country may be planning – no offence, I don't read the papers – and if his music is recovered from the musical time-capsule I am organizing here in Timbali – then it will stand as an explanation for the lunacy of the civilization that produced him. Trite, I know, but surely you follow me?'

'I don't know,' said McCray. 'I think so.' Again, McCray had the feeling he had just missed several minutes of Thwok's monologue, and soon found himself on his feet, shaking hands.

'I am grateful that we have had this talk. We have cleared the air, don't you think?'

'I'm sure we have.'

'Do think about staying longer. I'm sure you have found Timbali a beautiful place to live. And make sure, when you depart, that you take my helicopter. I will leave instructions with my staff to that effect. And now my doctor friend will show you back to your room.'

'Oh, yes. I'd like to have a word with him.'

'Your clothes will be ready. It is nearly dawn. Sleep, if you wish, or he will drive you back to your car at Mr Kastostis' house.'

'How did you know?'

'My spies are everywhere, Mr McCray.'

The brass doors opened, and Thwok left the room. The white-haired man entered in turn, and grinned knowingly at McCray. McCray stood up and followed him out of the dome-ceilinged room, back to the bedroom that looked like the inside of a human body.

★　★　★

As Eleanor neared the end of the piano piece, Kastostis conducted with one pudgy white hand, brushed at his tears with the other, lifted his wet eyes to the ceiling. At last, he thought, he could appreciate Schumann on Schumann's terms; no longer was it necessary for Kastostis to look back enviously at the great composer through the overgrown forest of musical history: today, with his overconfidence entirely restored, Kastostis felt that he and Schumann dined together at the table of greatness that transcended life and time, so attuned to one another's thoughts and music that they conversed without speaking. Kastostis had not wept while listening to music in such a long time that once he had begun great salty tears poured from his eyes as if they had been stored in his head in tiny rain-barrels. His face was contorted involuntarily into a mask of sheer despair; he felt the rare and lofty sensation of his emotions running out of control.

His white hand lilted in the air, protruding from the sleeve of his black turtleneck sweater, delineating the impeccable contours of his wife's playing. The piano sang and roared, its overtones pulsed and weaved together in a divine richness of sound. Through blurry eyes Kastostis watched Eleanor's lovely profile, which in its pure concentration seemed to embody all that was beautiful in the music, all that was touching and sweet in life; also, thought Kastostis, patting the pocket that contained his Opus 10, all that was treacherous and vile.

He first laid eyes on Eleanor Smythe when she was an eighteen-year-old contestant in a piano competition at which the angry young Kastostis served on a panel of eight male judges. Constrained by the constant imperative of fostering his already overblown reputation as an avant-garde composer, Kastostis had met the intense young performers' efforts with condescension and disdain – but uniformly so, meaning that his rankings were as valid as those of even the most traditionally inclined judge. The preliminary rounds of the competition were held in music classrooms before half of the judges and a small audience. Kastostis walked into one of these, after a long day of adjudicating excruciatingly intense performances of Rachmaninov and Beethoven, Ravel and Brahms, Chopin and Liszt, ready for yet more thundering brilliancies from the lightning fingers of a young performer eager to set the world on fire. Instead he found young Eleanor, seated at the piano sounding out its quirks, nodding hellos to spectators and judges alike, a picture of calm and innocence. Her wrists were as thin as oboes; her cheeks shone with excitement. Given the nod from the principal adjudicator, she introduced herself in a childish voice and announced that she would perform Schumann's 'Kinderszenen'. Before starting the piece, Eleanor met the eye of each judge and smiled, as if to say 'Isn't this going to be fun?' Each judge returned the smile in spite of himself, then hastened to restore the grim scowl that is the adjudicator's hallmark.

Kastostis sat with his pencil poised over his score-sheet, unable to take his eyes off the young pianist. The other judges scribbled their notes, but the entranced Kastostis remained motionless, drawn into Eleanor's performance as if he had slipped through time into the parlour of Schumann's house to find Clara at the keyboard performing for her husband. Since early on in his strict moral and musical education, Ludvik Kastostis had held the relationship between Robert Schumann and Clara Wieck on the highest-possible romantic and erotic plane. In young Kastostis' fantasy world, theirs was the ideal of love, the paragon of infatuation, and probably the hottest sex in the history of Western music. Even though MAXIMALISM had not yet smashed its way into his work, Kastostis had long been aware that he was destined for a MAXIMALIST love-affair on the scale of Robert and Clara's. The major component of his love would be obsession; its subject would be a fragile younger woman who played the piano like a dream. He had lived with this fantasy for years with no conscious expectation of its taking shape in reality, so that when he beheld the lovely Eleanor Smythe, and found that she had elected to play Schumann's 'Kinderszenen', dream became actuality.

Judging previous contestants, Kastostis had found in himself the facile vocabulary of the seasoned critic. The adjectives, almost all of them derogatory, flowed from the tip of his pencil as if he had done this sort of thing for years. 'Overbearing technique,' he might write. 'Affected', 'fraudulent', 'sycophantic', 'lush'. Kastostis found that, as in wine tasting, almost any adjective would serve in judging the art of musical interpretation. 'Histrionic', 'recondite', 'dogmatic', 'corrupt'. But there was no score high enough for Eleanor Smythe, no adjective soaring enough to describe his attraction to her and her playing. He prised his eyes loose from Eleanor's face and examined the expressions of his fellow-judges in an effort to gauge their impressions of her ability. Their stone faces revealed nothing. He closed his eyes and tried to wrap a cloak of objectivity around himself, to no avail.

When Eleanor completed the piece she curtsied prettily to the judges and left the room. When she walked within three feet of Kastostis he felt a shockwave of longing, and knew that he had no choice but to disqualify himself. He went straight away to the principal judge, an imposing elderly Russian hero of the piano, and announced his withdrawal.

'I cannot continue in good conscience,' he said in French.

'Can you not continue in *bad* conscience?' asked the weary Russian. 'It is only a piano competition after all. What is the reason for your decision?'

'I am in love with one of the contestants, with Eleanor Smythe,' said Kastostis. The sentence sounded awfully romantic in French.

The principal judge cursed in his own language, and waved a gnarly hand of dismissal at the rising Czech composer. 'I have given her slightly higher than average marks,' he said, breaching the first rule of adjudicatory ethics. 'In the first round of the preliminaries, her sight-reading was miraculous. But her playing is immature. She will not advance to the final round.'

Kastostis resisted a strong impulse to challenge the old man to a duel. 'Nevertheless,' he said instead, 'I have withdrawn.'

While he was new to infatuation on a cosmic scale, Kastostis knew enough to rip his score-sheets in half and cast them in the air as he strode from the room. His first stop on the way to finding the love of his life was a men's room, where he combed his long hair back behind his ears and brushed the dandruff from his black turtleneck. He found Eleanor Smythe in a common room, drinking a cup of tea with her father. Kastostis knew that in the mould of Robert Schumann, and in the spirit of nineteenth-century courtship, he should introduce himself first to Eleanor's tall bespectacled father, an accomplished British cellist. As he shook Mr Smythe's hand and introduced himself, he saw out of the corner of his eye that Eleanor was startled that a judge should be fraternizing with the family of a contestant. 'Mr Smythe,' said Kastostis, somewhat worried that his English was not what it should be, and that his harsh accent might put off an Englishman, 'I have resigned my judgehood, for I am in love with your daughter. It will not affect her chances in the competition, I assure you.'

Mr Smythe's spectacles fell down along his nose as he gathered in this information from the shorter Kastostis. 'How . . . unusual,' he said.

Kastostis turned to Eleanor, who was still sitting down, and reached out for her hand. Instinctively she gave it to him, but seemed to flinch when he kissed it. 'You will not see me again until the competition is terminated,' he said, still holding her hand. 'You played so beautifully. I will reach you through the organizers.'

196

Kastostis bowed curtly to Eleanor, shook Mr Smythe's hand, turned gallantly on his heel and departed. He spent the remainder of the competition week in his hotel room composing a highly abstract work for solo cello, which he hoped to present to Mr Smythe. Eleanor won the sight-reading honourable mention, but failed to place in the top three of the overall competition. By the time she returned to London there were six love-letters and an abstruse cello sonata waiting for her. She wrote Kastostis a sensible letter pointing out the unlikelihood of their having much in common, which prompted Kastostis to leave his homeland for the first time and rent a flat in London. This sign of devotion was sufficient at any rate to gain access to the Smythe home, where Mr Smythe complimented Kastostis on the cello sonata, while not showing any inclination to perform it. Low on funds, Kastostis fell in with a brutally angry crowd, and composed the most attention-getting music of his career. Much to her parents' chagrin, young Eleanor was inevitably drawn to the dangerous side of Kastostis' life and work. She learned how to smoke cigarettes and stay out late, how to drink fortified wine, how to equate atonal music with the wretchedness of life in a nuclear age, how to dress entirely in black. Her piano-playing began to show signs of maturity.

From the outset, Kastostis was above board about his Schumannesque obsession with Eleanor. In a variation on the theme of a gentleman voicing his intentions, he told Eleanor that he wished to devote his life and his work to her and to her alone. He told her that if she were four or five years younger he would wait for her to grow old enough for marriage; but as matters stood he needed to marry her immediately. Because times had changed since Schumann's day – and because no one really knew how even the most ethereally romantic people behaved when the sun went down – he explained to her that premarital intimacy was not out of the question. This accomplished, Eleanor announced to her parents that she had accepted Kastostis' marriage proposal. Eleanor later reported candidly to her husband that Mr Smythe had grasped his daughter by her slender shoulders and stared hard into her eyes and said that he had infinite trust in her instincts, and that this was her choice to make, but that for God's sake if she had the slightest doubt she should not hesitate for one moment to postpone a decision that might lead precipitously to nightmare. Weighing this advice with all the conscientiousness of a woman who has already made up her mind, Eleanor announced on the spot that she would accept the Czech composer's proposal. Mr Smythe sighed and smiled and patted Eleanor on the head and said that of course she had his blessing. He went upstairs and attempted for the tenth time to play through Kastostis' cello piece, then stabbed straight through the manuscript with his bow.

Kastostis and Eleanor were married privately in Paris, witnessed by a small assembly of Eastern-bloc émigré artists attired in the manner of the groom, in sooty black. Their honeymoon was spent in Normandy at the country house of Eleanor's godfather, taking walks along the Channel bluffs, discussing music and their future. Kastostis felt suitably fatherly towards his new bride, and took pride in guiding her into a deeper understanding of post-modernist music. Eleanor listened carefully, asked probing questions, seemed open-minded enough to accept that the sounds in which Kastostis believed were not only valid but also beautiful. Meanwhile, after dinner each evening, on her godfather's sun-bleached Bösendorfer, she continued to play Schumann.

Kastostis squeezed the last tears from his eyes as these memories drifted through his overstimulated imagination. Eleanor had already concluded the 'Kinderszenen', and waited patiently for him to get a grip on himself. He dried his cheeks with one black sleeve and motioned for his wife to come to him. She sat down next to her husband on the couch. He took her hands and kissed them, pressed his face into them, held them to his ears as if listening for the resonance of the piano in her bones. To his surprise, she lifted his head to her shoulder and stroked his hair. 'Darling Ludie,' she said. 'I adore playing for you.'

Kastostis shivered and sniffed, and raised his nose to the warmth of Eleanor's neck. He kissed her beneath her jaw. He put his arms around her waist and pulled himself closer. He kissed her mouth and felt her hip press against the cassette in his pocket.

14

DR LORD had never lost the nauseating tingle of anticipation that preceded any performance, and on the morning of the tenth-anniversary bash he arrived at the compound gripping the steering-wheel of his land-rover with white knuckles and sweaty palms. He drove first to the staff housing building where Mary Mbewa lived, then took her to the outdoor amphitheatre where his chorus would later open the ceremony with Dr Lord's own choral arrangement of the Timbalian national anthem, and excerpts from the B-Minor Mass. The amphitheatre lay between the headquarters building and the auditorium, forty-four semi-circular rows of steep white steps divided down the middle by a rushing rivulet of water which fed into a fish-pond in the centre of the marble stage below. It was just after dawn, and the white steps gleamed in the first rays of sunshine, washed clean by the previous night's rain. A pair of barefoot Timbalian women wearing simple blue Music Programme gardeners' smocks had been assigned the task of buffing the stage with sheepskin rags. On his way to the amphitheatre with Mary, Dr Lord had seen identically dressed women stooped at the waist, plucking weeds and blades of grass from cracks in the footpaths that zigzagged from building to building in the park-like centre of the compound. When Dr Lord and his secretary reached the amphitheatre they unloaded sheet music from the back of the landrover and separated the parts. Dr Lord noticed that Mary seemed tired and downcast, even though she had worn her nicest yellow dress.

'Don't look so down in the mouth,' he said. 'I mean, so blue. Think what this celebration means.'

Mary tried to smile. There were new lines under her eyes, which she had tried to camouflage with an extra coat of violet make-up.

'Come now, Mary,' said Dr Lord, who could not bear to see her unhappy. 'You are going to love our performance. Have plenty to eat and drink. Rub elbows with the Insiders. This is our finest hour. What could be the matter?'

Mary stacked another pile of sheet music, then looked her boss in the eye and spoke her mind: 'I have been worried about the Supreme Director,' she said. 'How can we celebrate when he is—?'

'Why, haven't you heard, Mary?' Dr Lord himself had been told only in the last hour, when an excited Dan O'Connor had phoned him with the news. 'The Supreme Director is free, unharmed. Our friend Mr O'Connor was instrumental in his release. All is well again.' Dr Lord knew Mary would be pleased to hear this, but he hadn't expected her to throw her arms around his neck and shout with joy. 'Mary, my dear, please, you must calm down.'

'Oh, Humphrey, Dr Lord, sah, this is *wonderful!*'

'Please, Mary. We have work to do. Help me distribute these parts.' Dr Lord had decided that the general-service staff of the Music Programme must look up to the Supreme Director as if he were a deity. If they saw him in the flesh today, it might put an end to Mary's unhealthy brand of mystical idolatry. Dr Lord felt no trace of his previous awe; since his promotion and his handshake with the white-haired Supreme Director at the French ambassador's residence less than a week ago, Dr Lord had begun to think of himself as one of the SD's closest confidants. 'Everything must be perfect,' he told his secretary. 'The big boss will be sitting right over there, watching us.'

Dr Lord pointed to the dais behind the fish-pond, facing the stage and the amphitheatre seats. Thirteen oak chairs had been installed behind the long table; the central wing-chair was noticeably larger and more ornately carved than the others. On either side of the dais round tables had been set up, extending to the Richard Wagner Courtyard on the right and the grassy park near the front entrance to the headquarters on the left. Banquet-tables lined the walls of the auditorium and the headquarters, and already the cafeteria staff had begun to heap them with artistically organized food.

'He will be right over there, really?' said Mary, who did seem mightily relieved that the Supreme Director had survived his ordeal.

'Yes. Now, remember. When the singers arrive, I will need your help to make sure they are all shod correctly. I don't want any coloured tennis-shoes this time. Sandals are fine. Barefoot is better than coloured tennis-shoes, do you understand?'

'Yes, Humphrey.'

'Next year I hope they will give us the white shoes I have asked for. I don't care if I have to pay for them myself, at this point.'

'They will be beautiful in their white clothes. I remember last year.'

'Yes. We will meet them down by the river where they can change and warm up, then we'll walk up the path, double file. I wish we could have rehearsed this part, but most of them have done it before, and I am confident it can be described to the rest.'

Dr Lord went over his plan with Mary, explaining how the singers would take their places in an orderly fashion.

'Is everything set here, then? Music-stands for the orchestra? Sound system for Grandmarie's bloody synthesizer? Do you think we ought to sneak a little food before we go? My goodness, look at the ice sculpture. It will be melted by the time the guests arrive – it won't look a thing like Mozart.'

Mary's spirits certainly had soared since being told of the SD's escape. 'It is so exciting, this year. Big tenth anniversary.'

'Oh, yes,' he said. 'Fireworks, elephant rides, champagne for everyone, a good time to be had by all.'

'And your music.'

'Yes.' Dr Lord bowed his head and hoped as hard as he could that the performance would come off as well as he knew it should. 'Only one letdown that I know of. I've heard rumours that the programme has been changed only in the past few days. That bloody lunatic Kastostis has been given half an hour to himself.'

'The Composer-in-Residence, sah?'

'Yes, that's right. The bloody fool.'

'I saw his show last year, sah. I enjoyed it very much.'

'I beg your pardon?'

'Yes, it was very beautiful, Dr Lord, sah. There were many animals on the stage, and costumes, and the music was terribly frightening. My children loved it, too.'

'My God, Mary, do you know what you're saying? I mean, you don't mean to suggest that his music could possibly compare with' – Dr Lord could almost not bring himself to think of Kastostis and Bach in the same group of synapses – 'with *our* performances.'

'Oh, no, sah. Mr Kastostis, his music is very different. Very exciting and different.'

'Please, please, do stop. I'm nervous enough as it is without thinking someone out there will actually *like* what that bloody little Czech has got up to this time.' Dr Lord had never heard anyone say anything the least bit appreciative of Kastostis' music, unless it was to point out that it seemed to make the flowers grow faster outside the auditorium where it was performed. 'Off we go now,' said Dr Lord, clapping his hands together. 'Lots to do, lots to do, plenty of music to be made.'

Wendell Skinner amazed himself with his sober productivity. In one day he had completed a slick and persuasive book-proposal; hired a new servant named Jonas; bought two new shirts and ties and a dapper fedora; posted an epic love-letter to Tina; serviced his trusty jeep in the compound garage. He awoke on the morning of the tenth-anniversary celebrations with his usual hangover replaced by an annoying but by no means unendurable trembling in his hands. His eager new servant hurried to bring him fruit juice and coffee in bed, while Skinner revelled in his clear head and settled stomach. He instructed Jonas to go to town on the bus and buy some scales: when he looked in the mirror he thought he could already detect a tightening of the flesh around his jaw, and he didn't want this improvement in health and appearance to go unrecorded. To complete the picture of his morning's happiness, a call came from Dr Lord bearing the wonderful news that the Supreme Director had been released at last, after long negotiations and the heroic intervention of Dan O'Connor.

On his way out the door Skip kissed a framed photograph of Tina he had brought home from work, cleaned his saliva off the glass with his elbow and donned his snappy fedora. The thoughtful Jonas had warmed up his jeep, and seemed to recognize the reforms his master had made: he smiled broadly and saluted, then waved encouragingly until Skinner had cleared the driveway on to the main road to the compound. Skip whistled a medley of Duke Ellington tunes and drummed on his steering-wheel as he drove. It was a cloudless morning, and the night's rains had turned the hillside soil a richer red. An unusual volume of traffic, including caterers' vans and diplomats' limousines, slowed his progress on the road to the compound. The open truck directly in front of Skinner contained a cargo of Mister K, which caused him momentarily to rethink his abstinence. Was this cold-turkey programme a good idea on the day of the bash to end all bashes, especially when all of his work had been accomplished in one day? Would it not be prudent to hold his health together with a cold bottle or two of harmless beer as he awaited a sign from his acquaintance the Supreme Director that he should plough ahead with the trombone book? The crates of Mister K in the van were presided over by a handsome young Timbalian with close-cropped hair wearing a dusty black dinner-jacket. Skinner recognized him as a barman frequently in attendance at Music Programme festivities, who sometimes substituted for no-shows at the Anthony Eden Room of the Acacia Club. Yes, Skinner thought, a cold bottle of Mister K or two would be just the thing to ensure that he remained composed during what was bound to be an especially taxing day and evening of celebration. When the Supreme Director gave his project the go-ahead, that would be the time to abstain altogether; but not now – surely – not now, when the Music Programme in general, and Skip Skinner in particular, had both the anniversary and the release of the Supreme Director to celebrate all at once. In a way, thought Skinner, his two or three cold Mister K's would amount to a toasting to his new life, his new leaf, his new leaf on life.

By the time the slow caravan of cars and lorries reached the main gate of the compound, Skinner had broken out in a sweat thinking about the four or five Mister K's he would drink so that he could carry on a normal conversation with the Supreme Director. Just this one last time while the heat was on. As he passed through the gates he bowed solemnly to the abstract sculpture of the Supreme Director and recited the words 'De la musique avant toute chose'. Spurning his usual parking-place, he followed the lorry full of Mister K straight to its unloading-point near the amphitheatre, where he was able to communicate to the understanding barman that a whole group of friends – including some very important people in the catering division of the Music Programme – awaited their morning beer, so could he please take a whole case with him, and a bag of ice. With these spoils stowed in the back of his jeep he repaired happily to a secluded picnic-area at the river near Dr Lord's mini-compound, copiously to refresh himself.

★   ★   ★

Dan O'Connor spent the morning of the tenth-anniversary celebration at home, revising his speech for the Supreme Director. Much to his surprise, a messenger had brought the earlier draft to his house at the crack of dawn, each page covered with amendments in the precise handwriting O'Connor had come to know as that of the Supreme Director himself. O'Connor thought it right in character with the legendary man that he should come back from his crisis in the desert and dive straight into work. What a titan of bureaucracy.

The Supreme Director's comments and additions to the speech were detailed and unambiguous. The man was clearly an editorial genius. O'Connor was pleased with the newly forceful and inspiring speech, and read excerpts aloud to Yvonne over breakfast on the terrace. It was during this dramatic reading that another car was heard in the driveway, and Charles McCray stumbled through the front door looking like a wounded cavalry soldier returning to the fort from battle.

'Late night?' asked O'Connor, who was the picture of comfort and composure in his white shorts and dark glasses. 'Coffee? Mango?'

McCray collapsed into a chair, nodded hello to Yvonne, and reached for the coffee-pot as if it were his first drink of water in days.

'Have you heard the good news?' O'Connor said. 'The Supreme Director is free.' McCray cocked his head towards O'Connor and eyed him as if assessing the alibi of a known criminal. 'That's right,' O'Connor said proudly. 'He was right here in this house not six hours ago. Perfect health. I saw to it that he was returned to the compound.'

'Is that right?' croaked McCray.

'You don't seem too impressed,' said the blithe O'Connor. 'This means all is back to normal. The anniversary bash will go on as planned. God, you look terrible.'

'I'm sorry about your shirt,' said McCray, gulping at his coffee. The right shoulder was torn in a triangular flap.

'You weren't mugged, were you? Not again?' After what he had seen through his telescope, O'Connor wondered if McCray hadn't been ambushed by the Composer-in-Residence or one of his hirelings.

'No. My fault. I tried to sneak into the palace overland.'

'Wow. Not a good idea. Why would you want to do a thing like that?'

'The Congressman likes surreptitious investigation. His phrase.'

'And? Can you tell me what you found?'

'I found an impenetrable security system. The dome looks like real gold, though.'

'I almost wish you'd gotten in. The SD wouldn't have been there, of course. He was right here in my humble home.'

'H'm.'

'Who knows, you may finally get to meet him today. He's one hell of a charming man. He will have to be there to deliver this speech.' O'Connor held up the sheaf of papers. 'I'm just putting the finishing touches to it now.'

'And why was he here?' asked McCray.

'A friend of mine picked him up in the desert. It's all a bit vague. I did what I could.'

'Did you?'

O'Connor thought McCray seemed to have lost some of his good humour, which suggested tension on the Kastostis front. 'You ought to get some rest before the party,' he said. 'A friend of mine, Durin Oakes, is staying in the room next to yours. Don't be surprised if he stumbles around in your bathroom later. I see you have a car. You won't need me to drive you to the compound, then. I must go early to drop off the speech.'

'You're right. A nap. I'll feel better in a couple of hours.'

'Off you go, then. Help yourself to more clothes. The party's informal, of course. Children and everything.' McCray looked at Yvonne, as if he thought O'Connor had referred to his girlfriend. 'No, I mean the staff will bring spouses and children, if they have any.'

'Ah.' McCray nodded a weary adieu and slumped off to bed.

O'Connor had in fact acceded to Yvonne's repeated requests that she be allowed to accompany him to the anniversary party. O'Connor had come to this decision after arguing to himself that he had nothing to be ashamed of, that no laws he knew of were being broken, that Yvonne was surely old enough to exercise free will, and that both of her parents were quite definitely out of the country.

O'Connor had toyed with the idea of attending the celebration in disguise, knowing that Mr Ng would be on the prowl, but rejected it in the spirit of his new self-confidence: if Ng wanted to track him down and badger him with paperwork, let him just try to do that with the SD watching – that was O'Connor's thought. Just let little Ng try to accost him in front of everyone, even as O'Connor's own words echoed over the compound in the SD's voice, words penned by the man who had entertained the big boss informally in his kitchen the night before – just let him try. Does the word *access* mean anything to you, Ng? O'Connor would ask, gathering the adorable Yvonne under one arm. Won't you just relax and enjoy the *party*, Ng, before my friend the SD gets the idea you are *hassling* me?' Meeting the Supreme Director had given O'Connor something of an ego boost.

Yvonne stretched and yawned and smiled at her American boyfriend.

'I never had fun in Africa before you,' said Yvonne.

'Fun, fun, fun. Now we don our party duds.'

He went over to Yvonne and picked her up out of her chair and carried her to his room. She helped him select a flashier wardrobe than he might normally have chosen – white trousers and a white polo-shirt – so that he would match her own white cotton dress. On the way out of the house he plucked a flower from a tree overhanging the driveway and gave it to Yvonne. They mounted his motorcycle, and she held the flower over O'Connor's belt-buckle during the breezy drive to the compound.

McCray's body was stiff from its various exertions of the previous day and night. Naked in bed, he heard the sound of O'Connor's motorcycle starting outside his window, buzzing uphill out of the driveway, dopplering down the road to the compound. He knew he wouldn't be able to sleep. He looked back at his visit to the palace through a foggy curtain of exhaustion; his hazy recollections were further muddled by the already dream-like qualities of the Supreme Director's pad, and by the white-haired man's inspired chemical concoction. Normally the most tight-lipped operator, he was dying to tell someone what he had seen – he was dying to tell Eleanor. He found it intriguing the way rumours seemed to grow like vines at the Music Programme, the way people like O'Connor seemed to swing from tree to tree by these sturdy-seeming whispers. Contradictions were swept aside in the name of mystery; inconsistencies served only as paradoxical proof of the lordly Supreme Director's omnipotence. McCray had to give Thwok credit: the little harpist seemed fully aware that his actions were interpreted as magic by his devoted and terrified staff.

McCray was slightly ashamed that he had become so preoccupied with Eleanor Kastostis. This wasn't right. It was unprofessional. If anyone found out, it might mean that his investigation caused more of a scandal than its results. Such an illegal entry wouldn't be tolerated for a moment back home, and McCray knew that anything Thwok had told him was useless, at least as far as Congressional testimony was concerned. A savvy little man, that Thwok, for all his airs of insulated musical genius.

And what if McCray's affair with Eleanor were to leak out? A Congressional spy assigned to unmasking outrageous waste takes up with the wife of a distinguished Iron Curtain composer, taking time out from his fornication to scale the walls of a private mansion. This would not go down well on the Hill. It was no way for the incorruptible 'Crack' McCray to behave.

McCray groaned as he pulled himself out of bed, enlivened only by the prospect of seeing Eleanor at the Music Programme's birthday party. He hoped she hadn't worried too much about him after he charged off into the night on his dangerous mission. Sweet Eleanor, trapped in her house with an unstable Czech.

Eleanor pulled her husband closer and traced his lips with her index finger. He opened his eyes and smiled.

'We must go soon,' she said.

'A little longer. I am an addict for this. An addict for you.'

Eleanor's guilt was terrific. She had been unable to close her eyes all night long. While Ludvik slept she had searched her mind for excuses, tracing her shocking behaviour back through its slow evolution from an early tendency towards flirtation, to her inexcusable tryst with Saint Thomas, to her headlong rush into romance with the visiting American. She had been kidding herself with the justification that in return for making her husband's life comfortable she deserved the physical attentions of those who could supply them. She had argued to herself that in the isolation of Timbali, in the absence of the kind of sex life she had been taught by books and movies that a young woman should expect, she ought to explore any attractive physical adventures that presented themselves. She had lived for two causes: for her husband and for the piano. Her mental health, she had told herself, and by extension the success of her two missions in life, depended on the occasional sexual outlet. It sounded good in theory, but now she had discovered the guilty pitfalls of its practice.

'You're right,' sighed Kastostis, turning to his wife and stroking her hair. 'We must go. I have a performance.'

'No,' said Eleanor, 'you were right the first time. Just a little longer.'

It had never been clearer to Eleanor that her experiences with Kastostis held a power that could never be rivalled even by the most titillating fling. Their early struggles together in London, the thrill of climbing the ladder to respectability, the shimmering fantasy of playing out musical history – such were the heady ingredients of their life together before the move to Timbali.

Eleanor now thought she had merely projected the slow deterior-ation of her husband's creative energy: it was her own impatience, rather than his musical impotence, which caused the tension between them; it was her own frustration, rather than his creative infertility, which led to her nagging doubts about the future of his music. Great lives are not written by a jealous and dissatisfied spouse; Eleanor had willingly placed herself in a supportive role, and dreaded now that by shallow entanglement with another man she might have put the fantasy at risk.

'My love,' said Kastostis.

'Yes,' said Eleanor, her head swimming with resolutions. 'What is it, darling?'

'I must go check the sound system.'

'Just a moment longer,' said Eleanor, holding his head to her shoulder, trying to ignore his anticlimactic remark. 'It's been so long since we held each other this way.'

For all her guilt and anxiety, Eleanor knew she had no choice but to trust in the adulterer's most common psychological escape-route: the hope of never being found out.

'Just a moment longer,' said Eleanor, holding Kastostis' head to her shoulder. 'It's been so long since we held each other this way.'

Kastostis is back, he thought happily – Kastostis the composer, Kastostis the *man*. When Schumann was my age his Clara was probably already schtupping Brahms, his brain had already begun to melt down.

Kastostis could feel the guilt vibrating inside his wife, could smell the burning odour of her regret; rejoined with his wife, he thought he had never felt so vivified, as if he drew breath through her young body. He had spent the night slipping in and out of deep dreamy sleep, waking now and then to the sight and smell of his wife close to him. She was his again.

It had occurred to Kastostis that because of their reconciliation it might be somewhat cruel to perform his Opus 10 containing Eleanor's breathy noises. Half an hour in the Computer Centre remixing his composition would eliminate her portion of the work, a job he could easily finish before performance-time. But, no, he decided, what he had written in the spirit of jealousy and obsession must remain so. Had Beethoven decided not to destroy his Third Symphony when Napoleon crowned himself Emperor? Certainly. Did Kastostis gut a masterpiece simply because he had forgiven his wife's infidelity? Certainly not. Kastostis had spent a lifetime digging a moat of artistic integrity around himself, and now was not the time to lower the drawbridge.

'All right, my love,' he said, kissing his wife. 'We must get dressed. We will make such a wonderful sight together. You, too, will wear black.'

Eleanor sat up in bed and smiled. 'I'm so looking forward to your piece today,' she said, then she frowned comically. 'There are no animals in this one, are there, Ludie dear? You know that's the one thing I can't bear.

He almost pitied her the shock she would suffer when she heard his Opus 10, but it was not the genius's place to take people's feelings into account.

'No, my dear – at least, no live animals. It's all on tape.'

15

ALL YEAR LONG in the Music Programme compound the shadows went vertical at noon. The sun shrank to a fiery pinpoint overhead, animals roaming the ocean of plain beyond the fence searched out the paltry shade of acacia trees, and in Dr Lord's corner of the compound the Colobus monkeys descended from their lofty perches and begged with angry white faces for food and drugs.

Dr Lord and Mary Mbewa had sorted the singers' cricket costumes by size, and now sat at the picnic-table under the eucalyptus trees waiting for the buses to arrive. Dr Lord drew nervously on his pipe, envisioning any number of disasters that might have interfered with the progress of his chorus on their way to the compound. Every few minutes he stood up and paced, listing these concerns aloud to his secretary. 'Punctures,' he said. 'Punctures and rock slides and carburettor trouble and driver heart-attack and military roadblocks and flooding and rebel crossfire.'

'Please sit down,' said Mary. 'It is just noon, and we did not expect them until now.'

'Land Pirates,' said Dr Lord. 'If they harm my singers, I shall call in the British navy.' He sat down again and tapped his pipe-bowl on the edge of the picnic-table.

'Don't worry,' Mary said. She busied herself with a needle and thread, letting out the waist of Dr Lord's white trousers. 'They'll be here soon.'

'Your country is so bloody disorganized,' said Dr Lord. 'You ought to go to Europe some day and see a well-structured society at work.'

'Don't be angry at Timbali,' Mary said. 'They will be here soon.'

'I bloody well hope so. Good, the monkeys are going to sleep. I was afraid they would bite one of my singers. Vile creatures.'

Skip Skinner took off his shoes to soak his feet in the river. He had started a pyramid of empty Mister K bottles, and he was fascinated that the bottles gave off no shade, as if they weren't really there. 'High noon,' he said, and laughed heartily at his pun. He rolled up his trouser legs and let out a whoop as his feet entered the cold water. 'Are there any fishies in there?' he asked. 'Little African fishies? Carnivores, perhaps?' He opened another Mister K and gulped it down. 'Here little fishies,' he said. 'Come nibble on my toes.'

O'Connor emerged into the noon sunshine from the headquarters building where he had submitted the finished draft of the Supreme Director's speech to his secretary for typing. He found Yvonne reclined on his motorcycle with her white dress gathered up around her haunches and her long brown legs over the handlebars, her face raised to the sun, not wasting a moment of tanning-time. Her ponytail, a new addition to her appearance, hung over the rugged back tyre.

'We can leave the bike here,' he said. 'Let's watch the arrivals.'

A string of six elephants, trunk to tail, had been led into the main car park by a safari-suited trainer. A line of limousines, boot to bonnet, discharged their passengers at the main entrance to the headquarters beneath the limp flags of the Music Programme's contributing nations. Musical ensembles occupied every nook of the compound: a wind quartet performed at the headquarters entrance; a lone pianist played at a crosswalk in the park; a jazz trio swung in the Richard Wagner Courtyard; a small *a cappella* group sang joyfully atop a pair of banquet-tables near the amphitheatre; an African percussion section could be heard drumming somewhere in the distance. Guests were encouraged to stroll the grounds to be serenaded by a smorgasbord of history's sounds.

The festivities were not officially scheduled to begin for more than an hour, but already the grounds were swamped with visitors. Arm in arm, O'Connor and Yvonne took the walking tour, pausing every so often to listen to musicians. O'Connor encountered several of his Music Programme acquaintances along the way, some watching, some performing, many of them with children and other relatives in tow. Everyone was glad to see Dan O'Connor. Word seemed to have spread that the young Irish speech-writer had risked his life to save the Supreme Director, a bit of hearsay O'Connor did nothing to dispel. He had started to believe it himself.

On a grassy knoll next to a brass quintet playing warm chorales, O'Connor stopped to give his girlfriend a hug. Over her shoulder he caught a glimpse of Mr Ng in his golf-cart, wearing a morning coat and top hat, cruising along an asphalt path in the direction of the headquarters building. O'Connor was virtually certain that on such an important day Mr Ng would be too busy to waylay a lowly speech-writer, but still he took the precaution of burying his head in Yvonne's hair until the top-hatted Ng had disappeared over a rise.

O'Connor's enjoyable hug was interrupted by the piercing sound of a siren coming from the direction of the main gate.

'Now, what could that be?' he wondered aloud.

'I know,' said Yvonne. 'It is the President of Timbali. He came with my father to visit our school once, and made the same noise.'

'The President-for-Life? Here?'

'You are very important, Danny.'

From their vantage-point on the knoll they could just see the long line of black limousines, for which the other cars and trucks had cleared the road by driving off into ditches and fields of grass. A lead car projected the wailing siren, as well as a man's voice on a loudspeaker shrieking hysterically at people and vehicles to get out of the way. The caravan of black cars raced unimpeded to the main entrance of the headquarters, and there was a great deal of confusion as bodyguards and aides opened and slammed car doors and organized a shielded but dignified entry for their leader.

'There he is,' said Yvonne. 'The extremely fat one.'

'Just like his picture on the currency. He's probably going straight in to see the Supreme Director. Offer apologies for the kidnapping. Perhaps he'll want to thank me, too.'

When the President-for-Life and his entourage were all inside the building the limousines raced off to the car park, and traffic was back to normal. O'Connor and Yvonne continued on their

212

walk, coming next to a group of madrigal singers in medieval costume accompanied by lutes and guitars.

'Say, look,' said O'Connor. 'It's Thwok.'

Thwok rode up the path on a rusty bicycle, wearing a dark flannel suit and a rather rakish blue tie.

'Hello, Thwok,' said O'Connor. 'Thanks for the poem. Keep 'em coming.'

Thwok bowed modestly, then looked enquiringly at Yvonne. O'Connor made the appropriate introductions, describing Thwok to Yvonne as the poet-in-residence of the Music Programme, and adding that he was a harpist of international repute.

'Isn't this party going to be fabulous?' O'Connor said.

'Fireworks at night,' said Thwok in his high voice.

'Really? I hadn't heard.'

Thwok nodded. 'Boom,' he said.

'Boom?' asked Yvonne.

'Boom,' O'Connor confirmed. 'Well, Thwok buddy, isn't this all super?' O'Connor didn't waste his Irish accent on the harpist/poet: despite an apparent written fluency in English, Thwok did not appear to possess a refined ear for verbal inflection. 'We'll be seeing you at the amphitheatre, then?'

'High table,' was all Thwok replied, before bowing again and pushing off on his squeaky bicycle.

'Funny little guy,' said O'Connor.

'He's cute,' said Yvonne. 'This whole place is cute.'

The singers' buses forded the river and climbed the hill to Dr Lord's office, spewing foul exhaust. Dr Lord coughed and gagged in the fumes as he helped them disembark, greeting each by name when breaks in his coughing allowed. When all the singers were unloaded and the buses had driven away to park across the river in the open field, Dr Lord began frantically to issue instructions in an angry tone of voice. The chorus members who had sung under Dr Lord's baton in the past were accustomed to his fits of irrational pique before a performance; novitiates were less sanguine about their leader's state of excitement, and some even looked hurt.

'I will *not* tolerate the *slightest* lapse in concentration,' Dr Lord shouted to the group. His kneecaps were chapped and red; his toes were encrusted with orange soil. 'From this moment on everything will be orderly. You will calmly, quickly put on your costumes, and assemble in ten minutes on the hillside here for warm-up. I want no talking, no dawdling. I see that some of you have worn improper shoes,' he scolded. 'For that reason we will all go barefoot. Is that clear?'

'Yes, Dr Lord,' said the sonorous group in perfect unison.

Dr Lord looked at his watch and expelled a sigh. 'We have one hour,' he said. 'Hop to it.'

Mary Mbewa helped her boss distribute the costumes. The singers undressed in the open and stepped into their bright white clothes. The youngest children were helped by their elders, and everyone carefully folded their street-clothes and brought them with their shoes into Dr Lord's office, where they would be safe from rain and monkeys. The men wore the white cricket costumes Dr Lord had ordered specially through the Indian embassy; the women wore simple white calf-length dresses with low square necks and ample breathing-room around the waist. The inhibited Dr Lord changed into his newly tailored cricket costume behind his hutch, then circled back around into the sunshine to gather his singers together.

'Places, places,' he said.

The singers formed a semicircle on the hill before him. Mary Mbewa placed a hand to her mouth and giggled when she saw how red Dr Lord's face and neck looked sticking out of a white shirt-collar. She thought the singers looked smashing: their joyful black faces shone in the sunlight; the men were slim and handsome, the women warm and pretty. Mary was so excited by the fresh clean look of the chorus that she even had the nerve to pipe up and suggest that Dr Lord go barefoot like everyone else. 'In due time, Mary,' he said with a frown. 'Places, everybody.'

Dr Lord reached into his pocket for his pitch-pipe, and when he held it to his mouth the chorus went silent. He produced an A that was barely audible except to the front row, but when those who could hear it hummed, the note travelled backwards through the chorus like hot gossip. He replaced the pitch-pipe in his pocket and raised his hands. Still humming the note in three octaves, the chorus raised their hands as well, palms slightly open to the sky. Dr Lord swept his eyes across the chorus, then issued a slow downbeat. The singers clapped in unison and stopped humming. Dr Lord conducted three slow beats of silence, and the singers clapped again on the subsequent down-beat. When they had repeated this figure a few more times, a rhythm was established; Dr Lord stopped conducting and followed his singers through the familiar warm-up routine with his own clapping and singing.

They started with a soft breathy 'Ah', and worked through the English vowels with mouths exaggeratedly agape. Their bodies swayed with the rhythm of their clapping. On the second pass through the vowels their singing increased in volume. On the third pass it split into harmony. On the fourth pass they added vibrato and some improved lyrics from old hands. 'Yes, yes,' a woman sang. 'Our Doc-tah Lord, he is a ve-ry good man.' 'Oh, yes, he is,' a man replied. 'He is a ve-ry good man.'

Dr Lord relaxed and tapped his foot in time to their singing. He winked at Mary, who stood to one side hugging herself with delight. The singers began to laugh and syncopate their clapping and inject lyrics about the sunshine, the cricket costumes and the anniversary. Dr Lord signalled for them to continue while he removed his sandals. When he stood up again, he raised a fist in the air and cued a prolonged 'Amen', which his singers harmonized according to their mood of high excitement and anticipation.

Dr Lord bowed his head and breathed deeply. All was quiet except for the purl of the stream. Dr Lord looked up again and said: 'You are all wonderful. I love every one of you. Please enjoy yourselves.'

'We love you, too, Doctah Lord,' sang the chorus.

Dr Lord returned to his expression of utmost severity. 'All right now,' he said. 'Double file, off we go.'

Skip Skinner poked into his ears with his index fingers and shook his head, quite disturbed that he could not make the sound of singing voices go away. His pyramid of Mister K bottles had collapsed under its own weight. His feet had gone numb in the cold stream. He felt good except for the annoying sound of singing and clapping that seemed to be centred in the right hemisphere of his brain. When he heard a soulful 'Amen' he looked up at the sky as if expecting a sign. When this was not forthcoming, and when the singing seemed to have stopped, he removed his feet from the water and began to dry them with his socks. He looked up from this chore to see a green mamba half in, half out of the water, just where his vulnerable feet had been only a moment before. He stood up slowly and took two steps backwards from the mamba's smirking head. The mamba slithered out of the water, its head low to the gravel, took a tour of the Mister K bottles, eyed Skinner with what the trombonist took to be a highly sardonic sneer, then sped silently into the underbrush.

Skip wasted no time picking up his shoes and jumping into his jeep and powering straight up the hill towards the centre of the compound with one hand on his fedora to keep it from blowing off his head. Halfway up the hill he stopped, put on his emergency brake, cracked open an iced Mister K, threw back his head and downed the bottle's contents in one go. When he

215

lowered his head with a long sigh and an explosive belch, he was confronted by the sight of Dr Lord, barefoot and dressed in a cricket uniform, trudging up the hill, followed by a procession of similarly dressed Africans marching in double file, clapping their hands in time to their dance-like gait. Skip stood up inside his jeep, removed his hat and placed it over his heart. When Dr Lord saw him and waved hello, the entire chorus followed suit. When Dr Lord said, 'Good afternoon, Skip,' the chorus chimed, 'Good afternoon, Mr Skip'. Skinner waved with his fedora as the long lines of singers passed.

'OK,' sighed Skip, when they were gone: a close call with a deadly snake, a hallucinated procession of black angels led by someone named Lord – it was all beginning to gel for Skinner. 'I guess that just about does it for the booze.'

Showered and shaved, but dizzied by lack of sleep, Charles McCray sat by himself at one of the round tables in the park, sipping a cup of coffee. At the centre of his table was a vase containing a single garish flower whose petals formed an almost human expression. Brightly dressed Music Programme staff and their families, as well as distinguished Timbalians and diplomats, strolled to and fro taking in the musical exhibits. The compound seemed to have been organized like a musical museum. In the short walk from the car park to his table, McCray had seen examples of instruments from conch shells to dulcimers to synthesizers, and heard types of music from a Gregorian chant to an *adagio* for sine wave and strings. He couldn't imagine where all of the musicians came from; because most were African, he guessed they had been trained right here at the Music Programme. McCray took in these sights and nodded to the occasional passer-by, including the Head of Personnel, who whirred along the asphalt path in his golf-cart, smiling gaily beneath an oversized top-hat.

A trumpet fanfare sounded from the amphitheatre, and the strollers began to drift in that direction. Many carried instrument-cases. McCray finished his coffee and followed along, scanning the milling crowd for Eleanor. Just as he reached the upper rim of the amphitheatre, the fanfare sounded again. McCray noted that among the five trumpeters was the black giant who had rendered him unconscious near the Supreme Director's swimming pool. Pennons bearing the blue-and-white Music Programme logo hung from the bells of their straight fanfare trumpets.

McCray heard the sound of hand-clapping behind him, and turned in time to see the red-faced Dr Lord coming over the rise, his wire-rimmed glasses glinting in the sunlight. Behind Dr Lord, two files at a time, appeared the chorus McCray had seen in rehearsal.

'Here we come,' sang some of the chorus members. 'We're coming now.'

'We're coming to sing,' sang some others. 'To sing for you, in outdoor clothes.'

Spectators cleared the path and let the singers pass, and many of them joined in the rhythmic clapping. McCray moved to one side and nodded hello to Dr Lord, who was so transported by his procession that he did not seem to recognize the American envoy. McCray found it hard to believe that these clapping, strutting, dancing singers could be the same ones who had performed Bach's music in the auditorium. Like everyone else nearby, McCray found himself smiling broadly at the sight of Dr Lord's spirited group, so much so that he cracked his sun-chapped lips.

Once the singers had entered the amphitheatre and started to take their places on the steps, McCray walked to a nearby banquet-table and requested a Mister K from a barman who wore a dusty black dinner-jacket. McCray had come to like this bitter brew. He thanked the barman, refused a plastic cup, sipped from the bottle, and turned back to the amphitheatre. Eleanor was easy to spot, tall and stunning in a black dress, eclipsing the black-caped Kastostis at her side. They made a dramatic entrance at the very top of the amphitheatre, and descended together along the narrow stream of water that divided the semicircle of steps in two. Some of the singers were forced to move out of the way, and McCray could see even from a distance the look of sheer loathing on Dr Lord's face as he waited for Kastostis to finish his entrance. At the bottom of the steps, Kastostis ushered his wife to a reserved table to the right of the central dais, neighbouring a table occupied by a man McCray knew from his stolen briefing materials to be the President-for-Life of Timbali. Conversation had fallen off perceptibly since the arrival of the Composer-in-Residence and his wife, but when they were seated it resumed in force.

McCray moved nonchalantly to a spot where Eleanor could not help but see him, then pretended to be transfixed by the label on his bottle of Mister K. He sneaked a glance at her every so often, only to find her staring intently into her husband's eyes, or holding his hand on the table in clear view of everyone, or fingering the pearls of her necklace while Kastostis spoke. The Composer-in-Residence looked different to McCray, gesturing grandly with his arms and fingers, nodding and winking hello to those who visited his table to pay their respects, and even – this McCray could not have imagined before seeing it – even *smiling* with warmth and self-assurance. His posture seemed to have improved, as if a weight had been removed from his back, and his obsidian mane of hair bounced healthily with each bob of his head.

The dais had begun to fill with the highest-placed Insiders, who by comparison to the colourful crowd looked somewhat stiff in their double-breasted wool suits. Soon only the central chair remained unoccupied, and from his vantage-point McCray could sense a general eyeing of that throne-like spot. The vacancy on the dais seemed to cause a gradual silencing of the crowd, until in a few minutes, without being ordered to do so, the crowd sat or stood in total silence, all attention fixed on the high table. Dr Lord's chorus stood rigidly at attention, chins proudly raised; the Insiders' faces were directed left and right towards the centre of their own banquet-table; Kastostis sipped from a champagne-glass and smiled reassuringly at everyone, as if he believed his own presence had caused the eerie lull; at his side, Eleanor studiously avoided looking anywhere but at her husband; near the main bar stood Dan O'Connor, his arm around the under-age French girl, in McCray's conservative opinion striking a rather cheeky pose.

It didn't take long for the silence to become uncomfortable. Even the Insiders were fidgety. Saint Thomas, impeccably overdressed in a navy pin-stripe suit and silk burgundy tie, raised a heavily bejewelled hand and used it to convey to Dr Lord that the ceremony ought to begin even in the absence of the Supreme Director. Dr Lord turned to his chorus and raised his hands. One hundred throats were cleared. The President-for-Life rose to his feet, and everyone noisily followed his lead. At last, McCray caught Eleanor's eye, just for the shortest moment, as she was lifted by the elbow to her feet by her newly chivalrous husband. She looked away quickly, towards the chorus, but the disappointed McCray kept his pleading eyes on her table. He concentrated so hard on making Eleanor feel his stare that he did not notice for several seconds that Ludvik Kastostis' eyes now burned at him beneath a lowered hateful brow.

The Timbalian national anthem combined the proud military march of its colonial roots and lyrics of liberation in the language of the ruling tribe of independent Timbali. Dr Lord had done what he could with its rather insipid melody; if he did say so himself, his counterpoint line could even be called stirring. In

218

the spirit of the Master, Dr Lord had injected a fugal accompaniment in the tenors and basses that, while lending a certain clutter to the song, would be sure to impress his musically sophisticated audience, if not the President-for-Life. For his own amusement, Dr Lord had made sure that the walking bass line in the last chorus, when played upside down and backwards, was 'God Save the King' in a minor key. In previous performances of this arrangement, only the astonishingly perspicacious Thwok had noticed.

'Oh shit,' said Skip Skinner. He had crashed his jeep into a black Mercedes limousine in the central car park. The damage appeared to be substantial. Steam rose from beneath the bonnet of his jeep. A squat chauffeur in the driver's side of the parked limousine looked at Skip through the steam with an expression of disbelief, as if the collision had been an intentional act of terrorism on Skinner's part. Skinner waved insouciantly at the chauffeur through his fogged windscreen, stepped out of his jeep, collected his half-empty crate of Mister K, and limped away, leaving the driver and his colleagues to clean up the debris.

Dr Lord turned and bowed to a chorus of bravos from the Music Programme staff and polite applause from the bemused Timbalians. He returned to his singers and cued them to sit down on the amphitheatre steps. He watched as a black giant, one of his own trumpet-players, carried a harp to the centre of the stage in front of the dais and the tables reserved for the most important dignitaries.

'Everyone will please be seated,' said Saint Thomas into a microphone. His voice was amplified through speakers on each side of Dr Lord's singers. 'It is time for a toast.'

Waiters circulated with trays of champagne-glasses. While everyone was served, Thwok came on to play soft arpeggios on his harp. Dr Lord made sure each of his singers had at least one glass of champagne, including the children. Thwok announced the time for toasting with a flourish on his harp, and as if on cue a voice, a high thin voice in an unusual accent, came through the loudspeakers.

'My friends, my dearest friends,' said the voice.

McCray recognized Thwok's voice. He searched the faces of the Insiders for telltale signs of this knowledge, but not one of them stole the merest glance at Thwok as the voice of the Supreme Director reverberated through the amphitheatre. Most looked up at the sky.

'Mr President, Mr Minister, distinguished guests, my beloved colleagues,' said Thwok's reedy recorded voice. Thwok himself sat silently at his harp, palms damping its strings, head slightly bowed. 'We raise our glasses now to toast ten years of striving, ten years of struggle, ten years of music.' Glasses were hoisted all around into the Timbalian sunlight.

O'Connor listened to the toast for snatches of his own writing. He couldn't understand why the Supreme Director had chosen once again to record his toast and speech, but reasoned that after his kidnapping he had felt the need for rest.

'To the generosity of our many supporters,' said the voice. O'Connor clinked his glass against Yvonne's. Yes, he thought he recognized the voice as that of the white-haired man. 'To the Board of Governors. To the world's musicians and composers, past, present and future, our inspiration and our joy.'

'I wrote all of that,' whispered O'Connor. Yvonne stood on tip-toe and kissed his cheek.

'And to all of you, my dear friends,' concluded the Supreme Director, 'may you meet happiness and success, and may our next decade prove as fruitful as the last. God bless you.'

From a window on the third floor of the headquarters building, brimming with love for all humanity, Skip Skinner stared down at the colourful celebrants. He sniffed the scent of cooking game on the air. He listened to the Supreme Director's amplified toast with a bottle of Mister K raised high.

'I've got the best seat here,' said Skip, which came out: 'I've got diabetes.'

He focused his swimming eyes on the tops of people's heads, searching for the familiar dash of white that would signify the presence of his friend the Supreme Director. 'It would be like him to be mingling at this point,' said Skip. 'A man of the people.'

Skip's single-minded fantasy was that the Supreme Director would search him out in the middle of this momentous gala in order to congratulate him on his book proposal. 'I shouldn't get too drunk,' he advised himself, sloshing a bit of Mister K over the sill. 'So I can still speak clearly.' He leaned out of the window in time to see his drops of beer splash into the hair of his faithful barman, and leaned back in time not to be identified when the man looked up.

'Vertigo,' said Skip. 'Dangerous.'

★　　★　　★

220

With the toasts completed, the waiters scurried from table to table bearing the usual Timbalian fare: barbecued game, sickly vegetables, fat perch. Eleanor watched with fascination as the President-for-Life of Timbali, only a few feet away at the next table, was fed his meal one forkful at a time by two terrified food-tasters, like mothers coaxing babies to eat their purée: one for me, one for you. The tasters worked swiftly, for the President-for-Life appeared to have an appetite that this tedious technique could not accommodate without the most expeditious execution.

Eleanor forced herself to look away from this morbid sight, and focused instead on Thwok, who plucked happily at his harp strings in the centre of the amphitheatre. Eleanor adored this little man, and was grateful for the moral support he had given her husband. When he looked up momentarily from his playing and caught Eleanor's eye, she gave him the tiniest finger-wave, and he smiled in return like a shy adolescent. She looked down again and picked at her perch, burdened by the necessity of avoiding eye-contact with Charles McCray, who was positioned all too conspicuously at a table near the side of the headquarters building. She knew that a confrontation with the American was inevitable, and wished her upbringing had equipped her with the tools of emotional straightforwardness.

Next to Eleanor, Kastostis carried on an animated conversation with the wife of an Indian Insider, a very dark and severe woman who wore a beautiful brass-coloured sari, and who seemed captivated by every word the composer uttered. Eleanor had not seen her husband so composed and outgoing since the days after his Opus 5 was favourably received by a majority of London critics.

'Pff,' she heard her husband say. 'The loneliness of the artist is hardly a sacrifice, not when he is alone with his gifts. When I am alone in my studio it is as if I were accompanied by all the masters and muses, crowded before me like . . . like . . .'

'Like a group portrait,' said Eleanor. 'Would you please pour me some champagne, love?'

'Ah, Eleanor my darling. You seem to have drifted into reverie for a moment. Isn't my friend Thwok "something"?'

'You learn so quickly, my darling.'

'Eleanor has succeeded in teaching me idiomatic English,' said Kastostis to the table at large. 'I am indebted to her in so many ways.' He gave her shoulder a squeeze with one arm as he filled her glass with the other. He filled his own glass and toasted his wife: 'To the most beautiful pianist in the world,' he said, and was readily seconded by his tablemates.

A constant stream of visitors excused themselves for interrupting, then shovelled praise and encouragement upon Kastostis as if they were Timbalian cabinet members and he the President-for-Life. Kastostis responded to this fuelling of his ego as if he spent every day basking in the plaudits of his many admirers. Eleanor had never known that her husband's work generated so much enthusiasm among the Music Programme staff. For her part, she could not imagine that in so short a time her husband had managed to wrestle a truly MAXIMALIST work on to tape, especially after the rigours of his mighty 'Flamedance of Euphorion'.

When her husband laughed out loud at something someone said, she realized that she hadn't heard the music of the Kastostis laughter in three years, but of course he had been terribly, violently drunk at the time.

The toasts at O'Connor's table were less lofty than the Supreme Director's, but no less heartfelt.

'To the Irish,' said Mrs Grayson, Skip Skinner's Venezuelan assistant. Yvonne giggled.

'To Venezuela,' replied O'Connor.

'To Timbali,' said Mrs Grayson's Australian husband, for the sake of the secretarial staff at their table.

O'Connor was about to launch into an expansive toast worthy of a speech-writer, when he felt a hand on his shoulder – definitely not Yvonne's, which held his own hand under the table. A tall shadow fell on the white tablecloth. In the time it took him to turn and inspect the hand, O'Connor was able to visualize the white-haired man and to hear the great man's protracted thanks for saving him from the kidnappers and preparing such a marvellous speech all in the same day.

The hand on his shoulder, protruding from a white cuff and grey pin-striped sleeve, was minuscule and brown. A gold wristwatch the size of a tarantula hung from an inch-wide band. O'Connor looked past the hand to Yvonne's upturned face and found on it an expression of the seen-a-ghost variety. He turned round and confronted the smile of Mr Ng, Head of Personnel, who seemed to be dressed like an undertaker. Conversation had stopped at O'Connor's table. In his top-hat and morning costume, silhouetted blackly against the sun, Ng was the picture of doom.

'May I please have a word with you?' said Ng, in a puny voice that contrasted markedly with his appearance. 'I have my car.'

Behind Ng was the electric golf-cart in which he crept silently around the compound and office corridors.

'Now?' asked O'Connor, attempting to fill the syllable with centuries of Celtic history.

Ng nodded.

O'Connor folded his napkin neatly and placed it beside his empty plate. Movies and literature had taught him to go to his execution with etiquette intact and posture erect. 'May I just have a word with my friend first?' he asked, instructed by the same sources that the executioner unfailingly grants last requests.

Ng nodded again and walked away to board his golf-cart.

'This is it, sweetie,' he said to Yvonne. 'The jig is up; my gig is blown.'

'That is the man you were afraid of?'

'It isn't his fault. It's all my doing. We have to be brave, face the music.'

'What will happen to you?'

'Next plane out of the country, no doubt. Unless of course the Supreme Director feels that he owes me his life, which I would argue he does.'

'Couldn't you tell that to the funny little man in the hat?'

'I'll do what I can. But there are undoubtedly rules that even the eternal gratitude of the Supreme Director may not be able to overcome.'

'Oh, Danny.' Yvonne squeezed his hand. Her eyebrows made little horseshoes.

'Don't worry,' he said. 'When they fire me, I'll head for the coast. I'll take you with me.'

O'Connor was thrilled by the romanticism of this proposal. It occurred to him that this was why he had taken the job at the Music Programme in the first place – so that he might some day be in a position to flee overland across Africa with a girlfriend on the back of his motorcycle. Everything had fallen into place.

With a kiss for Yvonne and a deep bow to his fellow-diners, he stood tall and walked away from the table to meet his fate in Ng's golf-cart.

When Thwok completed his performance, the black giant picked up the harp as if it were an overnight bag, and removed it to the shelter of the auditorium. Ludvik Kastostis continued his animated discussion of the artist's desperate struggle with his rapt audience of co-celebrants, but his thoughts were on his performance. He had checked with the sound engineers, he had handed over his digital tape, there was no turning back now. Just to make sure no one missed the portent of his composition, he decided that when the time came he would climb the amphitheatre steps and stand with his arms spread wide, his black cape open. All that remained was to call to mind the facial expression he would employ to lend his performance its maximum gravity.

After a stop in the men's room to slick his hair to the sides of his head, and to stand over the urinal thinking he might never finish relieving himself, Skip Skinner left the headquarters building by a discreet exit, his jacket pockets bulging with bottles of Mister K. His plan was to insinuate himself into a conversation with an Insider or two, and to keep his mouth shut, hoping the Supreme Director would naturally gravitate to the one employee who had truly outdone himself in the past week.

The first Insiders he saw were all seated together at a long banquet-table, where Skip noticed that one of the wooden chairs was conveniently empty. With some difficulty he managed to climb the steps to the raised table. 'Excuse me. Pardon me,' Skip said, as he moved to the centre of the banquet-table. He pulled back the heavy throne-like central chair and sat down. It took him by surprise when the man next to him leaped to his feet and helped him push his chair closer to the table, as if Skip were a long-awaited guest of honour. 'Thank you so much,' he said to the courteous Insider. He looked up and saw that his seat was particularly well placed to observe the proceedings. Directly in front of him was the amphitheatre, occupied by Dr Lord and his chorus. To each side were banquet-tables, one of them full of overdressed Timbalians, including a man Skip knew from the national currency to be the President-for-Life. The presence of the President-for-Life was not so surprising to Skinner as the fact that a hush had come over the crowd, and that everyone seemed to be staring at him, including the Insiders at his own table. Even the President-for-Life, now that Skip thought about it, seemed to be staring straight at him. What could be so wrong with his appearance, Skip wondered, that it would cause a major African leader, one of the world's richest men, to take expensive time from his feasting to stare at an American trombone-player? Have I had so much to drink, Skip asked himself, that I appear dangerous? Am I about to be wrestled to the ground by the President's thugs? Skip found that his natural response was to glare back at the President-for-Life, as if to accuse him of extreme rudeness. This seemed to work, for the President turned away to his fellows and spoke to them in an excited manner. Skip circled the crowd with the same expression of derision, and like a wave their faces turned away and the murmur of conversation rose again. The only face not to turn

224

away was that of Ludvik Kastostis, who still stared at Skip Skinner right in the eyes. To Skip's great surprise, Kastostis smiled at him, the first smile he had ever seen on the composer's face. Kastostis seemed to be on the verge of friendly hand-gestures when Skip scowled at him and forced him to abandon their eye-contact.

When Skip looked down again he saw that someone had brought him a glass of champagne and a plate full of appetizing food. This he dived into with relish, still conscious of the buzzing at his own table that seemed directly related to his presence. He wondered if his book proposal had made such a splash that the Insiders were simply awed by Skip's organizational abilities. He quaffed his glass of sweet champagne, grimaced despite himself at its unpleasant taste, and with a congenial glance to his tablemates on each side pulled a Mister K from his pocket, used his Swiss army knife to uncap it, and drank directly from the bottle.

16

'JESUS GOD said Kastostis in Czech, to no one in particular.
'Of *course!*'

Because Eleanor sat with her back to the dais, she had some
difficulty determining the cause of everyone's agitation. When
she heard her husband exclaim in Czech, she felt compelled to
turn around and take a look. There was Wendell Skinner, seated
in the Supreme Director's chair, wrestling with the cap of a
Mister K bottle. 'Oh, my,' she said, placing a hand on her
husband's forearm. 'Does this mean . . .?'

'Ah, my dear,' said Kastostis. 'It was so obvious all along, to
those of us who knew the truth.' Whether it was true or not,
Kastostis would not be the one to explode the notion that his
good friend was the Supreme Director.

'I will not keep you away long,' said the Head of Personnel.
O'Connor sat next to Ng in the golf-cart with his head bowed

and his hands clasped together in his lap, as if he were handcuffed. 'I have some papers here—'

'I know,' said O'Connor sadly, wondering to himself if Ng would be susceptible to a bribe or, easier still, to a pathetic soul-bearing plea for mercy.

Ng stopped his cart in the shade of the headquarters building and said: 'I wanted to get away from the others because – '

'I know, I know—'

'– this is not the time for – '

'I know.'

'– bureaucratic matters.'

O'Connor continued to nod contritely.

'Mr O'Connor, I apologize. But I have been trying to reach you by telephone, I have been coming to your office. I even follow you on your motorcycle in my little car. Not fast enough.'

'I know,' said O'Connor. 'I'm sorry. I'm really sorry as hell.' He spoke in his native accent now, completely resigned to his fate.

'Some people,' said Ng, 'they don't think this is important. They think they go about working and not to worry about paperwork. But I have my files, you know.' Ng's voice was soft and polite, despite the defensive nature of his remarks, but O'Connor suspected this was about as angry as the man had ever been in his life. 'I have a job, maybe not a music job, but I have files and I have to take care of them. I cannot do my job without co-operation.'

'I know.'

'So, please,' said Ng, 'will you sign these now?'

Ng proffered a sheaf of papers, which he had retrieved from a folder in the rear of his golf-cart, and a pen from his shirt pocket. O'Connor looked at the papers, but was so ashamed that he could not read them. I deserve this, he said to himself. I brought it all on myself.

'Oh boy,' said the frustrated Head of Personnel. 'Please sign, Mr O'Connor. It is for your own benefit.'

'I know,' said O'Connor, wondering how he ever thought he could get away with his deception. Typical, he mused, that they should wait for him to fall for a local girl before lowering the boom.

'You sign at the bottom of each page,' said Ng. 'Standard form. You are lucky I found you. You would probably be ineligible' – this was not an easy word for Ng to say, but he made a valiant effort – 'ineligible in a few days.'

Dan O'Connor had already put his signature on several of the sheets before he realized that he had signed not an elaborate confession, not his deportation papers, not even his 'voluntary' resignation: he had signed his health insurance forms.

'This is why you have been trying to reach me?' asked O'Connor, who now wanted to take Mr Ng into his arms for a crushing embrace. '*Health* insurance?'

Ng nodded impatiently. 'You have two more to sign ' he said. 'Go on.' O'Connor signed enthusiastically. 'I know you speech-writers are busy,' said the Head of Personnel, 'but I would appreciate it in future if you would make my job easy for me. I try to keep clean files.'

'I know you do,' said O'Connor warmly, in his normal voice. He was about to express more of his considerable gratitude when he realized that in Ng's files Dan O'Connor was still an Irishman. 'Well, then,' said O'Connor, in a brogue as thick as furze, 'if it's the signin' of the papers was all you wanted, I'll be away.'

Ng pursed his lips as the speech-writer loped off towards the amphitheatre.

'Well,' he said under his breath, addressing himself to a clip-board crammed with Things to Do. 'Under the circumstances, we need all the Americans we can get.'

At a signal from Dr Lord, the members of his orchestra left their tables and took their places on the amphitheatre stage. The versatile Thwok had agreed to sit in on timpani. Jean-Baptiste Grandmarie sat at the keyboard of a small synthesizer pipe organ borrowed from Kastostis' Computer Centre, whose size was so disproportionate to its gigantic sound that even Dr Lord had overcome his deep-seated mistrust of electronic instruments, and actually preferred the Japanese microchips to the real organ in the auditorium, Authentic Instruments be damned. The orchestra tuned their instruments and squinted into the glare of white sheet music on their stands.

Dr Lord had to muster all of his professionalism to stand still at the podium and raise his baton, when behind him Skip Skinner had seated himself in the Supreme Director's chair. He cleared his throat and swept his severe conductor's gaze across the faces of his singers. It took only this brief moment of concentration for Dr Lord to realize that old Skip could not possibly be the Supreme Director, that the trombonist had stumbled, as usual, into the chair he now occupied. Still, it was nice for the others to have something to believe in, and the situation gave Dr Lord special motivation to conduct the piece he had chosen to open his section of the programme.

'Credo,' sang Dr Lord's chorus, 'in unum Deum!'

'Wonderful,' Kastostis said aloud, and thought: Yes, how wonderful that my Opus 10 will follow one of history's titanic masterpieces, well performed. It did not occur to the Czech composer for a moment that his own work might lose some of its power by comparison to Bach's.

'Patrem omnipotentem, factorem coeli et terrae,' sang the chorus, 'visibilium omnium et invisibilium.'

An elated Dan O'Connor had rejoined his girlfriend in time for the start of Dr Lord's performance.

'I showed him,' he whispered to Yvonne. 'I straightened it all out.'

Yvonne's green eyes brightened. 'You will be staying, then?'

'Of course,' he said. 'I am indispensable.'

It was then that O'Connor glanced up at the Insiders' dais and saw the central chair occupied by Skip Skinner. 'Holy Mary, mother of God,' he said, his Irishness once again second nature. There was Skinner, six Insiders on either hand, at the focus of everyone's attention. A waiter hovered behind him, clearing away empty plates and bottles; the occupants of nearby tables were visibly alarmed, and while their heads were turned towards Dr Lord and the chorus their eyes strained in their sockets to take in more of Skinner's sudden ascension to power.

'That is the big boss?' whispered Yvonne.

'Yes,' said O'Connor. 'A close friend of mine, as I told you.'

I may be drunk, Skinner said to himself, licking a coating of melted butter from his fingers, but I'm not too drunk to know what's going on here.

He had learned long ago at the Music Programme not to question his promotions, and he was not going to begin doing so now that he had been made Supreme Director. Tina will be so proud of me, he thought. She might even quit her job and come live in the palace. We will make a family together, a family of little Supreme Directors.

'Dona nobis musicam,' sang Dr Lord's chorus.

Dr Lord did not consider it sacrilegious to alter the text of Bach's music, not since having convinced himself of the Master's atheism. He conducted conservatively, as was his custom in public peformances, and leaned slightly forward to expose as little as possible of his belly beneath his white

229

cricketer's shirt. Most of his signals to the singers were generated by facial expressions that ranged from beatific smiles to sadistic smirks. His red goatee spat in time to the music as he exhorted his tenors to their greatest heights.

Take that, Kastostis, thought Dr Lord, as his brave chorus and orchestra, including five powerful trumpeters and a fiercely determined Thwok on timpani, built a noble crescendo and sustained the final chord of the mass.

Dr Lord waited until he heard the reassuring applause from the crowd behind him, then turned to bow deeply. As he raised up from his bow, he looked at Skip Skinner, who stopped his wild clapping to insert two fingers of each hand into his mouth to produce a piercing whistle of approval.

The audience did not appear willing to cease their applause until Skinner stopped whistling, which gave the trombonist a giddy sensation of power. He whistled loud and long, then snapped his fingers at the waiter who had become so adept at uncapping bottles of Mister K. With beer in hand, he noticed that everyone was looking at him for word on what to do next. This duty he deferred to Saint Thomas with a regal gesture of his free hand. Saint Thomas in turn gestured to Ludvik Kastostis, and as the Czech MAXIMALIST rose to his feet aficionados of his music began to fill their ears with torn-off corners of paper napkins, bits of Timbalian currency, anything that could be moistened and crammed into an aural canal.

Oblivious to this activity, Kastostis climbed the amphitheatre steps between members of Dr Lord's retreating chorus. When he reached the top step he stopped and turned around to face the crowd, so that his black figure was silhouetted against the faded evening sky behind him. The most pregnant of silences hung over the amphitheatre, as if Kastostis were threatening to jump from a ledge. Kastostis had to remind himself that he lived for these moments of glory. 'I live for the rapt attention of my audience,' he told himself under his breath, for there was no longer anyone within earshot. 'World leaders, diplomats, the great Supreme Director himself: all of them await my performance in silence. Ah, and my dear Eleanor, you poor thing. What a *frisson* awaits you.'

Kastostis raised his arms from his sides, which was the prearranged cue for his sound engineer to roll the tape-recording of Opus 10. He closed his eyes and raised his face to the sun, and realized immediately that to hold this pose for twenty-eight minutes would constitute more physical exercise than he had undergone in his entire life up to this moment. 'Worth it,' he said to himself, as his bed of murmuring strings gurgled up from the speakers, 'worth it for the sake of my art.'

Fearing the onset of tears during Dr Lord's performance, Charles McCray had concealed himself behind a man-sized boulder in the Japanese rock garden of the Richard Wagner Courtyard. Sure enough, it had been necessary to brush two droplets from the corners of his eyes before returning to the banquet-area for the première of Kastostis' Opus 10. He sat as close as he could to Eleanor's table without being obvious about it, but also without sacrificing a clear view of her face.

A muffled murmuring sound drew McCray's attention to the amphitheatre, where he saw Kastostis standing atop the steps with his black cape spread wide. The general silence of the group, and their fixed stares, indicated to McCray that the sound he heard was the opening of Kastostis' brand-new composition. The burbling music grew steadily in volume, and soon was joined by a tuneful flute. He could sense neither rhythm nor beat, and despite his handicap of tone-deafness he was certain the melody never repeated itself sufficiently to establish a theme. It was unlike any music McCray had ever heard, but he could not yet say it was unpleasant.

There was something in the music that did not resemble any instrument he had heard before. A windy whispery sound, and an attractive one. Almost a *human* sound, McCray thought, to which he was drawn despite a fundamental unwillingness to be impressed by Kastostis' work. He squinted up at the composer, who stood as if crucified atop the amphitheatre, and listened closely to the novel noise that drifted in and out of his hearing. 'Oh,' said the sound, which was now definitely recognizable as a human voice, transmogrified by electronic tampering. 'Ah,' said the sound, which was now amplified loudly enough for McCray to be able to decide that the sound was that of a female voice. 'Charles,' said the sound, 'Charles, Charles, Charles,' and McCray thought he recognized the voice.

Dr Lord, sweaty and relieved, had expected to stand to one side with his hands over his ears during Ludvik Kastostis' 'perform-ance'. Instead he heard something intriguing in Kastostis' music, an unexpected remote quality which pried into his musical intelligence and demanded attention. Dr Lord had been as critical as anyone of Kastostis' previous musical perpetrations, and would readily admit to having long ago slammed the door on atonal music. But as he cocked an ear towards the nearest

231

speaker and listened he was surprised to hear that from the onset of the piece his musical senses were glued to the moody progressions of the murmuring electronic strings, moved by the sprightly flute, and alarmed by the ominous sound of a disembodied human voice moaning and whispering in the background. 'Jazz,' the high voice seemed to be saying. 'Jazz, jazz, jazz.'

Eleanor bit her lower lip and forced herself to look straight ahead at her husband. She could feel her face, her neck, probably her whole body turning crimson. Once she realized what Opus 10 contained, she found herself listening more intently than she would have if she were trying to commit the Sibelius Fifth to memory. She calmed herself, and kept herself from tears, by analysing each passage of the music, arranging it on a staff in her mind, visualizing the melody and miming it with her right hand on an imaginary keyboard. The tonal clusters in the murmuring strings moved in and out of dissonance in an intelligent manner, flirting occasionally with a central key but continually moving on to uncharted ground. The melody's beauty stemmed not from its harmonic relationship to the accompaniment, but from its constant striving to soar above and beyond it, an enterprise in which it had nearly succeeded when an invading army of brass entered the scene and seemed to drive the flute away. This was the Kastostis of old, the great post-everything MAXIMALIST, the Kastostis who made one's vision blur with sheer volume and dissonance.

Eleanor's relief at the disappearance of her own voice on the recording was quickly supplanted by terror when she heard a male voice accompanying the brass section. 'Oh,' said the voice, in time to the marching brass, 'oh, oh, oh.' Were these syllables noticeable to anyone else? Surely not, not with the pounding brass and the distracting three-against-four French horns. 'Ell,' said the voice. 'Ell.' Eleanor braced herself. 'Ah,' said the voice. 'Ah.' Just syllables, she told herself. Meaningless syllables. 'Nor,' said the voice. 'Nor.'

Kastostis' arms felt heavy as great tree-limbs, but the magnificence of his Opus 10 gave him the strength to hold them aloft. 'Bim-pom bom,' he sang along with the brass part, as sweat dripped from his temples, down his face and neck, and into his black turtleneck shirt. He dug deep down into his reservoir of artistic fortitude and transferred its great power to his shoulders.

In the middle of Kastostis' Opus 10, two of Dr Lord's youngest singers, a pair of brothers he had discovered in one of the capital's church choirs, came over to stand on either side of their conductor. He put a fatherly arm around their shoulders and looked down to see with some dismay that they were both transfixed by Kastostis' music. In the past he would have responded to their fascination with the Czech's MAXIMALISM the way a parent might react to discovering his pre-pubescent boys with pornographic magazines; now he could not deny that there was an element to what he heard from which no serious musician should be shielded. Despite this new understanding of Kastostis' work, when the music grew almost excruciatingly loud he put a hand over the boys' ears and squeezed their little heads to his body. One doesn't want one's sopranos deafened, after all.

Yvonne winced, and squeezed O'Connor's hand under the torrent of amplified sound that poured from the raised speakers. O'Connor could have yelled reassurances at the top of his lungs, and not even Yvonne, six inches away, could have heard him. Everyone at the banquet-table nearby had assumed a hunched aerodynamic position against the MAXIMALIST onslaught, and O'Connor almost expected Yvonne's ponytail to flail horizontally in the blast.

The tumult ebbed away to reveal the survival of the lovely flute, and the audience collectively relaxed. A duet of indefinite but rather sexual male and female sighs rose and then faded in the background. The murmuring strings waned in turn, and at last Kastostis' première disappeared into history. The composer dropped his arms to his sides and bowed his head in response to an outburst of applause derived partly from heartfelt relief, but mostly from genuine appreciation.

When Skip Skinner stood, everyone stood – even the President-for-Life of Timbali; the ovation lasted five minutes. Kastostis stood limply atop the amphitheatre and soaked up the adulation of his devoted audience. Eleanor rose to her feet with the others and stood on trembling legs, doing her best to avoid eye-contact with McCray; while her husband's Opus 10 bore no resemblance to any of the music that was so central to her life, it was safe to say no composition had ever affected her so profoundly. The Bloody Bolshies, at a table by themselves, clapped enthusiastically but leaned towards the centre of their table to make certain they agreed on the merits of the piece even before the applause subsided. When Skinner stopped clapping, everyone stopped clapping. When he settled down into his chair, everyone regained their seats, and the exhausted Kastostis descended the amphitheatre steps to warm expressions of praise.

McCray watched all of this behaviour with interest and

puzzlement. Good old Skip Skinner, his first contact at the Music Programme, and his partner in humiliation at the hands of the Land Pirates, seemed suddenly to be the focus of everyone's attention, more so even than Kastostis. McCray took advantage of everyone's distraction by stealing a glance at Eleanor, who looked as if she had swallowed a sizeable fish-bone.

During Kastostis' performance, Skip Skinner had given some thought to his first official act as Supreme Director, certain that his tenure would not last long. After polishing off the dregs of a Mister K, he stood up and left the dais, which caused something of a stir among the Insiders, who scrambled to be at his side when he reached the stage of the amphitheatre. Surrounded by sycophants, Skinner made his way over to Kastostis to shake his friend's hand.

'Ludvik baby, I love your stuff,' said Skip. 'You got a nutty wig.'

'Thank you,' said Kastostis uncertainly, bowing at the waist. 'I am so grateful.'

Skinner's congratulations were followed by more of the same from the Insiders, who had surrounded the breathless composer. Now that Skinner had issued his benediction they seemed on the verge of raising Kastostis to their shoulders. A maelstrom of well-wishers formed around him and swept him towards the Richard Wagner Courtyard: there was dancing on the agenda.

The amphitheatre area was cleared swiftly as staff and dignitaries followed in Kastostis' wake. This left McCray and Eleanor alone at their separate tables, along with some other stragglers and a crew of busy busboys clearing away debris. McCray dabbed at his mouth with a napkin, smoothed his hair with a palm, stood up, and walked over to join Eleanor.

'What a success,' he said, and then wished his voice hadn't come out in a timid squeak. He cleared his throat and asked Eleanor if he might sit down.

'Please do,' she replied formally.

McCray smiled in what he regretfully assumed was an idiotic manner, while searching his mind for something appropriate to say. Eleanor stared at her hands.

'Are you angry?' McCray was satisfied with his question.

'With whom?' asked Eleanor in return.

Good answer, thought McCray. He had begun to feel small and defenceless; this was not an accustomed sentiment for 'Crack' McCray. 'With your husband, of course,' he said, as if the sense of her question escaped him. 'Wasn't that cruel, what he did?'

'What *he* did?'

'Well. Let me put it a different way.' McCray could not think of a different way to put it.

'Let me try to place this in perspective for you,' said Eleanor. 'I behaved selfishly and recklessly, and I was caught in the act, as it were. Some would argue that my husband's retaliation was subtle and lenient. So far.' Eleanor spoke angrily, with her head lowered, as if her champagne-glass were a microphone. She did not look at McCray. 'I do apologize.'

'What, to me?'

'Yes, to you. You arrived at a confusing time. There was no way for you to know this. Perhaps you are used to behaving this way, but I –'

'Now, wait just a second, Eleanor—'

'– am new to it all.'

'That just isn't fair. You don't know anything about my—'

'Exactly,' Eleanor said firmly. 'I know nothing about you. I want you to know that I don't blame you in the slightest, but you must understand that it is my problem now. I am the one who must cope. You have no such difficulties. All you must do is return to your country and complete your mission. Say whatever you wish. I'm sure we will be able to carry on.'

'What makes you think—?'

'Have you decided the way in which you will describe our shortcomings?' Now Eleanor looked up. McCray was amazed to see that her eyes were completely dry.

'Is that all you care about?'

'I care about my husband. I believe I told you that all along.'

McCray was at least composed enough to know that it would be beyond bad taste to remind Eleanor of the non-verbal ways she had told him just the opposite.

'You know,' he said, issuing a sigh that indicated his capitulation. 'I had considered staying here for a while. Maybe even applying for a job with the Music Programme.'

'We have enough Americans,' said Eleanor. 'I'm sorry, Charles. I'm not trying to be ugly about this. Only direct.'

'You could not possibly be ugly,' said McCray.

'Please. It would be a great favour to me if you would leave.'

'H'm.' McCray steeled himself for manly behaviour. 'For you?' he said. '*Anything.*'

Children took turns riding elephants around the park; Dr Lord's chorus unwound with Mister K's, and relished their contact with the rich and powerful guests; while the rains had settled over the hills and the capital, the skies overhead remained clear, so that a complicated and colourful sunset blossomed in all directions; torches were lit on the park paths, and electric heaters warmed the dance-floor.

A pick-up jazz band had gathered on a raised platform in the courtyard. Among the musicians were Mr Aarndt on bass, Grandmarie on piano, a black giant on trumpet, and the ever-willing Thwok on drums. Skinner's trombone stood at the ready on its stand, but Skip had not yet joined them because he was too busy shaking hands with the departing President-for-Life and adjusting to his new role as centre of attention.

Dr Lord beamed with pride at his relaxed mingling singers, a pride that more than made up for his envy of the blandishments heaped on Kastostis. Mary Mbewa brought him a Mister K, kissed him on the cheek and toasted his successful performance. 'Next year,' said Dr Lord, 'we will have white shoes.'

Eleanor entered the Richard Wagner Courtyard alone and went directly to her husband. Kastostis had to sweep several well-wishers aside to greet his wife properly.

'Fantastic, darling,' said Eleanor, embracing her husband warmly. 'Your most daring work.'

'I'm so glad you liked it, my dear. I would have dedicated it to you, but . . .' Kastostis waved a hand in the air and realized others were listening to his remark. 'But all of my work is dedicated to you. Automatically.'

'You are too generous, darling.'

'And where would our Mr McCray be?' asked Kastostis innocently.

Eleanor shrugged. 'He said something about leaving. I don't think he was feeling quite well actually.'

'I do hope he's all right,' said Kastostis. 'Someone! Brandy!'

McCray was eyed suspiciously by the Timbalian President-for-Life's legions of bodyguards and chauffeurs as he marched through the main car park to Kastostis' white Peugeot. Behind the wheel, he fought off an urge to smash the car into the first solid object he came upon, and instead drove in a controlled manner as he wound up the road along the river towards the Supreme Director's helicopter pad. The road was bordered by trees, and although the sky overhead was still lit by the sunset it was necessary to turn on his headlights. He rounded a sharp corner, changed down, then accelerated uphill in the direction of the Computer Centre.

It was as he negotiated the next turn that he spied a snake on the road ahead. His instinct was to swerve, but the snake swerved, too. At the last instant the snake was illuminated in his headlights, a bright, almost phosphorescent green. McCray brought the car to a halt, shifted into reverse, and saw by his tail-lights that the rope-like snake lay wounded or dead in the road behind him. He backed down the road to one side of the snake, passed it, then put on his high beams to get a better look. The mamba had been crushed in the centre of its body, but its head still flailed about in circles. Now it was a simple matter of wanting to put a beast out of its misery – or so McCray told himself, as he guided his right tyre towards the mamba's darting head. He turned on the car radio, which received nothing but a loud buzzing static, to drown out whatever sound it might be that a snake makes while having its head crushed. McCray felt just the slightest bump as he passed over the snake, then reversed straight backwards again for good measure. This time his headlights illuminated a motionless cord of dead mamba.

'That's the old "Crack" McCray,' he said to himself. 'Slayer of snakes.'

The first of the fireworks went off with a loud report and decorated the sky with silvery light. O'Connor had fled the festivities after a quick twirling of Yvonne on the dance-floor, and now bumped across open country on his motorcycle in the eastern hills of the compound, with his girlfriend holding on tightly from behind. He stopped his bike on the crest of a hill to watch the fireworks, and provided Yvonne with a sweater from a compartment under the motorcycle seat.

For the first time since taking the speech-writing job for the Music Programme, O'Connor felt relaxed and at home in Timbali. This was not solely the result of having squared matters with the Head of Personnel, although that contributed to his sense of well-being; mostly it was because in Yvonne he had found an ally, a co-conspirator, someone to drive around with. They sat together on the parked motorcycle and watched the sporadic fireworks exploding overhead.

'With this sky you don't really need fireworks,' O'Connor said.

'Feu d'artifice,' said Yvonne.

'Right.'

The jazz group had started playing in the Richard Wagner Courtyard, and could be heard faintly from the top of the hill.

'Your parents will be back soon, won't they?' said O'Connor.

'I suppose they will.'

237

'We'll have to sneak around a little more than we have been doing for the last few days.'

'Yes,' said Yvonne. 'It will be like my father. He sneaks around, too.'

'Really?'

'Why do you think he is in Paris?'

'And your mother?'

'I don't think she has a lover in Iraq. But you never know.'

'Still, we'll have to be careful. You said he wanted to kill me.'

'That's not unusual. He says he is going to kill my older brother André almost every day. What is unusual is that he actually saw you there with me.'

'And with your little sister.' O'Connor shivered at the recollection.

Yvonne giggled, and rubbed his neck. 'Don't worry, Danny. My father is not going to kill you any more.'

'I hope not. Everything is going so well.'

More fireworks crackled in the starry sky; revellers could be seen dancing in the courtyard under torchlight; the red eyes of limousine tail-lights snaked along the road to the main gate; the lights of the capital created a hazy halo over the southern horizon. O'Connor sniffed at the cool dry air and smelt gunpowder.

Exuberant Music Programme staff gathered around the stage as Skip Skinner lubricated his trombone slide and prepared to play. Skinner had not held the mouthpiece to his lips for so long that it felt unfamiliar and cold as he settled it into his embouchure. The first few notes he played were uncentred and weak, but in no time he was swinging away through a blues chorus as if he had never quit the big-band circuit. Some people danced, but most stayed close to the stage and urged on their presumed leader through his histrionic solo. Kastostis, who was not a connoisseur of jazz, clapped delightedly when Skip quoted from the flute melody of his Opus 10 and playfully caricatured its poignant form. Skinner ended his chorus with a flourish of high-note falls, returned his trombone to its stand, and leaped youthfully from the stage to sweep Mrs Grayson into his arms and swing her about the dance-floor, as Thwok executed a thrilling drum solo.

The rotor blades began to turn as McCray settled into a plush armchair in the helicopter's passenger-cabin. A young African woman, wearing the white toga and crimson sash of the Supreme Director's personal staff, placed earphones on his head;

she then disembarked, leaving McCray alone with the music of a chamber group pouring into his ears.

The helicopter climbed slowly from its pad and into the night, then pushed away from the hillside. McCray leaned towards the nearest porthole to take in the view: first he caught a glimpse of the Supreme Director's palace, its golden dome reflecting a red flash of fireworks; next, as the pilot gained speed and banked to starboard, McCray saw the white headquarters building, the empty amphitheatre, and beside it, lit by torches, the Richard Wagner Courtyard, crawling with dancers. Fireworks exploded outside the helicopter window like bursts of anti-aircraft fire, until the pilot gained altitude and left the Music Programme compound far behind.

A journey that had taken hours two weeks ago – and cost McCray all of his possessions except for his wallet and passport – took only minutes in the helicopter. Soon the Timbalian capital was spread out below, a central collection of tall buildings and well-lit hotels, surrounded by enormous dark patches, which McCray would have taken for wasteland had he not seen the shanty towns in daylight.

McCray regretted having left without saying goodbye to the friends he had made at the Music Programme – the hospitable O'Connor, the hard-working Dr Lord, the sensationally restored Skip Skinner – but a manly exit had been called for. McCray thought it for the best that he had escaped with a semblance of control – or at least that was the way he hoped his departure would be construed by the rumour-drunk Music Programme staff.

The helicopter began its descent towards the airport. The music in McCray's headphones reached its conclusion, and Thwok's recorded voice came on, thanking the envoy for his visit and advising him that the Supreme Director's palace was McCray's palace. After a soft landing on the airport tarmac, McCray removed his headphones, unbuckled his seat-belt, stepped down a short staircase to the ground, and began for the first time to think about choosing a destination.

A group of Dr Lord's string players had replaced the jazz band on the stage in the Richard Wagner Courtyard, and proceeded to play a corny, sarcastic rendition of the 'Blue Danube' waltz. The dancers cleared the floor for Ludvik Kastostis and his lovely wife Eleanor, who waltzed together in a broad circle under the flickering light of torches. Kastostis' black cape hung dramatically beneath his outstretched left arm; Eleanor had kicked off her shoes so that she was only an inch or two taller than her husband.

Waltzing was one of the things Kastostis did extremely well.

The composer had not felt so elated in years – perhaps ever. He and his wife grinned at each other as they looped about the courtyard, focused on each other's eyes so that the crowd, the torches and the musicians in the background blended into a blur. Kastostis knew, just by the sensation in his thumb on the small of Eleanor's back, that the ugly episode immortalized in his Opus 10 would never be mentioned by either of them again.

Dr Lord lit his pipe and stood aside, as more waltzers joined in on the dance-floor. Even a few of his own singers, who still wore their cricket costumes and white dresses, decided to give it a whirl. He followed his pipe smoke into the air, and watched the finale of the fireworks popping and flowering brightly overhead. He had noticed the Supreme Director's helicopter banking away towards the capital half an hour before, and now it returned; momentarily it drowned out the small orchestra, then it descended into the hills near the Supreme Director's palace. Soon all was quiet again, and Dr Lord searched the crowd for Mary Mbewa so that he might enjoy a waltz. All was quiet except for the whoops of joy from the dance-floor, and the music.